Anointed

BethEl Book One

Anointed

BethEl Book One

H.R. Hutzel

Anointed

Anointed is a work of fiction. Names, places, and incidents either are products of the author's imagination or are used fictitiously. Any resemblance to actual events, locales, or persons, living or dead, is entirely coincidental.

ISBN: 978-0-9885036-5-6

Printed in the United States of America

Find out more at hrhutzel.com

TO MY READERS,

*May you unleash your Giftings, walk in your dreams,
and discover the adventure to which you are called.*

PROLOGUE

The road hums beneath the vehicle. It's been hours since the girl last stirred. The driver, Aleph, glances at the rearview mirror. The girl's white nightgown splays across the backseat and glows in the dim moonlight. Black waves of chin-length hair fall across her cheek. Her breathing is measured. Eyes dart back and forth behind closed lids, lost in a world of dreams. Aleph dares to hope they are sweet.

He casts a quick glance over his shoulder and reaches back to brush the hair from the girl's face. When he turns his attention back to the road, he slams on the brakes. The tires scream against the pavement, but the car won't stop. A man in a gray suit stands in the center of the dark country road, his smile illuminated by the headlights. Aleph recognizes him.

As if drawn by a magnetic force the man exudes, the vehicle careens toward him at an unnatural speed, but he doesn't move. Instead, the man holds up his hands to create an impenetrable and invisible wall. Metal buckles and groans at the impact. Glass shatters and sprays like confetti. Aleph yanks his hands from the steering wheel and tries to reach for the girl, but the impact is too great. Her body bursts through the back windshield as the car flips. Like a doll cast aside by a child, her limp body glides through the air. The white nightgown flutters like a kite. Aleph watches in horror from where he is pinned in the vehicle. He utters something under his breath, and as the words leave his lips, the night sky appears to open and swallows the girl whole.

***

The first time Cohen sees Rachel, she is facedown in a pool of her own blood. Dead or unconscious, the world can't tell, but he is able to detect the faintest heartbeat as he rolls her onto her back.

The starkness of her nightgown contrasts sharply with the violent shade of crimson that spreads like ink across the white garment. The wet gown clings to her delicate curves. She is beautiful—in a tragic sort of way.

Cohen focuses on the faint and erratic beating in her chest, hoping it's not too late. He shouts for help, screaming until he hears footsteps running toward them through the forest. The young woman's bright blue eyes open wide as he cups his hands against her beautiful face and assures her the Healers will be here soon. Then they will whisk her away to the place where all hope hangs by a thread—the middle world where death and life battle for the triumph over another soul. The girl's eyes roll back, then close.

Cohen curls up beside her, wrapping his body around hers, determined to transfer life into the growing void. Her time isn't up. It's not possible. She wouldn't be *here* if her life was ending.

He closes his eyes as her warm blood soaks his skin, and deciding to do the only thing he can, Cohen prays.

CHAPTER 1

The nightmarish sound of a shrill, animal-like scream rings in Rachel's ears. Her eyes fly open. Personnel in khaki-colored uniforms rush her down the hall on a gurney and into a bright, sterile room.

An urgent voice shouts, "We have a young female, looks to be sixteen or seventeen years old. Automobile accident. She was thrown from the vehicle."

"How did she end up *here*? Did anyone know she was coming?"

Rachel attempts to sit up on her elbows only to find that her arms are restrained.

A man wearing a medical mask shouts back, "I don't know, but I need you to sedate her!"

Realizing that the wails are coming from her own mouth, Rachel presses her lips together and tries to swallow. Her throat feels like sand, and the metallic taste of blood fills her mouth.

The nervous eyes of the medical staff are careful to avoid Rachel's as her frantic gaze darts around the room and scans the screens with dancing lines. A man switches out her IV bag and pats her shoulder as if to say everything will be all right, but the way he doesn't meet her gaze tells Rachel everything she needs to know.

Two women hover in the room just outside the ring of chaos, hands held outward toward Rachel's body, lips uttering incoherent words. A young man stands beside them. Concern fills his beautiful gray eyes.

The man with the mask mumbles something indistinguishable. Rachel's face feels tingly. She doesn't know where she is—doesn't understand what's happening. But one thing is certain: the red blotches in her vision are not due to the narcotic effects of the sedative. It's blood.

Her eyes fight to stay open, but Rachel knows she will soon lose the battle. She flutters her hand against the bed to get someone's attention. Anyone. But her gestures are slowed by the numbing medication that now flows freely through her veins. Before everything fades to black, Rachel makes one final attempt to make her voice heard.

Her papery voice cracks as she struggles to move her tongue. "The baby," she mumbles for anyone to hear. "The baby."

***

Strange images find Rachel in the depths of sleep. Nightmares meld with hallucinations. She drifts in and out of consciousness, never knowing what is real. Hands are placed on her broken body. Pain gives way to relief then returns fiercer than before. Someone sits beside her bed. Words are whispered. The voice is soothing. A hand squeezes hers. Shadowy figures hover in the room. Darkness comes then light. Night and day. Dark then light. Reality blurs with the dreamlike apparitions.

A desert wilderness fills Rachel's mind. White sand dunes roll into the distance then fade and give way to a cracked mirror with a blurry reflection of a girl. Beneath it is a sink filled with wet strands of hair. Cold steel walls replace the dingy bathroom image. Tiny shafts of light faintly illuminate the dark chamber. Eventually it too disappears, replaced by white walls and sterile smells. Rachel sinks more deeply into sleep.

Swirls of inky black dance before her eyes as she stumbles down the last few feet of the sandy desert dune. Her weary body longs to succumb to the heat. Struggling for balance, Rachel sits down before the faintness overtakes her. As she leans back, her right hand reaches for the ground while her left hand supports her heavy stomach. The white nightgown she wears stretches against her pregnant belly. She rubs her hand against it, but the baby doesn't move.

Sweat stings Rachel's eyes as it rolls down her forehead. A bead of perspiration slips off the tip of her nose and lands in the sand. She wiggles her tired, bare toes as she examines the valley that surrounds her. The hazy sun beats down on her scorched shoulders and exacerbates her thirst.

Fog fills Rachel's brain as her overworked body succumbs to fatigue and dehydration. Delirium sets in. The heat-induced daze brings panic and confusion, but the exhaustion is too great—her body so worn. She curls up on the ground and allows the heat of the sand to envelop her like a warm cocoon. Within seconds, her breath falls into a slow, steady rhythm. Before her eyes close, the world melts, daylight fades, and shadows stretch until they consume the land.

The dreams become less distinct. Again, the images blur. White walls and sterile smells give way to a dark, metal chamber. Tiny shafts of light filter through a vent in the ceiling. The desert scene returns, but this time it is night. The white nightgown flutters against Rachel's bare legs. Hands press against her swollen stomach. A man with striking features stands before her. His eyes are haunting. There's a flash of light, a sword, then a piercing wail. Rachel's nightgown is soaked with blood, and the baby is gone.

***

A steady beep breaks the silence of the otherwise quiet room. The high-pitched tone manages to reach Rachel in the murky nightmare world. It grasps like fingers, pulling her back into the world of the lucid.

Breath is the first thing Rachel recognizes. Though it is labored and painful, there is something familiar about the rhythmic rise and fall of her chest. Her mind comes alive, and her eyes long to open to the light of day. But they are glued shut. Rachel focuses all her willpower and energy on those two small parts of her body. She strains the muscles in her eyelids. Finally, a soft glow pierces through the cracks and reaches her retina. It's not a harsh light, but it blinds Rachel's tired and unused pupils. Her eyelids pause to allow the light to become familiar.

Through the crack, Rachel sees a blurred figure rush to her side. A cool hand grazes her forehead. A muffled sound enters her ears.

Rachel can't tell what the sound is or where it comes from. Her whole body is submerged, not in water—something thicker. The atmosphere presses on her skin like thick oil. With another deep breath, Rachel allows the liquid-like air to fill her lungs. She tries to speak, but her lips stumble over the movements. Her tongue is weighted down by an anvil made of sandpaper.

The muffled sounds around her begin to form and take shape. Like monstery shadows in a dark bedroom, they are frightening at first, but the longer Rachel focuses on them, the clearer they become.

A voice. Rachel blinks. She forces her eyesight in the direction of the figure by her bedside. A form appears in blurry khaki-colored blocks. Blink. A face with eyes and nose and lips. Blink. A woman—pretty. With green eyes and a soft smile. A kind face. Blink. Concerned. The woman's lips move, and Rachel matches the sound to the movements of her mouth.

"Ay-oh. An ewe ear lee?"

Blink. A dull hum fills her ears.

"Hey-o. An you ear me?"

Blink. The hum begins to dissipate.

"Hello. Can you hear me?"

The words sink into Rachel's ears. The sounds and syllables travel the distance from her eardrum to her brain. The response is delayed, but the sounds finally convert into something with meaning.

Her lips and tongue feel too fat and heavy to form her own words, so Rachel forces a nod. Immediately, she wishes she hadn't. Her mouth manages to form a grimace.

"You really shouldn't try to move just yet," the woman in the khaki uniform says. She pulls a penlight out of her breast pocket and flashes it across Rachel's eyes. Her lids squeeze closed, and her face forms another painful grimace.

"I need you to open your eyes. That's a good girl. Now, follow the light."

Rachel obliges begrudgingly. Her eyeballs throb and ache with every move of her ocular muscles. Up, down, side to side. There is a constricting pain in her pupils as the woman turns the light on and off. There's not a single part of Rachel's body that doesn't ache—her teeth ache; her fingernails ache.

Rachel swallows and attempts to move her tongue again. It loosens, and her lips part. She forces air against her vocal cords. They vibrate with a hideous sound.

"Easy there," the woman says. "You were intubated. Your voice needs to recover."

"Where?" A raspy whisper escapes Rachel's lips. Her own voice sounds foreign.

The woman helps. "Where are you?"

Rachel nods. She squeezes her eyes shut as pain shoots up her spine and neck.

"You're probably better off trying to use your voice than your neck. Here, let me help you sit up." The upper half of the bed raises with a mechanical whir. The shift in position provides instant relief. Rachel tries a gentle turn in her neck. One side then the other. It's painful, but no longer excruciating. She lifts her left arm to see an IV tube taped to the top of her hand.

"Hospital?" she manages to squeeze from her raw throat.

"We call it the Clinic, but yes, you are in a medical facility." The woman grabs a tablet from the foot of Rachel's bed. "I have a few questions for you. We can try to answer them now if you feel up to it."

Rachel doesn't hear the woman. She focuses on her body as she forces it to shift and move despite the agony. Rachel adjusts into a more comfortable, albeit still painful position. As she moves her head from side to side, she catches sight of a gray-haired man sitting in the far corner of the room. His eyes are closed, fingers splayed, palms faceup on his knees.

"Miss?"

Rachel redirects her gaze to the woman.

"Would it be all right if I ask you a few questions?"

"Sure." The word comes out stronger.

"Great. First question: Can you tell me your name?"

The question takes a moment to register. A thick lull lingers between Rachel and the woman as her brain processes the words.

"Rachel." The word sounds strained. She tries again. "My name is Rachel."

"Ah, there. You see? Your voice is already coming back to you. It's nice to meet you, Rachel. My name is Anna. I am one of the Menders. We have a whole team of Healers, Menders, and Intercessors who are caring for you." Anna's lips spread into a smile. "And how old are you, Rachel?"

Rachel presses her lips together. "Sixteen? Yeah, I just turned sixteen."

"Perfect." Anna taps the screen of the electronic tablet in her hand. "We suspected you were right around that age. All right if we keep going?"

This time when Rachel nods her response, it doesn't hurt as much.

"Wonderful." Anna smiles. "Rachel, can you tell me your last name?"

The question registers quicker as Rachel's brain becomes more alert, but this time, the processing of the question hurts. A sharp pain flares in the back of her head. Rachel's hand flies up to grasp the base of her neck. The motion triggers another shot of discomfort in her arm.

"Are you all right?" Anna steps closer to the bed, her face donning a look of concern.

"I think so. What was the question?"

"Your last name."

The pain in Rachel's head returns. She pushes past the throb between her temples and digs deep into her cerebral recesses. Images flash in her mind, but she doesn't recognize any of them. There is no pattern to the thoughts and imprints. They come to her too quickly and clump together like sticky noodles.

"Rachel?"

"I . . . I can't remember." Panic tints her voice.

"You can't remember your last name?" Anna glances back at the man in the corner, who now watches with curiosity.

A weight settles on Rachel's chest. Her lungs ache. Her heart races. The beep of the machine next to her synchronizes with the percussion of her body. Every physical system suddenly becomes loud—the blood in her veins, the breath in her lungs. They combine with the beating and beeping to form a haunting symphony.

"Wait. How did I get here?"

Anna checks her vitals. "Rachel, I need you to settle down. Your heart is racing."

Breath rushes in and out of Rachel's lungs. Her head swims. "I can't remember how I got here! I can't remember my last name! I can't remember anything!"

Anna tries to settle her. "Now, that's not true. You remember your first name and your age. And I am sure there are plenty of other pieces of information you remember as well. We just need to ask the right questions." Again, Anna glances back at the man. "This is very common after the kind of trauma you experienced."

"What happened?"

"Well," Anna pauses. "I can *tell* you what happened, but first, I need you to try really hard to *remember* what happened." Rachel takes a deep breath. "Can you do that for me? Can you try to remember?"

"Okay," Rachel whispers. Her gaze falls on the man who has settled back into his chair. His hands turn upward on his thighs.

"Great. Now tell me what you last remember before you woke up here today."

Her eyes slip closed as Rachel leans her head back against the bed, but behind her eyelids, she sees only blackness. Every fiber of her body wants to scream and demand answers from this woman, but Rachel is determined to conjure them up on her own.

She wills her memories to make an appearance—demands her mind to cooperate. Her eyes squeeze tighter. Colors begin to form and swirl. Her temples pulse in rhythm with her heart and the beep of the machine by the bed.

"I can't remember." Rachel's voice is hollow.

"Try," Anna says. "Just try."

"I can't."

Anna nods to the man in the corner then places a hand on Rachel's arm. She whispers something, but her words are too soft for Rachel to hear.

"Please?" Anna asks louder. "Please try just once more. I won't ask it of you again."

Her gentle request stirs Rachel. "Fine," she sighs.

Again, she closes her eyes.

As she sits in the silence, a wave of warmth rolls over her body. A strange sensation replaces the heat. It takes a moment for Rachel to identify it—relief. The pain has subsided. Her body no longer throbs as it had before. It's only for a few moments, but the temporary relief allows her brain the mobility it needs to roam her memory.

One second Rachel's mind is blank, the next, it is filled with a strange and startling image. An image of herself in a desert. And in it, Rachel is pregnant. The picture dances through her memory but never stops long enough for her to reach out and grasp it. Like an apparition, it soon turns to a hazy mist and slips from her brain's weak grasp. But for Rachel, it is enough.

Opening her eyes, she places a tentative hand on her stomach. Pain courses through her body. She can feel the outline of a large bandage underneath the paper-thin gown.

"Where's the baby? Is the baby okay?"

"The baby?" Anna cocks her head. "I'm sorry, Rachel, I don't understand."

"Is the baby okay?" Rachel tries to sit up straighter. Her abdominal wound screams. "I remember now. I was pregnant."

Anna backs away from Rachel's bedside and exchanges a glance with the man in the corner. She swipes her finger across the digital pad in her hand. "You were? Are you sure about that, Rachel? The Healers did a very thorough examination. There was no sign of pregnancy at all."

"That's not possible. I remember." Rachel's jaw clenches. "You asked me to remember. That's what I remember." The incision on Rachel's stomach throbs with every beat of her pounding heart.

"Listen, Rachel." Anna uses a calming voice. "You were in an automobile accident. You were thrown from the vehicle. You've experienced severe head trauma and have multiple wounds and lacerations all over your body, including one very large abdominal wound. You lost a lot of blood and have been in and out of consciousness for three days."

Rachel touches her forehead. Her fingers graze the gauze wrap.

Anna glances over Rachel's head at the machine that monitors her vitals and waits for Rachel's heart rate to come down. When it doesn't, she continues. "Sometimes, when traumatic things happen to us, our brains try to fill in the missing gaps to make sense of what happened. I think that's likely what you are experiencing. These could also be false memories or memories that you have of someone else. I can call in a Healer if you'd like. We can even schedule some time for you to talk to a Listener—"

"No." Rachel shakes her head. "No!" Her fist pounds the bed, the pain forgotten. "That can't be right. You must be looking at the wrong chart. I was pregnant! I can't remember anything else, but I remember that. Do you think I would make up something like this?" The man in the corner stands as Rachel's voice grows louder. She glares at Anna. "You think I'm crazy? You're the one who's crazy! What kind of place is this? I'm leaving!"

Anna backs toward the door. She sticks her head out and calls down the hall. "I need some help in here!"

Ignoring the pain, Rachel bolts upright and rips the IV out of her hand.

"Now!" Anna shouts. "I need help now!"

Rachel swings her legs over the side of the bed as two male Menders rush into the room. "Where's the baby?" she shouts as her bare feet hit the floor. The cool tile sends an icy shock up her legs. Rachel glances down and sees what looks like little red flowers blooming across the middle of her medical gown. The flowers grow.

"She tore her incision!"

Rachel feels lightheaded. She slides off the edge of the bed to put her full weight on her feet, but her knees buckle beneath her. One of the Menders catches her under the arm as Anna calls out, "We need to sedate her!"

"No!" Rachel protests.

The other Mender rushes to the side of Rachel's bed and helps his coworker force her onto her back. One holds her arms while the other presses down on her legs.

"No!" Rachel's voice is shrill as she arches her back. "No!" Blood seeps through the medical gown and onto the bed as she tries to pull her arms and legs free.

"This is for your own good, I promise." Anna pushes up Rachel's sleeve, punctures the skin, and pushes the burning liquid into her veins.

The faces of the Clinic staff blur like watercolors. The man in the corner utters words Rachel can't understand. The other voices become muffled, but Rachel can still make them out.

"What happened?"

"I'm not sure. She was insistent that she was pregnant before the accident."

"That's not possible."

"I know, I know. I tried to tell her, but . . ." Their voices fade.

The last thing Rachel hears before drifting into darkness is the garbled voice of one of the Menders as he says, "This whole situation is very strange."

CHAPTER 2

Blackness slowly fades to light as Rachel wakes from another nightmare. She's been in and out of consciousness for what feels like days. All concept of time is lost. She sleeps whenever she wants. Sometimes it is dark outside; sometimes it isn't. It doesn't matter. Each time Rachel fades from the world of the living, disturbing dreams greet her. And each time, she is pregnant.

Some time ago—days or weeks—one of the Healers came to see her. He was kind but firm about Rachel's situation. Rachel was never pregnant. There was never a baby. The dreams aren't real.

At first, the Healer's insistence made Rachel feel like she was crazy. In fact, she's still not convinced that she isn't because every time she sleeps, the nightmares still come. The Menders tell Rachel they will fade away eventually. Probably around the time her memory starts to return. But they haven't faded yet. Each dream is as vivid as before, and still Rachel can't shake the feeling that the dreams *are* her memories.

Now Rachel lies as still and silent as possible, wide awake but eyes still closed. There is a Mender near the bed. She can hear the shuffle of feet and the rustle of papers. Voices from the hallway float into the room. Her ears tune to the sound—curious, but not curious enough to care. Muffled laughter drifts toward her. Rachel's melancholy mood deepens.

Cabinets and drawers open and close as the Mender moves around the room. Rachel follows the sound of the feet as they move to the end of the bed. Her eyes peek open. A young brunette stands there, tablet in hand, reviewing Rachel's digital chart. She wears the same khaki-colored uniform all Clinic staff wear. She looks familiar. Rachel tries to conjure up the woman's name as she watches her swipe a finger across the screen then glance up at the bed.

"How are you feeling today, Rachel?" She sets down the tablet and makes her way over to one side of the bed.

"Okay, I guess." Rachel leans up on her elbows. Her body protests, but not as much as it used to. The last time one of the Healers stopped in, she said Rachel was making good progress in her recovery.

"Well, this is perfect timing." The Mender hands Rachel a cup of water. "Thirsty?"

Rachel hesitates with the cup in hand but eventually takes a sip. "What's so perfect about it?"

"Because," she draws out the word. "You have a visitor." The young woman's face lights up.

Rachel finishes the water and hands the cup back to the Mender. "Who?"

The Mender smirks. "I'll bring him in." Without another word, she sets Rachel's cup on the side table and breezes out the door.

Rachel smooths her hands over her wavy hair to tame any frizziness while she waits. She tucks and untucks the chin-length strands behind her ears, then adjusts the ill-fitting medical gown. It hangs awkwardly on her narrow shoulders and matches the same dusty color of the staff's uniforms. At least it's comfortable. She sits up straighter, clears her throat, then fixes her eyes on the door. A few minutes later, the Mender's voice whispers outside the room.

"Wait to see if she recognizes you before you say anything. She knows she has a visitor, but we haven't told her who."

An unfamiliar male voice replies, "I understand."

The Mender glances into the room as she passes in front of the door. She doesn't stop, but the boy behind her does. He looks to be about Rachel's age. Broad shoulders rise as he takes a deep breath. He steps into the room and stops just inside the door. Rachel scans him up and down, from his perfectly messy hair and light-gray eyes to his worn and muddy boots, but she can find nothing familiar about his handsome face.

"They tell me your name is Rachel."

"They didn't tell me your name."

He pauses and searches her with his eyes. When she doesn't say anything, his perfectly bowed lips curl into a smile. He glances back at the door then says, "I'm Cohen."

"That's a weird name."

"I know." He smirks. "Do you remember me?"

"Should I?"

Again he pauses and gives her a chance to recall before he shrugs and says, "I was the one who found you after the accident. I've been by to see you a few times over the past week. That was before we knew your name. Sorry, it's been a few days since I've been here." Cohen's smile falters.

"You're the one who saved me?" Gratitude fills Rachel's voice.

"Well, I guess I hadn't thought about it that way."

Rachel scans his face then looks at the chair beside her bed. "You were sitting there?"

He looks a little embarrassed as he nods. "We were really worried about you."

Rachel rubs her palms against the blanket that covers her, remembering the warmth of his touch as he sat at her bedside. She wracks her brain for any other details about Cohen's visits, but the past week is still blurry. Finally she says, "Will you tell me about the accident?"

Cohen steps closer to the bed. Rachel shifts farther back against the pillow. "I was only there after it happened." His smile fades and his gray eyes look far away. "It was a *bad* accident. I've never seen so much blood." He shakes his head and redirects his attention to Rachel. "I was out for a walk that night. When I found you, I didn't know what had happened at first. I tried to stop the bleeding, but I couldn't. I started shouting for help. That's when I noticed the car. It was so strange. We were right there on the edge of the city limit. The car was on a road just outside the tree line that marks the edge of the city, but you," he shakes his head, "somehow *you* managed to cross the city line."

Rachel furrows her brow.

"We assume you were thrown from the vehicle—there's no way you would have been able to make it out of the car otherwise. It was demolished. Just a pile of metal and glass." Cohen runs his fingers through his dark-brown hair. "There are some things that don't add up, though."

Nothing is adding up in Rachel's mind. But instead of saying that, she asks, "Like what?"

"To start, where that road came from and why I could see beyond the tree line. No one has ever been able to see beyond the city limit, let alone go outside it."

Rachel starts to ask a question, but Cohen continues.

"Then there's the biggest question," he sighs. "How did *you* end up inside the city?"

He pauses. Rachel isn't sure if he wants to give her time to process or if he's expecting an answer. She certainly doesn't have one. So she decides to ask a question of her own. Hesitancy marks her words. "What city is this, exactly?"

Cohen sighs. "Where to begin?" He starts to pace by her bed then stops. "The Healers thought it would be best if I was the one to fill you in on everything. Maybe that wasn't such a good idea," he mumbles to himself. "Okay, let's start at the beginning. You were in a car accident."

"We've covered that."

Cohen smirks. "Right. That was a week ago. You were in and out of consciousness for the first three days or so. I was here most of that time, but then I had to take care of few things. You had an . . . incident while I was away." Cohen pauses. Rachel looks down at her hands. "They told me you've slept a lot since then."

"Have they told you anything else?" Rachel rubs her hand over the tender wound on her stomach, thinking of her dreams.

"Patient confidentially. They tell me only what I need to know." Rachel wants to ask why he would *need* to know anything, but Cohen continues. "They said you're recovering well, by the way. They want to keep you here a little longer to see if your mind catches up to your body. One of the Healers said two weeks, but maybe sooner."

"Look," Rachel begins. "I'm really grateful for you saving me and visiting me, but I don't understand. I don't know you. Why are you the one telling me all this?"

"Because—" Cohen pauses and appears to struggle for the right words. "When they release you, you will be put under my care."

"What? No. That doesn't make any sense." Rachel shakes her head. "I'm going home." She tries to stand from the bed, but Cohen catches her by the wrist. The intensity of his gaze commands her to stop. She yanks her arm free.

He softens. "You're going to hurt yourself."

"I want to go home!"

"You can't." His voice is quiet.

"Why?" she demands.

"Where *is* home, Rachel? Where are you from? No one here knows. Do you?"

There is a tickle in her mind. The Healers have asked these questions of her. Multiple times.

Rachel searches Cohen's face. "Surely someone is looking for me."

"Rachel." His voice is gentle. "You can't remember who you are or where you're from. You didn't have any identification on you. As far as we could tell, there was no one else in the car with you. The only reason we know to call you Rachel is because it's one of the few things you *can* remember. If anyone has been searching for you, they will never find you here. To the outside world, you are a ghost." His words hang in the air.

Rachel feels lightheaded. "What do you mean, no one will find me here? Where am I?"

The Clinic is strangely silent. Cohen doesn't answer right away. He casts a quick glance in the direction of the door, takes a deep breath, then begins. "You are in a city called BethEl."

"BethEl?"

"You will not find BethEl located on any map," he continues. "As far as the world is concerned, this city doesn't exist. Only the people who live here have ever, or will ever, hear of it. Just like you, this city is a ghost. We call it a Cloaked City."

Rachel feels the color drain from her cheeks. "Am I dead?"

Cohen chuckles. "No, you're not dead. How you *aren't* dead is a miracle, though." He gestures to the bruises on her face.

"I feel like I'm dead," she whispers. "Or dreaming." Rachel's mind fills with the strange images that haunt her when she sleeps. She glances down at her stomach.

"I promise, you are not dreaming. In fact, I'd say you are more awake than you ever have been."

Rachel shakes her head. "I'm still not following."

Cohen takes a seat on the end of the bed. Rachel draws her feet toward her and winces at the movement. "Look," Cohen says. "I know none of this probably makes sense now, but you are about to encounter God and the supernatural in ways you've never imagined. Let me put it this way: People don't stumble into BethEl. They are brought here for a reason. God decides who enters and who leaves this city. No one can come and go on their own. He chooses us."

"For what?" Rachel asks.

"In your case?" Cohen shakes his head. "I'm not exactly sure." A smile forms on his lips. "But I promise to help you find out."

CHAPTER 3

Nothing about the chin-length bob feels familiar to Rachel as she gazes at her reflection in the Clinic mirror. She rakes her fingers through the thick black waves. The color is striking against her light skin. Her full lips don't smile, and her piercing blue eyes stare back with a haunting loneliness. That part is familiar. A knock on the open door makes her jump.

"You ready?" Cohen asks.

Rachel draws a deep breath. "I guess so."

Cohen leads Rachel down the white halls of what appears to be a normal medical facility—at least as normal as Rachel can remember. But she knows the truth now. This is no ordinary clinic because this is no ordinary city.

Though Cohen has been mostly tight-lipped about the mysterious town of BethEl during his daily visits, he alluded to the city's strange nuances. But whenever Rachel began to pepper him with too many questions, he would say, "Just wait. It's one of those things you have to see to believe."

Most of their conversations over the past two weeks were repetitive until Rachel's short-term memory began to improve. Each day she made a little progress, and each time Cohen visited, he tried asking her questions about her life before BethEl. Both he and the Healers encouraged Rachel to remember, but they never made much progress with her memory. When Rachel would finally become too frustrated with all the questions, Cohen would read to her from his Bible to help pass the time. Sometimes he talked about the stories as if he assumed Rachel knew them, but with the state of her memory, very little of it made sense. A handful of times, something from one of Cohen's stories would tickle her mind, but she was never able to place it. The stories fascinated her, but not as much as Cohen did. Though she struggled to cling to the details and new pieces of information he shared with her, Rachel never forgot Cohen's face and never forgot his name.

By the beginning of the second week, the Healers said Rachel's body had taken a turn in the right direction. She was able to remember the names of all the Menders and Healers and the details they shared about her accident. Over the next few days leading up to her release, Cohen began to tell her bits and pieces about the world outside the Clinic but never enough to satisfy her curiosity. He said he didn't want to overwhelm her.

When Rachel woke this morning, the Healers admired her recovery and said her only instructions were to take it easy physically and mentally. She overheard one of the Menders tell Cohen to make sure he doesn't let her overdo it.

Now, as Cohen leads her down the hall, Rachel fidgets with the pockets of her jeans. After wearing only a medical gown for weeks, the pants constrict against her legs. Cohen chuckled when she told him she'd rather have the gown back. She wasn't trying to make a joke, but she liked making him smile all the same. Over the past couple weeks, Cohen's smile has been the only highlight to the very long and confusing days.

As they reach the exit, Cohen pauses with his hand on the door. "You ready?"

Rachel's hands clench into fists. Her chest rises as she inhales and nods.

The door swings open. Light washes over her skin. She follows Cohen to where he stops on the sidewalk outside the Clinic. The sky draws her eyes upward.

"Whoa." The word slips from her mouth as all concerns about her prior life and the accident are forgotten.

The vast expanse above them has a distinct dome shape. Around the perimeter, a golden haze encircles the city. Wispy clouds fill the amber sky and take on a more distinct shape as they pull toward the center. They form a wall of perfect cumulous puffs, creating the illusion of a city in the sky. The clouds tower like white marble buildings and encircle the city in a wreath. The ring frames a scene Rachel can't wrap her mind around. In the center of the cloud circle, the sky opens like a portal to a distant galaxy. The opening reveals a midnight-blue expanse filled with stars, galaxies, and planets, all able to be seen with the naked eye. Jupiter hangs heavy in the sky, dwarfing everything in its presence. This close, the swirls of its surface are a deep bloodred color.

"Where are we?" The words escape as a whisper from Rachel's awestruck mouth.

Cohen steps beside her and follows her gaze. "Incredible, isn't it?"

She can't peel her eyes from the surreal scene. "Are we on another planet?"

Cohen chuckles. "No, we are on planet earth just as the good Lord intended."

"How is this possible? It's night and day at the same time. And I can see planets! They're so close."

"I know." Cohen sighs. "It's amazing."

"What is it?"

"It's a Thin Place."

"A what place?"

"A Thin Place." Cohen turns his attention to Rachel's wonder-filled expression. "A Thin Place is a location on earth where the Veil between the Spiritual Realm and the Physical Realm is incredibly thin. Sometimes, people outside BethEl use this term to describe places where they feel close and connected to God. In here, the concept of a Thin Place takes on a whole new meaning." He pauses. "You see why I said you have to see it to believe it?"

Rachel's head bobs. She manages to turn her gaze from the sky to focus on Cohen. "I have so many questions."

A smile spreads across Cohen's face. "I'm sure you do. Sometimes I forget how strange this place seems at first. Forgive me, this is my first time as a Finder."

"A Finder?"

"We talked about Finders, remember?" Rachel scrunches her nose, allowing her silence to answer his question. "C'mon. Let's take a walk," Cohen says. "I'll show you around and answer all your questions."

"All of them?" Rachel smiles. "I hope you're ready. I have a lot."

Cohen grins as he leads her down the sidewalk. "I'll do my best."

The city is a strange contrast to the Clinic. Beneath the surface, Rachel senses the oddity of the town. The air is different. Thicker. There's a buzz in the atmosphere—a hum that reverberates in Rachel's core. It fills her with anticipation.

"A Finder," Cohen begins, "is someone within the city who locates a new resident when they enter from outside BethEl." He recites the words as if he has told her many times, but there isn't a hint of irritation in his voice. "The Finder is then responsible for the person they find—we call that person the Disciple. It's kind of like an apprentice," Cohen explains. "I'm the Finder, and you are my Disciple."

Rachel's eyes drift back toward the sky as she processes the vaguely familiar information. "This may be a weird question—"

"In this place, all questions seem weird at first. And, well, so do the answers, I guess."

She casts a sideways glance at Cohen. "How can *you* be responsible for *me*?"

"You mean because you're sixteen and I'm seventeen?" He pauses as if Rachel should remember this information. "Here, age doesn't matter. If you live in BethEl, you're treated as an adult. Like I said, God chooses who enters the city. We don't judge who God chooses, especially not for something as trivial as age. If there is one thing in common with the people God selects, it's that they often aren't the expected. God chooses the unexpected, the unseen, and the unlikely because, through these kinds of people, he can do his greatest work. Yahweh does things differently."

"Yahweh." Rachel repeats the word, searching her memory for its meaning.

"God's name. In fact, God has many names. Don't worry, you'll learn them. *And* you'll remember them," Cohen adds. "Look." He stops beside an opening in the wall of evergreens they've been following. Columns tower beside them and mark the entrance to a park. A plaque on the portico reads: *Remember Eden. Hold fast for Zion.*

"I know this is a lot to process, especially with everything you've been through, but you'll get there. It's my job to make sure you do." Cohen's smile wavers, but his words give Rachel an ounce of confidence. He leads her to a building on the other side of the street. "I need to stop in here real quick. Then I'll show you the Central Gardens." Rachel casts a glance over her shoulder at the weird little town then follows Cohen into the building with a sign that reads: *Depot.* Inside, the walls of the small building are covered floor to ceiling with open cubbies. Each one is labeled with a name.

Rachel slowly spins in the center of the room. "What is this place?"

"This might just be one of the coolest places in all of BethEl."

Rachel tries to decide what word she would use to describe BethEl. *Unbelievable* comes to mind. Her eyes scan the room as she waits for Cohen to explain. She watches him walk to the far wall, reach into one of the open spaces, and pull out a pair of boots, a book, a loaf of bread, and a pouch of rice. Then he reaches into the open space next to it, removes more rice, another loaf of bread, and a small, paper pouch. Rachel's eyes scan the text printed on the label.

"Cherry tobacco?"

"It's not for me. These," Cohen holds up the boots, "are for me. This too." He shows her the book. "This is the Depot. Everyone in our city has their own MannaBox—it's like a mailbox that God fills with the things we need. We have no contact with the outside world, so this is one way Yahweh provides for us."

Rachel trails a finger along the edge of the nearest cubby. "Sounds like magic."

"It does at first, but for those of us who have been here for years, we've come to see that it is the love and provision of Yahweh. He knows exactly what we need and even what we want." Cohen flicks the pouch of tobacco. "My Finder has a bad habit, but it smells good, so no one complains." He grins as he examines his new book. "This is perfect. I wanted something new to read." He flips through the first few pages.

Rachel takes the time to peek into some of the other MannaBoxes. One contains a bag of candies. Some have small stacks of folded clothes. Books fill many of the cubbies, as do soaps, other personal hygiene items, bread, and rice. Rachel glances at Cohen's feet. The soles of his current boots peel away at the toes, and the threadbare laces have knots where he has tied them back together. He catches her staring.

"You have one too." He points to the open space above his. After watching Rachel reach on her tiptoes, he chuckles. "I'll see if I can get you a lower box." The fresh scent of soap greets Rachel as Cohen pulls down a small stack of items and hands them to her. She finds the standard bread and rice, a toothbrush, clean socks, and new undergarments. She unfolds a pair of the underwear and holds them out to look at them. Cohen turns away.

"What does *Manna* mean?"

"Manna comes from a story in the Old Testament. I read it to you in the Clinic. Remember?"

Rachel shakes her head.

"In the story, Yahweh's people lived in the desert. They were nomads."

With Cohen's words, desert images flash through Rachel's mind. Her hand grazes her stomach as she pictures herself pregnant, standing on a sand dune.

"God always provides for his people, even if it requires supernatural means." Cohen gestures to the wall of MannaBoxes. "Back then, God made bread called Manna fall from the sky."

Rachel bites back a grin. "That sounds crazy." She stacks her items and tucks them under her arm, realizing it doesn't sound any crazier than magical mailboxes.

"I know." Cohen kneels on the ground to unlace his current boots and try on the new pair. "Yahweh always provides for his creation. If we trust him, he'll take care of us." Cohen stands and picks up his other items. "Just like in the Bible, God provides for BethEl through supernatural means." He gestures to the wall of MannaBoxes. "But he also provides through the natural order of things too."

"How?"

"I'll show you." Cohen leads Rachel out of the Depot. She scans the small town as they cross the street to the park entrance. An abundance of greenery fills the spaces between the buildings. There seem to be more plants than anything else in the city. Rachel casts another wary glance at the strange, dual sky and wonders if she should pinch herself to wake from what has to be a bizarre dream.

"Now, if there is one thing you need to know about BethEl, it's that we love our gardens." Rachel follows Cohen through the entryway. Columns flank the path topped with a trellis of green. After several meters, the intimate trail opens into an even more lush botanical oasis.

Warm mist rises from the ground, sparkling in the golden light that twinkles through the tops of the trees. Splashes of red, purple, and yellow capture Rachel's eye. Moss creeps over every surface and creates a soft carpet. Songs drift through the branches as birds sing, and a graceful doe follows at a distance while chewing on some leaves.

Cohen points to the raised garden beds that are intermingled with the aesthetic foliage. The bedded plants are all labeled—peppers, tomatoes, carrots, and other varieties Rachel doesn't recognize. Several of BethEl's older residents tend the plants. A child is with them; he stoops to touch the vegetables and whispers strange words. At the touch of his hand, a pepper doubles in size. Rachel points, wide-eyed.

Cohen grins and nods. "He has a Gifting of Increase."

"What does that mean?"

"We'll get to that. Don't worry." Cohen leans in to pick a handful of small, ripe tomatoes. He hands them to Rachel then picks a few for himself.

The sweet and sour flavor fills her mouth. "If I've ever had a tomato this good," she whispers, "then I don't remember." There's a hint of sadness in her voice.

Cohen glances at her. His smile seems forced, like he is trying to hide the empathy in his eyes. "I know you would remember if you had a tomato this fresh. There's nothing quite like a fresh BethEl tomato. I can guarantee you've never had one." Cohen reaches over and places the few he picked for himself in Rachel's hand. She flinches when his fingers graze hers. Cohen doesn't notice. She watches him out of the corner of her eye then smiles.

Down the winding path, a few passersby greet Cohen, but their bright expressions fade when they notice Rachel.

Cohen reads her mind as they settle onto a moss-covered bench. “Don’t worry. They’re just curious. Your arrival in BethEl was, well, unprecedented. No one has ever come to BethEl unannounced.”

“But you made it sound like people are found here all the time.”

“Not all the time. We only have about three hundred people in the entire city. And Yahweh always announces when someone new enters the city. Then we send out search parties to find them. But with you, Yahweh hasn’t spoken a word. No one knew you were coming.”

“Great, so not only can I not remember, but I’m weird too.”

“I prefer to think of you as special.”

Heat spreads up Rachel’s neck and into her cheeks. She looks away. “I don’t feel special.”

“God doesn’t make mistakes, Rachel. There is a reason you are here, and together, we will find out why.” Cohen stands, takes a seat on the arm of the bench, then props his feet up on the seat to face her. Rachel shifts.

“Ow.” She tries to cross her legs underneath her.

“Still in a lot of pain?”

“Some. It’s not awful. Much better than it was.” She settles into a more comfortable position and glances around the garden. “Well, this place sure is weird. And unbelievable. I keep thinking that I’ll wake up soon.”

“I know what you mean. It must be even stranger for you than it was for me. At least I had my memories.” A dark look crosses Cohen’s face. “Then again, maybe it is better to not remember your life before BethEl."

Cohen leans forward, elbows on his knees. A soft breeze rustles his dark hair, and a smile lingers on his handsome face. The fragrant air drifts between them, heavy with the aroma of grass and flora. The scent of the Central Gardens stands out as a contrast to the smells of the Clinic. The sterile environment felt familiar to Rachel. Even though she was never able to access the memories, the antiseptic smells triggered something in her mind—images of white walls and muffled voices. But the stimuli of the garden infiltrates her brain as something fresh and new. There is no tickle in the back of her mind, no gnawing sense that there is something she is supposed to remember. It takes a minute to grasp what is different. Then it clicks. Rachel feels free.

"Yeah," she whispers. "Maybe you're right. For the first time, I'm actually glad I can't remember."

CHAPTER 4

After a few hours in the Central Gardens, Cohen leads Rachel down the remainder of the path. "BethEl has many gardens," he tells her. "This one is the biggest, and it's the most central." Cohen stops beside a large fountain in a circular clearing. Several paths radiate out like a compass. "Right now, you are in the center of BethEl," Cohen explains as Rachel examines the strange carvings on the fountain. Water spews from the mouths of four stone faces—three animals, one human. "From here, you can use one of these four paths to get anywhere in town." Rachel follows as Cohen selects the path across from the one they used to enter the Central Gardens. It winds through trees and flower beds. Eventually, they exit through a similar column-flanked passage on the opposite side. Not far off the path sits a residential area. Rows of townhouses form a square. Cohen leads Rachel down the sidewalk to stand outside one of the quaint duplexes. He holds out a key. "Here we are. Your new home sweet home." He drops the key into her hesitant hand.

"I'm going to live here?"

"Yup. C'mon. I'll show you the inside." Cohen trots up the three steps to the porch. "They're all fairly similar in layout," he explains. "I had some friends bring over furniture and set it up for you."

Rachel's words come as a whisper. "Thank you."

"Of course. And the girl next door, Jubilee—you'll meet her tonight—she's about your size, so I had her bring over some clothes for you." He gestures to the door. "Would you care to do the honors?"

Rachel replies with a nod and slips the key into the lock. There is a distinct click as the latch releases. The bright-red door sweeps open. Her feet hesitate on the threshold. Cohen gives her a tiny push and follows her inside.

"It's a little plain right now. I'm sure it will feel more like home as you put your personal touch on the space."

Rachel glances around. "If I ever remember what my personal touch is."

The front door opens into a spacious living area. The right side of the townhouse connects to an open kitchen. On the back wall, between the two spaces, a hallway leads to the rest of the unit. "This whole place is mine?"

"All yours."

She shoots him a quizzical look. "I don't have to live with you?"

"Of course not." He looks embarrassed by her question.

"Does everyone have their own place?"

"Pretty much. There are some married couples; they share living quarters. Otherwise, we have enough housing for each person to have their own living space." Cohen flops onto the couch as Rachel looks around. "It's a simple lifestyle, but I think you'll grow to love it like the rest of us. The homes are modest—not mansions—and each one is furnished by the belongings of other people within the BethEl community. And as I said, your clothes were also donated by the girls in our community. We even eat most of our meals together. No one is ever alone here, but we also give each other space for privacy and solitude, hence"—he gestures around him—"you get your own place."

Rachel glides her hand across the island countertop in the center of the kitchen. A knife block and cutting board sit off to one side. Her mind searches for something from her past to compare to her new life here in BethEl, but she can find nothing. "Sounds like the greatest place on earth."

"It's definitely the *thinnest* place on earth." Cohen chuckles.

Rachel glances around the dwelling. It's small, yet she feels swallowed in the space. She eases herself down onto one of the stools at the island. "Tell me more about Thin Places."

Cohen walks over to the island and rests his elbows on the counter across from Rachel. She leans back on the stool and draws her arms around herself. "Well, there are many Thin Places throughout the world, and there have been many throughout history, but never another permanent structure like BethEl. Typically, they come and go. They can also move. Actually, Jesus was a Thin Place."

"Jesus?" Rachel taps the island counter with her index finger. A bitter taste forms in her mouth. She remembers this happening in the Clinic when Cohen read to her. The name gives her an uneasy feeling.

"Yup." Cohen continues. "Wherever Jesus went, he carried a Thin Place with Him. Do you remember what a Thin Place is?"

Rachel's presses her lips together and thinks. "A place where the Veil between the Physical Realm and the Spiritual Realm is thin?"

"Exactly." Cohen beams. "So because Jesus was a Thin Place, while he was on the earth, miracles happened in his presence just like they do here in BethEl. Jesus healed people—the blind, the lame, the deaf. He was able to multiply food like an Increaser. He even raised someone from the dead!" Rachel's eyes widen. Enthusiasm fills Cohen's voice. She can't decide if it's exciting or intimidating.

"Any of this sounding familiar?"

She shakes her head. "Not at all."

Cohen pauses. "I can't imagine what you are going through. I remember what it was like for me when I came to BethEl when I was ten. Everything about this place seemed so unreal, but at least I had my memory."

Rachel doesn't respond as she stares into his kind, gray eyes. Finally she says, "Have you been here ever since?"

Cohen nods. "I've never left. No one has."

An uneasiness washes over Rachel as she remembers Cohen telling her in the Clinic that not only can people not enter BethEl on their own accord, they can't leave either. "Why exactly are we here, Cohen? What's the purpose for this place anyway?"

Cohen hesitates and glances down at his hands before peering up into Rachel's eyes. "To continue the mission of Jesus. To overcome the Darkness and bring Light-giving Thin Places to the entire earth. To manifest the *true* Kingdom of God. We are a remnant being reserved for a future time."

His face says there's more. Rachel waits for him to continue. He holds her gaze until she looks away.

"That's probably enough for today. Everything will be explained at the Academy. You start Monday."

"The Academy?"

"The Academy of Giftings—it's our school. I'll make sure they know you're still struggling to remember the basics of what we've talked about, but Rabbi will get you up to speed. We'll start fresh and continue with your education as if you're completely new to this whole faith thing." He raises his eyebrows and smiles. "And I don't want you feeling bad about that, okay?"

"Okay," she whispers.

"Don't worry, Rachel. You'll love the Academy. You'll learn more than you ever imagined could be real or possible."

Rachel shakes her head. "None of this feels real or possible."

"I assure you, it is all very real. More real than the life you lived before—whatever that was."

"But seriously? An invisible city?"

"Just because you can't see something doesn't mean it isn't real. Reality doesn't conform to our imaginations. But," Cohen pauses, "it *is* set free by our imaginations." He fights back a grin. "I've said too much. Rabbi, your teacher, will be upset I spoiled so many things."

Rachel sighs and glances around her new living quarters. "So this is my life now?"

"This is your life now," Cohen says. He holds her stare a little too long. "All right." He slaps the counter as he straightens his shoulders. "Dinner starts at sundown. I'll be back in about an hour to pick you up. I'll let you get settled. If you need anything, my unit is four doors to the left."

Rachel wavers. After being in the Clinic for nearly three weeks, she's ready to have some time alone. But she doesn't want Cohen to leave. His face is the only thing that feels familiar in her new home. As he reaches for the door to leave Rachel blurts, "Wait."

He stops, his hand on the knob.

Rachel smooths her hands over the counter, hesitates, then changes her mind about asking him to stay. Finally she asks, "Is this one of the community meals?"

A smile tugs at Cohen's lips. "It's Friday, Rachel. This is *the* community meal." His eyebrows punctuate the sentence. "Tonight is Shabbat."

CHAPTER 5

"The townhouse units," Cohen explains as Rachel follows him down the sidewalk, "are lined up in rows. Each strip of houses connects to another to form a square, and each house has a back door that leads to a shared green space." They turn a corner and start up the other side of the residential block.

"Then why would we walk all the way around? Couldn't we just use the door in the kitchen?"

"We could have," Cohen pauses, "but you'll see." She can hear the smile in his voice. She glances over at him but looks away before he can catch her staring.

After a short walk, the sidewalk turns again. Cohen and Rachel enter under an arborway covered with deep-green leaves and bold white flowers. Their fragrance mixes with the scent of roasting food and summer air. A wall of greenery conceals the scene on the other side, but Cohen can't hide his excitement as he leads Rachel through the entrance.

A gasp escapes her lips as lights, sounds, and smells reach out with welcoming arms and pull Rachel into the celebration. Her head spins as she steps into the lavishness. Women smile, dance, and toast drinks. Men stand over firepits, where the scent of cooking food mingles with hickory. A few young children run and play while dogs chase behind them. There's a large bonfire and musicians. Their melodic voices drift through the crowd to enrapture every soul with their song. Rachel spins, allowing every detail of the moment to seep into her pores. Now that she knows how fleeting memories can be, she wants to seal in this one forever.

Dancing fireflies draw her eyes upward. Connected to the roofs of the houses, along the perimeter, is a dome-like trellis that encapsulates the scene. It too is covered with snow-white flowers, their centers tinged with crimson red. Even the pattern in which they climb seems intentional, like delicate notes of a song. Nothing feels random about their placement. Each flower is right where it belongs. Strands of sparkling lights illuminate their soft petals in the night.

The center of the trellis holds nothing back. It opens like a telescope lens to reveal the magical BethEl sky. Through the trellis, Rachel can see that the perimeter of daylight has faded from the strange dual sky. Where sunlight used to shine on the outer ring, night now encroaches to highlight the display of planets and galaxies.

"What do you think?" Cohen's voice comes from beside her.

She doesn't turn her face from the sky. "It's beyond words."

"This is my favorite place in the entire world. I couldn't wait to show you."

"I can see why."

"You haven't even seen the best part yet."

"What's that?"

"The people." Cohen's eyes spark. "Come. I'll introduce you to your new family."

The word *family* strikes Rachel as odd as she once again tries to remember the people she knew before BethEl. She glances over at Cohen, realizing her Finder is the closest thing she has to family now.

Cohen leads Rachel in what feels like a choreographed dance through the crowd. His movements are fluid. He pauses, introduces Rachel to another BethEl resident, then glides her past the tables of food to meet another. One thing quickly becomes clear: everyone loves Cohen. Rachel watches the way the other residents speak to him. She isn't sure how to respond when they offer her the same respect. The kindness of each person she meets is overwhelming. For the first time since arriving in BethEl, Rachel feels truly happy, not overwhelmed. Her joy tapers only when she sees a few of the Menders from the Clinic. As they ask Rachel how she is feeling, she is reminded that nothing about her situation is normal, even for a place as strange as BethEl.

After Cohen introduces Rachel to another group of people, he leads her to a small table, its top covered with drinking glasses. An elderly woman stands behind the table with a ceramic pitcher in hand.

"Good evening, Elizabeth," Cohen says as they approach.

"Good evening."

"Two please," Cohen says.

The white-haired woman nods and fills two of the glasses with water. Rachel can feel Cohen's eyes on her.

"What?" Rachel asks.

"Watch!" He places a hand on her back and points to the glasses with the other. Rachel tenses under his touch.

Elizabeth picks up the glasses by their stems and lifts them in front of her. She mumbles something under her breath and swirls the liquid in the glasses.

Rachel's eyes widen, and Cohen's touch is forgotten as she watches the water shift from clear to cloudy to a deep red.

Elizabeth hands over the glasses to Cohen. "Shabbat Shalom!" She flashes a toothless grin.

"What is that?" Rachel whispers as Cohen leads her to a seat at a long, wooden table.

"Wine." He offers Rachel one of the glasses.

She takes a sip and slides onto the bench. "How did she do that? Magic?"

"Of a sort." Cohen laughs and sets his glass beside hers. "Remember, you're in a Thin Place. Miracles are the norm."

"That was incredible."

"You haven't seen anything yet."

On the bench across from them sits a petite teenage girl with wild, red hair. Rachel guesses she's around her own age. The girl's pretty face pulls into a smile as she stands and thrusts a freckled hand across the table.

"You must be Rachel! Cohen won't stop talking about you." The girl glances in his direction as Cohen walks away to grab food.

"Nice to meet you." Rachel hesitates then shakes the girl's hand.

Without taking her eyes off Rachel, the girl flops onto the bench and adjusts the layers of billowing skirts around her. "I'm Jubilee. I live next door."

"You're the one who brought over the clothes."

Jubilee's fiery curls bob up and down as she nods. "I wasn't sure if you were a wild soul like me," she gestures to her bangles and the layers of flowing fabric, "so Leah and Chloe chipped in some normal clothes."

She grins. "Anything colorful, you can bet, is from me."

Rachel feels suddenly self-conscious in the plain gray T-shirt and jeans Cohen brought to the Clinic earlier that day. "Thanks for sharing your clothes with me."

"Of course!" Her voice rings out like a song. There's something about Jubilee; Rachel can't put her finger on it, but whatever it is, she wants it.

Cohen returns with two plates piled high with an array of grilled vegetables, fruits, breads, and jams. He sets the platters down in front of Rachel and sits backward on the bench. Elbows propped up behind him on the table, he shifts toward Rachel so only she can hear. "Hungry?" His breath tickles her hair. Rachel's stomach rumbles as she shrugs away from him. He laughs and steals a grilled carrot from her plate. "I guess that's a yes."

Rachel tucks her short hair behind her ears, trying to shake off the feeling of his breath on her neck. He slides even closer on the bench. Rachel glues her eyes to her food, unable to decide if she wants him this close or not.

The music in the background fades, and an aged man rises from his seat at the centermost table. "I'll be right back." Cohen stands and jogs over to the elderly man. Rachel feels the cool void of his absence beside her and decides she wishes he would have stayed.

Cohen pats the old man on the back and lines up beside him at the table. They remain standing while everyone else finds their way to a seat. A thick, brown robe drapes the old man's shoulders—a dull color in comparison to his richly black skin. Rachel watches as the man's warm smile greets Cohen and flashes bright against his dark face.

"Thank you all for gathering here with us this evening." The man's deep baritone bellows into the night air. "Tonight, we celebrate Shabbat." Every eye is fixed on him. "We remember that Yahweh created the earth and all that is in it in six days, and on the seventh day God rested." The light from two candles on the table warms his ebony skin and flickers in his strangely blue eyes. "We also remember the way Yahweh saved us from our slavery to sin through Yeshua our Messiah."

The man's strange words pull Rachel into a trance. Everyone seems mesmerized.

The man's voice rumbles into the night as he recites prayers and blessings over the people gathered in the sacred space between their homes. At one point, he begins to speak, pauses, then glances at Cohen. He strokes his gray stubble of a beard and whispers something between them. A wave of uncertainty flashes across Cohen's face, but he nods then reaches for a loaf of bread in the center of the table in front of him. At every other table, someone reaches for a similar loaf and holds it high for everyone else to see.

Cohen clears his throat. "On the night he was betrayed, Yeshua—that is, Jesus—ate the Passover with his disciples." Cohen's voice carries across the crowd with power. It holds as much weight as that of the sage-like man beside him, but from where Rachel sits, she can detect the slightest quiver in his hand. "While they were eating, Jesus took the bread, and when he had given thanks, he broke it and gave it to his disciples, saying, 'Take and eat; this is my body.' Yeshua did this as a symbol of the way his body would soon be broken for humanity. And so today, on Shabbat, we remember his sacrifice."

The sound of her Finder's voice brings Rachel comfort. Though everything taking place around her is foreign, the constant of Cohen's voice remains, just as it was at her bedside in the Clinic. Rachel smiles as she watches him lift the bread high above his head. He hesitates then tears it in two.

"This is the body of Christ," he declares, "broken for you." He tears off a piece and eats it then serves the man beside him. The old man's haunting blue eyes reflect his approval as Cohen passes the two halves of bread down either side of the nearest table.

A soft murmur rises from the crowd as bread is passed between hungry hands. A strange emotion envelops Rachel as she watches people serve one another. Though she has little context for the story, she wants to know more. There is something powerful in those simple words whispered between friends.

Rachel's turn comes. Across from her, Jubilee now holds half a loaf of bread. It looks enormous in her small hands. "May I serve you?" she whispers across the table.

Before Rachel realizes what she is doing, she nods, stretches her longing hands across the table toward Jubilee, and cups them into a bowl. The name *Jesus* floats through her mind and grasps at something forgotten. She doesn't know this man, but she wants to. His name stirs something inside Rachel. Before, it was fear and uncertainty. Now, intrigue mingles with the strange sense of danger. A chill races down her spine. The evening summer breeze slips across her neck and wraps her body in goosebumps. "We do this to remember," Cohen had said. Rachel rubs her hand over her stomach thinking of her dreams and the baby she isn't sure existed. Though the loss of her past still lingers and though her mind struggles to grasp what is true, something in this city calls to her. There is a resonance of truth in the things Cohen has told her, and her spirit reaches toward it.

As she glances up at her Finder, Rachel decides she doesn't want to remember. Not anymore. All she desires is here now—with Cohen, in this city, in this moment, wrapped up in this humble piece of bread. She watches Jubilee tear the loaf and place a piece in her hands, hoping some of Jubilee's fire will be passed to her with the bread.

"The body of Jesus was broken for you," Jubilee whispers.

Rachel's hands are filled. She wraps her fingers around the bread as if it is the last scrap she will ever eat. She brings both hands to her lips and consumes the bread hungrily. Jubilee's eyes spark as if her soul was suddenly fanned into an inferno. The corners of her lips turn upward as she watches Rachel chew. Rachel's not sure why, but Jubilee whispers that name one more time as if it alone were a prayer: "Jesus."

"Jesus," Rachel repeats. She doesn't understand, doesn't know what it means, but there is just something about that name.

CHAPTER 6

The celebration continues into the cool parts of the early summer night and concludes with a final announcement from Francis, the presider of the ceremony. "I want to thank you all for keeping this city running smoothly while I was away on Sabbatical and for granting me the privilege of these times of solitude." Smiles and nods are directed toward him. "I know four weeks is a long time to be away and much can happen in that time period." Rachel shifts as the man's piercing eyes seem to stare directly at her. "But I have exciting news. Tomorrow morning, we will all gather in the Chapel." He pauses. "I received a message from Yahweh." A hush falls over the crowd. A few audible gasps fill the quiet space. Rachel watches Jubilee. The girl is on the edge of the bench, hands pressed under her legs, tense with anticipation. "For the first time in our history"—Francis draws out the words—"we will be sending a group of people outside BethEl—our first Apostolic Mission!"

The hush of the crowd is broken by the sounds of celebration. Laughter bellows from Francis as he joins in the city's joy. Though she doesn't understand what they celebrate, Rachel can't help but smile as she watches her new friends' elation.

Francis holds up his hands to settle the crowd. "We are all excited, I know, but Yahweh has provided specific instructions for choosing the members of this team. As I said, tomorrow morning, we will gather in the Chapel. There, Yahweh will show us who he has chosen to send from our city. Everyone must be present." The crowd mumbles their agreement. "You are now free to depart. May the peace of our Lord be with you all. Shabbat Shalom!"

"Shabbat Shalom!" the crowd echoes as some disperse to clean up the evening meal and others return to their homes.

Cohen returns to Rachel's table. "Ready to go home? I'm sure you're exhausted."

A long yawn slips from Rachel's mouth as she nods. She says goodnight to the people she met at her table.

"See you in the morning!" Jubilee calls, as Cohen leads Rachel back through the arborway and onto the sidewalk.

"What did you think?" Cohen's voice is filled with excitement.

"It was amazing. I didn't follow everything during the ceremony part, but it was still really cool. And that guy . . . what was his name?"

"Francis."

"Yeah. There's something about him. He seems so—"

"Wise?"

"I was thinking magical."

Cohen chuckles. "He's definitely different."

"Yeah, but so are you."

"And so are you," Cohen retorts.

"Not in a good way."

"In a great way," he says. Rachel feels his eyes on her. "Everyone in BethEl is unique and special, including you." Cohen walks closer to Rachel.

She wraps her arms around her waist. "So, what is an Apo—what was it called?" Rachel sidesteps, creating more distance between herself and Cohen. "The Mission?"

Cohen glances at her. "Apostolic Mission?"

"Yeah. What is it?"

"That's a good question." Cohen runs his fingers through his dark hair. "I'm not exactly sure. Like Francis said, this is our first Mission. From the day I arrived in BethEl, I've been told that Yahweh is reserving us for a special purpose in ushering in his Kingdom. For some of us, that purpose will take place outside the walls of our city, though no one knows exactly what that means or what it will look like. Like I said, no one has left BethEl since arriving here. What we do know is that one day, some of us will be called back outside the city to be Apostles—people who share the good news of God's story with the outside world." Excitement flashes in Cohen's eyes. "We've been preparing for this since we arrived, and it looks like that day has come."

"How did you know this was going to happen?"

"Yahweh speaks to Francis. He and Rabbi are the city Elders. We have regular meetings in the Chapel where Francis shares with us what's he's heard. He usually has a lot to share when he comes back from Sabbatical."

"What's Sabbatical?"

"Time off. Both he and Rabbi take regular Sabbaticals to connect more deeply with Yahweh and hear from him how to lead the people of BethEl. They usually go somewhere remote within the city to get away—like the woods—and we do our best not to bother them."

Rachel nods as she tries to take it all in. "I still have so many questions," she sighs.

Cohen casts Rachel a sideways glance. The moonlight illuminates his perfect smile. "That's why I'm here," he says. He pauses a little too long as he stares at her. The lingering silence and his smile make Rachel look away.

"I'm glad you're here," she whispers. They walk the next few minutes without speaking.

"Hey." Rachel stops. "What's that?" She points to a dirt trail that veers off from the main walking path. It dead-ends into an open field. Beyond that, Rachel can see a thick tree line in the distance.

"That," Cohen laughs, "is a dirt road. No one knows why it's here."

"Really? Who put it there?"

"I suppose Yahweh did when he established the city. Ask anyone in BethEl, and they will tell you it has been here as long as they can remember."

"But what's the purpose of it?"

"Everyone has a theory. I think it's one of Yahweh's mysteries, something to keep us guessing. Francis always jokes that it's an expansion project." They continue walking.

"Why were you helping Francis with the bread?" Rachel remembers the look on Jubilee's face as she tore a piece of the loaf and placed it in her hands.

"Francis and I have a relationship like ours." Cohen gestures between himself and Rachel. "Francis is my Finder. I'm his Disciple. He found me when I was ten." Cohen shoves his hands into his pockets.

"How did you end up here?"

"Well," Cohen begins, "I was adopted as a baby, so I don't have any memory of parents before the man and woman I called mom and dad."

The word *baby* brings an unexpected wave of emotion for Rachel. Her hand grazes her flat stomach. The healing wound throbs.

"You feeling okay?"

Rachel drops her hand from her stomach. "Yeah. I'm fine," she says. But the phantom sensation of being pregnant doesn't fade.

"You sure?"

"I'm fine." But Rachel can't quite meet Cohen's eyes.

Cohen shrugs. "Anyway, they were good parents. Took me to church, taught me about God, but they didn't get me. They always said there was something different about me."

"I told you!" Rachel jabs.

Cohen narrows his eyes at her, but a smile tugs at the corner of his mouth. "One day my dad told me that he and my mom decided to send me to a boarding school. They thought it was best for me because I was advancing out of the school system in my hometown. Said I needed something that would challenge me. I don't know if that was true or not. At that age, I thought they were just trying to get rid of me." Cohen pauses in his story. "Anyway, I was mad and kind of blew up on them." Regret fills his voice. "I didn't want to go away and leave my friends and family, but I was a good kid, so I packed my bags.

"It was the first time I ever traveled by myself. First time on an airplane too. I hated it. When the plane landed, someone from the school was supposed to pick me up and drive me to the campus. But," Cohen raises his eyebrows, "the driver didn't take me to the school."

"Where did they take you?"

"Here."

"How?"

"Later, I learned that the driver wasn't from the school. He wasn't even human. He was a Malak—an angel." The strange word stirs something in Rachel's memory. Cohen continues. "I fell asleep in the back of the car, and when I woke, I was curled up on a bed of moss in a forest on the outskirts of BethEl. Not too far from where I found you, actually. Francis showed up right around the time I woke up."

Rachel shakes her head. "That's a crazy story. It sounds so—"

"Unbelievable? I know. I can't imagine what I would tell my parents if I ever saw them again."

"Did your parents actually know they were sending you here, to BethEl?"

Cohen shakes his head. "Nope. As far as they knew, they really did send me to a boarding school. I guess God had a different school in mind for me."

"What about your parents, though? Don't you think they were scared after they realized you never made it to the school?" Rachel wonders if there is anyone outside BethEl worried about her.

Cohen bites his lip. "I've always wondered that myself."

"You don't know?"

"No one in BethEl knows what happens to the family and friends we leave behind. It's one of the sacrifices we make."

"That has to be painful." Rachel stares at the sidewalk. "I guess it's not all bad that I can't remember."

Cohen glances at her then shifts the conversation. "Anyway, back to Francis. After he found me, he took me into his home for a few years. Then when I turned thirteen, I moved into my own house. Since I arrived in BethEl, Francis has been my Mentor and my father figure. That's why I help him with Shabbat—I am his Disciple, and I am also his protégé."

"What do you mean?"

"Francis is the town Priest. In BethEl, we all have roles based on the Giftings God has given us—like the Healers and Menders who helped you. Some of them were doctors and nurses before they arrived, and Francis was going to school to be a pastor." He glances at Rachel and seems to read her mind. "But don't worry, not everyone's past life translates directly to what they do here. Even if you can't remember your life before BethEl, I am confident we will discover what your role is here."

Rachel bites her lip and nods. Just like at the Shabbat celebration, a part of her wants to abandon her past and weird dreams and embrace this strange new world and the comfort she has in her Finder. But her vivid nightmares from the Clinic linger in her mind like a foul scent and taunt her with the truth she can't remember. Rachel stifles a shiver. Instead she says, "So what's your role in BethEl?"

Hands still in his pockets, Cohen shrugs. "Just training to be a future Priest. That's why I couldn't visit you in the Clinic those few days. I had to help out with some things while Francis was on Sabbatical. Other than that, I'm still waiting to see if Yahweh gives me another assignment."

"Oh." Rachel watches him from the corner of her eye.

"But I'm a Finder now." Cohen forces a smile in Rachel's direction then stops and points to a townhouse unit that looks exactly like every other one on the street. "That's my place, just so you know."

They walk to Rachel's doorstep in silence.

"Hey, thanks. For everything," Rachel hesitates. "Since I woke up from the accident, you are the only thing that has been constant." She meets his gray eyes. "For what it's worth, the fact that you're my Finder feels like a big deal to me."

Cohen's eyes dart down then back to Rachel's. "You're welcome."

"I feel stupid telling you this . . ." Rachel's voice trails off. Cohen waits for her to continue. "I don't know what I'm missing by being here," she finally says. "I don't have memories of a family like you do. At first it bothered me, but now"—she shrugs, ignoring the instinctual urge to touch her stomach and pushes past the images lingering from her dreams—"the feelings I have here are so new. I can't explain it, but I know I've never felt this way before."

Cohen folds his arms across his chest. "What do you feel?"

Rachel peels her eyes from his. The covered porch partially hides the magical BethEl sky, now completely filled with the dark of night. No daylight remains. In the distance, a star tumbles from its heavenly palace. It seems to bounce through the darkness like a ball spilling down the stairs, passing visible planets and galaxies on its way to earth. Rachel shivers, but even the chill can't steal the warmth that spreads through her body as she glances back at Cohen. With a deep breath, Rachel says the four words she is certain she has never said before in her life. "I feel at home."

CHAPTER 7

Rachel enters the dark townhouse and doesn't bother to turn on a light. She shuffles over to the front window in the living room and peeks through the curtains to watch Cohen walk home. He's nearly past her house when he stops and turns. A girl with bouncy hair runs up the sidewalk toward him. Rachel watches as Jubilee touches Cohen's arm. Curls dance about her shoulders as she tosses her head back and laughs. A smirk spreads across Cohen's face. Jubilee leaps into his arms and hugs his neck. They linger. Rachel's eyes shift to the floor. She leans back from the window to make sure they can't see her before she dares another peek. Cohen pulls away. Jubilee hesitates, waves goodnight, then turns back toward the townhouse next to Rachel's.

The curtain swishes back into place as Rachel jumps away from the window. She holds her breath and listens to Jubilee's feet pound up the front steps. The door of the adjacent townhouse opens and closes, and a lyrical voice seeps through the walls. Jubilee sings a refrain from one of the songs played during dinner. Rachel feels a twinge of jealousy as Jubilee's voice fades to a soft hum then melts into the silence of the night. She rubs her burning eyes and plops down on the couch. A dull pain works its way across her abdomen, reminding her again of the dreams she is trying to forget. She glances down at her body and tries to shake the strange sensation that her stomach should be larger than it is.

"It's not real," she whispers to herself. But even as she says the words, she isn't sure she believes them. Her emotions feel as muddled as her mind. Now that the excitement of the day has dissolved, Rachel is left with an ache in her body and fear of the nightmares that are sure to come.

She reaches for a blanket someone draped over the corner of the couch and wonders what generous BethEl resident contributed it to her new home. The soft fabric promises to make everything better as Rachel wraps it around her shoulders and pulls it tight against her chilled body. A comforting scent lingers on the blanket—old wood, fresh air, and a hint of cherry. She brings a corner of the fabric to her face and breathes deeply. It smells like Cohen.

Rachel hesitates then wraps the blanket tighter around her shoulders. She stretches out on the sofa and digs her bare feet in between the cushions. Though she tries, Rachel knows she won't be able to keep her eyes open. Even the fear of falling asleep can't hold it at bay. Eventually, sleep will come, and so will the dreams.

As Rachel drifts in and out of consciousness, a strange emotion emerges from deep within the recesses of her memory. Anticipation and fear flood her body each time her heavy eyelids flutter. Her heart rate quickens then slows as the oppressive weight of sleep takes over. Her pulse accelerates as her body flinches, not allowing slumber to win so easily. Before she can protest, a wave of fatigue washes over her and transports Rachel to a world where memories and nightmares fight for her devotion.

***

Familiar images drift toward Rachel in sleep. A cracked mirror with a blurry reflection of a girl. This time, Rachel recognizes the face—it is hers. The mirror is replaced by an image of a sink filled with wet strands of hair—Rachel's hair. Scissors sit on the ledge. Steel walls come to enclose her on every side. The cold floor presses against her back and sends a shiver up her spine. Eyes trace the matching metal ceiling where tiny shafts of light filter through a vent. A muffled voice says her name. The walls fade to white. Sterile smells assault her nostrils. A man in a white jacket stands before her. Black glasses frame his eyes. A smile curls on his lips then fades as he crumbles into a pile of sand. The sand bubbles then gushes like a geyser, spewing in all directions. The force throws Rachel to the ground; the sand surrounds her like a desert wilderness.

Rachel presses her palms against the ground and pushes up into a seated position. Sand clings to her arm and cheek. She wipes it away and dusts off the white nightgown that stretches over her pregnant belly. Her fingers graze the lace hem of the nightshirt before taking in the landscape. A midnight-blue sky wraps around the land. The chirp of crickets is the only sound she hears. Everything else in the desert remains still and silent. Rachel shivers.

A howl in the distance brings her to her feet. With a hand on her belly, Rachel stumbles through the thick sand. Another howl echoes, this time closer. Rachel takes off in a sprint.

The haunting wails are all around her now. Her heart races. Feet stick in the sand. She tumbles to the ground but jumps back up. On the distant horizon, a faint glow beckons her. She lengthens her stride and runs as fast as her heavy stomach will allow. The growing sounds of the night predators encroach from every direction.

Rachel scrambles over the top of the dune where she saw the glow, stops, and looks around. There is no light source, no safe haven. Nowhere to hide. She tries to push past the panic, but fear creeps in like a parasite needing a host. A foggy feeling fills her head. Breath is too rapid. Palms sweat.

A beastly growl urges her forward, down the sandy dune. The ground slips from beneath her. It undulates like a wave and throws her down the mountain of sand. Arms flail, but her fingers find nothing to which she can cling. Rachel tumbles down the hill and rolls to a stop. The howls cease, and a voice greets her. “Hello, Rachel.”

She stifles a scream. A man towers over her in his gray suit. There is a sort of glow about him. Hair dark as the starless sky frames his striking face. Blood turns to ice in Rachel’s veins as she shuffles away then stands.

“Rachel,” he coos, “don’t be afraid.” Despite his consoling tone, Rachel takes another step back. “I have been searching for you.”

“Who are you?”

He tilts his head curiously as he steps closer.

“Who are you?” she repeats, this time with force.

The man ignores her question. “You shouldn’t be out here all alone, wandering around in a place like this.” He holds out his hand. “Come.”

Rachel turns to run, but her body slams into something solid in the darkness. She stumbles back and peers up into the shadowed face of another man. Before she can recognize him, he spins Rachel around and pulls her close to his chest. A hand clamps over her mouth and muffles her scream.

Still gripping her against him, the second man steps out of the shadows and into the glow being cast from the man in the gray suit. "You must be careful, Rachel," the man holding her whispers. "Even the Darkness can masquerade as Light."

He directs his attention to the man in the suit. "You are too late. I have the child now." He places a protective hand on Rachel's pregnant stomach. "The child is under my care, and so long as it is, you shall not lay a finger on it." Rachel's defender reaches to his side and draws a flaming sword from its sheath. Heat radiates from the weapon as he advances forward, still holding Rachel.

The suited man opposing them unleashes an icy-black blade with a hook on the end. The strange onyx metal is nearly camouflaged by the night. "Too late?" he mocks. "No. I am afraid you are the one who is too late."

Before Rachel's guardian has time to react, her attacker lunges. She hears the screams of protest, sees the flash of the fiery blade, but it *is* too late.

The assailant steps back with his sword at his side. A look of pleasure spreads across his face as beads of dark liquid cling to the blade and drip into the sand. Pain sears through Rachel's body. Stumbling backward, she looks down at her pregnant belly. Blood puddles around her feet. She can't tell what is skin and what is fabric.

The sensation fades from her arms and legs as all feeling centralizes in her gut. Rachel crumples to the ground and curls around the wound. The man who tried to protect her kneels beside her. His massive hands cup her face.

"This is not the end," he whispers over her. "For this child will be called a Prophet of the Most High. It will go on before the Lord to prepare the way for him." The man's voice becomes distant as the dream loses its hold.

"To give his people the knowledge of salvation through the forgiveness of their sins because of the tender mercy of our God, by which the rising sun will come to us from Heaven."

His face fades.

"To shine on those living in darkness and in the shadow of death, to guide our feet into the path of peace."

The darkness consumes her.

***

A deafening crack of thunder shakes the tiny townhouse. Rachel bolts upright. Hands clutch her stomach and rub the tender but nearly healed wound. Sickness fills her gut as she pictures the image of her pregnant stomach torn open and the baby taken from her. Her heart knocks against her rib cage as rain pelts the house. She looks around the living room, confused. Lightning dances outside. The room lights up. Seconds later, a deep growl of thunder echoes through the night.

Rachel catches her breath and considers moving to the bedroom, but her body is too stiff and sore. She shifts uncomfortably on the couch then rolls over to face the window. Her arms wrap around her abdomen as she tries to shake the sensation of the nightmare.

Eventually the rhythmic downpour lulls Rachel back into a half-asleep state. The white noise comforts her as she watches the window light up with another series of dancing lights. Eyelids flutter as the intensity of the light show increases. Her brain begins to conjure the initial making of dreams.

Rachel's consciousness jumps awake as the windowpanes rattle with a violent crash. Her eyes shoot open, and for a split second, she sees a shadow outside the living room window. The sky outside is black again, but Rachel can't ignore the undeniable feeling that she saw something outside the window that was not there a minute ago. She stares at the glass, willing her eyes to see what her mind hopes is not there.

The rain slows in intensity. Wind whistles against the house. Rachel draws her knees to her chest and makes herself as small as possible. Hands clutch her ears to shut out what sounds like words whispered in the gale. Another flash of lightning, this time accompanied immediately by a crack of thunder. The light illuminates the window. Rachel's breath catches in her throat.

Backlit against the raging storm is the silhouette of a man directly outside the house, hands pressed against the window. Rachel's hands fly to her mouth to stifle a scream as the light disappears, replaced by the night sky. Not even a second passes before the storm illuminates the window again. The shadowy figure is gone.

Fear springs Rachel's body to life. She manages to leap over the back of the couch and shuffle backward into the shadows of the kitchen. She snatches a knife from the counter, stumbles toward the front door, and nearly trips over a pair of shoes she left in the entryway. A half-wall separates the front entrance from the living room. She crouches behind it and reaches up to the door. Her fingers slide over the deadbolt and flip it into a locked position. Rachel peers around the corner to the window where she'd seen the figure. The night sky lights up the panes again. Still, nothing is there.

Rachel crawls from the entryway to the back of the couch. Adrenaline surges through her veins. With eyes fixed on the door, she waits, knife gripped firmly in hand.

The house is quiet. Thunder is distant now. At least thirty minutes pass before Rachel begins to wonder if the figure outside the window was just a dream.

She crawls around one side of the couch with the knife still clutched tight. She grabs the blanket off the cushion and drags it with her. As she comes around the side table, she notices a book she hadn't seen before. Rachel slides it down to the floor and carries it around to the back of the couch. She wraps the blanket around her shoulders, draws it close to her face, then lays the knife beside her on the floor.

Though the room is black, Rachel can make out the bold words on the front of the book. Her eyes, now well-adjusted to the darkness, trace over the letters as her index finger follows. Unsure what might happen if she dares to flip open the pages, Rachel hesitates.

The cover opens easily, as if the motion is familiar for the book. Her eyes land on a handwritten note on the title page, but the script is too small. She brings the book closer to her face. A scent lingers on the pages. Something familiar. The scent stirs her. Images of large wooden bookcases race through Rachel's mind then vanish. She hesitates then decides to take a moment to try to place the fleeting memories as the Healers taught her, but they disappear like mist.

More curious about the handwritten note in the book than the forgotten memories, Rachel reaches for the lamp on the side table. Her fingers pause on the knob as she glances one more time at the empty window before flipping on the light. A soft amber glow bathes the worn title page.

Next to the words *Holy Bible* the handwriting is illuminated.

Rachel, while you may not remember the truth of who you are, may you never forget God's goodness and love for you. Yahweh made you for a purpose. I can't wait for us to discover what that is. Reach out to him. Ask him for the answers. Seek him. Yahweh is eager to answer those who call on him. Cohen.

Rachel's left hand smooths the Bible's cover back into place. She lays her palms against the worn leather as she tries to guess how many items in the house once belonged to Cohen. Now looking at it closely, Rachel recognizes this book as the exact Bible Cohen read from when he visited her in the Clinic. At times when she was too tired, Cohen sat with the Bible in the corner, reading silently and scribbling notes. Rachel didn't realize he was writing a note to her.

Once again, Rachel's Finder is the only source of comfort and peace in this strange and sometimes frightening new life. Her eyes close as she listens to the sound of the fading storm.

As the minutes tick by, Rachel's breathing deepens. Eyelids fall. Her chin hits her chest as her head droops, jarring her awake. The Bible falls from her knees and lands open on the floor.

Rachel stands, deciding it's now safe to move back to the couch. As she picks up the Bible, something on the open page catches her eye. Pencil marks underline a small section of words. Rachel stifles a yawn as her tired eyes scan the ancient scriptures.

The words jolt her mind awake. Panic grips Rachel as she tries to make sense of the words Cohen underlined in the Bible that once belonged to him. Her trembling voice reads the haunting words.

"And you, my child, will be called a Prophet of the Most High; for you will go on before the Lord to prepare the way for him, to give his people the knowledge of salvation through the forgiveness of their sins, because of the tender mercy of our God, by which the rising sun will come to us from Heaven to shine on those living in darkness and in the shadow of death, to guide our feet into the path of peace."

CHAPTER 8

An impressive and ancient building towers above Rachel. Her heart stirs. Something about this place speaks to the deepest recesses of her mind and soul. It awakens something hidden, but what that something is, she isn't sure. Rachel stifles a shiver.

The dark stone of the Chapel is inlaid with intricate designs and patterns. A massive steeple on the front and centermost part of the Chapel stretches to the visible cosmos of the BethEl sky, holding a cross high enough for all the world—or at least all of BethEl—to see. The proud steeple is flanked by twelve smaller ones, each topped with its own cross to bear. The heavenly bodies of the universe hover like spectators.

Carved columns flank the sides of the building. Menacing gargoyle-like creatures lay slain atop the capitals. Each head is crushed by the foot of a carved and terrifying winged soldier. The faces of the strange beings unnerve Rachel. She jumps when Cohen appears beside her.

"Malakim," he whispers.

"Angels?"

"Archangels to be exact. Your recall has improved."

"There are seven of them?"

"That's what legend says." Cohen glances over at Rachel. "You feeling okay today?"

Her eyes don't meet his. "Just didn't sleep well. I'll be all right."

Rachel can feel Cohen's stare. After a minute he says, "You ready to go inside?" He nods in the direction of the Chapel doors. "It's even more incredible in there."

Rachel tries to swallow against the tightness that has formed in her throat. Her insides bubble. Skin prickles. Cohen walks ahead and leads her up the grand entrance.

Massive slabs of stone pile on top of each other to create the path for anyone who dares to enter the sacred space. At the top, Cohen disappears inside the dark doorway. After a deep breath, Rachel follows.

The entry leads into a small, dark room lit only by candles. The soft glow dances on the walls and casts curious shadows as the residents of BethEl file past. The room ends in a stone tunnel where more candles flank the hall. They whisper to Rachel as they guide her feet. Their beckoning flames conjure up now-familiar images from her dreams. Rachel's mind lingers on them until she stumbles forward and runs into the back of Cohen. He catches her arm.

"Sorry." Embarrassment warms her cheeks. Cohen only smiles.

The tunnel before them opens into a brightly lit sanctuary. Rachel's eyes are instantly drawn upward. Her lips betray her with an audible gasp. The barrel vault ceiling soars above, covered with a fresco of a heavenly scene. Images of Malakim match the sculptures in the stone on the front of the Chapel. The gargoyles make a second appearance as well—this time, even more sinister. Their eyes judge Rachel as they discern her secrets—even the ones she can't remember.

The culmination of the images tells a story and carries Rachel's eyes from one scene to the next. Her gaze drifts to the front of the Chapel, behind the altar. There the mural crescendos with a painted image of a throne surrounded by a rainbow. It appears empty except for the brilliant-white light that occupies the seat of power.

A man behind Rachel clears his throat.

"Oh." Rachel steps out of his way. The man smiles then walks down the aisle to take a seat. Several of the pews are already occupied.

Cohen appears beside Rachel and grabs her elbow. "Take a seat anywhere. It's about to start." Rachel slides her arm away from his hand.

Cohen takes a seat on the right side of the Chapel. Rachel turns, walks to the left side, and finds a seat in a nearly empty row across from him. She watches Cohen shift in his seat then fold and unfold his hands in his lap. He glances over at Rachel and forces a smile. She draws a shaky breath and for a moment wishes she would have sat closer to her Finder.

As they wait to begin, the Chapel is quickly filled as the rest of BethEl enters for what is sure to be a momentous occasion in their town's history. A couple times, Rachel catches Cohen glancing at her across the aisle. At first she avoids his gaze, but when Francis enters the sanctuary from a doorway behind the altar, she allows her eyes to meet Cohen's and returns his smile. Francis clears his throat and draws every eye to the front, even Cohen's.

"Thank you all for being here on this truly historic day." Francis's deep voice echoes off the vaulted ceiling. "For the first time in the history of BethEl,

Yahweh has chosen to send out a team of Apostles from our city. Today, Yahweh will indicate those select individuals. Here's how it will work. I will come around and place my hands on all of you, to pray and listen for Yahweh's will. His instructions, not mine. I am told that if you are chosen, Yahweh will make that known to both you and me. How? I guess we will find out!" His eyebrows dart up as his full lips part into a smile. "Of course, it is up to you as to whether or not you will say yes to the calling. But keep in mind, it is a great honor to be chosen as an Apostle. This assignment will not be without its challenges, but it will be highly rewarding. I am honored to serve with all of you. Please remain in your seats until after I have prayed over everyone. Then I will call our newly appointed team forward. We will pray a blessing and commission them." He pauses. "This evening we will have a send-off celebration in the Common Gardens behind our homes. The team leaves tonight." Whispers drift through the crowd. "Any questions?"

Rachel holds her tongue. No one else speaks up either.

"Wonderful. Then let us begin." Francis descends the stairs, his priestly robe in one hand while he balances himself with the other. He makes his way down the right side of the Chapel first.

Rachel watches Francis place his hands on the residents of BethEl, young and old alike. The eyes of everyone else in the sanctuary are closed. A girl who looks to be no more than ten years old sits in the second row. Her tiny shoulders look even smaller under the weight of Francis's massive hands. Arms are held out in front of her, palms open like she is ready to receive a gift. The murmur of Francis's voice echoes through the marble room yet never lands long enough for Rachel to make out his words. She wishes she could see the face of the little girl. Could someone so young be chosen? Could Rachel be chosen?

Francis approaches Cohen.

Rachel sits on her hands as a thought strikes her: what if Cohen is chosen to leave and she is not? Or equally as bad: what if she is chosen and Cohen is not?

Francis pats him on the back before he rests his hands on Cohen's shoulders. Rachel turns away and forces her eyes closed.

When she looks up again, Francis is several rows behind Cohen, where he prays over another young man. Cohen is still, quiet, and visibly unchanged. Rachel's lungs exhale the tension.

As the hours pass, Rachel becomes more attuned to the details and strange nuances of the Chapel. An odd aroma fills the sanctuary from the two bowls on the altar. Smoke wafts and curls like a snake into the air. The scent of the incense tickles Rachel's memory and attempts to conjure images from her nightmares. Rachel closes her eyes to shut them out. She feels nauseous.

There is a light touch on her shoulder. Francis chuckles from behind Rachel as she jumps. He pats her back to reassure her that she is not the first one to be startled by his presence. He begins to whisper under his breath and places his hands on Rachel's shoulders. She wants to shake them off. Instead she inhales, holds the breath, then lets it out. Not sure what to do or what to expect, Rachel slows her breathing and quiets her mind.

As Francis prays, Rachel's closed eyes peer into the dark of her mind. Black turns to swirls of color, and the color turns to images. The fingers of Rachel's memory grasp at the pictures, willing them to come into focus. The swirls and shapes slide into place, painting a picture—a sand dune that looks over an arid valley.

The searing sun beats down on the familiar desert. There is not a tree or even a blade of grass in sight, only sand and stone. A shiver slithers up Rachel's spine as she realizes that what at first appeared to be rocks strewn across the desert floor are actually bones of a skeleton—human bones. Thousands of them. As far as she can see in any direction, dry bones litter the valley floor in heaps of decay.

Rachel furrows her brow, the presence of Francis already forgotten.

In the vision, a bubbling feeling forms in Rachel's gut and rises in her throat. Before she can stop them, sounds spew from her lips. Incoherent syllables form and pour out like a song. She can't hold them in. Like resonating glass, the sounds pierce the air with a noise haunting and beautiful, then they shatter. More sounds, more notes. They have no sense or rhythm, yet they are perfectly strung together. Rachel's hands rest on her pregnant belly. The baby inside her moves.

A haunting rattle fills the desert valley as Rachel babbles. The bones shake. Their movements are slow at first, but as the ramble of sounds flow from Rachel's mouth, the bones come together, bone to bone, to reassemble into their original skeletal structures.

Gaping holes where eyes used to be stare back at Rachel from the bleached skulls. She withdraws from the horror and stumbles. Firm hands catch her. The baby inside her kicks as Rachel peers up into the face of the guardian who tried to save her in her dream. He spins her back around to stare at the army of skeletons. His hands press against her stomach.

"Speak," the man whispers. "The child must speak!" Heat radiates from Rachel's gut and shoots through her body.

The vision before her blips in and out, replaced by a dark, metal cell. A voice whispers her name.

The scene before her fades from black to light to the sink filled with hair.

The metal cell again, then back to the desert.

A chatter arises from the horde of ghastly skeletons.

"Speak!" the bones shout. "Speak!"

The dream blips in and out again. White walls. Sterile smells. Desert sands.

The army of skeletons chants. Hollow caverns where eyes used to be stare longingly in Rachel's direction. Their jaws hang slack, mouths agape. Rachel's heart races. Her breath is ragged. The skeletons tremble before her and stomp their feet. Dust swirls about their sticklike ankles.

"Breathe!" one of the skeletons commands. "Breathe into us!"

Rachel's body shudders. Tiny beads of sweat form on her upper lip, but she doesn't notice. She's fully entranced in the vision. It has become her only reality.

"Speak!" The skeletons chant louder. "Breathe!"

The guardian clutches Rachel's pregnant stomach. "This child will be called a Prophet of the Most High," he whispers into Rachel's ear. "For it will go on before the Lord to prepare the way for him. To give his people the knowledge of—"

His words are cut short as an invisible force throws him back.

The sinister man with the gray suit materializes where Rachel's protector once stood. He reaches to his side and unsheathes a hooked sword. Rachel tries to scream, knowing what is about to happen.

The man lunges forward and slashes open her pregnant stomach. Water and blood pour to the ground.

Pain rips through her body and yanks Rachel from the vision.

***

She can feel Francis's desperate grasp on her shoulders now. His nails nearly dig into her skin. He lets go as if being thrown from her. His breath is labored. Rachel turns and looks up into his face. The warm coloring of Francis's dark skin has drained to ash, his blue eyes wide and wild.

Rachel glances around the sanctuary. No one seems to have noticed their bizarre encounter. She clasps her hands together to calm the shaking. It doesn't help.

"I'm sorry," she whispers. "I'll leave." She starts to stand.

"No!" Francis's voice is hushed but insistent. "Please. Stay. I would like a word with you." With that, he backs away from Rachel and moves on to the next person. Francis places his hands on the shoulders of a woman in the row ahead, but his gaze is fixed intently on Rachel.

She bows her head but keeps her eyes open for the remainder of the time, fixated on a crack in the marble floor. All the while, she can feel the gaze of Francis boring into the top of her head.

Rachel's stomach flips. She's not sure what she experienced when Francis laid his hands on her. She wasn't chosen as an Apostle, she's sure of that, but *something* happened.

After what feels like several more agonizing hours, Francis takes his spot in front of the altar. "I am amazed by the goodness of our Lord, Yahweh," he begins, "and I am honored to see the people he has chosen as Apostles for this mission. I suspect Yahweh is up to something good." Francis pauses, glances in Rachel's direction, then continues. "Those of you who have been chosen, if you accept your calling, please come forward."

Starting with the front row on Rachel's side, the chosen individuals stand and make their way to the front of the Chapel. Rachel is caught off guard when the tiny blonde-haired girl near the front of the other side stands and walks forward—a child. Cohen said that everyone is treated as an adult in BethEl, but it still doesn't make sense how a girl so young could be chosen for such a seemingly significant role.

Rachel counts five pairs of individuals as they file in a line beside Francis. A sixth pair walks from the back. They take their spot, but Francis continues to wait. His eyes well with joy as he watches the aisle. Cohen exits his row, pauses, then walks toward his Mentor. When he finally reaches the altar, Francis pulls him in for a strong embrace. It would be a heartwarming moment if Cohen weren't Rachel's Finder.

Rachel doesn't hear anything Francis says as he commissions the team. There are words, applause, then Francis asks the rest of the residents of BethEl to extend their hands forward in a sign of blessing. Rachel follows their lead. Her eyes find Cohen's. The smile he flashes her is forced.

A few seats over from where Cohen was seated, Jubilee wells with pride. Her bright-pink lips beam against her porcelain-white skin. Rachel wishes she could be happy for Cohen like Jubilee is; instead she wonders what will happen if she doesn't have a Finder.

Without her memory, Rachel is disoriented. Without Cohen, she will be lost.

The blessing ends. Francis dismisses the crowd and reminds everyone to attend the send-off dinner at dusk. He shakes the hands of each newly appointed Apostle then sends them home to prepare and pack. He embraces Cohen again and places a fatherly kiss on his forehead.

Jubilee stands in the center of the aisle, ready to hug Cohen. She wraps her arms around his neck, whispers something in his ear, and plants a kiss on his cheek. Rachel bites the inside of her lip. Jubilee casts one last glance at Cohen as she leaves the Chapel.

Several other people wait to congratulate the Apostles. Cohen hurries through the crowd and makes his way to Rachel. Francis watches from the altar.

"Hey," he nearly whispers.

"Hey."

"I, uh, I wasn't expecting to be chosen."

"Congratulations," Rachel offers.

"Look, this changes a lot of things, not just for me, but for you too." Rachel doesn't respond. "The first thing you need to know is that I'm still your Finder, you're still my Disciple, and I'm still here for you. Well, sort of."

"You won't exactly be here for me."

"But when I come back—"

"What do I do in the meantime?"

"You will be in good hands. Don't worry. Francis offered to fill in as your Mentor while I'm away."

Rachel's stomach sinks. "Are you sure that's a good idea?" Francis continues to watch them from a distance.

"Are you kidding? It's a great idea." Rachel catches Francis's eye and looks away. "Look," Cohen says, "I know this isn't ideal, but God moves in mysterious ways."

"What does that mean?"

"It means something bigger is at work here. The intersecting of our lives is not coincidence. And even though we've only known each other a short time," Cohen takes her hand in his, "I'm so thankful to know you."

Rachel yanks her hand back. Cohen flinches. A look of hurt creases his face.

"I'd like to introduce you two now, if that's okay." He nods his head toward Francis.

Rachel offers a weak "Sure," and follows Cohen to the front of the Chapel.

Francis finishes a conversation with one of the other chosen Apostles then turns to Rachel. He speaks to Cohen but doesn't take his eyes off her. "My boy, I am so proud of you."

"Francis, this is Rachel—my Disciple."

"Ah yes, the mysterious Rachel. I am sorry we are just now meeting. I was away on Sabbatical when you arrived and didn't return until yesterday right before Shabbat." He pauses. "You have caused quite a stir in our little town, my dear. No one knew you were coming. I'm sure Cohen has told you how unique that makes you."

She nods. "I feel more weird than unique."

"My dear, all of God's chosen people are a little weird, as you say. But it is the weird who change the world."

Cohen stands closer to Rachel. "Francis, thank you for offering to keep Rachel in your care while I'm away. I know she is in the best hands."

"It is my honor, dear boy." Never leaving her gaze, Francis's eyes flash with some untold secret.

"I guess I better go home to pack." Cohen shakes the hand of his Finder and Mentor.

"I couldn't be more honored to send you away on such a journey. May the Lord bless you, my son, and everything your hands touch."

Cohen bows his head then looks to Rachel. "Are you ready to go? There are a few things I'd like to set in place for you before I leave—"

"Actually," Francis interjects, "I'd love a moment with your Disciple if you don't mind."

Cohen beams. "Of course. Rachel, I'll come by your place this afternoon."

Her voice comes out strained. "Okay." All she can think about right now is being left alone with Francis. What happened when he touched her shoulders?

"Great." Cohen walks away and waves. "See you soon." The soles of his new boots squeak against the marble floor and echo through the now-empty Chapel. Rachel catches a glimpse of one of the monstrous figures on the ceiling fresco. Glowing eyes glare at her, hungry and desperate. A shudder travels the length of her body. The gonging of a church bell causes her to jump.

"Are you all right, my dear?" The swish of Francis's robe accompanies the question as he takes a seat in the front row of the Chapel. He pats the spot on the pew beside him. "Come have a seat. My bones are weary."

Rachel slides into the row, leaving enough space for three people between them. He turns to face her, rubbing the gray stubble on his cheeks before speaking. "How are you adjusting to life inside our little town?"

"Well, it's definitely strange."

Francis grins and nods. "May I ask you a question?"

"Sure," Rachel answers, not sure she has a choice.

"Do you believe in coincidences, Rachel?"

She clears her throat. "I, uh, I suppose so."

"I don't." He raises his eyebrows. "There are no coincidences with God, only divine appointments. And this, my dear, is one of them."

Rachel doesn't know how to respond.

"You see, Rachel, I know who you are, and I have been waiting for you." The vaulted ceiling repeats his words.

"You've been waiting for me?" Fear mixes with hope. Rachel doesn't even know herself, and now, here before her sits someone who claims to know her.

"Yes, my dear," the old man chuckles. "I have been waiting a very long time."

"How do we know each other?"

Francis smooths his hands over his robe. "Well, maybe *know* is a bit of a stretch. I don't personally know you." Rachel's stomach relaxes. "But I know *of* you."

She angles her body toward his.

"Are you familiar with the story of Simeon in the Bible?"

Rachel thinks back to the stories Cohen read to her in the Clinic. "I don't think so. I'm having trouble remembering things."

Francis waves a hand. "Not to worry. You'll get caught up at the Academy. Simeon," he continues, "was a righteous and devout man. The Holy Spirit was on him. He lived in Jerusalem during the time Jesus was born. But long before Jesus was ever born, Simeon was made a promise by Yahweh."

Rachel's curiosity is piqued at the mention of that now familiar name—Jesus. The tone of Francis's voice and his mysterious nature prompt her to ask, "What kind of promise?"

"The Lord promised Simeon that before he died, Simeon would see the one who would redeem humanity."

"And did he?"

"He did." There is a spark in Francis's eye. "One day, the Holy Spirit told Simeon to go to the temple. So he did. And guess who was there?"

"Jesus?"

"Yes, but not just any Jesus. Baby Jesus."

An unexpected and sharp pain flashes along the healing wound on Rachel's abdomen.

"When Simeon entered the temple, he saw Mary and Joseph carrying baby Jesus. They were there to present him to the Lord, because according to the law, every firstborn belongs to Yahweh. When Simeon saw them, he immediately took up the child in his arms and declared, 'Sovereign Lord, as you have promised, you may now dismiss your servant in peace. For my eyes have seen your salvation.'"

Silence lingers between them as the eyes of countless Malakim peer down from their painted positions.

"That's a nice story, but—"

"But you're wondering what this has to do with you, am I right?"

"Right," Rachel whispers.

Francis shifts in his seat and turns to face her more fully. One arm rests along the back of the pew as he leans in closer.

"Rachel, I am not so unlike Simeon." He sees the confusion etched in her face. "I am old now." He chuckles. "Well, seventy, but this arthritis makes me feel older than I am. Anyway, when I was younger, shortly after I arrived in BethEl, I heard the Lord speak to me in an audible voice. It was only one of two times that has ever happened to me, and I have been following the Lord for a very long time." His eyes drift as if remembering the moment.

Rachel sits up straighter. "What did he say?"

"He said, 'Francis, you are my servant. In you I am well pleased. Because of your devotion and love for me, I swear by myself that you will not depart from this world until you see the Lord's Anointed.'"

Rachel has no response.

"Now let me assure you, my dear, I am not crazy. I didn't make it up. I heard the voice of the Lord, and that's not all he said."

Rachel uncrosses her legs and leans toward him. "What else did he say?"

"He said, 'In your old age, Francis, a child will be brought before you, and this child will be called the Prophet of the Most High God." Rachel stiffens. "For this child will go on before me to prepare the way for my return. This child is the one I have chosen, the Anointed.'"

Rachel pulls back and shifts her gaze to the ground.

"When I placed my hands on you, Rachel, I saw a vision that leads me to believe that you are the mother of the Lord's Anointed, the child we have been waiting for, and—"

"No. You're mistaken."

"I just—"

"No." Rachel's hair swishes as she shakes her head. "You have the wrong girl. I'm sorry. I need to leave." Light-headed, Rachel jumps to her feet, knocking a Bible off the pew in the process. Pages splay open.

Francis stands, hands extended in a peace offering. "I didn't mean to upset you. Please forgive me."

"It's fine. Really." Rachel backs down the aisle; fog fills her head; a stampede echoes in her chest. She turns and quickens her pace. The eyes of the menacing creatures glare down from the ceiling. The doors at the end of the aisle stand open. Through the candlelit hall, daylight beckons her.

Rachel bolts out the door and down the steps of the Chapel, taking them two at a time. She casts a glance backward; her foot trips on the pavement as her body crashes into a boy at the bottom of the stairs. Her hands scrape the concrete as she falls backward onto the steps.

Embarrassed, she blurts out, "Sorry!" She brushes her hands against her jeans. "I didn't watch where I was going. Are you okay?"

Eyes wide with shock, the boy, only a few years older than her, doesn't respond. Heat rises in Rachel's cheeks. "Are you all right?"

He nods his head and runs a hand through his sandy-blond hair. "You, uh, surprised me." He reaches down to offer Rachel a hand. "Here."

"No!" Rachel shifts away. "I mean—no, thanks." She offers an awkward smile, unable to hide the torrent of emotions Francis stirred. "Sorry again."

Rachel backs away, turns to trot down the sidewalk, and places as much distance as possible between her and the Chapel.

***

The blond-haired boy watches Rachel disappear into a crowd of people. When he is certain she's out of earshot, he reaches into his pocket and pulls out a communication receiver. He brings the small device to his ear.

"Please work this time," he mumbles.

After nine rings, an eerily calm voice answers, "Where the hell have you been?"

The blond-haired boy casts a quick glance in either direction then casually walks around the side of the Chapel. "Sir, I'm not sure exactly." He lowers his voice. "I tried to reach out several times. This is the first time I've been able to—"

"What do you mean you're not sure where you are? We've been trying to reach you for months—"

"Wait. Months?" The boy peers around the corner then ducks back.

"You better have a good explanation." The voice on the other end is like ice.

A smile creeps across the young man's face. "I think I have something you'll like even better than an explanation."

"This better be good."

"Oh, it is. *I found her*."

CHAPTER 9

The front door slams behind Rachel as she enters the townhouse. Shoes flop to the floor. She marches straight down the hall to the bathroom, stripping her clothes off as she walks. Jeans and a T-shirt leave a trail behind her.

Rachel cranks up the water in the shower as hot as she can stand then slips under the thundering stream. Water pounds the back of her neck and shoulders. Steam fills the small bathroom. Rachel thumps her head against the shower wall and begins to tap her forehead in an almost soothing rhythm.

Not even sure how to process her conversation with Francis, Rachel tries to force her mind to go blank. She wishes she could talk to Cohen about it, but he still doesn't know about her weird dreams. The Healers told Rachel it was up to her if she shared that information with her Finder, but she hasn't been able to bring herself to tell Cohen. The Healers' insistence that the dreams aren't real makes Rachel feel like *she* is the one who's crazy. But the vividness and persistence of the nightmares—and now her conversation with Francis—make her wonder if the Healers are the ones who are wrong. Her head thumps harder as she tries to decide what to do.

Rachel traces her finger across the jagged wound on her lower abdomen. The scab starts to peel, leaving behind a bright-pink line that will one day fade into a silvery scar. The Healers told her it was a piece of metal during the accident that punctured and tore her body.

"I was never pregnant," Rachel whispers into the water. "It's just a dream. A nightmare. It wasn't real."

Then why is Francis so convinced otherwise? And why won't the lifelike dreams go away?

For the first time, Rachel allows her mind to really consider the possibility. If she were pregnant, how would she have ended up in such a situation? Who would the father have been? Did she love him?

Rachel shoves the thought from her mind and instead questions how Francis came to the conclusion that she is the mother of some special baby. He doesn't know about her dreams. Or does he? He told Rachel he saw a vision when he placed his hands on her. Rachel saw a vision too.

"I wonder what he saw," she whispers into the water. Her head throbs from thumping it against the shower's wall. "Can't I just move on?" She sighs.

Things were just starting to take a turn for the better. Then Cohen was chosen to leave.

Her confusion turns to frustration as she realizes the only thing that feels familiar and safe is being torn away. The frustration turns to anger. Rage bubbles inside her. Rachel swipes her arm across the shelf in the shower, knocking over a bottle of shampoo. She throws a bar of soap against the shower wall. It lands with a hollow clatter in the tub. Rachel clenches her jaw and grits her teeth. She grasps the shower curtain then pulls, ripping down the curtain and the bar that holds it. The crash jolts her from her outburst.

Rachel's heart races in her chest. Water sprays onto the bathroom floor. She shuts off the shower and scans the mess. Fear grips Rachel as she stares at her trembling hands. "Why did I do that?" she whispers. The rage ebbs as quickly as it came, but it takes more than a few deep breaths to settle the horror of how quickly she snapped. For the first time, Rachel can remember the looks of fear on the faces of the Menders when she lunged at them from the Clinic bed.

Rachel closes the door to the steamy bathroom, not sure how she will explain what she did to Cohen, or now, Francis. She shivers.

With a towel wrapped around her, Rachel tiptoes into the living room to grab the Bible she found the night before. Water drops dot the carpet behind her as she takes it back to the bedroom. She glances at the closed bathroom door as she passes.

In the bedroom, Rachel searches through her closet of clothes. After trying on a few different things, she opts for a simple black cotton dress. On the bed, Rachel pulls the Bible onto her lap. She draws a ragged breath. The pages flop open, and as she anticipated, the book opens to the same passage she read last night.

"And you, my child, will be called a Prophet of the Most High," she reads aloud. "For you will go on before the Lord to prepare the way for him." Her insides flip as she recalls the sound of Francis's voice echoing through the Chapel as he recited these words.

As Rachel rereads the passage, she notices a handwritten note in the margin. The handwriting is the same as the note on the title page of the Bible. An arrow points to the underlined passage. The note reads: *The Lord's Anointed: the second forerunner who will come before Jesus's return. BethEl's mission: find the Lord's Anointed.*

One of Rachel's hands finds its way to her stomach. She presses it against her flat belly. "No," she shakes her head. "No. This is stupid!" she shouts through gritted teeth. She slams the cover of the Bible closed and throws it across the room.

Her black, wavy hair splays across the pillow as she flops back. "I don't even know what is real," she whispers.

Rachel fixes her gaze on the popcorn ceiling, forcing her mind to stop trying to make sense of all the nonsense. Eventually her mind relaxes, and her eyes begin to find shapes and faces in the patterns overhead. One directly above her head looks like a lion.

A wave of exhaustion comes over Rachel like a thick blanket. She forces her eyes to stay open. Transfixed on the ceiling, she whispers, "Don't fall asleep. Don't fall asleep." It's the only solution to the nightmares. She knows she needs to get out of bed, take a walk, or at least sit up, but her arms and legs are lead. Blinks are slower, breathing deeper, thoughts stranger. Darkness dances around the fringe of her vision. It closes in and covers her eyes. Despite her desire to resist, Rachel succumbs.

***

Slate gray forms behind Rachel's closed eyes. Steel walls surround her. Again, the vision tugs at her mind. The metallic scent mixes with the smell of urine and stings her nose. Eyes drift to the vented slats in the ceiling. Beyond the steel room, the world gives way to a pale-gray sky. Wisps of clouds breeze past the tiny openings. Like curls of smoke, the clouds drift into the metal cell and fill the small space. The haze floods Rachel's field of vision until it consumes the image of the metal chamber. The dream morphs.

Now flat on her back, Rachel stares unhindered at the hazy sky. Stalks of grain encircle her body and sway in the wind. Hands press into the cool, soft ground as she sits up. As far as Rachel can see in every direction, she is engulfed by fertile fields. All the way to the horizon line stretches golden grain ready for harvest.

Rachel stands to examine the circular clearing, its diameter not much larger than the length of her body. As she brushes her hands on her thighs, she notices the familiar white nightgown that hangs loose around her thin body. She smooths her hands over her flat stomach. The rich soil leaves a dark stain on the almost sheer fabric.

Grains bend and point south as a powerful gale gusts in from the north. The nightgown presses against Rachel's body. Hair whips into her face. She pulls a dark strand from her mouth and strains her eyes against the bits of soil and grain that pelt her.

As the wind gains intensity, a sound like rushing water pours down from the sky. Rachel spins around the circle. The sound of the watery torrent grows louder, but she cannot find its source. Instead it bellows from all around—the ground, the grain, the sky all cry out with the roar of a multitude, but amidst the chaos, there is one distinct and haunting voice. "Come!" it bellows.

Her hands fly up to cover her ears.

"Come!" the voice urges again.

Rachel crouches. The wind whips her hair. The nightgown slaps her legs.

"Come!" The voice is insistent.

Rachel drops to the ground. She clutches her head and hides her face. Her heart thumps against the cool earth and pulses in her eardrums.

"Come!"

"No, no, no," she whispers into the earth.

The voice hears her objection. "Come!"

"No!"

"COME!"

Through her arms, Rachel peers out at the small clearing, expecting to see the menacing man with the hooked sword. Through the shower of windblown soil and whips of hair, something vibrant red catches her eye. It's almost iridescent. A lone flower, it pushes up through the black soil.

"COME!"

She buries her face again. Her body trembles. The ground quakes. The earth growls its protest to Rachel's resistance. She flattens her body and digs her fingers into the ground, overcome by an instinctual urge to hide.

"COME!" the voice demands one last time. The rumbling of the earth drowns out its sound.

The ground beneath Rachel's cowering body cracks. Her hands press into the soil and strain, but she cannot keep the ground from splitting. As the earth opens to swallow her whole, Rachel grasps in futility for anything to hold on to. Her fingers wrap around the red flower. The stem bends. For a second, it seems to hold her weight, then the roots give way and release from the soil.

With the red flower clutched tightly in hand, Rachel plummets into a world of darkness.

CHAPTER 10

Moonlight illuminates their path as Rachel walks through the Central Gardens with Cohen to the rendezvous point. The trail ends, Cohen told her, in the woods where Francis found him so many years ago, near the same place where Cohen found Rachel. Yahweh chose that exact spot for the newly appointed Apostles to meet their Malak leader who will escort them out of BethEl.

Warm night air mingles with the scent of the garden flowers, yet a chill still manages to wrap itself around Rachel. She shivers.

"Cold?"

"No, just thinking."

"About?" Cohen pauses under the branches of a weeping willow. Stars illuminate the tree-lined path that leads to the Apostles meeting point, but even the beauty of BethEl can't erase the uncertainty and fear in Rachel's gut.

The send-off celebration had been warm and joyful, but the terrors from her nightmares prevented Rachel from enjoying the evening with her new friends. Even now, the darkness of her dreams clings to her.

She draws a shaky breath. This is it; she has to tell him. "I've been having nightmares lately—a lot of nightmares. I've been having them since the accident."

Cohen's eyebrows pull together. "That sounds awful."

"Do you ever have nightmares?"

Cohen is quiet while he thinks. "Not since I was a kid, I guess. Are these dreams about the accident?"

His gentle prying unsettles her. She can't do it. She doesn't want her last few moments with Cohen to be tainted by the darkness of her dreams. "Forget about it. I'm sure they'll go away eventually." Unable to look Cohen in the eye, Rachel starts back down the path.

"You should talk to Francis about your dreams." Cohen follows a step behind her. "Sometimes, in this place, the images we see when we sleep have meaning."

The mention of Francis sends a shiver across Rachel's shoulders.

"Sure you're not cold?"

"I'm fine." She forces a smile.

"Something else is on your mind." Cohen's eyes remain fixed ahead as they walk.

"What makes you say that?"

"I'm not sure. Maybe it's a Finder-Disciple connection or something." A smile spreads on his face.

Heat fills Rachel's cheeks. "It's dumb."

"I doubt it." He hoists his bag on his shoulder.

A long silence passes before Rachel fills it. "It's just, you are the only thing that feels familiar to me." She hugs hers arms to her chest. "When I was in the Clinic, you visited me every day, and now that I'm out, you're leaving." She tries to hide the frustration in her voice. "I still don't know why I'm here, and to be honest, I'm not sure I want to be here," she spits.

"What happened to 'feeling at home'?"

"It's different now."

"You know, there is a reason you were brought to BethEl. Maybe if you focus on discovering what that is—"

"I don't want to!" Rachel explodes as she turns to face him. "I'm lost, okay? Can't you see that? I'm lost, and now I don't have a Finder!"

Cohen looks as hurt as if Rachel had struck him with her fist. He quickly hides it, nods, but doesn't respond. Rachel saw the same look on his face in the Chapel earlier that day, and like that time, she is the one who caused it. Her eyes drop to the ground. The two of them continue down the path in silence.

"Sorry I didn't have a chance to take you to see the Academy today," Cohen finally says. "There were a lot of preparations to be made for our trip. Jubilee will help you get settled on Monday." Rachel clenches her jaw. "Well," Cohen stops. "This is as far as you should go. I want to make sure you don't get lost on your way back home." He winces at his choice of words. "You think you can find your way from here?"

"I hope so." Rachel swallows her regret, wishing she could start the day over. "When will you be back?"

He hesitates. Creases form on his forehead. "I don't know. Whenever Yahweh sends us back. God chooses who comes and goes from this place—and when. He brought you here, Rachel, and he's taking me away, but I believe he will bring me back. God has a plan."

"God's plan sucks."

Cohen bites back a grin. "It seems that way sometimes, doesn't it? But don't forget, God moves in mysterious ways. I'll be back before you know it."

"See you soon, I guess."

"Yeah." His voice is quiet. "See you soon." A hint of doubt flashes in Cohen's eyes. He wavers then reaches over to squeeze her hand. This time, Rachel doesn't pull away.

Without another word, Cohen turns down the path and disappears into the forest.

***

No lamps flank the path on Rachel's walk back to her townhouse. Though daylight has disappeared from the perimeter of the sky, it seems the glow of the heavenly bodies in the center of the mystical night sky should be enough to light her way. But the night feels as dark as Rachel's mood.

Rachel's feet shuffle down the sidewalk. Her pace slows as she sees Cohen's townhouse in the distance. She draws a deep breath then continues.

Dread begins to overtake the feelings of regret as she thinks of going to bed. She can't hide from sleep forever, and once she enters that empty house, she knows it will find her.

Wind rushes through the trees and stirs the hair around Rachel's face. The hem of the black dress tickles her legs. The sensation conjures images from her nightmares and fear so real she can taste it. She wraps her arms around her waist and quickens her steps.

A burst of wind sends a few leaves tumbling down the street. As they swirl about her ankles, one of them sticks to her bare leg, held in place by the forceful gust. Rachel reaches down to peel it away and discovers not a leaf but an unusual flower blossom. The large petals nearly embrace her ankle. Its deep-red color shimmers under the light of the heavenly bodies.

"How?" she whispers. Petal by petal, Rachel frees the flower from her leg, careful not to tear the delicate object that seems to have materialized from her dream. The last petal comes free. The flower falls to the ground, but before Rachel can retrieve it, another gust of wind whips down the street and steals it away.

Down the sidewalk it tumbles, out of reach. Rachel hesitates before following.

Curiosity dissipates and fear intensifies as the mysterious dream flower seems to know the way to Rachel's house. It crosses the threshold of the yard Rachel shares with Jubilee, drifts across the grass, and tumbles down the side of the house. She stops in the front yard. Alarms fire in her head. Something isn't right.

She runs up the front steps, enters the house, then slams the door behind her. Back pressed against the front door, Rachel wavers. "This is stupid," she huffs. "It's a flower. BethEl has tons of flowers. I did not make it appear from a dream."

Rachel throws open the door and stomps down the front steps. She rounds the side of the house and pauses. Her eyes search the darkness, but the flower is gone.

A flash of red catches her attention in the plants along that side of the house. The flower dances in the wind, caught in the branches of a shrub. Rachel takes a step toward it then stops, overcome by the sense that someone is watching her.

Her eyes peer into the darkness that stretches toward the back of the house. The Common Gardens is completely dark. Everyone has gone home from the send-off celebration.

"Hello?" Silence responds. "Jubilee? Is that you?"

Rain begins to drizzle as Rachel makes her way to the flower. She snatches it from the branches, gaze still fixed toward the backyard.

At the corner of the house, a shadow hovers. Rachel's eyes play tricks on her. She blinks. The shadow wobbles, then it slinks around the corner toward the back of the house.

She stumbles back and falls into the shrub. She scrambles to get up. The flower falls from her clutched fingers and lands in an imprint in the mud. Breath catches in her throat.

There, directly below the window to the living room, the same window where Rachel thought she saw a person looking in the night before, are two perfectly formed boot prints.

CHAPTER 11

Thunder crackles through the small town. Rachel's chest heaves as she pants. Her legs burn from the run. The Chapel seemed closer when she walked with Cohen that morning, *and* it wasn't raining. Her body, still weak from recovery, screams at her as she makes her way up the Chapel steps. Her mind plays tricks, making a monster out of every shadow in the dark.

Her cold, wet hands tug on the handles of the giant wooden doors. They're locked. Rain soaks Rachel's face as she stares up at the menacing tower. Monsters and Malakim glare down from the top of the building, backdropped by an ominous sky.

The dress she wore to the send-off dinner is soaked through. It clings to her trembling body like a second skin. A distinct chill marks the early summer night. Shivers glide up and down her spine.

Rachel heaves one more time on the mammoth door and wonders why, in her panic-stricken state, her feet would choose to bring her here. A hollowness forms in her stomach as she realizes that with Cohen gone, she has nowhere else to turn. She folds her arms over her chest and hugs her thin shoulders as she turns to walk away, but a warm glow from a window in the adjacent parsonage beckons her.

Now on the front step of Francis's home, Rachel hesitates and glances over at the Chapel. The hands of the clock tower passed midnight long ago.

"What am I doing?" she whispers. She sucks in a deep breath and, before she can convince herself to leave, knocks on the door. It groans open.

The familiar form of Francis fills the doorway. A deafening crack of thunder covers any words he might have said, but his lips don't move. There is no look of surprise on his face, just a simple gesture for Rachel to enter. He closes the door behind them.

Without a word, Rachel rubs her hands against her bare arms and follows Francis down a narrow hallway. As they pass a small kitchen on the left, Rachel realizes the glow she saw in the window comes from the room up ahead. The hallway ends in a small but open area. A large stone fireplace is its central feature.

The charming cottage is adorned with Francis's simple belongings: a broom in the corner, a small table with a hand-carved chess set, and a rusted and curved farm tool that hangs over the mantle. Rachel shivers when she sees it. Two plain, wooden rocking chairs wait in front of the fire, a blanket draped over the back of one. Vapor curls from a cast-iron kettle on the stone hearth. Two mugs of steaming liquid sit beside it. Despite it being early summer, the warm room is a welcome reprieve from the storm.

"Unseasonably cold tonight with the rain. Would you care to warm yourself by the fire? I have some tea ready for us, and of course, there is the blanket. You are soaked, but this fire should have you dry in no time."

Rachel starts to speak then stops. Francis chuckles, waves away her unspoken question, and shuffles over to one of the chairs. He picks up a mug and begins a methodical rock. "The Lord tells me things, my dear." Rachel hesitates near the entrance to the room. Francis's rocking chair comes to a stop. "Come have a seat. You'll catch your death if you don't dry out."

Rachel's feet squeak against her wet sandals as she takes a seat across from Francis. She wraps the blanket around her shivering frame.

"Now, I am sure you have some questions—"

"I do—"

Francis holds up a hand. "Right now, I have a question for you."

Rachel sips the warm tea. Its heat spreads through her body like an intoxicating drug. "Okay."

He leans forward. Knobby fingers stroke his gray beard. "Do you dream, Rachel?"

She shifts under his gaze. "Doesn't everyone?"

"Yes, of course. Everyone dreams, but did you know that for some people, their dreams have meaning?"

Rachel recalls that Cohen told her the same thing as he left BethEl. A fresh wave of guilt comes over her as she thinks of their last conversation. She glances away.

"God likes to speak to his people, Rachel, and sometimes, he will speak to his people through their dreams."

Rachel takes a long sip of the tea so she doesn't have to respond. The fire cracks and pops, interrupting the silence that fills the room. Francis waits. When Rachel doesn't respond, he changes the subject.

"Tell me about the child you carry. You are obviously not far along. You aren't even showing yet."

The question slips from Rachel's lips. "What makes you think I'm pregnant?"

"The vision I saw of you earlier today." He pauses to watch her. "In it, you were pregnant."

A lightheaded feeling washes over Rachel. "Did you see anything else?"

"Yes." Francis hesitates. "But given the prophetic nature of visions, I'm not sure how literally to take the rest of what I saw. When I saw you pregnant, though, there was an insistence in my spirit that the Lord's Anointed—the child we have been waiting for—is inside you."

Despite the tea, Rachel's mouth feels dry—as dry as a desert. She closes her eyes and sighs, wishing it were Cohen here and not Francis. She gazes into the fire. The hypnotic dance of the flames lulls her mind as she fights to find words. "I was in a car accident a few weeks ago."

"Yes, I heard. How awful."

"Has God already told you everything about me?" It comes out more sarcastically than she intends.

"My apologies, my dear. Please, continue with your story."

Heat floods Rachel's body. She's not sure if it's embarrassment or if the fire is finally thawing her frozen limbs. She sighs and shakes her head. "I'm sorry. I don't know how to process any of this." She gestures around her. "BethEl, your vision, my dreams—"

"Your dreams?"

She presses her lips together. "I'm not pregnant."

Francis furrows his brow. "No?"

"No. I'm not pregnant. Not *now*."

Francis sits up straighter in his chair.

"Look, I don't know what Cohen's told you since you've been back, but I experienced severe head trauma from the accident. I can't remember anything." Her eyes drift back to the fireplace. “Anything,” she repeats. Thunder punctuates Rachel’s words, followed by a silence that consumes the room. “But I did have a dream.” Rachel allows her gaze to meet that of the old man across from her. The amber glow of the fire reflects deep within his eyes, contrasting against their cool, blue color. For the first time, Rachel notices something in those eyes. Something Cohen must see every time he looks at his Finder and Mentor—kindness. Fear and hesitation begin to melt with the chill in Rachel’s body. “A recurring dream, actually. I first had it in the Clinic. In the dream, I’m in a desert. I’m never sure how I end up there. I don’t know if it’s a place that is real—”

“From your memory?”

“Right. Or if it’s just a dream.”

Francis shifts.

“Every time I’m in this dream, I am pregnant.”

Francis raises an eyebrow.

“Really far along.” She gestures to show him the size of her stomach in the dreams.

Francis scratches his chin as he listens.

Rachel allows her mind to drift back to those first few blurry days in the Clinic. Parts of the dream she previously couldn’t remember now flow fluidly as she picks through the images. “I fell asleep.” It comes out almost as a question.

“In the Clinic.”

“In the dream. I remember now.” She squints and dredges up more images. “I was lost in the desert. I remember feeling so tired. I had been walking for a long time. I sat down and fell asleep in the dream.”

“A dream within a dream. Interesting.” Francis leans forward. “Go on.”

"When I woke—in the dream—it was nighttime. The desert had changed. The whole experience felt . . ." Rachel searches for the word. "Creepy." Her shoulders shiver. "There was a man there with strange, glowing skin. I had a weird sense about him from the moment I saw him. But there was another man. He was good."

"How do you know?"

"He tried to save me."

"From what?"

Rachel sets the mug down and stands. The wool blanket falls from her shoulders and lands on the chair behind her. The still-soaked dress clings to her shivering frame.

"From the evil man," she nearly whispers. "He used a sword to rip open my stomach. And when I woke from the dream in the Clinic—" Without hesitation, Rachel tugs the wet dress over her head, removing it completely. Unfazed, she stands before Francis in nothing but her bra and underwear. The glow from the fire dances across her wet skin. Goosebumps dot her flesh as shadows grab like hungry hands at the crude laceration across her stomach.

Francis straightens his shoulders and shifts back into his chair. A confused expression forms on his face. He begins to say something, then presses his lips together. Without a word, he leans forward to examine the nearly healed wound. After a moment, he looks up into her eyes, uncertainty etched into the lines on his face. "What happened?"

"The Healers told me it was from the accident. That I was torn open by a piece of metal."

"And the child?" Apprehension fills his voice.

"They told me there was no child. I was never pregnant. It was just a dream."

Francis can't hide his shock this time. He leans back into the chair to resume his methodical rock, averts his eyes, and gestures for Rachel to cover herself. She wraps the blanket around her shivering shoulders and hangs the soaked dress on the back of her chair to dry.

"Cohen knows all of this?"

Rachel shakes her head.

"Why not?"

"The Healers left it up to me to tell him about my dreams. At first I thought I was crazy. I didn't want Cohen thinking that too. Everyone at the Clinic was so insistent that the dreams aren't real, but—"

"But what?"

Rachel shakes her head. "They feel real. And they won't go away."

Francis reaches for a pipe that hangs from a hook on the stone mantle and chews its end before lighting it. "They are certain you were never pregnant?"

Rachel shrugs. "That's what they kept telling me."

She resumes her quiet observation of the fire as Francis puffs away. The scent of cherry tobacco fills the room as he ruminates on everything she has told him.

The rhythmic sound of Francis's chair and the seductive warmth from the fire lull Rachel into a trance. She tries to imagine her fears and worries burning away like the embers beneath the flames. Perhaps she was wrong about Francis.

"There is more," he says, interrupting her thoughts. "You are not telling me everything." There's an urgency in his voice. "I can sense you are not telling me the whole story. What else has happened?"

Rachel hesitates, then spills. After three weeks of holding everything in, it feels good to let it all out. Even if it is Francis and not Cohen.

Rachel tells him everything, starting with the other images that haunt her when she sleeps, the shadowy figure outside her window, and the boot prints she found moments before arriving on his doorstep.

With each layer of the story, the creases in Francis's face deepen. Eyebrows knit together, his puffing and rocking become more erratic, and Rachel becomes more unsure about the state of both her and Francis's mental stability. But his eyes beg her to continue. So she does. It's cathartic in a way she doesn't expect. Rachel shares every nightmare and dream she can remember, from when she first had the accident to the one she had that afternoon. She even tells him about the frightening voice that called to her from the sky. When she gets to the part about the flower, she uncurls her fingers to reveal the shimmery, red bloom she snatched from the ground before she ran to the Chapel.

Francis leans forward and takes the flower from her hand. "Where ever did you get this?"

"I saw it in my dream—or I saw one like it. Then when I was walking home tonight, it sort of"—she shrugs—"found me."

"My God," he whispers.

"What?" Rachel tries to steady her voice.

Francis takes a long draw from his pipe and places the flower back into her hand. He wraps her fingers around the bloom. "Keep it."

She searches his face for answers but finds none. With a loud sigh, Francis leans back into his chair. When he doesn't say anything more, Rachel says, "Now you understand why I was so upset this morning." Francis nods. "I'm sorry for running out like that. Cohen would be so ashamed if he knew."

He waves her words away. "Trust me. That boy could never be ashamed of you. And that's not important now. What is important is your safety. That and finding out what happened to your child."

His words are like a knife to Rachel's already wounded gut. "Don't do this to me." Her hushed voice is barely audible.

"Do what?"

"Don't pretend you believe me just to make me feel better."

"What makes you think I don't believe you?"

Rachel doesn't know how to answer. Instead she says, "Tell me I'm crazy like the Healers did. Tell me it's my brain's way of making sense of the trauma." Suddenly this feels like the easier reality to come to grips with. Because if she was pregnant, that means there was a real baby, and if there was a real baby—

"My dear, this may come as a surprise to you, but I don't think you are crazy."

Her jaw clenches.

"I don't," he insists.

"But what about the Healers and what they told me?"

"That is a very good question, my dear. One I plan to investigate myself."

"Would they lie?" Rachel asks.

"Of course not. But they may have missed something."

"How could they miss something like that?"

Smoke billows about Francis's face as he shakes his head. "I don't know. But the urgency in my spirit is too strong to ignore."

"What do you mean?"

Francis hesitates then says, "Strange things have been happening in our city lately. And not just the things you've told me."

Despite the heat from the fire, a chill manages to wrap itself around Rachel. “Like?”

“Just this afternoon, thirteen new people were discovered wandering around the city. No announcement that they were coming. No Finder. No explanation.”

Rachel’s eyes widen. “Like me.”

“No. You had a Finder. Rabbi and I have no idea what to make of this. We are trying to figure out what to do with them. We’ve never had this many people show up at once. Oh, and please,” his eyes are insistent, “not a word of this to anyone. We will explain it to the city soon enough. As best we can anyway.” Francis rubs a hand over his beard. “All that to say, something is going on in our little town, and I am concerned not all of it is good.” He must see the fear in her eyes. “But I don’t want you worrying about that.”

“Too late,” she mumbles. “I’m worried about it.”

Francis rubs his brow. “Let’s put it this way, BethEl has been waiting for the Lord’s Anointed since, well, for a very long time. This child is important, and I would not be surprised in the least to discover that something sinister and supernatural is trying to keep us from the truth.”

Rachel tightens her grip on the blanket.

“Do you want to know the truth, Rachel? About your dreams? The mysterious wound?” He waves his pipe through the air. “The baby?”

She wraps her arms around her body.

Francis continues. “I’m sure Cohen told you that people do not stumble into BethEl. We are brought here by Yahweh because he sees a potential in us to fulfill a purpose, but we must also say yes to that purpose. And trust me, you will not find that purpose until you first decide to look for it.” Smoke curls around his face. “So, what will it be, Rachel? Are you ready to discover the truth and the reason why Yahweh brought you here?"

Rachel allows her gaze to drift into the flames. Images from her dreams play through her mind. She turns her head to meet Francis's stare. His haunting blue eyes are almost the same shade as hers.

"I need to know the truth," she whispers. "I *have* to know."

Francis gives her a slow nod. He sets his pipe on the mantle. "You will sleep here tonight. In the morning, you can go back home and gather some of your belongings. I would like to spend some time in prayer and discernment before we bring this to the attention of anyone else in the city. In the meantime, you will stay here until we know you are safe."

"But—"

Francis holds up his hand. "Follow me. It's time for you to get some sleep."

The mere mention of sleep makes Rachel's stomach flip. She stands with the blanket still wrapped around her shoulders.

"Leave your clothes to dry. I will stay up until the fire dies. Come with me. I have something you can wear."

Rachel follows Francis down a second hallway that leads away from the hearth room. He opens the first door on the right. "Wait here a moment."

Rachel peeks into what she assumes is Francis's bedroom. She watches him open a closet door, pull out a small, dusty box from the top shelf, and set it on the bed. He lifts the lid with care and reaches inside. The floorboard creaks beneath Rachel's feet as she shifts to get a better view. Francis turns, but Rachel has already ducked out of sight. He returns a minute later with a small white nightgown in hand.

"It should fit." He places the carefully folded garment in her hands.

"Thank you," she whispers as she runs her fingers over the hem. A strange sensation tugs at her mind like a memory. Or a dream. Rachel's eyes widen in realization.

She wants to give the nightgown back, but Francis is already at the end of the hall. He stops at the last door on the left, opens it, and gestures for Rachel to step inside. "You will sleep here. If you should need anything, please don't hesitate to ask."

Rachel wants to ask for something else to wear to bed, but instead she mumbles, "Thank you. I was wrong about you."

Francis offers a forced smile then shuffles back down the hall. As he passes the door to his own bedroom, he pauses. "Oh, and Rachel," he says over his shoulder, "you mentioned that a voice called to you in your dream this afternoon. If in your sleep tonight you hear a voice beckoning you once again, you should answer it."

Rachel watches him from the bedroom doorway, the nightgown clutched in her balled fist. "Answer it? How?"

Francis chuckles and shakes his head. "It's easy, my dear. All you have to say is, 'Here I am. Your servant is listening.'"

CHAPTER 12

Heaps of rubble decay like carcasses and litter the floor. Cohen kicks at the charred remains of the building. A tiny gray mouse scurries away. A spark of vibrant red catches his eye beneath the surface of the debris. He reaches down and pulls out a soot-covered rosary. The beads, made from real stones, survived the inferno. The crucifix, on the other hand, is a molten metal blob. An omen and foreshadowing of the world he has entered.

The team of Apostles paces the decimated church. Charred pages of scripture tumble across the floor as if the Holy Spirit were trying to breathe new life into the hollow shell of a body. Pieces of broken stained glass crunch beneath their feet. Cohen watches his new teammates carefully. Their ages range from eleven to fifty-three, both men and women, all with different Giftings, all called to be Apostles in this foreign world.

"This is where we're supposed to live?" Kate, the youngest of the group, asks.

"Camp. This is where we are supposed to camp," one of the older gentlemen corrects her.

"But we don't know how long we will be here. What if we do end up living here? Forever?" Kate voices the concerns of the entire team. No one was prepared for what they would encounter outside BethEl.

"Don't worry." Adrielle, a girl close to Cohen's age, helps Kate unpack her sleeping bag. "We're in this together, and Yahweh is with us too. He chose you for a reason. Uriel will be back soon. He will explain everything."

After she helps Kate settle in, Cohen sees Adrielle approach him from across the Chapel. He kneels and pretends to busy himself with his backpack. Her booted feet stop beside him. Cohen stands. Adrielle brushes her hands on her olive-green pants and extends one to him. "Hey, Cohen. It's been a while." She blows a strand of loose hair from her face. Her grip is firm, posture relaxed but confident. She's eye to eye with Cohen.

"It has. I guess we haven't really talked since the Academy."

"Hard to believe it's been so long since we graduated." Adrielle shakes her head and rests her hands on her hips.

"Yeah." Cohen doesn't remind her that it hasn't been that long for him. The truth is that Cohen and Adrielle started at the Academy the same week, but she graduated almost a full two years ahead of him. Cohen doesn't feel the need to correct her or mention the fact that his stint at the Academy was nearly one and a half times the length of the average student.

Adrielle's strong shoulders flex as she crosses her bare arms in front of her chest. "So, Francis put you in charge, right?"

Cohen clears his throat. "Uh—"

"Just kidding," she grins. "Wouldn't put it past him, though. That guy loves you—so does everyone else." Adrielle glances around the skeleton of a building. "Looks like they think you're in charge." She nods to the rest of the Apostles. Cohen follows her eyes to the nervous faces of his teammates. Questions burn in their eyes as they seek his face for answers.

"Anyway." She shoves her hands into her pockets. "If you need any help, I'd love to jump in. I have some experience with this sort of thing. My Gifting is Pastoring. I'm a Shepherd back home." Cohen remembers what a great leader Adrielle was at the Academy. She was quickly promoted to Shepherd over some of his classmates. Unlike him.

"I think I'll leave the whole leadership thing to Uriel," Cohen finally says. After transporting them outside the Veil of BethEl, the Archangel left them to set up camp, saying he had pressing matters to attend.

Adrielle shrugs. "Looks like a pretty good flock, though." She slaps Cohen on the shoulder as she walks away, flips a chestnut-brown braid over her shoulder, and turns to smile back at him.

The team continues to unpack their sleeping bags and mosquito nets as they settle in for their first night outside BethEl. Cohen notices that several Apostles still watch him with a look of expectation. Adrielle's words unsettle him.

With his backpack slung over his shoulder, Cohen wanders away from the group to where the altar of the church used to be. Beams that once held up the ceiling of the chapel cave in like broken ribs. He walks up one to test its strength, jumps down, and tests another that has fallen across it. Confident they will hold, he strings up the hammock he brought from home. With mosquito net in place, Cohen lays down and waits, the hammock dangling from the crude crucifix.

Night descends through a few gaping holes in the roof, the lackluster sky a pale shadow of the one Cohen is used to inside BethEl. It's a grim reminder that he is far from home. As sleep begins to settle over the group, a few team members stir. Warm light bounces off the jagged remains of the building and illuminates the shattered faces of saintly statues, peering like ghosts from hollow eyes. One of the nearly intact statues, a Malak with a drawn sword, looks even more fierce in the light of the haunting glow. No sound enters the demolished church, but a distinct figure can be seen as it walks over the rubble. He carries a candle in his hands, but the radiance comes from his body. Cohen slips from the hammock as the others rouse from their makeshift beds. They follow the light to what used to be the front of the church, find a seat among the rubble, and wait. Adrielle nudges Cohen as she plops down beside him.

"Welcome Apostolic Assembly of BethEl. As you now know, my name is Uriel." He sets the small candle in the only usable cup of a melted candelabra. "I'm sure you are wondering why you have been called here. I will get to that in a moment. First, let me tell you what an honor it is to be called by Yahweh as an Apostle. Each of you has been uniquely chosen for this mission because of the Giftings Yahweh has placed inside you." Cohen shifts his gaze to his hands. "Your presence here is not a mistake.

"I'd also like to say what an honor it is for me to serve with you. We are all members of the family of Yahweh. This is how it was always meant to be—the celestial and terrestrial family working and living together in harmony. Thank you for this honor."

"Thank *you*," one of the women calls out.

Uriel nods his acceptance of the compliment. "Now let us begin. The world outside BethEl is hardly what you remember. It is a pitiful shadow of the beauty that once was humanity. Since the day of the fall, humans have been on a slow descent. Instead of establishing Heaven on earth, they have manifested Hell. The world that remains is unrecognizable. Yahweh is grieved. He came to earth to do what humans cannot. He gave to humanity his Spirit so they would turn back to him and turn back to his plan—on earth as it is in Heaven. But the wickedness of humanity is too great. Every intention of the thoughts of their hearts is evil all the time. For as it was in the days of Noah, so it has become today. As wise Solomon once said, 'There is nothing new under the sun.'

"The Darkness is so thick in the world, it seems there is not even a sliver of Light that remains. But you, children of BethEl, you are the Light of the world. You are the proverbial city set on a hill. You have been hidden, but soon, no longer. Just as people do not light a lamp and put it under a bowl, but on a stand so that it may give light to everyone in the house"—Uriel nods to the dripping candle beside him—"so too, Yahweh has called you to let your light shine before others, so they may see your good deeds and glorify your Father in Heaven.

"The true light that gives light to everyone, Jesus, entered the world. Though the Darkness tried, it was not able to snuff out his Light. For while he was in the world, Jesus used his light to kindle the flames of others. To this day, a remnant remains. *You*. Now you are the Light of the world. And your Light will shine in the Darkness, and the Darkness will not overcome it." Uriel's presence glows brighter.

"This dilapidated church will be your base camp. Do not be dismayed by its state. For as you know, the Lord no longer dwells amidst temples and tabernacles. Now he dwells in the hearts of men. BethEl—it means house of God—but the House of Yahweh is not in a church building. It is not even in your beloved cloaked city. It is in your midst. You," he gestures to the whole group, "you are BethEl. You are the house of Yahweh. You are his temple."

Cohen looks around the group and sees the mood of his teammates visibly lift.

"But know this," Uriel pauses. "The temple is not complete, and the Darkness will do everything in its power to keep it from being rebuilt and restored. That is why this once-sacred space looks as it does."

Everyone shifts their gaze to the debris around them. Once a majestic chapel, now a graveyard for Bibles, hymnals, and hope.

"Across the globe, all true remnants of Christianity have been snuffed out. In fact, all religions have been banned, except one." Murmurs echo off the fallen beams.

"As Darkness increased throughout the earth," Uriel explains, "the world powers began talks of peace and unity. And as has been speculated by many throughout history, the world has now come under one power, one governing body. And with that, one religion."

"How is that possible?" Jesse, the oldest man on the team, speaks up.

"Yeah, how could so much have changed in such a short amount of time?"

"I was ten when I entered BethEl," Cohen adds. Everyone turns to look at him. Expectation hovers on their faces. He shakes off their uncomfortable stares. "I was old enough. I would have remembered these things about the outside world." The group mumbles their agreement.

Uriel holds up his hands to silence the team. "You are a step ahead of me. I was just getting to that point." He clears his throat and straightens his shoulders. "With the Lord a day is like a thousand years, and a thousand years are like a day."

"Second Peter three eight," Adrielle responds.

Uriel nods. "Very good."

"But that's just allegory."

"You're right. It is. At the same time, it isn't." The team waits for Uriel's explanation. "It's not an exact equation. One day is not equivalent to a thousand years, but time does pass differently for Yahweh."

"I'm confused," Kate interjects.

"When you are in BethEl, you are in a Thin Place. There is only a fine Veil that separates you from the Spiritual Realm. Time is . . ." He searches for the word. "Ambiguous. It's not the same."

"Not the same as what?" Adrielle asks.

"Not the same as time outside BethEl."

Understanding where the conversation is headed, Cohen pipes up. "How long have we been gone?" Again, everyone turns to him. They fall silent and wait for Uriel to respond.

The Archangel pauses. "Roughly one hundred and fifty years."

An uproar rises from the team. Next to Cohen, Adrielle is silent, eyes fixed on him. Cohen doesn't shift his gaze from Uriel.

"How is that possible?"

"All things are possible with Yahweh. Because of the way time elapses within BethEl," Uriel points to Cohen, "it seems only seven years have passed for you. It's been twenty for you." He points to Jesse. "The truth is that you all were brought to BethEl within a span of three earthly months of one another."

The team continues to talk over each other. "But our families?" someone shouts. "Our friends?"

"They have been laid to rest with the Lord long ago." Uriel's voice is empathetic. "You are surrounded by a great cloud of witnesses. They spur you on from their place in eternity."

Adrielle folds her arms over her chest. "Does anyone inside BethEl know about this?"

"Yes." Uriel pauses. "Francis and Rabbi. They have known for quite a while, but in order to protect you and the other residents, they were told not to speak of it until the appointed time."

A somberness drifts from team member to team member. No one has a response. Tears fill the eyes of some. Cohen swallows the lump that has formed in his throat. Everyone expects him to be strong, even when he feels like he can't. But it's what they need.

Adrielle sees the shift in his demeanor. She reaches over and squeezes his forearm. Straightening his shoulders, Cohen looks to Uriel. "Forgive us. This is a lot to take in. We will come to grips with our reality. In time," he adds, not fully understanding what those words mean anymore. "But right now, there are clearly more pressing matters. We are Yahweh's servants. What is our mission?"

The tension fades. Cohen feels the strength of his team members begin to return. They mimic his poised posture and follow his lead as he stands. Uriel glances from face to face and smiles. Fixing his eyes on Cohen he says, "To bring Light to the Darkness."

CHAPTER 13

"You look well this morning!" Jubilee chirps.

"Thanks." Rachel offers a genuine smile. "This is the best I've felt in weeks. I haven't slept well lately, but this weekend was pretty restful."

"I didn't know you weren't sleeping well." Jubilee furrows her brow. "Because of the accident? How are you feeling by the way?"

"Yeah, because of the accident." Rachel keeps her answer vague. No need to bother Jubilee with her weird nightmares . . . or visions? Whatever they are, Jubilee doesn't need to know about them. Especially since they might be going away. For the past two nights at the parsonage, Rachel's sleep was uninterrupted and uneventful. "And I'm feeling about the same. Thanks for asking, though."

"Well, I'm glad you're well rested. Today will be a busy day." Fiery curls bounce about Jubilee's heart-shaped face as she thrusts a neatly folded stack of gray fatigues into Rachel's hands. "Here's your uniform." It matches the simple slacks and tunic Jubilee is wearing. "Bathroom is to your left. I'll wait here."

Rachel returns a few minutes later. "Does everyone wear a uniform in the Academy?"

"Yup." Jubilee tugs her wild mane back into a ponytail. As she watches Jubilee, Rachel runs her fingers through her own short hair then tucks and untucks the loose pieces behind her ears. She smooths her hands over the sharp creases in the new pants. Jubilee's uniform doesn't have so much as a wrinkle. Rachel tugs down on the tunic then removes her shoes as Jubilee does.

"How long have you trained at the Academy?"

"About three and a half years."

"And how long before you—"

"Graduate?" Jubilee finishes the question. "Most people are at the Academy about four years. Some progress faster than others. A few are here longer, like Cohen." Rachel shifts her gaze to the ground. "He was the longest standing student," Jubilee continues without taking a breath. "He studied and trained for just over six years. Rabbi still wasn't ready to release him for graduation, but Francis insisted." She smirks. "One of the perks of having the town Priest as your Mentor."

"Why wouldn't Rabbi release him?"

The gonging of a bell interrupts their conversation. Jubilee claps her hands together. "Time to start your first class!"

Rachel wants to ask Jubilee about her relationship with Cohen but instead follows her through a wide doorway and steps down onto the sandy floor of the Academy's training room. A group of thirty or so students, all different ages, huddle together. Bare toes dig into the sand as Jubilee leads Rachel to the center where the students are gathered. Rachel tries not to think about the last time she felt sand beneath her bare feet.

Windows cover the perimeter of the room and allow natural light to illuminate the training space. Metal rigs and fitness equipment stand out against the floral background of the garden outside. Stacks of ancient texts are piled in what seems to be strategic places about the room. There are more books than people or equipment. Possibly even more books than flowers in all of BethEl's gardens. The scent of aged paper tints the air and teases Rachel's mind with a brief image of a familiar wooden bookcase. The memory flees her mind as Jubilee grabs her hand and introduces her to a fellow student.

From the entrance on the far wall, a woman—regal, in every sense of the word—glides into the Academy's training room. Ivory fatigues compliment her sleek mocha skin. The chatter ceases as she takes her place in front of the students.

"Who is that?" Rachel whispers to Jubilee.

"Good morning." The woman's voice thunders through the room before Jubilee can respond.

"Good morning, Rabbi," the group echoes.

She folds her hands in front of her. "I'm told we have a new student today. Rachel, will you please step forward."

Heat floods Rachel's cheeks as she pushes her way through the group to stand beside the statue of a woman. Rabbi shakes Rachel's hand. "It is a pleasure to meet you, Rachel. We have heard much about you. Jubilee has agreed to help guide you during our lessons so you don't fall behind in class. We are about to get started. Follow her lead. You'll catch on." Rabbi turns and looks to the students. "Please make Rachel feel welcome, and as always, jump in to help if you see that help is needed."

Rachel shuffles back to Jubilee, her cheeks still pink.

"Don't feel bad. She singles everyone out on their first day. She's tough, but she's kind."

"She's intimidating."

"She's awesome."

"And still a little intimidating—"

"Shhh." Jubilee points to Rabbi.

"This morning, we will pick up where we left off in practicing our Giftings. This afternoon, you need to spend at least two hours preparing physically on the equipment and two hours reading a text of your choice." She points to the stacks of books.

Jubilee leans over. "We exercise ourselves physically and mentally, as well as spiritually."

"That would explain why everyone here is so fit."

Jubilee flexes her bicep. "You'll catch up."

"All right." Rabbi's voice echoes. "Who would like to go first?" Murmurs float through the group before a hand shoots up. "Silas. Thank you. Come on up. What will you practice today?"

A boy, maybe a few years younger than Rachel, walks to the front. With the back of his hand, he brushes his hair out of his eyes. When he notices Rabbi's gaze on him, he straightens his posture then says, "Interpretation."

"Okay, we need a partner for Silas. Who would like to give a word from the Lord this morning?" Two hands go up. Rabbi points. "Ethan. We haven't heard from you recently." An older man walks to the front to join Rabbi and Silas. He rubs the gray stubble on his cheeks and closes his eyes.

"Now we are silent and listen," Jubilee whispers while she bows her head. "Silas is the only one who will give the Interpretation, but we should all listen for it."

"I don't understand."

"You'll see. Close your eyes. Just listen."

Rachel follows Jubilee's lead. With her head lowered and eyes closed, she listens. The sound of Jubilee's rhythmic breath comes from beside her. Somewhere in the room, a fellow student pops her knuckles. In the background, a very faint but familiar sound resonates—the sound of rushing waters. It is quickly masked by the sound of Ethan's voice filling the room. After a few sentences, he stops. Rachel hears the crowd stir as they open their eyes.

Rachel taps Jubilee's shoulder. "I don't get it."

"That's okay. No one does on their first try. Sounds strange, doesn't it?"

Confusion etches Rachel's face. She shakes her head. "Into what language are we supposed to interpret?"

"English."

She furrows her brow. "He *was* speaking English."

Jubilee cocks her head. "What do you mean?"

Rachel hesitates. "He said, 'Hear, O Israel: The Lord our God, the Lord is one. Love the Lord your God—'" Rachel stops. Jubilee's eyes go wide.

Silas begins to speak. "I have the Interpretation. It is the Shema. 'Hear, O Israel: The Lord our God, the Lord is one.'" Jubilee doesn't take her questioning eyes off Rachel. Silas continues. "'Love the Lord your God with all your heart and with all your soul and with all your strength.'"

"Thank you, Silas." Rabbi gestures for him to return to the group. "Can anyone confirm the Interpretation?"

Jubilee raises her hand, gaze still fixed on Rachel.

"Thank you, Jubilee. Now, who's next?"

The morning practices continue. Other pairs of students take turns repeating the exercise. Each time,

Rachel's confusion grows, and so does Jubilee's strange behavior.

They break for their afternoon strength training. "You get started. I'll be right back." Jubilee leaves Rachel at the pull-up bar.

All around, Rachel's classmates begin their physical training. She watches for a moment then decides to join. With a big leap, she grasps the bar above her and tries to squeeze out a pull-up. Her body dangles, arms weak from recovery. She can't lift her body even once. The throb of the incision on her abdomen only pushes her to try harder. She fights to make her elbows bend. Legs kick, arms burn. Finally, her chin scrapes the top of the bar. Her fingers immediately slip. Clutching her incision, she flops to her back, panting. Everyone else continues their workout, breath steady, foreheads free of sweat.

She catches her breath, flips over, and watches another girl roll through her workout with poise and strength. Rachel grits her teeth and tries to hide the tremble in her arms as she walks her hands out for a push-up. She forces out six before her arms collapse.

"Your strength will return." Rabbi hovers nearby and watches Rachel's arms shake as she tries to push out two more. "You've been through a lot. It will take time, but soon you will be as strong as your peers. Perhaps," she pauses, "even stronger."

"Thanks." Rachel sits back on her heels and stretches her arms. Jubilee lingers behind Rabbi, shoulders hunched, arms wrapped around her chest. The expression on her face worries Rachel.

"Do you have a moment to talk while your classmates continue?"

Rachel hesitates. "Sure." She rises to her feet and follows Rabbi like a shadow to the door on the far wall of windows. She casts a glance back at Jubilee and waves to her new friend. Jubilee just stares.

In the garden, Rabbi's graceful bare feet pad against the stone path as she leads Rachel to a fountain. She takes a seat on its ledge and pats the space beside her for Rachel to join.

"We are so happy you've joined us at the Academy of Giftings, Rachel. Are you enjoying your time in our lovely city?"

Rachel shifts on the stone ledge as she decides how to answer the question. "Yes. It's an interesting place."

Rabbi's lips form a stiff smile. "That it is. And you are getting settled in?"

Rachel shrugs, not sure how to answer. "I suppose."

Rabbi nods. "Well, I'm not one for small talk, so I won't waste your time or mine by dancing around the subject. I brought you out here this afternoon to test you."

"Test me?"

"Yes. We typically give our students several months to settle in and become familiar with our program before we test them for a Gifting, but I have reasons that suggest we should"—she searches for the words—"expedite the process."

Rachel's stomach twists. Perspiration forms on her palms. "I'm not prepared for a test."

Rabbi waves off her words. "This is an easy test. It's based on your raw ability, not your knowledge."

"I still don't know—"

Rabbi cuts her off. "Let's start with this. How many languages do you speak, Rachel?"

"I don't understand."

"It's a simple question. How many languages do you speak?"

"One. At least, one that I know of." Rachel's gaze drifts into the bubbling water of the fountain. "I don't remember much since the accident."

"Yes, I heard." Rabbi's big eyes narrow.

"Is there a problem?"

"No. Not at all." She trails an elegant finger through the water. "Are you up for a little experiment?"

"I'm guessing no isn't an option?"

"You're a quick study." Rabbi's full lips offer a warm smile. "Here's what we're going to do. I'm going to speak in another language, and you are going to tell me what I'm saying, as in the exercise this morning. You give the Interpretation in English."

Rachel's confusion returns. "But they were speaking English. There was no Interpretation. They just repeated what was already being said."

"This is precisely why we are doing this experiment. Now, listen closely."

Rabbi bows her head, eyes closed. She draws a deep breath then turns her face to the sky, eyes still shut. At first, unfamiliar words flow from Rabbi's lips. Again, the sound of rushing water returns. The sound melds with the bubble of the fountain, but it quickly distinguishes itself as something separate. Rabbi's words switch to English. She concludes and opens her eyes. "What did I say?"

"Well at first I wasn't sure. You were speaking in a different language, as you said you would. Then you switched back to English."

"What did you hear me say?"

"Blessed are You, O Lord our God, King of the Universe."

Rabbi's eyes narrow. "Anything else?"

"Only those first few words that were in another language."

"It's Hebrew."

"Oh."

The rumbling sound of water drifts through the garden. Beside them, the fountain gurgles as Rachel waits for what is next. No words come from Rabbi, but she doesn't take her eyes off Rachel. Eventually she says, "Let's try another."

"Okay, but I'm confused. What language am I supposed to translate into? I told you, I don't know any other languages."

"First, it's an Interpretation, not a translation."

Rachel clenches her jaw.

"Second," Rabbi continues, "you're doing fine." She offers an empathetic smile. "Let's try again. I promise to explain when we're finished. Are you ready?"

"Fine." Rachel tucks a strand of wavy, black hair behind her ear. Her shoulders straighten as she waits for Rabbi to speak.

Again, Rabbi lifts her face toward the sky. A soft breeze ruffles the curls of hair closest to her face. She pauses then shifts her gaze to Rachel. Eyes deep as canyons peer into Rachel's. Ancient knowledge resides in every pore of this woman's being. She speaks. Wisdom falls from her lips. Again, English is the language of choice. At first, Rachel is frustrated. It feels like a cruel joke. Is there a deeper meaning to the words? Is there some secret she needs to interpret? Frustration gives way to confusion, confusion to intrigue, and intrigue to fear as Rabbi concludes.

Rachel feels the color drain from her face.

"Rachel? Do you have the Interpretation?"

Rachel nods.

"Then please." Rabbi crosses one long leg over the other. "Enlighten me."

Rachel's mouth is too dry to swallow. Her pulse throbs in her throat. Rabbi is silent, lips pursed as she waits.

"Here is what I heard you say." Rachel's voice quivers. As the words leave her mouth, she knows this moment will haunt her forever. "'Blessed is she who has believed that the Lord would fulfill his promises to her.'" Rabbi's head tilts to the side. Intrigue washes over her face. Rachel continues. "'Blessed are you among women, and blessed is the promise inside you."

Rabbi's eyes go wide as she draws in a sharp breath. She jumps to her feet and paces in front of the fountain. After a moment, she composes herself, straightens her tunic, and turns to Rachel. "That's what I said? I mean, that's the Interpretation?"

"You don't know what you said?"

Rabbi's gaze drifts to the pool of water before she turns back to Rachel. "Every time I spoke . . . every time anyone in class spoke, we were all speaking a different language."

"I don't understand."

Rabbi returns to her seat. "You, Rachel, have a Gifting. You can understand or interpret other tongues and languages. You hear foreign and angelic languages in your own tongue. You said you heard me speak in English?" Rachel nods, still not understanding. "The entire time, I spoke in another language."

"Hebrew?"

"The first time."

"And the second?"

"It was a different language, not an earthly one. A heavenly language. I didn't even know what I spoke, but you did." She pauses. "I have to admit, I am unsettled by what you claim is the Interpretation. Do you know what it means?"

"No," Rachel lies. Surely she made up those words. There's no other explanation. Her subconscious is betraying her.

Rabbi seems to sense that Rachel is withholding something, but Francis told her not to say anything. To anyone.

Rabbi's stare tries to break her, but Rachel won't give in. Rabbi breaks the silence. "I'd like to try one more test with you." Before Rachel can object, Rabbi reaches into the pocket of her tunic and pulls out a knife. Its silvery blade slips from the sheath and glides across the palm of Rabbi's hand. Red liquid clings to the blade and pools in her palm.

Rachel jumps to her feet. "What are you doing?"

Blood drips onto Rabbi's crisp, white pants as she extends her hand toward Rachel. "Heal me."

"What? Are you crazy?"

"No." She stands. "Heal me."

"Everyone in this town is crazy! Let me go grab a towel or something."

"Don't you dare leave, Rachel. Take my hand." Rabbi forces her palm against Rachel's as if to shake her hand. "Now, heal me."

"You're insane! I can't heal you!"

"Oh, I believe you can. Trust me. I wouldn't have cut myself if I weren't so confident."

"You made a mistake. I don't know how to heal you."

"You do. If what I suspect is true, then the power is inside you. We just need to pull it out."

Blood drips from between their clutched hands. Warmth spreads to Rachel's palm as Rabbi's life leaks from her body and puddles on the ground. Rachel's stomach flips. She looks away and tries to prevent her mind from drifting to the nightmares filled with her own blood as it spills from her belly.

Rachel sighs and bites her lip. “What do I need to do?”

“Why don’t you start by closing your eyes.”

“Doesn’t that hurt? You’re so calm.”

“As a matter fact, it does hurt, but sometimes discovery and growth require pain.”

“Let’s just get this over with. You’ll see.”

Rabbi smiles. “No, you’ll see. Now, eyes closed. Good. Take a deep breath, and tell me what you see.”

“Nothing.”

“Try harder.”

“I’m trying.”

“Not hard enough.”

“Fine.”

Breath fills Rachel’s lungs. She attempts to ignore the sensation of Rabbi’s pulse in her hand and the fact that every throb is another pump of Rabbi’s heart, another gush of blood that seeps from the gash in her palm. Rachel is feeling more confident that she is the sane one, and it is everyone else in this town who is crazy. She tries to clear her mind. A picture begins to form.

“I see a man,” Rachel finally whispers.

“Good. Tell me about him.”

“He’s covered in blood.” Rachel hesitates. “He looks like he’s been beaten. He’s naked, and he’s wearing something on his head. I can’t tell what it is.”

“Go on.”

“There’s another man. Like a soldier or something. He’s grabbing the bloody man and—” She pauses. Like the vision in the Chapel, the scene takes over her mind. It becomes more real than Rabbi’s presence, more tangible than her spilling blood. Rachel's other hand flies to her mouth.

"What do you see?" Rabbi urges.

"I can't," Rachel's voice quivers.

"Tell me."

"His hands." Rachel swallows. "The soldier is driving spikes through the man's hands."

Rabbi says nothing.

"No!" Rachel screams. "No!" Against her will, she succumbs to the vision. No longer can she hear the soothe of Rabbi's voice as she urges Rachel to continue. "No! He can't do that! He's taking their pain. He's taking their scars, their wounds. He's taking their evil!" The vision is too much. The sound of her own voice pulls Rachel from her mind. Her eyes fly open. Through tear-filled eyes she sees a blurred image of Rabbi, who smiles.

"Why?" Rachel pants. "Why are you smiling?"

Rabbi clasps her other hand on Rachel's shoulder. She doesn't say a word. There is a spark in her eyes as her gaze shifts to their joined hands. Rachel follows her stare. Rabbi pulls her hand away. It's clean—not a drop of blood in sight. The wound is gone.

CHAPTER 14

The guest bedroom at the parsonage feels like a holding cell. Rachel places her ear against the door and strains to hear Rabbi and Francis. Murmurs float down the hall.

"Why didn't you tell me?"

"I was going to, but—"

They lower their voices. Rachel can't make out the rest of their words.

She sits back down on the bed and runs her hands over the plain brown blanket. It looks like it may have been cut from the same piece of fabric as Francis's robe. In addition to the bed, there is a plain wooden nightstand with matching dresser, both as tiny as the bed they accompany. The only other adornment in the room is a simple crucifix on the wall directly over the bed. Rachel faces it, legs crossed beneath her. There is a miniature metal man nailed to the wood. Rachel shivers and picks up the red flower from where she left it lying on her pillow. She twirls the unwilted bloom between her fingers then tucks it into her pocket when she hears Rabbi's voice call for her to join them.

Her finger trails along the wall as Rachel tiptoes down the hallway and enters the hearth room. Rabbi stands only slightly shorter than Francis. Her hands are folded in front of her, covering part of the brick-red bloodstain on her pants. She didn't bother to change her clothes, didn't explain anything after the miraculous healing of her hand—just said, "Come. We're going to see Francis."

Rachel wants to ask Rabbi why she seemed so confident that Rachel could heal her self-inflicted wound, but Francis speaks before she can ask any questions.

"Hello, my dear." Francis welcomes her with his raspy voice. "I hear you caused quite a stir at the Academy today. Please, come have a seat."

Rachel bites her lip and slips into the extra chair they have set across from the two rockers by the fireplace. A chill settles over her as cold as the empty stone hearth.

"Francis and I discussed your behavior from this afternoon," Rabbi begins. "He also told me that you came to see him two nights ago and have slept here ever since. You lied to me." Rachel shifts in her seat. "He told me about your dreams. We've been out here discussing and praying to discern what the Holy Spirit is saying."

"Did the," Rachel hesitates, "Holy Spirit say anything?"

Francis chimes in. "He did. He said that you, my dear, are a very special girl. We've known that since you arrived, but we didn't know just how special."

"Francis told you that he believes the child from your dreams is real?" Rabbi questions.

Rachel hesitates then nods. She doesn't need to lie anymore; Rabbi already knows the truth.

"Did you have any more dreams about the child last night?"

"No. I didn't dream at all last night. Or the night before."

Curiosity crosses Rabbi's face. "I think it's time you learn a few things about BethEl and the group of people who live here, Rachel. There is a reason we are here. We have been given a very important mission. We are not brought to BethEl because we are so special or so holy. We are brought here because Yahweh sees a willingness in our hearts and wants us to partner with him in manifesting the fullness of his Kingdom, and we believe you and the child are to be a part of it."

"You think my dreams are real too?"

"Whether or not they are actual memories or simply a way God is trying to communicate with you, we are not sure. But Francis and I both sense that there is something very special and significant about the child."

Rachel fidgets with the drawstring on her uniform.

Rabbi looks to Francis. "Would you like to start?"

He takes his pipe from the mantle, offers one of the rockers to Rabbi, takes his own seat, then begins. "Last night when you were here, you may not have dreamed, but I did." Rachel sits up straighter. "Now, this dream was not particularly vivid or visual. I saw only one image—a desert. There was also a voice. It called to me from the sky."

Rachel shifts in the chair. "What did you do?"

"I did what I instructed you to do. I said, 'Here I am, Lord. Your servant is listening.'"

"Did the voice respond?"

"Yes."

"And?"

"It said, 'Francis, I have sent you to help the girl.'"

"Me?"

"Yes, my dear, you. So I asked the voice, 'Lord, am I to help her find the child?'" Francis pauses. Rachel holds her breath. "He said yes, Rachel."

A fog fills Rachel's head. She swallows then leans forward. "What happened next?"

"I asked the Lord, 'Is the child safe?'" Rabbi glances between them as Francis continues. "Yahweh said, 'For now, but danger is coming.'"

Rachel's knuckles are white, her fists tucked in her lap. "So you're saying the baby is real?"

Francis gives a silent nod.

"Then are you suggesting the car accident wasn't an accident?" she asks.

"I'm not sure."

"And the wound on my stomach?"

Francis sighs. "Exactly. As I told you, I would like to conduct an investigation into some of the mysterious and missing details surrounding your accident. But with the unannounced arrival of thirteen new residents—without Finders—well, let's just say we are doing all that we can right now."

"Rachel," Rabbi interjects. "I don't want to alarm you, but you need to know that Francis and I are concerned that our city has been Breached."

"What do you mean *Breached*?"

"Francis told me about the figure outside your window, and how you thought it was a dream until you saw the footprints. Here in BethEl, we are in a middle ground. We are not technically in the Physical Realm or the Spiritual Realm. Yahweh holds us somewhere in between. This is a Thin Place. Good spiritual forces can enter freely here, and of course, it is not unusual to experience supernatural phenomena and even miracles in our city." Rabbi unconsciously rubs the palm of her hand. "But we are protected from the evil forces of the Spiritual Realm. They cannot enter here unless—"

"Unless there is a Breach?"

"Exactly. We don't know how it happened, but we are concerned that it *has* happened. And we believe this incident is not separate from you and your child."

Rachel notes the first time Rabbi calls the baby *her* child. "What about the thirteen people who arrived after me? Are they somehow connected?"

Francis and Rabbi exchange glances. "We are trying to find out what we can about them," Rabbi says, "and why Yahweh brought them here. But without Finders, it is making the process of introducing these individuals to our city—and investigating them—quite challenging."

"Many things are not adding up, my dear," Francis adds. "Which is why we must find your child." Francis's voice grows louder.

"How?" Rachel questions.

"You, my dear. You are the one who will find the child. You must! This baby is important. It's the one we have been waiting for!" Rabbi places a hand on Francis's shoulder. "Forgive me." He chuckles as he composes himself. "I am zealous in my old age.

"In my dream last night," he continues, "I asked the Lord, 'How will we find the child?' The Lord replied, 'The girl. She must come to me, then I will tell her great and unsearchable things she has never known. I will reveal the truth and answers to her. If she asks, seeks, and knocks, I will help her. I will help her find the child.'"

Rachel is silent, not sure what to believe. At the same time, a fire burns inside her. A deep, unquenchable thirst to know what is true.

"How do I meet with—" Rachel doesn't quite know what to ask. "I mean, how do I seek—"

"The Lord?" Francis fills in the gap.

"Yes, how do I seek him?"

He sighs. "You will not like the answer."

"Tell me."

"You must meet him in your dreams."

Rachel leans back in the chair.

"Do you know what happens when we dream, Rachel?" Francis asks.

"Scientifically speaking?"

"No, spiritually speaking."

Rachel shakes her head. Rabbi leans back to listen as Francis takes the lead.

"Rachel, this world you see here," Francis gestures around the room, "is not all there is to reality. In fact, you might even call this place an alternate reality. Not just BethEl but outside our city walls too.

"There is a story in the first book of the Bible, Genesis. In it, the first man and woman, Adam and Eve, defied God and rebelled against him. They were originally created to be one with God, to stand in his presence face-to-face. God's presence was their reality, their place of dwelling—"

"But then the snake came and tricked them," Rachel blurts out.

"You remember the story?" Francis asks.

Rachel's voice softens. "Cohen read it to me when he visited me in the Clinic." His face fills her mind now, along with the hurt that filled his eyes as he left her alone in the Central Gardens.

Francis nods as he chews his pipe. "The Nachash was much more than a snake, though."

"Nachash?"

Rabbi jumps in. "It's the Hebrew word used for this creature."

"The Nachash was a spiritual being," Francis says. "The Shining One. He was also a deceiver, as malevolent as they come."

Rachel's mind fills with memories of the story Cohen told her.

"His intentions were nothing but pure evil," Francis continues. "He lied to Adam and Eve and tore them away from Yahweh to imprison them."

"Imprison them where?"

"In an alternate reality. In another dimension, some might even say. The book of Genesis tells us that when Adam and Eve rebelled and ate the fruit that Yahweh commanded them not to eat, their eyes were opened."

"To what?"

"That is precisely the right question no one asks. To what were their eyes opened?" Francis takes a long drag from his pipe. The smoke unfurls around his face. "To everything but God. Before, Adam and Eve were face-to-face with Yahweh. His presence and his love filled their vision both in a physical and metaphorical sense. But when they chose *not God*, they chose to close their eyes to him. They turned away from him. They were no longer face-to-face."

His words stir something inside Rachel. While everything about BethEl feels like fantasy, she can't deny the resounding yes that bubbles within her.

He notices the faraway look in her eyes. "Shall I continue?"

"Please."

"When we dream, we all have the ability to fall asleep to the world around us, the alternate reality. But most people are so inundated with the lies of this world that they believe them to be true. They internalize them.

Then their sleep merely becomes an extension of this world.

"But for others of us, we are different. We seem to instinctually know that this world is but a dream, that there is something more, something real. It's hiding just out of sight, beneath the surface. We crave it. We know it's there, but we don't know how to reach it. We are the people who are turning."

"Turning?" Rachel asks.

"Turning to Yahweh. And it is in the midst of this turning that he can reach us."

Francis continues. "For some of us, when we close our eyes in sleep, we exit the physical reality and enter the Dream World, a portal to the Spiritual Realm. It is a wonder-filled and almost magical place to be, but it is also dangerous and frightening." Rachel shifts in her chair. "For in our sleep, it is not just Yahweh who can reach us, but all of those who dwell inside the Spiritual Realm. We become ethereal and therefore susceptible. Able to cross time and space, defy gravity, and all laws of physics. And more importantly, we are able to enter more fully into Yahweh's presence."

Rachel shakes her head. "Cohen didn't share any of this. What do you mean more fully?"

"Well," Francis begins. "The presence of the Lord can be entered while awake on earth, but as first Corinthians tells us, that reality is but a faint reflection in a mirror. The Apostle Paul tells us that one day, humanity will stand face-to-face with Yahweh, even in our physical form. It will be the most glorious day of all, the Wedding Supper of the Lamb." Francis pauses and smiles. "I'm getting ahead of myself." He clears his throat. "In our dreams, we have the second best. We can stand face-to-face with Yahweh in spiritual form. In our dreams, we can be turned toward him as we were always meant to be. We can enter that reality, even if only for a brief time." Francis folds his hands in his lap. The pipe dangles from his lips. "Yahweh chooses us, but you, my dear, must also choose him. To find the answers and your child, you must decide. Will you turn?"

The question lingers like a scent, the room so silent, Rachel can hear the soft ticking of a clock from somewhere else in the parsonage. Francis's words hang in the air, waiting to be seized or dashed to the ground.

Rachel clears her throat. "I have to be honest with you. I don't know that I ever was turned toward God. I mean, maybe I was. I don't remember."

A soft chuckle rumbles in Francis's chest. "My dear, that's just the thing. From the beginning, Yahweh's will was for humanity to be turned toward him, but very few of us remember."

"So, in order to find the child—*my* child—"

"The Lord's Anointed," Francis adds.

"Right. The Lord's Anointed." Rachel glances between her Mentor and teacher. "Why me? Why am I the one who has to do this?"

"You were brought here for a purpose, my dear. Did you not just two nights ago say you were ready to discover what that purpose might be—"

"Yes, but—"

"And did I not say that you will not find that purpose until you decide to look for it?"

Rachel folds her arms over her chest. "Yeah—"

"You see," Francis's eyebrows dart up, "you are already seeking and searching. And Yahweh is eager to answer those who call on him."

Rachel has heard those words before. "But why go through all this trouble?" she protests. "Why doesn't

God snap His fingers and bring the baby—my baby—back?"

"God can," Rabbi speaks up. "But in a sense, he also can't." She continues. "Francis mentioned the Nachash—"

"Right, the Shining One."

Rabbi scolds Rachel's interruption with her glare. "Yes, the Nachash is the Lord's adversary, his enemy, and the Nachash is not alone. He has rallied his own army, both in the Spiritual and Physical Realms. Yes, God can put an end to the spiritual battle once and for all, but Yahweh has already made an irrevocable move."

"What did he do?"

"Yahweh gave both humans and spiritual beings free will. Yahweh is love, Rachel. It's not just what he does; it's who he is, and real love requires a choice. God could not establish a creation that was a true reflection of him if he did not give us that free will. Yes, at any point in time, God can choose to revoke that free will from both humans and celestial beings, but then he would also revoke our ability to truly love him."

Rabbi reaches behind her to pull forward a small table. On it sits an intricate chess set. "To use simplistic terms," Rabbi says, "it's like a game of chess." Her long fingers pick up one of the hand-carved game pieces. "Do you know that if you were to ever play a game of Chess against God you would lose every time?"

"Why is that?" Rachel asks while examining one of the pieces.

"Because Yahweh is infinitely intelligent," Rabbi says. "While you and I can only anticipate a handful of moves our opponent can make, Yahweh can anticipate every possible move we could make from the beginning of the game to the end."

She pushes a pawn forward. "Think about it this way. In any game of chess there are two opposing sides. Yahweh and his people are the Light pieces. The enemy is the Darkness." She peers up at Rachel. "We must choose on which side we will play, because guess what?" There's a spark in Rabbi's deep-brown eyes. Her lips purse with a smile as she says, "The Light always wins. Every move of the enemy, regardless of how cleverly or meticulously orchestrated, leads to one result." She knocks over the mahogany king.

"Checkmate," Francis whispers.

Rachel stares into his cool blue eyes. A fire burns beneath their placid surface. Rachel knows exactly which side these two are on.

Rachel slides to the edge of her chair. "Light," she whispers. "I choose the Light."

Francis smiles. "Ah, my dear, your words are like music to my old ears." He rests his pipe on the hearth and smiles warmly at Rabbi. "We haven't had this much excitement in our little town in a very long time." He turns back to Rachel. "You will continue to stay here at night until we are sure you are safe. We will begin an investigation concerning the possibility of a Breach and set precautions in place. We'll also find out what we can from the Clinic. During the day, you will split your time between specialized training and traditional studies one-on-one with Rabbi."

"But we'll be kicking it up a notch." A smirk forms on Rabbi's lips. "Sleep well, Rachel. You start tomorrow." She stands. "I'll let myself out." She pauses and turns. "You have chosen what is right, Rachel. It will not be taken from you. Welcome to the Light."

CHAPTER 15

"From the time you were first brought to BethEl, you've been taught that you were called by Yahweh to come against the powers of the Darkness." Uriel paces the front of the church. His striking face is illuminated from his inward glow. "In BethEl, the Darkness is a concept, an idea. It is a monster in a bedtime story. Out here, the story is real; you are the child in the bed, and the monster lurks in the shadows nearby." A few team members squirm. "You have been taught that your enemy is not flesh and blood but the powers of Darkness and the spiritual forces of evil in the Heavenly Realm. That remains true. But out here, the lines are blurred. It is hard to know who the enemy is because the enemy hides in plain sight, disguised as flesh and blood."

"You're saying that, out here, the evil spiritual entities look like humans?" one of the Apostles probes.

"That is correct. But not just any humans. They have disguised themselves as the elite. In the Spiritual Realm, they were given titles such as Thrones, Rulers, Powers, and Authorities. They have carried those positions over into the Physical Realm. Some of the world's leading powers are not human at all.

"When the world came under one leading power, the Unity, that movement was orchestrated and led by the Darkness. Many resisted at first, but as you know, the Darkness is ever so crafty. At that point in history, the benefits of a one-world governing body so far outweighed the costs that very few resisted in the end. And like slowly boiling a frog in water, the powers that be began to make subtle but perilous changes. Humanity was being cooked alive, and they didn't even realize it. Why? Because the ones with their hands on the temperature control masqueraded as the heroes.

"When terrorism and violence increased to the point where it was no longer safe to go to the grocery store or send children to school, who was there to save the day? Why the Unity, of course. The humans didn't realize that their beloved world government was the one behind the terrorists' masks. Violence in the name of a god became so widespread, so prominent, that when the suggestion was made to ban all public declarations of religion—even attending a church service—everyone, even the Christians, jumped on board. 'You may still practice in your homes,' they were told. And the dial on the stove moved up another notch.

"The trick with deceit is that once the water becomes so hot, it's hard to detect the increase in temperature. Bubbles began to form. Small at first, until the once-placid surface rolled with a steady boil. Many years later, after the religious and governmental landscape had been drastically altered, a universal world religion was formed, and humanity all but begged for it."

"Christians wouldn't buy into that idea," one of the team members says.

"Oh, but they did. It was *their* idea."

"That doesn't make any sense."

"Sure it does," Cohen chimes in. "If the universal religion was Christianity."

Understanding registers on several faces. Uriel smiles his approval. "Well done, young man. Yes, Christians have wanted the government to adopt their religion since, well, since the days of Emperor Constantine. All of you lived in America before being brought to BethEl, correct?" The team nods. "Can any of you remember a time when Christians did not want to vote in a Christian president?" No one responds. "You can't," Uriel continues. "And that is what happened. The Kingdom of God intermingled with the Kingdom of the World.

"Humans need a belief system," Uriel explains. "So after years of having their religious expressions sterilized and stifled, humanity clung to this new movement as a gift from God—or the gods, as it later became.

"With the new world government came the abolition of separation of church and state. *Oneness and Peace* is the motto of the Unity. Christianity, or rather, some variation of it, was selected because it was the most peaceful of the religions."

"History would tell a different story," someone interjects.

"Yes," Uriel agrees. "We all know that, throughout history, Christians have been guilty of some of the most heinous bloodshed. And in the name of Yahweh," he adds as he shakes his head. "But since peace is a core theme in the New Testament, it gave the Unity something to work with.

"The picture was painted slightly different for each people group. To the Muslims, Christianity was given a distinct Islamic flare. To the new agers, Jesus was a mystic. You get the picture. The most important piece to the puzzle was to get the buy-in from the Christians, the people group the Darkness most needed to deceive. So they gave them exactly what they wanted: the gospel spread to every corner of the earth. Christianity became the world religion."

A shiver works its way through Cohen as understanding sets in.

"From there, the dial on the stovetop was notched up another increment. Each year, slight changes were made to the governing theology. New archeological discoveries were made that changed scriptural interpretation. And—"

Cohen cuts him off. "And the pot began to boil over." The team is silent, all eyes fixed on Uriel as they wait for him to continue.

"Over the course of one hundred and fifty years, Christianity morphed into what is now called the Path. It looks nothing like the Way of your brothers and sisters in the first century church. Yeshua is a distant memory, not Lord, but there is world peace . . . on the surface," he adds. "The water has cooled. Now all that remains is a still pot of lukewarm water. Very inviting." Uriel looks from face to face. "But beneath the surface, floating belly up, is one very dead frog.

"Across the world, the remains of antiquity's chapels and churches, like this one, lie in heaps of decay. The old-world sanctuaries, mosques, and temples have been destroyed. Now they exist as abandoned artifacts, places where certain sects of Path followers come to indulge in their legal drug use and orgies. They see it as a sacrament to come to these once-holy places to gratify their every fleshly desire. They believe that in marrying the old with the new, they redeem their past, and in turn, secure their future.

"Sadly, as disturbing as it may sound to you and me, the Unity has given humanity exactly what they want—bread and circus. They are fed, entertained, and cared for. Given enough treats and distractions to make them dependent and placate their desires. They have legalized every indulgence you can imagine, and above all, they have given humanity peace. They have erased the concept of fear from the human psyche. They have humanity so numb, they don't even realize they are in the midst of the greatest war ever fought.

"Thanks to the Unity, World War III never happened, but the battle between the Darkness and the Light erupts all around them. They are the victim and the prize. The spoils of war will be the look on humanity's face when they realize they've been duped. The enemy is playing for keeps, and he's craftier than ever."

"How?" Adrielle raises her voice beside Cohen. "How are we supposed to bring Light to that kind of Darkness? It sounds hopeless, too far gone." Others mumble their agreement.

Uriel interlaces his fingers behind him and straightens his shoulders. "The same way Yahweh has always brought Light to Darkness. Carefully, quietly, subtly as one tiny flicker. Something that will go unnoticed by most. Like a peasant baby being born in a manger. Or an infant child floating in a basket down a river. Or a crazy man shouting in the wilderness. Like a tiny mustard seed, Yahweh is planting the people of BethEl into the unfertile soil of the world. And you will grow. Slowly at first, hidden and underground, but before the Darkness can realize what is happening, you will be a sprout, and then a seedling. Before long, you will be the largest garden plant of all, with roots that reach down into the earth, drinking up every ounce of water so that nothing else can survive. And once again, the Tree of Life will be the tallest and most majestic of all the plants in the garden. Nothing will be able to rival it."

A sly smile spreads across Uriel's face. "The enemy may be crafty, but Yahweh is wise. You are the Lord's Trojan horse, and the Darkness has no idea you are coming."

CHAPTER 16

"What happened yesterday? I saw you and Rabbi leave. Did she talk to you about Interpretation? Is it one of your Giftings? Where'd you guys go?" Jubilee bounces like a puppy while she peppers Rachel with questions. "I haven't seen you at home for a few days. Is everything okay?" They enter the training room of the Academy and join the rest of the students.

"We just discussed my training." Rachel's not sure how much she can reveal. Or wants to reveal.

"I'm so jealous! First, you get to work with Francis, and now you're receiving special attention from Rabbi."

Rachel waves good morning to some of the students she met the day before, but they all seem distracted. There's a buzz in the Academy as the existing BethEl students file in and notice a row of new faces in the center of the training room. One of them, a young man with sandy-blond hair, nods to Rachel. She recognizes him as the boy she bumped into outside the Chapel.

"Good morning, class," Rabbi's voice bellows through the room. She wears a clean white uniform with no blood stain or evidence of Rachel's bizarre encounter with her the day before.

Rabbi's gaze settles on Rachel before she continues. "It seems we are living in exciting times. Yahweh has once again surprised us with not just one, but thirteen new BethEl residents.

Murmurs fill the room as Rabbi begins to introduce each new face.

"He's not bad to look at." Jubilee leans over and nudges Rachel in the ribs.

"Ow." Rachel rubs the spot, still tender from the accident.

"Sorry! I forgot." Jubilee apologizes under her breath.

Rachel follows Jubilee's finger. She points to the blond-haired boy—Hayden.

The class listens with intrigue as Rabbi explains the mysterious arrival of these thirteen new individuals.

"This is only the second time anyone has ever entered BethEl unannounced." Rabbi catches Rachel's gaze. "And the first time we've ever had a group this large. Also unlike a typical situation, there was no Finder for any of these individuals."

Rabbi goes on to explain how the newest residents were discovered one by one while wandering through the town lost and confused. As Rabbi speaks, Hayden catches Rachel's eye. He offers a timid smile.

"Do you know him?" Jubilee whispers.

"I bumped into him outside the Chapel after the prayer service." More like crashed, but Rachel doesn't tell Jubilee that. Instead, she returns the smile to Hayden.

A student interrupts Rabbi. "Why didn't Yahweh announce their arrival? Or Rachel's?"

"Is it because we sent out thirteen Apostles from the city that we gained thirteen new residents?" another student asks.

Several others throw out questions at the same time.

Rabbi holds up her hands. “These are all very good questions—ones that Francis and I are actively investigating. Which leads to my next announcement. You all know Deborah, my protégé.” Rabbi gestures to a thin, young woman with Asian features. “Over the next several weeks, she will lead during class time. Those of you who are Shepherds—your assistance will be needed as well. Deborah will fill you in. With all that has happened recently, my presence is needed outside of the classroom. I will pop in from time to time, but please direct your inquiries to Deborah whenever possible. Everyone’s cooperation will be needed. In fact, Deborah will be pairing each of you up with one of the new students.”

Quiet chatter drifts through the room, but Rabbi’s voice breaks through the whispers before any rumors can take hold. “All right, let’s get started for the day.” Her smile looks forced. “Please do all that you can to make our newest residents feel welcome.”

Rabbi glides across the room as the students disperse. “Jubilee?” She speaks in a low tone so only Jubilee and Rachel can hear. “As of today, Hayden will be your new partner during class.” Jubilee meets Rachel’s eyes with a mixture of confusion and surprise. “I know I assigned Rachel as your partner yesterday,” Rabbi continues, “but from here forward, she will train as a Dream Walker.”

Jubilee’s eyes widen. “A Dream Walker?” Rachel is equally surprised about this news.

Rabbi presses a finger to her lips. “Yes, but for now, let’s keep that between the three of us.”

“Okay,” is all Jubilee can manage for a reply.

“Good. I am grateful for your help, Jubilee. I know I can count on you.”

Jubilee beams. "It will be an honor."

"Thank you." Rabbi turns to walk away. "Rachel, please come with me," she says, not waiting for her to follow.

"Sorry," Rachel whispers as she leaves her friend behind with no explanation. She waves to Hayden as she passes him.

Outside in the garden, Rabbi waits for Rachel under a vine-covered pergola. "Come with me." She leads Rachel through an unfamiliar part of the garden. "As I said to Jubilee, today you will begin your training as a Dream Walker. Francis and I discussed this before inviting you to join our conversation yesterday afternoon. He, in particular, is convinced that you are ready to begin this kind of advanced training." Rabbi casts a glance over her shoulder at Rachel. "We shall see if he is correct." Rachel quickens her pace to keep up with Rabbi.

"I doubt Cohen told you anything about Dream Walkers before he left." She doesn't let Rachel respond. "Dream Walkers are rare in BethEl. Currently, we only have three active in the entire city.

"Yesterday, Francis explained that for people who are gifted in dreams, such as yourself, their sleep becomes much more than a fantasy world. It becomes an extension of reality. Dream Walkers enter the Dream World when they sleep, but because of their training, they can use their dreams as portals to enter the Spiritual Realm. In a sense, the Spiritual Realm and Physical Realm mirror one another. Not a direct mirror . . . more like a representation. Even still, because of the connection to these two realms, the Dream Walkers' actions *there* have consequences *here*. That is why we believe it is possible for you to use your dreams to locate your child. Yahweh has already made it clear that the Dream World holds the answers. We will do our best to train you for the journey ahead and provide you with a team to support you in this quest, but ultimately, you must be the one to find your child." Rabbi pauses as the path widens. "We are here."

Up ahead, the garden opens into a clearing with a large pond. A small island of land rises from the center with an open-air shelter situated in the middle. Tall grasses and foliage create a barrier where walls cease to exist. An intricate stone bridge creates a path to the mysterious floating island.

"Where is here?" Rachel whispers.

"This is the Sleep House, the place where your dreams will become your reality."

Rachel tries to swallow her nerves.

"Are you ready to meet the team?"

CHAPTER 17

From the open-air Sleep House, Rachel peers out at the pond as she waits with Francis. Hand in her pocket, she rubs the silky petals of the flower bloom between her fingers.

Three rectangular tatami mats are arranged side by side in the center of the floor with a small square mat set apart from the others. Rabbi brings in a fourth. "They should be here any minute," she says as she arranges the mats into a new configuration.

Early morning daylight casts a warm glow into the room. No walls exist to separate it from the garden life that creeps in on every side. Francis shuffles toward Rabbi as she finalizes the new pattern for the mats. Now, the small square mat is at the center with the other four placed around it to create a larger square. Rabbi sets a cushion on top of the center mat, takes Francis's hand, and helps him into a seated position. The sound of footsteps shifts Rachel's attention.

"Rabbi. Francis." A young man with dark hair and even darker, narrow eyes enters. His appearance suggests he is in his mid-twenties, but his presence is that of one much older. He bows his head in respect and greeting.

"Micaiah, a pleasure to see you, my friend." Francis welcomes him from his seat on the pillow. "Thank you for coming."

The man walks toward Rachel and offers her a slight bow. "Rachel, I presume?" He glances over at Francis who nods his response. "So young," Micaiah comments. "Much younger than I expected."

"The youngest," Francis's raspy voice answers from his place on the floor.

"It is an honor to meet you," Micaiah says to her. "Francis believes you will make an excellent Dream Walker. Are we doing her skill test today?" He directs the question to Francis.

"No." Francis pauses and glances up at Rabbi.

"We start her training today," Rabbi explains.

"Today? Without a skill test?" Micaiah doesn't hide his surprise. "How do we know she has the raw Gifting to begin training?"

Rabbi's face is set. "She does. Francis is confident." The conversation comes to an end as another young man and woman enter the room. They approach Rabbi first, greet her with a bow of the head, then repeat the gesture toward Francis.

"It's good to see you all in one room again." Francis says to the three Dream Walkers. Then he directs his words toward Rachel. "This is Elias and Rivkah, but everyone calls her Rivi. Together with Micaiah, they will be your teammates."

Rachel wants to ask why everyone has such unusual names in BethEl; instead she says, "Nice to meet you."

Elias offers a deep bow, lifts his head, and winks. Rivi's full lips pull into a tight line as she mimics a smile then offers a barely detectible nod of her head. She narrows her eyes.

The Dream Walkers are an impressive crew, all three dressed in black fatigues with white embroidering. A closer look reveals little stars stitched in white thread all over their uniforms. Rachel glances down at her plain gray Academy tunic.

"All right"—Rabbi takes control of the room—"let's proceed. Rivi, can you please begin by reciting the BethEl mission?"

Rivi adjusts her shoulders and straightens her already perfect posture. "To overthrow the enemy and set the captives free."

"And who is our enemy?" Rabbi probes.

"The Darkness." Rivi's response is militant.

"Who are we?"

"The Light," Micaiah snaps.

"And our strategy?" Rabbi continues.

"The Light shines in the Darkness, and the Darkness cannot overcome it." Micaiah's face is stoic.

"Our tactic?" Rabbi turns to Elias as he runs a hand through his perfectly combed, brown hair.

"To prepare the way for the Lord's Anointed." Elias conceals a playful smile as he speaks.

"Why?" Rabbi drills.

Elias puffs out his chest. "So the Anointed can prepare the way for Yeshua's return."

"Amen," the voices of the three Dream Walkers chant in unison. Rachel takes a step backward.

Francis clears his throat. "Rachel, these are my former trainees. When I first arrived in BethEl, I was also a Dream Walker, but I have since abandoned that post to take on other duties." There is a hint of regret in his voice. "But these three individuals carry on my legacy, and now, you will too. When you first arrived, we planned for you to enter the Academy and begin training like any other new BethEl resident, but it seems your Giftings have already begun to make themselves known. Given the situation, Rabbi and I believe it makes sense to train you in the skill of Dream Walking. As we told you yesterday, you will continue to train one-on-one with Rabbi at the Academy in the basics of discipleship, but effective immediately, you will also train with me and this team." He gestures to the three Dream Walkers. "It will be a grueling schedule. Are you up for the challenge?"

Rachel glances at the three Dream Walkers. She wants to say no, that she is really not up for any of this, but her hunger to know the truth won't go away. "I am," she says.

"Team," Francis addresses the three imposing figures, "allow me to formally introduce to you Rachel, one of the newest members of BethEl. As I'm sure you have heard by now, she, among others, came to us in quite an unusual way. Yahweh did not announce her arrival. No one knew she was coming. Cohen, my Disciple, found her, but as you know, he has been dispatched as an Apostle on our first mission outside of BethEl." Rachel grips the flower in her pocket and bites her lip. "I am Rachel's Mentor in the interim," Francis continues. The three Dream Walkers nod their understanding. "It has come to my attention that this young lady is quite gifted. As you noted, Micaiah, she is the youngest Dream Walker we've ever had."

"How old is she?" Rivi asks. She folds her smooth, brown arms across her chest.

"Sixteen," Rabbi answers. Murmurs drift between the team members.

"That's a whole two years younger than me when I started," Elias comments.

Francis ignores him and continues. "We believe that Rachel has been sent here by Yahweh specifically to help us locate the Lord's Anointed." Curious expressions form on the faces of Rachel's new team members. "We knew it would be soon. Rabbi and I believe the time is now. Yahweh's hand of blessing is clearly on this young lady and her child."

"Her child?" Rivi questions with narrowed eyes.

"Yes." Francis clears his throat. "Her child is the Lord's Anointed."

Rachel doesn't hear what Francis says next. Instead, she tries not to break under the weight of the Dream Walkers' stares as Francis explains the car accident, the mysterious abdominal wound, the dreams, and the lost baby.

"I hate to bring up her age again," Micaiah interjects, "but a child? The Lord's Anointed? She's only sixteen." Elias and Rivi nod their agreement.

Francis glares. "Is this the first time in history that Yahweh has brought forth a very special child through such a young woman?" Micaiah is silent. "As with every mission Yahweh has placed before us, we must have faith. Rarely do his commands makes sense. Yahweh's favorite way to work is through the unexpected. You know this." The team visibly softens—even Rivi—convicted by Francis's words. "Do you trust me?" Francis's voice echoes off the cedar rafters.

"Of course we do," Rivi replies without hesitation. She drops her arms.

"And do you trust Yahweh?"

"Without any doubt." Elias flashes a smile in Rachel's direction.

"Then tell me"—Francis folds his hands in his lap—"are you willing to accept this mission?"

The team exchanges a few quick glances. Micaiah steps forward and stands before Rachel. "It will be an honor to serve with you, Rachel. We will do whatever is required to find the Lord's Anointed." He extends his hand to her. "Welcome to the team."

Francis beams with pride. Rabbi offers a rare smile. The three Dream Walkers bow their heads in respect to Rachel. She returns the gesture.

"What are we waiting for?" Elias moves toward the mats.

Rabbi clears her throat. "There is one last thing we need to discuss."

Elias pauses when he hears the hesitation in Rabbi's tone. "What's that?"

She sighs and folds her hands in front of her. "Francis and I are concerned that BethEl has been Breached by an evil entity."

Rivi speaks up. "How is that possible?"

"We're not sure, but we have compelling reason to believe it is true. As you know, there has been strange activity in our city as of late."

"What makes you think it's an evil entity?" Micaiah asks.

Rabbi and Francis exchange glances. "The nature of Rachel's dreams," she says. "There are other reasons too but none you need to concern yourselves with now."

The three Dream Walkers whisper among themselves.

"Yahweh spoke to me in a dream." Francis interrupts their chatter. The Dream Walkers fall silent. "We know very little at this time," Francis continues. "Only that the child is in danger, and as the mother, Rachel is the one Yahweh has chosen to speak to and direct to find the Anointed. We assume the Darkness has the baby, though we are not quite sure how they obtained it. There are some mysterious and missing details regarding Rachel's accident." He pauses. "We're beginning to question whether or not it actually was an accident. As far as we can tell, the Darkness is trying to prevent us from knowing the truth and locating the Lord's Anointed."

"What else is new?" Rivi sighs. "The enemy is always trying to keep us from the truth."

"This sounds like a suicide mission—"

"What Elias means to say," Micaiah cuts him off, "is that the Darkness will fail." Micaiah shares a confident smile with Rachel. "The news of the Breach does not alter the mission. It only makes it more crucial that we begin immediately."

Rabbi folds her hands at her waist. "Agreed."

Micaiah looks to his teammates. "Agreed?"

Rivi crosses her arms in front of her chest.

Elias rubs his hands together. "Totally. Let's get this show started." He looks to Micaiah. "You didn't let me finish, bro. I love a good suicide mission. Death can't stop me!"

Rivi rolls her eyes.

Micaiah waits for her agreement. "There is inherent risk for any mission. You know this, Riv."

She sighs and mumbles, "To be martyred for the cause of Yahweh would be an honor."

Micaiah grins. "Yes, obedient unto death, just like Yeshua."

Their words usher in a new level of fear. Rachel never imagined sleeping could be so dangerous.

"You have trained them well." Rabbi looks to Francis. "They are all yours."

"Actually . . ." Francis reaches a hand up from the floor. Elias helps him to his feet. With a grunt, Francis says, "I need to speak with Rabbi privately. Micaiah, can you take over from here?"

"Yes, sir." Micaiah bows to his elder as he shuffles from the room.

Rachel watches as Rabbi takes Francis's arm and leads him toward the garden. They pause before leaving.

Rabbi calls over her shoulder, "Oh, and not a word about the possibility of a Breach to anyone outside this room? Understood? We don't need to bring unnecessary fear on the city." She doesn't wait for a response as she and Francis make their way out and leave Rachel all alone with her new and frightening teammates.

CHAPTER 18

An eerie quiet settles over the room in the absence of Francis and Rabbi. The palms at the edges of the room rustle and sway. The scent of the pond blends with nectar in the air. Rachel wraps her fingers around the flower bloom in her pocket and draws a deep breath.

"So, Francis was a Mentor to each of you?" She tries to fill the awkward silence. "How many people has Francis found?"

"Trainer," Rivi corrects as she runs a hand through her dark-brown hair. "He was our Trainer. There's a difference. A Finder," Rivi explains, "is the person who finds you. They automatically become your Mentor. Sometimes, as in the case of your Finder, Cohen, his Mentor also became his Trainer. A Trainer is the person who trains you in a particular skill." She explains it as if she were talking to a child. "Usually, the skill for which you train is related to your Gifting, but again, to reference that special exception, our very own BethEl golden boy"—she smirks—"he doesn't have a Gifting." Rivi shrugs. "But Francis does claim to see things we cannot."

"Wait. What do you mean?" Rachel asks.

"A Gifting is your spiritual gift," Elias says. "Like a superpower." He raises his thick eyebrows and flexes one arm. Rivi punches him in the bicep. "Ow!"

"Yes, I understand that." Rachel observes their banter. "But Rivi said Cohen doesn't have a Gifting?"

"Didn't he tell you?" Another smirk takes over Rivi's perfect face. "Cohen doesn't have any spiritual gifts." Rivi chuckles when she sees Rachel's surprised expression.

"All right, that's enough." Micaiah steps in and the conversation dissolves. "All that to say, Francis was our Dream Walking Trainer. For a time, he was the only Dream Walker in BethEl, but he quickly realized that as the Priest of this city, it wasn't wise for him to continue to take such huge risks."

"I don't understand how it can be so dangerous? It's just a dream."

"But you see, it's never *just* a dream," Micaiah explains. "When we Dream Walk, we can transcend time and space. It's more like an alternate dimension." He allows his words to linger. "Anyway, two years ago, Francis decided it was time to train others to do what previously only he could. He selected the three individuals from BethEl who were the most gifted at dreams, visions, and dream analysis."

Elias takes a bow. "Yours truly. Your very own Dream Team!"

Rivi rolls her eyes again. "You know I hate when you call us that."

"Ignore them." Micaiah waves them off with his hand. "So, Francis is ultimately your Trainer, but as the leader of the Dream *Walking* Team"—he shoots a glare at Elias—"I will also help with your training. As well as these two. Don't worry. They will grow on you." Micaiah pauses and looks over at his teammates. "Well, maybe." He laughs at their expressions then focuses on Rachel. "Ready to get started?"

All three fix their eyes on her. "No, but I guess I don't have a choice."

"Nope. You don't." Elias takes her hand and all but drags Rachel to the center of the room where the tatami mats are arranged. She tries to free her hand. "Here, you can lie on my bed." Elias grins.

"Oh, for goodness sakes." Rivi strides over and swats him away. "Here, Rachel. This mat is yours." She shoots a glare at Elias. "It's brand new. Unsoiled by this creep."

"You know you love me." Elias bats his eyelashes at Rivi.

"Only because Jesus tells me I have to."

Micaiah shakes his head as he takes a seat on the floor beside Rachel. Elias and Rivi's playful banter continues in the background. "There are a couple basic principles you need to learn before you dive into a dream. First, how to get into a dream; second, how to stay in a dream; and third, well . . . let's start with the first two. Those are often the hardest.

"To get into a dream"—Micaiah folds his legs beneath him—"we use advanced meditation techniques. All three of us can fall into a deep REM cycle in less than one hundred seconds, on command, anywhere, anytime. When we're finished with your training, you will be able to sleep anywhere at the snap of a finger."

After trying to avoid sleep for the past few weeks, Rachel isn't sure she likes the idea of being able to enter her nightmares so easily.

"This certain skill comes with its disadvantages as well. While we can fall asleep easily, it is not often a restful sleep. Once you are trained to Dream Walk, it is nearly impossible to sleep and dream normally."

Micaiah sees the look on Rachel's face. "Don't worry. The pros outweigh the cons. To be a Dream Walker is an honor. It is a calling very few receive."

"Right," she whispers.

"Let's begin with the breathing technique," Micaiah suggests. The banter in the background fades, and silence returns to the Sleep House. Elias and Rivi fold their legs beneath them on their mats and join Micaiah as he models the practice. "Just watch," he commands. Rachel obeys and listens carefully to Micaiah's breath pattern. After a couple minutes of inhaling and exhaling in varied lengths, he opens his eyes. "I'll stop there. Any more and I will begin to slip into a trancelike state we call Twilight. It's the moment right before you fall asleep. It's a critical stage. I'll explain in a moment. First, you try."

Seated on her mat with her new teammates, Rachel tries to mimic the breath pattern.

"No, not quite like that," Micaiah says. "Listen to Elias." Elias is now flat on his back, eyes fixed on the cedar rafters while his chest rises and falls in a very specific pattern. Rachel syncs her breath to his.

"Whoa." She starts to fall backward. Micaiah reaches out to catch her hand, but Rachel braces herself. The quick contraction of her abdominal muscles sends pain shooting across her incision.

"You did it!" Micaiah beams. "Twilight. You were almost there."

"I feel light-headed." Rachel casually rubs her hand across her stomach. The pain lessens.

"That's it. Normally, we'd be lying down, but I don't want you to slip in too quick." Micaiah nods to Elias. "He's already there. Elias is the fastest on the team."

"But his eyes are open."

"He's a bit of a show-off if you haven't already guessed."

"Too handsome for his own good," Rivi mutters. A smile twitches in the corner of Elias's lips.

"Elias can dream with his eyes open," Micaiah explains. "He's mastered some pretty advanced techniques, but you don't need to worry about those."

"Can he hear us?"

"Yes. He can hear and see everything that takes place in this room while also dreaming. He's still in Twilight, though. When regular people dream—sorry"—Micaiah corrects himself—"when people who aren't trained dream, their subconscious minds take over. Dream Walking is the process of turning the subconscious into conscious. Elias has mastered the technique of holding two conscious realities at the same time."

"Party trick," Rivi chimes in. "Hardly useful."

"What she means to say"—Micaiah shoots her a look—"is that Elias is very skilled. He used to be the youngest Dream Walker before you arrived."

"How old is he?"

"Twenty," Elias says from his mat.

"He can talk while dreaming too?"

Rivi shakes her head. "Twenty. Just a baby. It explains so much." She pulls her long hair back into a ponytail.

"Yeah, those three extra years make you so much more mature," Elias jabs back.

"Let's move on." Micaiah straightens his shoulders. "Once you enter Twilight, you must choose your destination. Oftentimes, it is a dream we have entered before. Sometimes, we picture a physical location."

Rachel leans back on her hands. "Why physical, if we're entering the Spiritual Realm?"

"Good question. Every physical location has a corresponding spiritual location that can be intercepted through Dream Walking, but that doesn't necessarily mean it looks like the physical location. It just has the same coordinates." Micaiah pauses. "Does that make sense?"

"Not really."

Micaiah shrugs. "It will make sense once you start to practice." He shifts on his mat. "To choose your destination, you must picture it in your mind while in Twilight. Imagine it as vividly as you possibly can. The colors, the sights, the sounds—smells even. The more real it becomes in your imagination, the more fully the location will manifest in your dream. This part usually isn't difficult. Humans use their imaginations all the time. It's the next step, Lucidity, that is a bit tricky."

"What's Lucidity?"

Rivi takes a seat closer to Micaiah and Rachel. Still on his mat, Elias's breath sighs in the background. "Lucidity," Rivi explains, "is the moment you realize you're in a dream. In the beginning, this is incredibly difficult to do."

Rachel challenges Rivi. "Why?"

"Because"—Rivi returns the intensity of Rachel's gaze—"you have to wake your conscious mind while your body remains asleep. Waking the mind is hard, but to stay in the dream is the real challenge."

"Once our brains realize we are in a dream," Micaiah adds, "our natural tendency is to wake up. The mind and body like to be one. To split the two is foreign for most, but it can be mastered. And to Dream Walk, you must master it. Otherwise, if you don't know you're dreaming, your mind will perceive your dreams as reality. In a Dream Walking state, that can have dangerous implications.

"You must become Lucid and stay Lucid, so you can manipulate the dream just as you manipulate the physical world around you. That is the reality we want to master. There are some daily exercises you'll begin to practice immediately that will help you with this. We call them checks.

"First, you need to recognize when you are in a dream and when you are awake. To the untrained person, a dream feels real when they are asleep, but when they wake up, they start to recognize all the things that were off. For example, look at your hands." Micaiah waits for Rachel to follow his command. "Look at them closely. Count your fingers."

Rachel examines her hands. "You want me to count my fingers?"

"Yes." Micaiah holds out his own hands. "How many fingers do you have?"

"Ten."

"No." Micaiah shakes his head. "Don't tell me how many fingers you know you have. Count them. Out loud."

"Is this a trick?"

"It's a technique. I need you to do this every day. Ideally, whenever you step into a new location."

Rachel counts her fingers out loud. "Why did I do that?"

"Because in subconscious dreams, details are often lost or confused," Micaiah says. "In a dream, you might have three fingers or twenty fingers. Or your hands will look distorted. We train the conscious mind to look for oddities while we are awake. When you practice them enough, the subconscious mind learns to do these checks as well. Then you'll find yourself counting your fingers in a dream, realize you're missing a few, and immediately recognize that you are dreaming."

"Weird."

"I think what you mean to say is cool." Elias jumps up from his mat and joins them. "There are other checks too. Here." Elias drops a large book into Rachel's lap.

It grazes her stomach. "Ow."

"Read that," Elias commands.

"Where do I start?"

"Anywhere."

Rachel opens the Bible to the beginning and starts to read silently.

"No." Elias shakes his head. "Out loud. And slow. Examine each letter and word carefully."

Rachel runs her fingers under the line of text. "In the beginning, God created the heavens and the earth—"

"Good news," Elias interrupts. "You're not dreaming."

"You can't read in dreams?"

"To read real text in a dream is next to impossible," Elias says. "Your brain can mimic reading. You might look at words and know what they mean, but to make out actual letters and words . . . it doesn't really work that way. If for some reason you can read text, look away and try again. That's usually when you realize that you weren't reading at all. The text will change or become illegible at a second glance."

"You're looking for clues," Micaiah says. "Anything that can tip off your brain to the fact that you are in a dream. You must study the Physical Realm to recognize the Dream World. The best way to do that is to practice checks throughout the day, and the best time to perform these checks is whenever you enter a new location. For example, when you first step into the

Academy or the Sleep House or when you return home after a long day."

"Why is that?"

"Because when you first fall into a dream, you are thrown into a location that is different from the one you just left." Micaiah gestures around him. "Like this room. You want to train yourself to conduct your checks whenever you notice that your surroundings are different from where you were previously. That way, you enter the dream, conduct your check, and immediately recognize that you are in a dream. Eventually, this will become second nature, and you won't even have to think about doing it. Now, as I said, once you recognize that you are in a dream, the greatest challenge you will face is to stay asleep."

"How do I make sure I stay in the dream."

"Practice, darling." Rivi's long legs stretch out in front of her. "Lots and lots of practice."

"Speaking of which." Micaiah stands, walks across the room, and returns with a tiny box. "Here." He holds the box out to Rachel. "A gift from all of us."

She sits up on her knees. "Really? That's nice of you."

"Don't get too excited. It's also a necessary tool for Dream Walking." Elias rolls onto his stomach and knocks out a few push-ups. Rivi props her feet up on his back.

The lid to the wooden box slips off and reveals a uniquely designed gold ring. The sides of the band are plain, but in the center of the ring, the metal swirls into an intricate symbol. "Wow. It's beautiful."

"We all have one." Micaiah slips his from his finger and holds it up. "Each is unique, and only the wearer knows its pattern. When you conduct your checks throughout the day, study this ring. Memorize its pattern. It is far too detailed for your subconscious mind to recreate. It will eventually be the only thing you need to recognize that you are in a dream."

"It's also the thing that connects us to one another." Elias grunts as he drops to his belly and rolls over. "The rings are blessed by Yahweh. They allow us to walk in each other's dreams, but don't ask me how they work." He throws Rivi's legs off him.

Rivi folds her arms behind her head as she lays back on the mat. "The Lord moves in mysterious ways."

Rachel notes the familiar phrase. "Mysterious ways, indeed."

"Are we gonna do this or what?" Elias slaps his hands together.

"That's up to Rachel." Micaiah returns his ring to his finger. "What do you say? Are you ready to try Dream Walking?"

The ring falls into the palm of Rachel's hand as she overturns the box. She examines it, traces the lines with her eyes, and tries to commit every swirl and swoop to memory. The ring slips over the index finger of her right hand. Her eyes follow the pattern once more before they meet the eager expression of Elias.

"I'm ready. Let's do this."

CHAPTER 19

"All right, here are the basics." Micaiah readjusts on his mat. "One person is the Dreamer, the others are the Walkers."

"He's usually the Dreamer," Elias whispers to Rachel while pointing to Micaiah. "But not always."

"When you Walk in someone else's dream, you focus on the person not the place while in Twilight."

Elias leans over again. "You can think about me if you want."

"Leave her alone." Rivi grabs Elias by the collar. "You focus on the person whose dream you plan to enter. So, in this case, Micaiah. Yahweh help you if you have to enter this one's dreams."

Elias winks.

"Thanks, Rivi. So, to clarify," Micaiah continues, "the Dreamer focuses on the place, the Walkers focus on the Dreamer. If done correctly, we will all enter the same dream space. When we arrive, we conduct our checks and become Lucid."

"What do we do after we become Lucid?" Rachel spins the new ring on her finger.

"Let's focus on the first few steps for now. Once we are in the dream and you're Lucid, we can go from there. Most beginners drop from the dream within seconds of becoming Lucid. As Rivi said, it takes practice."

"I was Lucid for over a minute my first time," Elias says, looking pleased with himself.

"Micaiah, take us somewhere spacious," Rivi says. "We need plenty of room for Elias's head."

Rachel tries to hide her smile.

"Moving along." Micaiah unfolds his legs and stretches them out on his mat. "No pressure, Rachel. Dream Walking isn't easy. If it were, everyone would do it. The four of us have trained for years. Francis is confident you have what it takes. I believe him, and I believe in you. You ready?"

Rachel's breath trembles as she inhales. She can't believe she is voluntarily entering sleep, the very thing she has avoided since she arrived in BethEl. "I'm ready."

"Perfect." Micaiah grins. "Everyone lie down, eyes closed. Relax your body from the top of your head to the soles of your feet. We will begin the breathing technique. Rachel, follow our lead. Elias, can you give us a countdown from one hundred?"

"You got it."

"All right, Rachel. Here we go." There is excitement in Micaiah's voice. "Focus your thoughts on me."

The room fills with the sounds of their breath. The pattern is difficult to follow at first, but Rachel catches on. Lightheadedness quickly follows. Elias's voice becomes distant as he counts. Rachel reaches into her pocket and clutches the red flower.

The sensation of the mat is the first thing to disappear—first from beneath Rachel's feet, then from under her head. Her breath takes over, her chest rising and falling without focus or thought. As she slips from the conscious realm, the image of Micaiah slips from her mind.

A familiar sensation washes over her, a memory from a nightmare. Rachel is falling. Her arms want to flail. Fingers wrap tighter around the bloom.

The depths of unconsciousness suck her in. Beneath Rachel, the ground opens to swallow her whole. Terror grips her chest. Darkness fills her mind. Rachel tries to return her focus to Micaiah, but she can't. Unable to hold onto one thought long enough to make the connection, Rachel tumbles through nothingness until her body jerks to a halt. She is grounded. Sensation returns. She opens her eyes.

***

The world unfolds, vapory at first as amoeba-like shapes take form. Concreteness and substance take over and reveal a world of triangles. Mountains evolve. Coniferous trees stretch to the cold slate sky and race to the heights of Heaven. Patches of white litter the thawing ground. The scent of soil and earth fills the crisp air.

The team awakens on their backs, heads pointed toward each other's feet. Their bodies arrive in the same pattern they left. Each Dream Walker rises to a seated position, looks at their hands, and examines their rings. They become Lucid. They stand, look to one another, and peer around at the world they've entered.

"This place again?" Elias groans.

Rivi rubs her arms. "Can't you pick somewhere warmer?"

"I vote that I pick our locations from now on. All in favor?" Elias's right hand shoots toward the sky.

"Shut up, Elias." Concern fills Rivi's voice as she looks around. "Micaiah, where is Rachel?"

"I was just going to ask the same thing. She must not have made the Jump."

Elias opens his mouth to speak, but Rivi cuts him off. "Whatever smart remark you're about to say, don't." She looks to Micaiah. "I guess we need to go back?" He nods.

"I was going to say"—Elias raises his voice to be heard—"don't you find it odd that she didn't make the Jump? The Jump isn't the hard part."

"Yeah, well, it's her first time." Rivi shrugs.

"We all made it on our first try," Elias says.

Micaiah holds up his hands. "Let's not worry about her skill level. Francis is confident she has what it takes. She'll need practice just like we did. Let's go back and get her so she can try again."

Elias folds his arms over his chest. "Something doesn't feel right."

Rivi takes her place beside him, leans over, and whispers, "It's you." Elias shoves her.

"Guys, c'mon."

Elias salutes. "Sorry, boss."

With their right hands held in front of them, the team forms a tight circle with their bodies. Each examines their own ring, notices the flaws their subconscious creates in the metal's pattern, and whispers, "This is a dream. I'm ready to wake up."

The forest scene fades around them as the dream crumbles. Mountains tumble as they disintegrate into sand. Limbs from the towering pines fall away as easily as petals stripped from a flower. The cool air is replaced by the warm embrace of the garden as sensation returns to them in the Physical Realm. Solid ground takes shape beneath the Dream Walkers as they wake.

Elias is the first to sit up. "Uh, I think we have a problem."

Micaiah and Rivi sit up as well.

"Well, that's interesting," Rivi utters under her breath.

"Very," Micaiah says as he examines Rachel. Her body is still; her chest rises and falls with the measured breathing of one who is in a deep sleep. Her eyes dart back and forth behind closed lids.

"She's in deep REM. She made the Jump."

"Yes, but to where?"

"Rachel, can you hear me?" Micaiah crouches over her body.

"Wake her up," Elias commands.

"What do you think I'm trying to do?" Micaiah lightly shakes her shoulders. "Rachel, wake up." She doesn't stir. He raises his voice as he shakes harder. "Rachel, wake up! It's time to wake up." Micaiah looks to his teammates. "Wherever she is, she's in too deep."

Elias watches the movement of Rachel's closed eyes. "But she'll drop from the dream as soon as she becomes Lucid."

"Right," Micaiah sighs. "But this is her first time. There is a chance she might not become Lucid. She hasn't had a skill test or any of the normal drills we'd run through with a new Walker. That's why we were supposed to be there. To remind her to do her checks. She doesn't have any practice under her belt. On her own—"

"She's stuck," Rivi interrupts. Micaiah nods. "Because she's not in a regular dream. It's a forced dream. She can't wake until she realizes it's a dream."

"I was afraid you'd say that. How long will it take?" Elias nudges Rachel's body with his foot.

"Minutes, hours, days . . . I have no idea. This never happened with any of us. This is one of the reasons we never Dream Walk alone." Micaiah sighs.

Elias flops to the floor. "So, I guess we wait?"

"That's all we can do." Rivi crosses her arms in front of her. "How did this happen?"

Micaiah shakes his head. "She must have focused on something other than me while in Twilight."

"Can you blame the girl?"

"Elias!" Rivi's glare silences him.

Micaiah stands, eyes still fixed on Rachel. "I should find Francis. He will want to know about this. She could be anywhere."

CHAPTER 20

A bead of sweat rolls off Cohen's forehead and slips into his eye. He wipes the sting away and grunts as he picks his way through the debris. When he reaches the corner of rubble he calls his room, he thrusts the backpack from his shoulders and collapses to the ground. Exhausted, he leans back against what used to be a church pew and closes his eyes. A half-full water bottle flies at him and thumps against his chest.

"Bad day at the university?" Cohen opens his eyes to see Adrielle. A mischievous smile curls on her pretty face.

He takes a long drink from the bottle then throws it back to her. "I guess you could say that. How was your day?"

She flops down next to him and unlaces her boots. "From the look on your face? About the same." Cohen follows her lead and unties his laces. Even though his boots are already a couple months old—a couple earthly months—they show no wear. In fact, none of the Apostles' clothes do. Day after day, Cohen and the team see miniature miracles of God's provision. Like in the food rations and other supplies that show up as they did back home in the MannaBoxes. Every morning when the team wakes, they find enough food for the day sitting on top of the old church altar.

As he loosens his laces, Cohen considers how timely these new boots were, as was the backpack he received almost a week before he was chosen for this mission. Other Apostles have shared similar stories.

"This doesn't seem to be working," Cohen mumbles.

"It takes time," Adrielle sighs. "We have to integrate ourselves into their world first."

"Right. It's just taking longer than I thought."

Adrielle finishes what's left of the water. "We can't bind Yahweh with time constraints."

"Clearly." Cohen kicks at a crumbling brick. On at least two occasions, Cohen tried to get a more comprehensive explanation of the time difference from Uriel, but all he told Cohen is that, inside BethEl, time is ambiguous. There is no direct conversion to time outside BethEl and time inside. While two months have elapsed for Cohen and his teammates, they have no way of knowing how that converts inside the city they once called home.

Cohen watches Adrielle beside him as she scans the wreckage they now call their home. None of the other Apostles have returned yet. "I still can't get over how big the campus is," she says. "It's bigger than BethEl. We attend the same university, and I never see you."

"I guess that's what happens when you merge all of the schools into one per region."

"Sector, not region," Adrielle corrects him.

"Right." Cohen shakes his head. "The world is so different now."

"And dark," Adrielle says. "Where do you think the Unity gets the money for government-funded education?"

"Government-funded everything." Cohen shakes his head. "I almost don't want to know." He sighs as he tries not to think about some of the more disturbing innovations humanity has made. "Uriel was right, though. There is no threat of danger. Everyone is so—"

"Stoned?"

Cohen chuckles. "I was going to say placid."

"Catatonic?"

"Apathetic," Cohen says.

"Dead."

Cohen pauses. "Yeah."

Adrielle unfolds her long legs. "I wonder how the other assignments are going."

"Kate says middle grade is awful. Maybe even worse than the university based on some of the things she's told me."

"Of course it is." Adrielle crosses her ankles. "At that age, the Unity is still indoctrinating the students with the ways of the Path. Personally, it sounds like mind control."

Cohen casts her a sideways glance. Adrielle's face stares ahead unchanged. "I hadn't thought about it that way."

Adrielle's eyebrows dart up. "No?"

"No, because"—Cohen searches for the words—"to them, they are just going to school and learning the ways of the world like we did when we were kids. There is nothing weird about it to them. And to be honest, based on the texts we are reading and the modified histories—"

"Modified histories." Adrielle huffs. "That's putting it politely. I'd call it BS."

Cohen nods. "But they don't know that. Think about it . . . if from the time you are born, your authority figures, who you trust, insist that what they teach you is the truth. Why would you ever suspect that it's a lie?"

"Creepy."

"It is."

"And wrong."

"But they don't know that."

Adrielle clenches and unclenches her jaw. "What about the herbs all the students take? Uriel said it is some sort of government-rationed drug."

"Yeah." Cohen pauses. "I guess that part does sound like mind control."

Adrielle glances at him. "Told you." She stretches beside him. Her arm brushes against Cohen's. "Any news from those in the workforce?"

"As far as I know, they face the same struggle we do. They need to establish themselves and build relationships without succumbing to the Darkness around them."

"Not an easy task." Adrielle runs her fingers over her braid.

"If the gospel is going to take root in this cesspit, we first have to lay down a better soil."

"Fancy metaphor. You sound like Uriel." Adrielle chuckles and shoves Cohen's shoulder.

He shakes his head and grins. "I suppose he is rubbing off on me."

"You have the best smile." Adrielle narrows her eyes, but her playful grin lingers. "And the most perfectly bowed lips. Anyone ever tell you that?" She pokes Cohen in the cheek. Her gesture catches him off guard. As her eyes lock onto his, Cohen allows himself to embrace the desire he's buried and the attraction that has slowly built over the past several weeks. He stands, almost too fast, when he hears someone enter the campsite.

"Hola, amigos. Hope I'm not interrupting anything." Jesse's chipper voice echoes off the rubble.

"Hardly." Cohen puts distance between him and Adrielle as he welcomes the oldest member of their team. He can feel Adrielle's stare as he wraps the gray-haired man in a bear hug. The other Apostles begin to trickle in from their assignments outside the camp. "Seems like you're in a good mood," Cohen says. "You should share it with the rest of us."

"I guess I have some good news to share." Jesse's full lips curl upward. "Might be small, but it feels like a win to me."

"Let's hear it. I could use some good news."

Jesse rubs the gray stubble on his chin and puffs his lips. "Well, some of the guys from work go to the bar after our shift ends." He shrugs. "So I joined them today. I thought, you know, I'll have a drink, get to know them a little better, build some relationships, that sort of thing. But when I got there, they were already yapping away." Jesse makes a talking motion with his hand, rolls his eyes, and smiles. "Couldn't get a word in. Then I noticed this guy to my right. Doesn't work with us, quiet, kinda nerdy looking. Like you!"

Cohen pretends to slug Jesse in the shoulder.

"I joke! I joke!" He holds up his hands. "You're *muy guapo*."

Cohen laughs. "Handsome?"

"Of course! The ladies love you." Jesse pretends to be sneaky as he whispers in his thick accent and points to Adrielle.

"Back to your story." Cohen folds his arms.

"Anyway." He draws out the word. "You know me—never met a stranger in my life. So, I introduce myself, get to know him, and bam! Turns out, this guy is high up." Jesse dangles his hand above Cohen's head for emphasis. “A Unity scientist.” He waggles his eyebrows. “Calls himself Orthodox. The conversation was”—Jesse steeples his fingers—“very interesting. And, best part, he wants to continue our little chat. We’re meeting again next week.”

“Jesse, that’s great!” Cohen pulls him in for another hug.

“Ah, it’s nothing. Just had a beer with the guy. I’d do just about anything for a cold *cerveza*.”

“It’s more than that.” Cohen places a hand on the older man’s shoulder. “You planted a seed, and right now, it’s the only seed we have.”

Redness forms in Jesse’s eyes. He blinks a few times. “Thank you. You see, this is why you’re gonna be a great leader someday.” Jesse’s thick finger taps Cohen on the chest. “I know you don’t think you will, but one day, it will happen. You know what to say to give us hope and keep us going. That’s important in a leader. You got all the right stuff.”

Jesse’s words make Cohen smile despite his inner denial. “I don’t quite have all the right stuff. There’s a certain set of skills I’m still missing.”

The older man’s tone turns serious. “Your time will come. You might not see it, others might not see it, but I see it. You were born to be a leader.” Jesse’s words linger in the space between them. Cohen can’t muster up the guts to tell his friend he is wrong.

Cohen glances back at Adrielle. “You’ll have to share your story over dinner tonight. It will fill the others with hope.” He pats Jesse’s thick arm and catches up with the rest of his teammates as they enter. With each one, he lingers longer than necessary to avoid Adrielle. His attraction to her confuses him almost as much as her aggressive pursuit of him.

Dusk creeps over the chapel ruins and peeks in through a few open spots in the roof. The Apostles finish their meal and settle in for the night to await Uriel's return. He is later than usual.

A restlessness unsettles Cohen as he makes his way to his corner of the church. He's managed to avoid Adrielle all night, but it wasn't easy. She tried to sit beside him during dinner, but he quickly formed an excuse to get up and talk with someone else. Now, he rubs his temples as he hauls his tired body back to his private space and begins changing his clothes for bed.

"Cohen?"

He turns, shirt in hand. Adrielle's eyes sweep over his bare chest before quickly darting back to his face. Cohen snatches a clean shirt from his makeshift clothesline and yanks it over his head.

"I'm sorry," Adrielle says. "I didn't realize you were changing."

"Do you need something?" Cohen extracts all emotion from his voice.

"I was hoping we could talk."

"Can it wait until morning? I'm exhausted."

Before she can answer, they both hear the familiar voice of Uriel echoing through the fallen rafters.

Murmurs drift through the camp as the Apostles drag themselves from their beds and trudge over to the designated common space. Cohen prays Adrielle can't see the relief on his face as she follows him to where the team has gathered.

"Please forgive me for my tardiness." Uriel surveys the group to ensure everyone is present. "As usual, it is wonderful to see you all." He pauses. "But I have some unfortunate news to report." The residents of BethEl lean forward in their seats. "I am being reassigned."

"Reassigned?" One of the men speaks up. "What does that mean?"

"You, the Apostles of BethEl, you were my assignment for a time, but effective immediately, that will no longer be the case. It was always the plan to help establish you on this mission. I was never meant to stay."

Now fully awake, the team members whisper among themselves. Cohen fixes his gaze straight ahead, feeling Adrielle's questioning eyes burn into his cheek from beside him.

"Who will lead us then?" someone asks.

"Thank you. I was just getting to that. I think you all will be very pleased to know that one of your very own will take over the leadership of this team."

"One of us? We need someone like you."

Uriel folds his hands in front of him and ignores the protest. "Cohen? Can you please step forward?"

Heat floods Cohen's face. His stomach turns. This can't be happening.

"Cohen?" Uriel repeats as he waves him over to stand beside him.

Adrielle shifts in her seat. Everyone's eyes are on him. After hesitating a moment longer, Cohen rises from the heap of ash to join Uriel in front of his teammates. The Archangel speaks directly to him. "As I said, Yahweh is reassigning me. When I asked him who to place over this team in my stead, he specifically asked for you."

"Me?" It comes out as a laugh.

"Yes. He thinks very highly of you, as do your peers."

Cohen's mind races. Sure, the residents of BethEl like Cohen, but that doesn't necessarily mean they trust him to be their leader. Though Jesse smiles proudly, hesitation lingers on many of his teammates' faces. Adrielle's expression is devoid of emotion.

"I can't lead these people," Cohen says.

Uriel's countenance is warm. "Oh, but you can."

Cohen shakes his head. "You don't understand." His eyes dart to the team. They already know his secret, but they don't realize how debilitating the weight of it is. "I can't lead." Cohen lowers his voice. "I don't have a Gifting."

Unfazed by his confession, Uriel reassures him. "You may not have the skills others seek in a leader, but the truth remains. You were made for this. You were born to be a leader."

Jesse whispers loudly to the person next to him, "I just told him that today!"

"These people respect you," Uriel says. "They believe in you even though you don't believe in yourself, and I am certain they will follow you."

"Surely someone else would be better suited for the task. What about Jesse or Miriam? They are older. They have so much more experience and wisdom."

Uriel shakes his head. "On the day Francis found you, you were destined to become his protégé, a Priest, someone who would one day lead the people of BethEl. You have apprenticed under him for years. You knew this day would come."

"I've trained as a Priest, not an Apostle. I'm not qualified for this, and I'm certainly not ready. I'm not ready to lead, and because I have no Gifting, they aren't ready to follow."

"Yahweh chose *you*." A sternness fills Uriel's voice. "Have you forgotten that Yahweh chooses the unexpected, unseen, unlikely, and dare I say, the unqualified?"

Cohen's mind drifts to the conversation he had with Rachel shortly after she arrived in BethEl. Guilt washes over him as he pictures the lost look on her face the last time he saw her. "I can't do this by myself."

"You will not be alone. Yahweh will be with you, and you will have the support of this team." Uriel looks to the other Apostles and speaks directly to them. "Your support is not optional. You will honor and obey those whom the Lord appoints."

"I can help him." Adrielle stands, posture rigid and voice determined. "This is a large group, and our mission is critical. It would be an overwhelming responsibility for even an experienced leader. Yahweh tells us two are better than one, for if they fall, one will lift up the other."

Uriel's eyes narrow on Adrielle before he turns to Cohen. "What she speaks is wise. Would you like a coleader?"

Cohen wonders how he can communicate that, yes, he would like a coleader but not Adrielle. The existing tension between them is more than enough. He needs distance, not more time with her. Still, he knows he can't turn down the offer for help.

"Adrielle is wise," Cohen says. "She has experience and has already proven herself as a capable leader." He pauses. "I'd be both honored and grateful for her help."

Adrielle's face lights up.

"Very well then. Let it be so. Adrielle, will you please join us?" Uriel waits for her to make her way toward the front. Looking out at the eleven faces illuminated by the glow his presence casts, Uriel declares, "Team, these are the newly appointed leaders for the Apostolic Assembly of BethEl. Do you accept them?"

A unanimous chant rises from the group. "We do."

He turns to Adrielle first. “Adrielle, do you accept your role as leader of these people?”

Without hesitation, she replies, “I do.”

“And Cohen.” Uriel places a massive hand on Cohen’s shoulder. His eyes burn like embers. “Yahweh has appointed you as leader of these people. Do you accept the calling?”

All eyes are on Cohen as they wait for his response. Clearly, there is only one appropriate answer to the question. With his shoulders pressed back, Cohen tries to summon the confidence he is usually able to fake. Francis always called him a born leader. Today, two others echoed that same calling.

Cohen has dreamed of this day, played it out in his mind a hundred different ways, but it never looked like this. In his dreams, he was always much older, wiser, and gifted. He always imagined the Gifting would come before the day of his calling, not the other way around. Silently, he prays that, one day, he will see the potential Francis has always seen, and more importantly, that the potential will be fulfilled and manifested in his life.

While everything within him screams no, Cohen looks out at the moonlit faces of his peers, then back to Uriel as his lips utter the words, “I do.”

CHAPTER 21

Flat on her back, a pale-gray sky greets Rachel. Wisps of clouds drift past her field of vision. Stalks of grain encircle her body and sway in the wind. Hands press into the cool, soft ground as she sits up. As far as she can see in every direction, Rachel is engulfed by fertile fields that reach to every corner of the earth. All the way to the horizon line stretches golden grain ready for harvest.

She has been here before.

Rachel comes to her feet in the center of the small circular clearing and brushes her hands on her thighs, fingers hesitating as she feels the fabric beneath her hands. Rachel pauses and stares at the two familiar soil stains that now mark the white nightgown. It hangs loose around her body.

Her heart thrums in her chest as Rachel takes in the scene. The images tug at her memory. Fear creeps in as the grains start to sway, and the nightgown whips against her bare legs. Beneath her, the earth rumbles.

Small pebbles rattle in the loose soil. Rachel stoops, eyes drawn to a splash of red in the dirt. Fingers wrap around the base of the flower as she snaps the stem. She brings it to her face, traces the unusual shape with her finger, and marvels at the strange, iridescent color.

"I've seen this before." Her voice is like a breath.

Beneath Rachel's feet, the earth shudders. She braces herself. The vibrations encompass her, strumming against her ribcage like fingers across guitar strings. The sound of rushing water surrounds her. In the distance, a voice booms, "Come."

The flower falls as her hands fly to her ears. Rachel drops to the ground and covers her head. The bloom curls in the dirt.

"Come."

The lustrous-red color taunts her memory. Silk petals evoke emotions, smells, and images.

"Come." The ground quakes and begins to crack.

Fingers reach for the petals.

"Come!"

The ground splits beneath the flower. Rachel snatches it before it falls. Something unlocks in her mind. Words come to her. Jumping to her feet she shouts, "Here I am!"

The tremors cease. The grains are stilled.

"Here I am," she repeats quietly. "Your servant is listening."

The silence lingers then breaks with the sound of the voice, this time a whisper. "Look." The voice comes from the sky.

A stormy gale rushes through the field. Rachel peers up, holding her wind-whipped hair back from her face. Clouds begin to part. A form takes shape. Clouds separate like layers of tissue paper to reveal a house floating in the sky.

Silence returns, then the voice beckons, "Come."

The earth swells beneath Rachel and tosses her into the air. A scream escapes her lips as her feet are swept out from underneath her. She is lifted higher and higher until the house is no more than an arm's length away.

Now overcome with awe, Rachel reaches out to touch the house. Outstretched fingers wrap around the simple handle on the front door. She pulls. The door swings open, and an unseen force throws her body backward. An invisible power pours from the house and ushers her even higher into the sky. A petal from the flower breaks off as Rachel clutches tighter to the bloom. She watches the spot of red shrink beneath her, past the house and field that now fade from view. In what feels like seconds, the earth is already a tiny blue-and-white ball, but the force that carries her doesn't stop. It continues to pull Rachel through space, bringing her before another marble-like planet—this one a clear, pale blue, like a perfect sphere of water. A gasp falls from her lips as the force draws Rachel closer and pulls her into the planet's atmosphere.

Gray, wispy clouds obstruct her view at first, but as Rachel is pulled closer to the surface of the planet, the haze begins to clear. As far as she can see in either direction, there is nothing but water. The calm sea stretches like a piece of glass and disappears into the pale-gray sky. A thin fog hovers.

As the mist parts, dark shadowy figures emerge, rising and falling through the water. Fear washes over Rachel, but as the force pulls her closer, the serpentine shapes become clearer. Stone archways create bridges, each one connected to another by a stone pavilion with pillars and a roof.

"What is this place?" Rachel whispers.

Without an answer, the force sweeps Rachel across the sea and suspends her above the surface of the water. As she nears one of the colonnades, she recognizes the forms of two humans standing in the center. She strains to get a better look and reaches for the side of a bridge to pull her toward the gazebo where the figures stand. As her fingers graze the cool stone, the bridge disappears. Around her, the other bridges vanish and the floating platforms with them. The two figures fade into mist.

An invisible force barrels into Rachel. She tumbles through the air, but her body is halted right before her feet hit the surface of the ocean.

The atmosphere around her darkens. Waves form. Salt water sprays her face and soaks the hem of her nightgown as the sea becomes turbulent. What was once a hazy fog now turns into a thick, angry storm. Fear returns as the land growls its disapproval.

The sky opens and unleashes the floodgates of Heaven. Rain pelts Rachel's face. The force that holds her in the air tightens like a vice around her body. Arms are pressed to her sides, legs frozen. She can't even turn her head.

Maniacal laughter bellows from the storm. Though it doesn't speak, Rachel can tell this voice is different from the one that beckoned her to this land. She tries to scream, but her tongue struggles against the roof of her mouth. Her lips won't part. Her heart seems to be the only part of her body still able to move. Her head throbs with every rapid thump.

The force sweeps her up in its invisible hands and yanks Rachel through the realm at a speed faster than before. It carries her to a place where the sea finally ends then suspends her over the shore.

The stench of the beach is unbearable, the sand blackened. Nauseating heat emanates from it.

Along the shore, people shuffle through the sand with long sticks in their hands, raking the beach. As Rachel watches, she realizes it is not sand they rake. It's rice, millions of grains, all burnt beyond the point of consumption. The rakers drag the grains out of the ocean and onto the shore where they can continue to burn in the scorching sun. Despite the heat that radiates from the seared beach, a chill washes over Rachel.

At the center of the beach stands a wooden structure. Hanging from it by its feet is a beast with the body of a bear and the face of a pig. It's dead. A sudden urge to vomit overcomes Rachel. Bile rises in her throat. She swallows to keep it down.

As the people on the shore continue to rake the beach, Rachel notices chunks of rotting meat mixed within the rice. The stench intensifies, but no one notices she is there.

A soft chant rises from the people as they work. "Unclean, unclean," they repeat in a monotone. "They have no part in the unseen. Separated from sea and love, they cannot enter the place above. Banished to burn, they shall not return. Unclean, unclean."

A bellowing roar breaks through their words. The beast is not dead, and now it is awake.

Suspended by its feet, the creature reaches with both hands for the burnt grains. It shovels the rice and putrid meat into its mouth, laughing as it eats. Then it locks eyes with Rachel. As if on cue, every person on the shore turns to stare at her.

Blood drains from her face. Legs pump as if she is running, but her body cannot move from its fixed position in the air. Rachel flails her arms to try to stop the force that now drags her toward the beast.

There's a flash of gold on her right hand. Rachel stares at the interlaced swirls on her finger. Then she remembers. This is a dream.

Rachel scans the beach for Micaiah, Elias, and Rivi, but they aren't here. She can only see the haunting faces of the rice rakers, their stares like the hollow gaze of the desert skeletons.

Locking her eyes on her ring, Rachel screams, “Help! Please! Wake me up! Wake me up! I want to wake up!” She clutches her hands against her flat stomach.

Immediately, Rachel wakes flat on her back. Steel walls enclose her on every side. A metallic scent mixes with urine and stings her nose. Eyes drift to the vented slats in the ceiling. A face glides into view. Skin like onyx, eyes like death. “Hello, Rachel.”

Rachel screams and bolts upright. Sand consumes her. The desert surrounds her. She glances down at her swollen, pregnant belly that presses against the nightgown. It’s soaked in blood.

Again, Rachel jolts awake, this time nearly ramming her forehead into Elias’s face as she jumps up from the mat.

“Whoa!” He jumps back from where he hovered over her.

Perspiration beads on Rachel’s face. Her breath is ragged. Hands tremble.

“Are you all right?” Concern fills Rabbi’s voice.

“I—” Rachel heaves. “I don’t know.”

Everyone is silent as they wait for Rachel to catch her breath. Her toes grip the mat as she prays for the ground to remain beneath her. Her mind sorts through the images of the dream. “Unclean, unclean,” she whispers.

Micaiah and Rivi stare at her curiously.

“They have no part in the unseen. Separated from sea and love, they cannot enter the place above.”

Everyone is quiet. Rabbi’s eyes widen.

“Banished to burn, they shall not return. Unclean, unclean.”

Francis is motionless. His pipe dangles from his lips.

Rabbi breaks the silence. “Where did you hear that?”

“We need to talk,” Rachel whispers. “I need you to tell me about the banished ones.”

CHAPTER 22

"The first rule of Dream Walking: You never Walk alone!" Rabbi's bare feet pace up and down the floorboards.

"She wasn't alone," Micaiah defends himself. "At least she wasn't supposed to be alone."

"Where was she?" Rivi stands nearby, arms crossed.

"And how did she end up there?" Elias is flat on his mat, fingers tracing the lines of the rafters on the ceiling. Rachel sits next to him on her mat, knees drawn to her chest. Francis hovers at a distance, noticeably silent on the matter.

Rabbi stops. "Tell me again what happened." Her slender arms fold in front of her.

"I told you! We did a trial run so she could practice Lucidity." Micaiah clears his throat. "Forgive me. I'm as confused as you are. Perhaps we moved too fast. We should go back and do the skill test."

Rabbi ignores Micaiah's suggestion and focuses her attention on Rachel. "Do you know where you were?"

"In the beginning, the dream looked familiar." Rachel hesitates when she sees the surprised faces of her new teammates. "The first scene was from another dream."

"Which one?" Francis shuffles closer.

"The dream with the wheat field and the voice."

"Ah yes. The voice that beckoned you?"

Rachel nods.

"And what did you do this time?"

"I answered as you told me."

A proud smile tugs at the corners of his bearded lips. "Were you thinking of this place while in Twilight?"

"No." Rachel shakes her head. "Well, wait."

Elias slaps his thigh. "See, Micaiah, she just didn't want to think about your ugly face." Elias is silenced by a glare from Rabbi. Francis tries to hide a smirk.

"The sensation of Twilight made me feel like I was falling." Rachel unfolds her legs as she explains. "It reminded me of that other dream. I didn't do it on purpose."

"Of course you didn't, my dear, but it did happen, and now we can learn from it. Come, you must tell us everything."

***

Silence fills the small hut-like structure Rabbi calls her home. It sits on the island a short distance away from the Sleep House. Colorful tapestries decorate the walls. Windows open to the fresh air of the garden. Tatami mats and vibrant rugs cover the floor where the six of them sit on cushions.

Rachel's eyes scan the kimono-like tapestries as Rabbi stares out a window and Francis chews his pipe. She waits to hear their reaction to her dream.

"May I?" Francis looks to Rabbi.

"Please." She motions for him to continue.

"My dear, as I suspected, it seems you are already quite gifted in the skill of Dream Walking. This is good news, but it can also prove to be quite dangerous. Though you are skilled, you are also untrained. This is my fault. I implied to Micaiah that we should do things out of order.

"What frightens me is what you have already seen and the implications of such things. You have no context for it, which means you don't realize how dangerous it is."

"Are you talking about the banished ones?"

The pipe finds its way back to Francis's mouth. He reaches into his robe and pulls out a match. Smoke curls as he kindles the bowl. The scent of cherry tobacco fills the small space. "Where did you hear that term? In your dream?"

"Not in my dream, but as soon as I woke. I had a thought, like I suddenly understood what the dream meant. The words *banished ones* popped into my head."

Francis and Rabbi catch each other's gaze. Rabbi gestures to give Francis the floor. He grunts as he shifts on the cushion. "Before Yahweh created human beings upon the earth, he created a heavenly family."

"Angels?"

"Malakim, yes, but others as well. All spiritual beings, celestial in nature. The Nachash I told you about was one of them. He was the first to rebel against his Creator, but he wasn't the last." Thick smoke envelops Francis's face as he considers his next words. "A faction of Yahweh's spiritual family betrayed him."

Rachel's mind uncurls. New memories begin to unwind.

Francis continues. "It happened on more than one occasion. These beings did things so heinous, they were banished from Yahweh's Assembly. They were cast from his presence and imprisoned in Tartarus."

"Tartarus?" Rachel asks.

Rabbi clarifies: "Hell."

"What did they do?"

Rabbi and Francis exchange glances through the curtain of smoke between them. "A story for another day, my dear."

Rivi shifts on her cushion. Elias and Micaiah look to each other then stare at their hands. Rachel's stomach flips. "Then what is Yahweh's Assembly?"

Francis stretches one knobby leg out in front of him. A sandaled foot peeks out from the hem of his robe. "What you need to understand, my dear, is that Yahweh is the Most High. He is the Almighty. He doesn't need anything or anyone to accomplish his will, yet because his nature is relational, being three in one, God chooses to use his relationships with other beings to manifest his will and Kingdom. A God who is love must have someone to love if he is to express the fullness of his character. Therefore, he invites other beings, both human and celestial, into the divine existence of his love. It's quite beautiful, actually."

Rachel leans toward Francis, removes the red flower bloom from her pocket, and twirls it between her fingers as she listens.

"Whoa! Where'd you get that?" Elias snatches the bloom from her hand.

"Hey! Give it back."

"Is that what I think it is?" Micaiah takes the flower from Elias.

"Be careful with it."

"I've never seen one in the Physical Realm before." Rivi examines the bloom as Micaiah holds it up.

Francis sighs. "Give it back, Micaiah." He hands the flower over with care. Francis clears his throat. "It has come to my attention that Rachel may also have the Gifting of Manifestation."

"Impressive." Elias glances at Rachel. "The only other person who can do that in BethEl is Francis."

"I don't know how I did it."

"And we're still not sure she actually did." Rabbi ends the conversation. "Back to the Assembly."

"Right," Francis continues. "Human beings were created to be among Yahweh's Assembly, but our rebellion separated us from Yahweh, just as the rebellion of some of Yahweh's spiritual family led them to be cast from his presence. But not all Elohim revolted."

"Elohim?" Rachel shoots a glare at Elias, who watches her tuck the bloom into her pocket.

"Spiritual beings," Rabbi offers. "It's Hebrew. Translated, most would say it means 'gods,' but the way it is used throughout scripture gives us a more accurate way to understand the word." Rachel wonders why she was able to understand Hebrew words on her first day at the Academy but not now. Rabbi continues, "Elohim refers to a being that lives in the Spiritual Realm. Yahweh is called an Elohim but so are the other members of his Assembly. One thing is clear from the scriptures, though. While there may be other spiritual beings, there is none like Yahweh. He alone is the Creator, the only uncreated one."

"As I was saying, not all Elohim revolted." Francis waves his pipe through the air as he speaks. "Yahweh still has an Assembly, those who remain loyal to him and his divine mission. In the cosmic world, those who are devoted to Yahweh make up the Light, and those whose loyalties have shifted . . ." Francis's voice trails off.

Rachel pieces the information together with her dream. "So, the banished ones are the ones cast from Yahweh's Assembly?"

"Not just banished from the Assembly, my dear. Banished from Yahweh's presence, banished from what most people would call Heaven. Forever."

"The rice."

Francis nods, urging Rachel to continue.

"In my dream, the rice symbolized the ones who have been banished. They were being pulled from the ocean, a place of peace and love." Rabbi peaks an eyebrow. "They were laid out on the beach to burn under the scorching sun until eventually"—Rachel shudders as the image of the beast takes shape in her mind—"they are consumed."

Elias whistles. "She has a Dream Analysis Gifting too? She's a regular ol' Dream Girl."

Rivi sighs. "What about her baby?"

"She's right." Rabbi pauses to consider the implications. "If what Rachel says about the dream is true, then you know who we are dealing with." She exchanges a glance with Francis.

His eyes stare into the smoke as he rubs his weathered cheeks. "Watchers," his gravelly voice whispers.

The team doesn't respond, but the word brings a sharp image to Rachel's mind. It retreats as fast as it came, but the terror from the apparition lingers. A face, not fully human or creature, the makings of nightmares. Skin like onyx, eyes like death. Rachel recognizes it. It's not a dream or a vision. It's a memory.

She feels the color drain from her face and hopes no one notices. For the first time since she arrived in

BethEl, Rachel has a distinct memory from her past, not a momentary vision. The face of the beast morphs in her mind with the man who tore open her pregnant stomach in the dream. She can't shake the image of her bloody, pregnant belly.

"What about when I woke up? I didn't wake up here at first. I woke up, but I was still in a dream."

Rabbi's eyes question her. "You didn't share that with us before."

"Wait, you were two layers deep your first time Walking? Nice." Elias holds out his hand to high-five Rachel. She hesitates then slaps her hand against his, deciding not to mention that it was actually three layers, not two. After watching Rabbi and Francis's silent exchange, she's not sure she should tell them about the creature from her memory.

"Not her first time as it turns out." Francis ignores Elias and leans toward Rachel. "This happened in your dream at the Clinic, yes? You slept while in your dream? You awoke from a dream within a dream?"

"Yes, but this time—" Rachel hesitates. She wants to tell Francis about the monstery face from her past, but clearly, this creature is not a part of the Light. "When I woke, I was in the guest bedroom at the parsonage. I threw back the covers. I was pregnant."

"And?"

"My stomach and the bed were soaked with blood. I screamed, and it woke me up."

Elias watches her with a strange expression. Francis sits back. His face nearly vanishes behind the billows of smoke. Micaiah breaks the silence. "We have to go back in."

"No," Rabbi cuts him off. "No more untrained Dream Walking. It's reckless. I won't allow it."

"But what about her baby! What if we were close to finding the Anointed? If we wait, we might never—"

"Micaiah"—Rabbi's voice sounds too loud for the small space—"we will find the Lord's Anointed." She looks to Rachel. "But we won't find her child if our irresponsibility leads to Rachel coming down with Sleep Sickness or getting lost in some unknown realm."

Rachel tries to steady her voice. "Can that really happen?"

Rabbi ignores the question. "She will train just like anyone else. Given her natural Giftings, we can likely expedite the process, but I will not allow any horseplay or reckless behavior on my watch. Understood?" She fixes her gaze on Elias. He shrugs. "And from now on, you must always have an Intercessor while you sleep."

"Every time we sleep? Not just Dream Walk?"

"Correct."

"That's unreasonable!"

"Elias, if today's little incident revealed anything, it's that we need to take extra precautions. The stakes are higher than we realized."

Elias folds his arms. "Who in all of BethEl is willing to intercede for us every time we sleep?"

"I will." Rabbi forces a smile.

"And so will I," Francis adds.

"Then when will you sleep?" Micaiah asks.

"When we can." Rabbi is firm.

Rachel looks to Francis. "There were Intercessors in my room at the Clinic. What do they do exactly?"

"An Intercessor is someone who prays or intercedes on behalf of another," Francis says. "Our words hold great power, you know. They can move mountains in both the Physical and Spiritual Realms."

"Like incantations?"

Francis cocks his head. Rivi shoots Rachel a strange look. "Not exactly, my dear. In this case, the Intercessor, myself or Rabbi, will pray for the safety and protection of the team while you Dream Walk, or in this case, every time you sleep."

Elias whistles. "That's quite the task. Do you realize how many hours I sleep a day? It's not just a hobby; it's my profession."

Rabbi rises to her feet. "It's temporary. Francis and I can survive on a few hours of sleep."

"Not for long," Micaiah mumbles under his breath.

Rabbi ignores him. "I'll prepare the Sleep House. You will all stay and sleep there until we are certain everyone is safe."

"We can't go home to our own beds at night either?" Irritation fills Rivi's voice.

"Not until we are certain everyone is *safe*." Rabbi repeats her words. "Pack your bags." She pushes through the bright-red fabric hanging in the doorway.

"She's in a mood."

"Shut it, Elias." Rivi stands and follows Rabbi without another word.

"Are all the women in a bad mood today, or is it just me?"

Rachel tries to hide her grin. "It's just you."

Elias clutches his chest. "Ouch. That hurts, Dream Girl." He jumps to his feet. "Better go pack for the slumber party." He slaps Micaiah on the back as he darts through the cloth.

"Guess I'll see you both later this evening." Micaiah nods a farewell to Rachel and Francis. "Rachel, it's been a pleasure." He pauses. "It's also been really interesting." Micaiah waves as he exits the hut.

Left alone with Francis, a foreign feeling grips Rachel. It starts as a tingle in her legs then spreads through her body like a warm liquid. Anticipation mixes with the desire for truth and a fear of what she might find. Adrenaline courses through her veins and bolsters her to ask the next question. "What happens now?"

The pipe never leaves Francis's lips. The smoke parts and curls around his face as if making way for the words of its master. A smile tugs at his dark, bearded face. Mystery kindles in his ancient eyes. "You go back in."

CHAPTER 23

"Are you sure this is a good idea?" Rachel follows Micaiah into the open-air room of the Sleep House.

"You have to go back in sometime. Might as well be today. I thought you said you were ready to try again?" The familiar mats are arranged in the center of the floor. Elias and Rivi are already there. Their muffled banter echoes from the cedar rafters.

"That was yesterday."

"You've had several days to run through drills and practice your checks. You'll do great."

Wind whistles through the rafters of the Sleep House. The vapory residue of ancient dreams lingers in the atmosphere, longing to share all the magical worlds that have been encountered from this room. It seems the thinnest of the Thin Places. Rachel rubs her hands together as goosebumps creep up her arms.

"Here she is!" Elias's arms spread wide as he approaches. "My Dream Girl!" Before Rachel can get away, Elias wraps her in a tight embrace and squeezes her arms to her sides. He ruffles her short black hair. "You ready for this?"

Rachel manages to shove him away. “Ready to try Dream Walking? Maybe. Ready for your hugs? Definitely not.” She straightens her tunic and smooths her hair.

A wicked grin flashes across Elias’s face. “She speaks my love language. She really is my Dream Girl!” Rivi folds her arms over her chest and shoots him a glare. “Don’t worry. You’re still my girl too.” Elias pulls Rivi in for a side hug. She struggles to break free.

“All right, children, let’s get started.” Micaiah takes his place on his mat.

“Yes, father.” Elias takes an exaggerated tumble to the floor as Rivi shoves him. Rachel joins them on her mat.

Micaiah clears his throat. “Now that Rachel has had several days of drill practice, she will once again attempt to enter a dream as a Walker, become Lucid, and stay Lucid. We are here to support, guide, and train her. I’d like to request that we all take this seriously.” Micaiah fixes his gaze on Elias. “No goofing off, please.”

Elias salutes. “I agree to your terms, sir.” Micaiah rubs his brow and sighs.

Francis and Rabbi make their way across the room. “Positions!” Francis declares through clenched teeth on his pipe. His voice echoes off the cedar beams. Rabbi helps him to his cushion in the center of the other four mats. Micaiah takes his place, and the other team members join him, followed last by Rachel.

She leans back, her head directly in front of Francis as she stretches out her legs. He pats her shoulder. “You will do great, my dear.” Rachel offers a nervous smile.

Rabbi begins to walk in a square around the perimeter of the team. She splays open her fingers, palms faceup in front of her as she whispers prayers of

Intercession. Her bare feet are nearly as silent as her lips.

"Close your eyes," Francis says. "Begin your deep breathing. I will give you the countdown."

Rachel follows her teammates' lead, mimicking their body posture and breath. She tries to forget the image of the monstrous face that has dominated her thoughts since she retrieved the memory a few days ago. A nightmarish creature is the last thing she needs to focus on while in Twilight.

By the time Francis counts down to thirty, the lightheaded feeling takes over. Rachel's body sinks into a deeply relaxed state. Thoughts in her mind melt, stripped of concreteness, but she manages to hold tight to a mental image of Micaiah. As she slips deeper into Twilight, other pictures vie for her attention. In her mind, giant leaves fan out around Micaiah's face; a sweet scent fills her nostrils; splashes of red fill her vision. Then she falls.

***

Rachel bolts upright. She is alone, cross-legged on a damp, earthen floor, surrounded by the most beautiful flowers she has ever seen. They're as big as her hand and an unearthly shade of red. The color triggers something in her mind, but it vanishes when the foliage parts and Micaiah walks through. He waits and watches her.

"Micaiah, where are we?"

"I was about to ask you the same question." His face remains composed.

Rachel stands and turns. Rivi is behind her. "Rivi, how did you get here?"

"Good question, but how did *you* get here, Rachel."

Rachel ignores her teammates and trails her fingers across the wall of greenery and blooms. Her mind stirs as she walks the perimeter of the clearing. She collides with Elias.

"Hi, Dream Girl." A mischievous grin spreads across his face. The words fall from his lips in slow motion. Rachel's brain reels. It can't make sense of what's happening.

"How did I get here?" She spins in place, trying to comprehend the environment. "Where am I?"

"Those are all great questions, Rachel." Micaiah places a hand on her shoulder. "How did you get here?"

"I just . . . wait. No." Rachel rubs her temples. "This is new. I've never been here before."

"Very good, and what do you do when you enter new places?"

Rachel looks to each of her team members for a clue. Elias balls his hands into fists and releases them. He does it again. Not sure why, Rachel copies him. Her eyes focus on her hands as they open and close.

"Wait." She splays her fingers, palms upward, studying the lines of her hands. Her fingers are odd—longer, like spaghetti. The noodle-like appendages unravel from her hands and spill onto the ground. Something falls with them. Rachel stoops to pick it up. A ring. At first it is familiar. She studies it, made curious by its strange design. "This isn't right," she whispers. Rachel peers up at her teammates. "This isn't my ring." They smile simultaneously. "This is a dream. I'm dreaming."

As the words leave her mouth, Rachel's fingers return to normal. The ring takes on its familiar form as she slips it over the index finger of her right hand.

The earth beneath her trembles. "What's happening? What's happening!"

"Breathe. Stay calm," Micaiah coaches. The garden-like scene shakes violently. Flower petals rain down all around her.

"You're losing your grasp on the dream. Stay calm—" Rivi's words are cut short.

Rachel's eyes fly open. She is back in the Sleep House.

Too embarrassed to sit up and face her teammates, Rachel stares at the ceiling as she listens to them stir. Heat flushes her cheeks. Her hands ball into fists. She failed.

"Rachel? Are you awake?"

She sighs and finally sits up. "You know I'm awake, Micaiah."

"You did great."

Her jaw clenches. "I fell out immediately."

"That's normal. I told you that."

"Yeah, well, I'm not normal," Rachel says. "At least, that's what everyone keeps telling me." She jumps to her feet. "I'm done."

The room fills with Micaiah's commanding voice. "No."

Rachel stops and turns, arms fold over her chest. Everyone stares.

Micaiah stands and points to Rachel's mat. "Lie down. You'll try again."

She narrows her eyes at him. "I said I'm done."

"And I said you'll try again."

"Don't tell me what to do. I'm sick of everyone telling me what to do!" Rachel storms across the room to leave. Behind her, the team's muffled voices echo in the rafters.

"Rachel, wait." Elias trots up behind her and catches her hand. She yanks it back.

"Leave me alone."

He darts in front of her, walking backward to face her as Rachel pushes past him and bursts into the garden.

She quickens her pace. “What do you want?”

“Just to talk.”

“Don’t touch me.”

“Fine.” Elias holds up his hands. “You sure are feisty.”

Rachel stops. “You want to talk? Then talk.”

Elias runs his hand through his thick hair. He offers a goofy grin then winces. “I’ll be honest, I didn’t think this through. I just followed you. I didn’t have a plan.”

“Of course you had a plan.” Rachel narrows her eyes. “You came out here to make me go back in there.” She jabs him in the chest with her finger then points it at the Sleep House.

“I’m not here to make you do anything.” Elias jabs back, poking her in the shoulder. Rachel swats his hand. “I’m out here because you’re right.”

Rachel hesitates. “Right about what?”

“You aren’t normal.”

She rolls her eyes and crosses her arms.

“And I can’t understand why you would want to be normal.”

“Yeah, well, I’m not,” Rachel says. “And I’m not gifted at Dream Walking either.”

This makes Elias laugh.

“I’m not. Francis is wrong about me. He made it seem like I would be a natural, like you, but he’s wrong. About everything.” Rachel’s hand instinctively touches her stomach.

Elias tries to hide a smile. “Francis isn’t wrong about you.”

“How do you know?”

He lowers his voice. “Can I tell you a secret?” Rachel doesn’t respond. “Let me see your flower.” Elias holds out his hand.

“No. You’ll break it.”

Elias makes a show of looking offended. “I will not. Give it here.”

Rachel sighs, reaches into her pocket, then carefully places the flower bloom in Elias’s hand.

“You’re worried about me breaking it? If anything happens, it’ll be you who squishes it in your pocket.”

“Look at it,” Rachel says. “It doesn’t look any different than the day I found it.”

“Exactly. That’s the point. Now, here’s the secret about this flower.” Elias twirls it under Rachel’s nose. She swats him away. “These flowers are special. Like you,” he adds. “These blooms only grow in the Spiritual Realm. That dream you just entered, it’s one of the few places they can be found. Francis suggested we take you there.”

Rachel softens. “What are you saying?”

“I’m saying you *are* gifted at Dream Walking. Because somehow, on your own, you managed to find an incredibly rare flower, and not only that, you Manifested it.”

“I made it physical?”

“You made it real. And if you can do that”—Elias raises his eyebrows—“there might be other things you can find and Manifest.”

Rachel hesitates. “Like my baby.”

Elias’s tone shifts. “There’s this concept we have here in BethEl; we get it from the Bible: on earth as it is in Heaven. The biblical idea is that we are called to bring the Kingdom of Yahweh to the earth. That’s why BethEl exists. That’s why we sent out a team of Apostles. But as a Dream Walker, I have a theory.”

Rachel can't hide her curiosity. "What is it?"

Elias grins. "What if there is a deeper layer to that idea. What if it has something to do with literally Manifesting things from the Spiritual Realm—the Heavenly Realm—on earth."

Rachel waits for him to continue.

He shrugs. "That's all I have so far. But the point is, you did something awesome that not many people can do. You are gifted. Yahweh brought you here to Dream Walk and, through that, lead us to the Anointed."

Rachel lets her arms drop to her sides. "You think that's my purpose here?"

"Definitely." Elias scans her face. "What do you say? Want to give it another try?" He pulls out his cheesiest grin. "Please? For me?"

Rachel huffs. "Fine."

Elias does a silent fist pump then grabs Rachel by the arm to lead her back inside.

"What did I say about touching?"

"Whoops!" Elias holds up his hands and backs away. "Don't do it."

"Right. Don't do it." Rachel hides a smile.

"Were back in business!" Elias shouts as he trots into the Sleep House. Rachel follows behind. No one asks what was said between the two of them.

"Everyone on your backs." Micaiah pretends the interruption never happened. Francis and Rabbi watch Rachel but say nothing. "Begin deep breathing," Micaiah says. The raspy rumble of Francis's voice begins the countdown.

Everything happens much faster this time, including the moment Rachel falls out of the dream. Mere minutes pass before everyone is again staring at the ceiling. No one moves.

"Again," Micaiah says.

Rachel enters the dream, becomes Lucid, falls out.

"Again."

Dream. Lucid. Fall.

"Again."

The cycle continues for what feels like hours. Rachel loses count of her failures. Each dream blurs into the next. Her mind and body become less cooperative with each try.

"Again."

"Wait." A new voice fills the room. The team sits up. "I'd like you to try something different this time." Francis shifts to a more comfortable position. "This time, Rachel will be the Dreamer."

"Begging your pardon, Francis, but that is a terrible idea."

Francis turns to Rivi, a stern expression fixed on his dark face. "And why is that, my dear?"

"You saw. She hasn't even Walked yet. Can't stay Lucid. To make her the Dreamer, well, it wouldn't be wise."

"Don't tell me about wisdom." Francis's rebuke is gentle but assertive. "Yahweh chooses the foolish things of the world to shame the wise. For the foolishness of Yahweh is wiser than human wisdom."

"Touché." Elias's comment is met with an icy stare from Francis. "Sorry." Elias mimes zipping his lips.

"My decision to place Rachel as the Dreamer may not make sense to you, but nothing about her circumstances makes sense. We are not preparing her, or any of you, for a normal mission." He glances at Rachel. "We are on a quest for the Lord's Anointed. To find her child, you must eventually enter her dreams. We might as well begin now."

"To remain Lucid in someone else's dream is difficult, to do it in your own dream—"

"Micaiah, I do not ask for your understanding. I ask for your cooperation."

He lowers his eyes. "Yes, sir."

"Do I have everyone's cooperation?"

"Yes, sir."

"And trust?"

"Yes, sir."

Francis turns his attention to Rachel. "And you, my dear? Do I have your consent?"

Rachel glances at Elias then back to her Mentor. "You really think I can do this?"

"My dear, I know you can," Francis says. "I know all of this is still so new to you, but trust me. You were not sent here by Yahweh to learn to walk in the dreams of others, but to peruse the depths of your own. I believe you will be quite surprised at the things you are able to do when you are operating in the will of Yahweh." Francis glances at the other Dream Walkers. "Now, let's try this again. This time, with Rachel as the Dreamer. I will join you."

Concern creases Micaiah's face. "Are you sure that's a good idea?"

"Of course I am. Don't be preposterous. I may be old and arthritic, but I'm not incapable." Francis settles into a seated, meditative position.

Rachel watches him as he closes his eyes. "Don't you need a mat to lie on?"

Francis peeks his eyes open. "My dear, don't let Elias fool you into believing that he is the most skilled Dream Walker in all of BethEl. Why, I can all but dream standing up while I eat my breakfast, but for safety's sake, I'll sit down." He flashes a mischievous grin. "Now, let's not completely abandon everything you were doing before. I want you to reenter the location Micaiah took you. The Crimson Gardens, yes?" Micaiah nods. Francis grunts his approval. "As I instructed. Very good." Francis glances at Rabbi. "You will continue to intercede?"

"Of course." Rabbi nods.

Francis closes his eyes. "Very well. Picture the dream, Rachel. Picture it as vividly as you can. We will follow you there."

***

Within seconds, Rachel is back in the land of red flowers. She comes to her feet and glances around. She's alone.

A thought gnaws at the back of her mind. How did she get here? Where was she before? An image of large ceiling rafters forms in Rachel's mind—the Sleep House. This place is familiar yet new.

Rachel holds her hands straight out in front of her, palms down to see her ring, eyes tracing the pattern. Its true design is more familiar now, and this one is not right.

"This is a dream," Rachel whispers. She steadies herself and braces for the world to crumble, but it doesn't. The ground remains firm beneath her feet.

She looks up, pinches her nose, closes her mouth, and waits for her lungs to burn, but they don't. Somehow, Rachel is still able to breathe even while her breath is held. "This is definitely a dream."

On all sides, towering walls of lush foliage enclose her. Rachel takes a couple cautious steps. Splashes of red garnish the scene as if someone splattered paint all over a green canvas. The sweet scent of nectar is intoxicating; her senses cling to it. At the same time, Rachel's mind begins to wander.

The garden enclosure reminds Rachel of somewhere she has been before. She can't place it until sections of the living wall begin to morph into stalks of wheat. A memory of a different dream creeps in. "No," Rachel whispers. She focuses on the scent of the flowers. "Crimson Gardens." The wavy stalks of grain vaporize. The giant blooms return.

Applause startles Rachel as she turns to see Francis clapping his hands. The rest of the team waits awestruck behind him.

"Bravo, my dear. An exceptional display of skill. I am impressed with your ability for self-control. The mind is a difficult thing to wrestle. It does like to wander, especially in dreams. You'll have to fight your subconscious. It's an angry sea monster, ready to overturn the ship of sensibility and pull you into the murky depths where all matter of strangeness abounds. Team?" Francis turns to the three other Dream Walkers. "What did I tell you? Pretty good, eh?"

Micaiah shakes his head. "I'm sorry, Rachel. I underestimated you."

"It's okay. I think I underestimated myself." Rachel casts a quick glance at Elias. "Now what?" she asks Francis.

"Now we begin your training."

"I thought we already started."

He shrugs. "Yes, but this is where the real training begins." Enchantment kindles in his icy-blue eyes. His feet dance in place. "Look at that! No pain at all! I forgot how agile I am in this world. Oh yes, we are going to have great fun." Francis slaps his thigh. "Right then. Let's get to it. First things first. You must learn how to control the dream. Micaiah? Would you like to take over with the first test?"

“My pleasure.” Micaiah steps forward. “In dreams, even the simplest of tasks require great focus. Take, for example, this.” He reaches forward and plucks one of the giant blooms from the garden wall. “Anything that requires a conscious choice will also demand great focus. Manipulating a dream isn’t hard in theory, but it can be very difficult in practice.”

“Because of the subconscious mind.”

“Exactly. Give it a try.”

Rachel thrusts her hand forward into the greenery. When she pulls it back, it is covered in red paint. Elias chuckles. All around them, the flowers melt into red puddles and drip from the leaves.

“Your subconscious mind thinks the flowers are painted onto the garden wall,” Micaiah says. “You’ve already proven you can manipulate a dream, now we need to help you do it on purpose. So, tell me. What was different when you waved away the grain stalks that were beginning to form?”

“I focused on what was already here in the dream—the smells, the images.”

“Great. You made a conscious decision to make the current dream more concrete. With that in mind, try again.”

She does, only to end up with more paint on her hands.

“Again,” Micaiah says.

Rachel huffs. She doesn’t want to try again, but she catches Elias watching her. He prods her with his eyes.

Her shoulders rise as she takes a deep breath. She stares at the red splatters on her hands, rubs the paint between her fingers, and notes the almost silky texture. The image stirs something in her memory. Her eyes get lost in the strange shimmer then close. Rachel imagines the red flower bloom she found the night Cohen left, the same night she said yes to all this nonsense. In her mind, she says yes again.

She opens her eyes and fixates on the paint stain. A minute or two passes. Nothing happens. Then the paint on her hand begins to bubble.

The team watches, amazement glued to their faces as tiny orbs of paint evaporate off Rachel's skin. The same happens with the paint on the garden wall. Excitement builds, but Rachel clings to the world. All around the team, blood-red raindrops float suspended in the air. They swirl and coagulate into shapes and forms. Flowers materialize in the air. They swirl about the center of the garden and dance around Rachel's head in a crimson fury before being flung against the leaves in a strange but distinct pattern.

With a now-clean hand, Rachel reaches out again, mind fixed on the scent of the bloom. She remembers how smooth the petals feel between her fingers, how much more fragrant the scent will be as she holds the flower up to her face.

Leaves rustle as her fingers lock around the base of the biggest flower. She snaps it from the vine and offers it to Micaiah. His face is unreadable.

"That was—"

"Awesome?" Elias offers.

"Yes, awesome. What you did with the paint, how it evaporated—that takes a level of skill that can take months to master."

"She's not just consciously altering what is already here," Rivi speaks up, "she is consciously adding to the world."

"This experience," Francis says. "It was not so unlike the moment you healed Rabbi, yes?"

"She's healed someone?" Elias asks. "Man, most people only have one or two Giftings, but she—"

Francis holds up a hand to quiet Elias. "It was similar, yes?"

Rachel's eyes search the faces of her teammates.

"Rachel?"

"Yes. It was very similar."

Francis nods. "Yahweh has gifted you, my dear, in quite a unique way, I might add. But we must ensure you know how to use these gifts properly."

"You really are a Dream Girl. Ow!" Rivi elbows Elias in the ribs.

Micaiah holds Rachel's gaze. "It seems you've discovered the reason Yahweh brought you here. You are a Dream Walker, Rachel." He tucks the oversized bloom behind her ear. The gesture feels familiar. "And because of you and your Gifting, we will now be able to find the one we have been waiting for—the Lord's Anointed." He pauses. "I think I speak on behalf of our team when I say, we are with you. To the ends of the Physical Realm and the Spiritual Realm. We will help you find your child."

CHAPTER 24

Mist hovers and wraps its thick, warm arms around the land. Droplets glimmer and cling to the grasses of the field like a plot of land to harvest precious jewels. They shimmer in the light of the hazy, amber sun. The heavy orb hangs so low, it appears the field has to hold it up with its outstretched, grassy fingers. Gravel crunches beneath Rachel's feet as she turns to follow the winding path with her eyes. Like guardians of the land, three statuesque trees watch over the field from the other side of the road. They stare at her solemnly and promise no safety beyond the bend in the road where they stand guard. She wonders what lies beyond that point. If this were her dream, she would simply imagine herself farther down the road where the path disappears into the rolling hillside. But this is not her dream.

"What's on the other side of the hill?" she asks Francis.

"Nothing you need worry yourself with today, my dear."

"What is this place?"

"A land from an old dream—a dream from antiquity, I daresay. I revisited this place often while training these fine folks." He gestures to the three other Dream Walkers. "It is a wonderful training ground."

"Why?"

"I'm not sure." He chuckles. "It just is." Francis observes her. "Your concentration has improved. Your conscious mind is much stronger than when we began your training, even while Walking in another's dream. You have made excellent progress, which is why we are here today. Team." Francis signals to Rachel's companions. They line up side by side across the gravel road. The heavy sun behind them outlines their silhouettes with fire. All three are composed. Even Elias wears a strangely serious expression.

"Draw your weapons," Francis says.

A wave of heat pulses from her team members and forces Rachel back as they unsheathe the swords at their sides. Fiery blades made almost entirely of light stand menacingly rigid before her. Her heart races in her chest as she watches the flames dance upward from her comrades' hands.

Another rush of heat envelops her from behind. Francis holds out his weapon. Rachel recognizes these swords. Her feet shuffle backward. Images bombard her mind. Pictures of desert sands and two men. Each holds a sword—one light, the other dark. The swords clash. Sparks sizzle. Rachel pictures the face of the man in the gray suit. She tries to compose herself, but in her mind, the man's angular face morphs into the beastly creature. Skin like onyx, eyes like death.

Pieces of jagged gravel rattle beneath Rachel's feet as her hand presses against her flat stomach. The team braces themselves. The ground trembles and quakes like the fear that courses through Rachel's body. In the distance, the hills roll and heave. Rivi catches Francis's arm before he tumbles to his knees.

"What's happening?" Micaiah shouts over the rumble of the earth.

Francis shoots a horrified glance in Rachel's direction. No one else sees it, but she reads his expression. It's not possible. This isn't her dream. Yet Francis's reaction makes it clear; somehow, Rachel is manipulating this world.

She slows her breath and fixes her eyes on Francis. The tremble subsides to a gentle purr. He nods discreetly. The team regains their footing. The tremors cease.

"What in BethEl was that?" Elias looks to Francis. "Was that you?"

Francis shrugs away Rivi's arm and brushes the front of his robe. "A test," he says casually. Rachel doesn't miss the warning he shoots her from the corner of his eye. "This is a training ground after all."

"What was the point?"

"To keep you on your toes." Francis straightens his shoulders. "An old man need not have reasons for the things he does. Now, where were we. Ah yes, swords. Please use caution as you wield your weapons." Rachel suspects his comment is directed more toward her than the rest of the team. On more than one occasion during her training, Rachel's reckless lack of control has seemingly turned her Gifting into a weapon. Elias watches her then holds his sword in front of him.

"This, Rachel, is the Sword of the Spirit," Francis bellows, "our mighty weapon in combat."

Rachel's conscious mind grasps at Francis's words while holding tight to the essential and constant reminder that she is in a dream. At the same time, now, she must fight back the nightmarish desert images that bombard her. "I thought the people of BethEl were a people of peace," Rachel questions. "Isn't that what Jesus taught?"

"Very good, my dear. Your lessons with Rabbi have paid off. Have you read Ephesians yet?" She shakes her head. "Micaiah?" Francis gestures for him to take the lead.

"We are a peaceful people," Micaiah begins, "but we are also a people of war. Though we do not wrestle against flesh and blood, but against the powers of Darkness and the spiritual forces of evil in the Heavenly Realm."

"The Darkness," Rachel says.

"Yes, my dear, the Darkness. There are real, nonhuman, evil entities that exist, and as a Dream Walker, you are sure to encounter them." Rachel doesn't offer to tell him she suspects she already has. "Today you enter the next portion of your training—combat. You must know how to fight."

"With a sword?"

"Yes, the Sword of the Spirit, the Word of Yahweh."

"And your fists when necessary," Elias says.

"But only in dreams and the Spiritual Realm," Rivi says. "We are never to use violence in the Physical Realm."

Rachel nods as she takes in their words. "The Word of Yahweh? That's Jesus—he's the Word of God."

"Right again. The Sword of the Spirit contains within it the power of Yeshua, the Son of Yahweh." Francis's eyes spark. "Are you ready for a story?"

Elias flicks his wrist, and the blade of his sword disappears. "A story? We should sit down. This might take a while." Micaiah and Rivi sheathe their weapons.

Francis snaps his fingers dramatically and five chairs appear in the middle of the road. They're identical to the rockers in the hearth room at the parsonage.

"These again?" Elias moans. "The back is so stiff."

"What can I say, I am a creature of habit." Francis sheathes his sword and settles into his familiar rocking pattern. "Now." He reaches into his robe to retrieve his pipe. "Parts of this story may be familiar." He shrugs as he chews on the tip. "But I'm old, and I forget things. So you get to hear it again."

Elias leans over to Rachel. "Old people are funny." She hides a smile.

"Before humans walked upon the face of the earth," Francis bellows in his best storyteller voice, "in fact, before the earth was created, Yahweh created a beautiful Spiritual Realm—a lush garden-like land high upon a mountaintop. It was his dwelling place. The expanse of this creation reached into the farthest recesses of the deepest galaxies and universes. It was a land of harmony and peace. The entire realm was created by the power of Yahweh's spoken word. His utterances erected a great city, a Kingdom, and formed into existence a vast countryside with a majestic palace, a temple where he dwelled. But as you know, Yahweh is a God of love. It's not just an attribute of his character; as the Three in One, it is his identity. So, he created beings to love.

"With no more than mere syllables, Yahweh brought forth the Elohim, celestial beings who dwelt in the Spiritual Realm with him. They appeared in all different shapes and sizes, striking yet odd creatures with forms that looked neither fully human nor fully animal. They were assigned different ranks and positions, roles and responsibilities. From the humblest of Malakim, the Angels and Messengers, to those called Rulers, Thrones, Powers, and Authorities. All were given assignments in the Kingdom, and though some were given great power and authority, none were like Yahweh. For he alone is the Creator. There is no other. He is Yahweh Most High, and there is none like him. He is the one who was and is and, of course, is still yet to come. He adored his creation, and so he offered them the gift of his love."

"Free will," Rachel says.

"Very good. Yes, love in its purest form, the essence that fills Yahweh, requires a choice, and a choice requires free will.

"In the beginning, the Elohim used that free will to love Yahweh in return. The hosts of Heaven adored him. Their praise and worship were willingly given, never forced. They were his celestial family. So Yahweh gave them areas of dominion, just as he would later do with humanity."

"Because God likes to work through relationships?"

"Precisely, my dear. Very good. Yes, each created being was given a territory or position. Some were assigned to distant galaxies, some served on the Mountain of God, some worshiped unceasingly in the temple, and others, the most loyal, consulted with him amidst the Assembly. From among these, seven rose to be among Yahweh's closest and most trusted confidants, the Archangels."

Rachel recalls the statues on the façade of the Chapel and the monsters they crush beneath their feet. She shifts in her chair.

"Yahweh bestowed upon these seven an extended amount of dominion and power. The Archangels became the keepers of the Swords of the Spirit, though at that time, they weren't weapons so much as scepters, symbols of Yahweh's power. It wasn't until much later that they would become flaming blades as you saw here today, with the very words of Yahweh engraved upon their hilts." Francis pauses to take a long draw from his pipe.

"A mere fraction of the power of Yahweh's Word was placed within these scepters, though it was still much more authority than many other Elohim had been given.

"As Yahweh later did with humans—though I must say, not in the same capacity—he gave these trusted leaders the gift of partnering with him to expand creation and reflect to it the essence of his being."

"Love," Rachel whispers.

Smoke curls around Francis's face as he nods. "So the Archangels and other Elohim partnered with Yahweh, and his love filled creation. And thus, Yahweh looked upon his spiritual Kingdom, and it was good.

"I'll skip over some details, but sometime later a cosmic rebellion ensued. War became an unfortunate reality amidst the Spiritual Realm. The seven scepters were reforged in the furnace of Yahweh's holy power and became the seven Swords of the Spirit. Where once they contained the power of Yahweh to expand his expression of love, now that love was in opposition to a will that was not Yahweh's. To all who opposed it, God's love was perceived as a weapon.

"I think you know how the story goes from here. Yahweh later created a Physical Realm with an earthly family, but with us, he did something very different.

"Yahweh didn't just give humanity a portion of his power and authority by handing us a sword or scepter. He gave us the fullness of his identity by breathing into us his Spirit. Yahweh placed himself inside us. Though humans were made lower than the Elohim, even a little lower than the Malakim, we were given a status that was unrivaled. We were the Imagers."

Questions swirl in Rachel's mind, but Francis continues. "But of course, after another rebellion, this time in the Physical Realm, the image of God was not able to be revealed in its fullness until Yeshua."

"The Word of God."

"Indeed, my dear. And before Yeshua left us, he did something quite remarkable."

"What's that?" Rachel asks.

"He gave us the full power of his Word. All authority in Heaven and on earth had been given to Yeshua, then, he gave it to us. The Archangels, or other Elohim for that matter, were never meant to embody the Word of God. That was reserved for Yeshua, but because of his great love for us, now we, like Yeshua, can be filled with the fullness of Yahweh."

Rachel blinks as she processes Francis's words.

He continues. "In the Physical Realm, the Word dwells unseen within us, slipping out when we open our mouths and speak in accordance with Yahweh's will of love. But when Dream Walkers enter the Spiritual Realm through our dreams, we are able to wield the Word as the sword and weapon it truly is in defeating the Darkness."

Rachel leans forward in her chair. "Every human has this sword?"

Francis crosses his ankles. "No. Only those who receive it."

"Is that why I don't have one?"

Francis nods.

"But it hasn't been offered to me," Rachel says. "How can I receive what hasn't been offered?"

"My dear, it is always being offered, but you must turn toward him to receive what he offers."

"What do you mean I must *turn*?" Rachel narrows her eyes.

"Turn back to face-to-face," Francis says.

"I thought I already did that when I said yes to all this!" She throws her hands in the air and gestures to the world around her. "I told you and Rabbi I would do this dream thing and help you find my baby. I chose the Light! How can you say I haven't turned?" Even as Rachel spits the question, she knows the answer. It hovers in her memory.

The rest of the team shifts uncomfortably.

"You've said yes to us, my dear, but have you said yes to him?"

Rachel flops back in her chair. "Sometimes you don't make any sense."

"Have you even met him?" Francis questions.

"Who?"

"Yeshua, of course. Jesus."

"What do you mean have I met him? He's dead."

"Ah, but see, that's where you are wrong. He is very much alive, and until you come to grips with this reality, it will be nearly impossible for you to meet him."

"Reality," Rachel mumbles. "I don't even know what that means anymore. I said yes to you, this mission, my purpose—or so I thought." Her voice trails off. "I thought I turned, but apparently I haven't." She shakes her head. "I'm done! With you, these dreams, this stupid city, all of it!"

In a dramatic gesture, Rachel mimics Francis's snap of the fingers and is immediately transported down the gravel road to the other side of the trees. Micaiah and Elias jump from their chairs. "Don't follow me," she barks over her shoulder.

As Micaiah and Elias near the trees, the ground cracks before them. Elias shoves Micaiah backward to avoid being swallowed by the earth.

Rivi rises from her chair, a look of wonder on her normally stern face. “How?” she whispers. She turns to Francis. “Rachel’s manipulating your dream.”

He sighs. “Yes. It seems as though she is.”

“But that’s impossible.”

“Clearly not.”

Francis and Rivi join Micaiah and Elias by the gaping pit. Francis waves his hand over the hole, and solid earth returns. His eyes fixate on the road ahead where Rachel’s form quickly shrinks. Francis rubs the thick stubble on his cheek. “Go after her, Elias. She’s listened to you before. Perhaps, she will do it again.”

CHAPTER 25

Cool water laps at Rachel's toes. Her eyes scan the horizon. Shades of lavender and periwinkle fill the sky before melting into the deep blues of the waterline.

"Beautiful, isn't it?" Elias comes to stand beside her. The breeze ruffles his brown hair.

"I'm not really a fan of the beach." Rachel scrunches her toes in the sand, thankful she is not standing ankle-deep in burnt rice. "Where are we?" She scans the dreamscape.

"You're in one of my dreams." He flashes a mischievous grin. "You've been in them before, you know." He waggles his eyebrows.

Rachel rolls her eyes. "I know this is your dream. I willingly chose to come here with you. But why'd you pick this location?" She flicks a seashell into the surf with her toe.

It didn't take Elias long to catch up with Rachel after she stormed off from Francis and her teammates. She tried to avoid him by simply waking herself from Francis's dream, but of course Elias followed. He offered to take her somewhere where she could let out her frustrations.

Now, Elias shrugs. “You may not like the beach, but I do. And it’s my dream, so I get to choose.”

“Too much sand,” Rachel mumbles under her breath. She tries not to let her mind drift to the desert images that haunt her dreams.

“What was that?”

“Nothing. You mentioned something about letting me punch you?”

Elias grins. “I knew I’d win you over with that offer.”

Rachel folds her arms. “You realize you’re only making me angrier, and you’re the only person around to take it out on.”

“I don’t see the problem—ow!” Elias rubs his shoulder. “What happened to no touching?”

“That wasn’t touching, that was punching. What? Do I hit hard for a girl?”

“You hit hard for anyone.”

Rachel rolls up her uniform pants and wades out into the waves. In the distance, whitecaps surge. The colors of the sky captivate her. “You know,” she calls back to him, “it’s not as bad as I thought.”

“What’s that?”

“Rivi once said, ‘Yahweh help me if I’m ever in one of your dreams.’ But it’s not so bad.”

Elias joins her in the water. Rachel stops when the waves hit just below her knees. The hem of her gray pants darkens as the salt water soaks through.

“I come here to surf.”

She casts him a sideways glance. The light reflects off the water and highlights his strong jaw.

“You asked, ‘Why here?’ This is a place I come often. It’s where I learned to surf.” He points to a craggy rock formation that juts out from the land farther down the beach. “Nearly cracked my head open over there. Thankfully, just some bad scrapes." He runs a hand through his hair to show her a scar along his hairline.

"So, this is a real place? I didn't realize you could create real locations in your dreams. I thought they were only representations of the Physical World."

"Right, so"—Elias looks to the sky and squints—"this is a dream, but it's also a memory." Rachel shifts. "It's hard to explain. I created this place from a memory because I entered it from a memory."

Rachel folds her arms. "That doesn't make any sense."

He turns to face her. "When entering a dream as the Dreamer, you focus on the location—"

"Right. And the Walkers focus on the Dreamer—"

"Correct." He hesitates. "But the first time I came here, I wasn't just focused on the image of the location. I fixed my mind on the memory of the location and the memories that filled it."

"So, I'm Dream Walking in your memory?"

He winces. "Basically."

"Is that"—she searches for the word—"allowed?"

Elias turns to walk back toward the shore. "I don't know."

Rachel chases after him. "What do you mean you don't know? Elias, don't ignore me!"

He flops down in the sand. "I've never told anyone about it."

"Why?" Rachel joins him on the beach. She folds her hands in her lap so she doesn't have to touch the sand.

"I've never heard of someone entering an actual memory," he says. "I didn't want Francis to tell me I couldn't come here anymore."

"Is it dangerous?"

Elias shrugs. “Dream Walking is a powerful Gifting. Our actions in the Dream World have ripple effects in the Physical and Spiritual Realms. I don’t know what kind of impact a memory can have.”

Rachel’s stomach turns. She knows the impact memories can have. She tries to shake the image of the beastly face that has haunted her mind for the past two weeks. “So why come here if it’s potentially dangerous?”

Elias digs a stone out of the sand and skips it across the water. “Because this place is important to me.” His gaze remains fixed ahead, but his expression darkens.

Rachel lowers her voice. “Then why did you bring me here?”

His lip twitches. He doesn’t look at her. “There’s a lot going on in your life, Rachel. Things you don’t understand. Things no one understands. You’re confused and angry, but you’re also scared. You need to be somewhere that feels safe.” He pauses. “This is the safest place I know.”

They sit in silence for a long time. Rachel twirls the golden ring on her index finger, noticing the incorrect pattern in the metal swirls. She could choose to wake up right now, to leave behind the sand and beach that stir nothing but horrifying images. She glances at Elias. His legs are out in front of him, feet in the water, hands propped up behind him. Watching his face, Rachel can tell he sees more in this dreamscape than she does. She only sees what Elias chooses to show her, but he is lost somewhere else, somewhere deep in his memory. Rachel decides it’s finally time to get some answers about hers.

“So, this sword . . . does it always look the same?”

Elias’s eyes are fixed ahead. “The Sword of the Spirit?”

"Yeah."

"What do you mean, 'does it always look the same'?"

"I mean, does it ever look different? Instead of the blade being made of fire, is it ever made of something else?"

Elias looks at her and shakes his head. "Why are you asking this?"

Rachel sighs. "When Francis first introduced me to the team, he told you guys about my dreams."

"He didn't tell us much, only that your dreams led him to believe your child is the Lord's Anointed."

"Right." Through her tunic, Rachel rubs her thumb against her scar. "In one of those dreams, there were two men. One had a sword like yours. The other had a sword made from a strange, black metal." Elias watches her but doesn't respond. "The man with the fiery sword tried to save me."

"Sounds like Yahweh sent you a Guardian Angel."

Rachel considers his words, wondering if she should tell him that this Guardian has made an appearance in more than one dream.

"But to answer your question, I've never seen a sword like the one you described. I've heard stories, and as I'm sure you've already guessed, that type of weapon is not associated with the Light."

Elias goes back to staring at the ocean while Rachel plays the dream through her mind. The scar on her stomach aches with a dull throb as she remembers the moment it was created. She drifts from dream to dream, replaying each vision she's had since arriving in BethEl.

"Elias?"

He doesn't look at her. "Hmm?"

"Tell me about the Watchers," she whispers.

The turn of his head is slow. When his eyes meet Rachel's, they frighten her.

"My first time Dream Walking," she explains, "that time when I was stuck . . . afterward, Francis and Rabbi mentioned something about Watchers. I'm not familiar with that story."

Elias takes a deep breath, blows out the air, then jumps to his feet. "Didn't you say you were ready to punch me? I promised Francis I'd start your combat training today."

Rachel stands. "Don't ignore the question."

He scratches his forehead. "Right." He glances around the beach. "Well, let's at least begin your first lesson while we talk."

"Fine."

"Fine," Elias mocks. He snaps his fingers and two foam swords appear in his hand. He tosses one to Rachel. "It has the weight of a real sword," he explains, "without the ouch factor."

Rachel narrows her eyes at him. "I'm not a child, Elias." She snaps her fingers, adding a big flourish at the end. The swords in their hands morph from foam to metal. "Where's your sense of adventure?" she teases.

He shakes his head. "Don't do that. This is my dream. You shouldn't even be able to do that."

She shrugs and grins. "I'm special, remember?" She takes a pretend swing at him with her sword. "Now, talk!"

"Hey! Watch where you point that thing!" His feet and hands are quick. Within seconds, he has knocked Rachel's sword from her hand. "Look, if you want to play with the big kid swords, you have to act responsible and mature. I'll tell you about the Watchers"—he pauses—"but you have to take your training seriously."

"Coming from a man who is never serious."

He picks up Rachel's sword and hands it to her. "Let's start with the basics. Watch my feet, my stance, my hands, everything. And copy me."

Rachel slides next to him to follow his movements.

"No, no. Face me." He places his hands on her shoulders and redirects her. She tenses at his touch but doesn't shove him away. "Sorry." He pulls his hands back. "I want you to face me, so you can mirror me." Rachel nods. "You ready? We'll start slow."

Elias begins with footwork only. At first, it's disorienting to copy from a mirrored perspective, but Rachel soon falls into a fluid rhythm.

"Before Yahweh created humans, he created an entire realm of spiritual beings."

"The Elohim."

"Correct. Francis told you that some of these Elohim revolted against Yahweh."

"The Watchers."

"Yes—pay attention to my feet—Watchers is a term that comes from the Book of Enoch."

"I've seen that book in the Academy before."

Elias nods. "It's an ancient Jewish text, but it's not in the Christian canon—the Bible. It is, however, referenced in some New Testament writings. Which shows that, even though the Book of Enoch isn't in the canon, it was a text that influenced the biblical writers. You're doing great, by the way. Let's add the arms." Elias holds his sword out in front of him. "The account in the Book of Enoch is a strange one. It sounds like fantasy, and throughout history, many Christians have written it off completely."

"So, it's not a true story?"

"Well"—Elias taps his sword against Rachel's—"it's hard to say what in Enoch is true and what isn't. It has a lot of details you won't find anywhere else, but—your arm is dropping—the essence of the story is believed to be true."

Rachel corrects her posture. "Why is that?"

"One reason is because many of the basic themes in the Book of Enoch are found in stories from ancient cultures across the globe, but more importantly, the story is found in the Bible." Rachel stumbles in the sand. Elias's eyes are wide as he catches her hand. He quickly releases it. "Please don't fall and gut yourself with that sword."

Rachel composes herself. "Tell me the story."

"Right." His chest rises. "Follow my lead. Your goal this time is to keep your sword touching mine." He steps toward her. Rachel shuffles back, keeping her blade against his. "Good." Elias sidesteps. Again, Rachel mirrors him. "Genesis six is where the story is found in the Bible. In it, the Watchers are called the sons of God."

The phrase stirs Rachel's mind. She focuses harder on Elias's movements.

"Some suggest that the term Watcher was given because these Spiritual beings were supposed to watch over humanity. But instead, they used their authority in opposition to Yahweh rather than use it to serve humanity."

"What did they do?"

Elias steps back and Rachel steps toward him. He draws back his sword, she drives hers forward. "The story says the sons of God, the Watchers, thought the human women were beautiful—"

"Are you blushing?"

"What? No! I'm twenty years old; I don't blush!"

"What does your age have to do with blushing?"

Elias narrows his eyes. "You need to pay attention." He quickens his pace. "Try to keep up." He blows out a sigh. "Where was I? Oh yes, the human women were beautiful, so the Watchers decided to take them as their wives and, uh, reproduce with them."

There's a piercing clash of metal as Rachel fumbles her sword against Elias's. "Did they succeed?"

"New footwork pattern. Pay attention." Elias shuffles forward, to the side, then spins, stabbing and arcing his sword as he moves. "They did succeed. They produced hybrid humans that were both celestial and terrestrial. Demigods basically, and they were giants."

Rachel's mind spins. She tries to follow Elias's lead, but something in her body feels off, awkward.

"Throughout most cultures, there are stories of gods, angels, or spiritual beings reproducing with human women. Take Greek mythology for example." Elias's movements are too quick to follow. Rachel shuffles through the sand, making up her own footwork to keep pace. "Zeus, one of the gods in the Greek pantheon, had quite the reputation as a ladies' man."

"But you just said that's mythology." Something clicks in Rachel's body. The muscles of her legs unlock, and the motions flow out like a dance. It doesn't match what Elias is doing, but he's too occupied with the story to notice.

"Yes, but when myths from all over the world have a common thread like that, we should take notice. Especially when it matches a story we have in the Bible, which we in BethEl consider to be true." Rachel's blade nearly clips Elias's arm. He blocks it. "You're a natural," he says. "Of course, I would expect nothing less from someone so special." Rachel lunges with a jab, but Elias is too quick. "Toss your sword down. Let's work on hand-to-hand. Mirror me."

"Why would the Watchers do that?" The motion of punching and jabbing with her fists is freeing.

Elias models a block. "There are theories, but no one is certain."

"What's your theory?"

Elias throws out a slow punch and lets it linger. Rachel blocks it harder than she intends. Her body immediately responds with a counter. Her feet shuffle forward at the same moment her fist extends. The fabric of her uniform makes a distinct snap as her body lunges. Rachel hears the thump of her fist against Elias's sternum then the gasp of his lungs as he tries to suck air.

"My theory," he wheezes, "is that you're going to be a great fighter."

"Sorry."

He waves away her words and catches his breath. "No worries, Dream Girl. It comes with the territory." He straightens up. "Let's kick it into the next gear." Elias moves around Rachel in a slow circle. "This is a fight now. I'll go easy on you, but not too—ow!" Elias rubs a finger across his now split lip. "We're not trying to draw blood!"

"Sorry. I'll go easy on *you.*" Rachel grins. "Now, what's your theory on the Watchers?"

Elias shakes his head. "This is not how I imagined you in my dreams." His posture changes. Shoulders hunch forward. The bend in his knees deepens. "When the Watchers"—Elias hesitates—"did what they did, they disobeyed Yahweh and became enemies of God." Elias throws out a kick. Rachel dodges. The motion is familiar. Again, she feels something unlock in her body. The movements flow. Elias huffs. "To me, the explanation that makes the most sense is that the enemy knew he would one day be defeated by a human. So—"

Elias backs up to dodge a punch then lands one in Rachel's gut. Air rushes out of her lungs. The scar on her abdomen throbs. He nods to her. "You okay?"

"Don't baby me."

Elias laughs. "I'm hardly babying you. I've never fought like this with anyone on their first day."

"I'm fine." Rachel wipes her sleeve across her sweaty forehead then clenches her hands into fists. "C'mon." She fakes a jab then spins backward, extending her leg at the same time. Her bare foot almost connects with Elias's shoulder, but his hands are too fast. He catches her foot and pulls her leg out from underneath her. Rachel's back smacks into the sand.

He hovers over her. "You want a hand?" He leans down and extends his arm to her. Rachel nods, pretends to reach for his hand, then grabs the collar of his uniform instead. Before Elias can react, Rachel grips his tunic with both hands, pulls him toward her at the same time she extends a leg. Her foot presses into his chest as she rolls backward and flips him over her. She hears him moan behind her.

Rachel stands and hovers over him. "You need a hand?" she mocks.

Elias squints up at her. "No, thank you." He stands and brushes his hands on his tunic. "I was saying," he pants, "that since the enemy knew he would one day be defeated by a human, maybe he thought he could prevent that from happening by corrupting the human gene pool. It's just one theory." He shrugs. "The important thing is that, for whatever reason, these beings willingly chose to revolt against Yahweh and forsake the Light." He heaves a sigh. "I think that's enough for today. You pick up fast."

"You said it yourself: I'm a natural." Rachel folds her arms over her chest and smiles.

Elias watches her. “Right.” He draws a deep breath as he glances out over the ocean. “Is your curiosity about the Watchers satisfied? Because I’d like to get back for lunch if that’s okay with you.”

“One last question.”

“Make it a quick one.”

“What did they look like?”

Elias shakes his head. “Why would you want to know that?”

She shrugs and avoids his scrutinizing gaze. “Just curious.”

He mops his forehead with his sleeve. “No one really knows, but some legends say they had a reptilian appearance, like a serpent.”

Rachel is careful to make sure her face doesn’t reflect what she is thinking. An image that fits his description fills her mind—a face with deathly yellow eyes and skin the color of onyx.

“Now that I’ve answered all your questions”—Elias pauses—“and kicked your butt, can we please go get some food?”

“I was the one who kicked your butt!”

“That’s not the story Francis is going to hear.”

“It will be if I get to him first!” Rachel thrusts her right hand out in front of her. Elias does the same. They glance at their rings and, at the same time, say, “This is a dream. I’m ready to wake up.”

***

Back in the Sleep House, Rachel jumps off her mat before Elias can even sit up. She nearly bumps into Rabbi as she runs across the open-air room to where Francis is seated in a chair reading his Bible.

Rachel kneels in front of him. He glances up from the text. “How was your combat training?”

“I have something else I need to tell you first.” She glances down before meeting her Mentor’s piercing eyes. “I’m sorry, Francis. I’m sorry for losing my temper.”

He offers a warm smile. “You are already forgiven, my dear. Now, tell me about your training?”

Rachel can’t hold back her smile. “I beat Elias.” Francis raises an eyebrow. “He says I’m a natural.”

“Good for you, my dear. Elias needs a good humbling every now and then.” He glances over her shoulder at Elias, who hovers nearby. “Now.” Francis closes his Bible. “Let’s grab lunch, shall we?” Francis calls to Rabbi. “Feel free to catch some sleep after you eat. I will take the next intercessory shift.” Rabbi nods and glides out of the Sleep House. “Go on, my dear,” he says to Rachel. “I’ll be there shortly. Micaiah and Rivi are waiting for us.”

Once Rachel is out of earshot, Elias walks over to Francis and offers him a hand up from his chair.

“You have brightened her countenance.” Francis grunts as he stands. “Thank you. She is a girl with many moods. Is she really a natural as she says, or were you taking it easy on her?”

“No, she’s quite a good fighter.” Elias glances in the direction where Rachel exited. “But, Francis, what I saw in her today, that wasn’t just natural talent.”

Francis furrows his brow. “What was it?”

Elias lowers his voice as he meets Francis’s questioning eyes. “That was muscle memory.”

CHAPTER 26

"All right everyone, let's gather around." Adrielle's voice bellows as she traipses across the chapel floor toward the meeting area. She gestures for Cohen to follow. After several months at the campsite, the Apostles have cleared walking paths through the rubble, but Adrielle still seems to prefer to climb over the lingering piles of debris. Cohen watches her determined gait. She stops near the front of what used to be the church altar. Arms cross in front of her chest as she flips her long braid over her shoulder. The rest of the team stop what they are doing and follow her lead without question.

On his way to the front, Cohen pauses to engage a few of the Apostles. Exhaustion rings their eyes. Cohen told Adrielle on more than one occasion that they should give their team time to rest at the end of the day before they debrief.

"Cohen?" There's irritation in Adrielle's voice as she beckons him once again. He ignores her, smiles at his teammates, and takes his time to make his way to the front. After greeting everyone, he comes to stand beside Adrielle.

She casts him a quick glance then addresses the group. "All right, team, it's time to revise our strategy—"

Cohen places his hand on her shoulder, leans in, and whispers, "We agreed I would lead the conversation tonight."

"I know," she hisses. "I just have a few quick things I need to say." She turns back to the team. "I have some ideas I'd like to present to you this evening."

Cohen tries to swallow his irritation, but he can't do it anymore. His hand locks around Adrielle's wrist. He whispers through gritted teeth. "Not now."

"It will only take a minute." He sees the muscles in her jaw clench.

"Don't make a scene. You are not the only leader on this team. We agreed. Tonight, I'm leading."

Cohen can feel the awkward stares of his team watching him and Adrielle. He wants to explain that they aren't fighting; he's simply allowed Adrielle to dominate the team, including him, for too long. His friends crumble beneath the weight of their calling. They're weary. They don't need someone to lead over them, they need someone to come under them and lift them up. There is a time to issue commands, but that time is not tonight.

Adrielle holds up her hands and backs away from Cohen. She takes a seat behind him on the altar. Cohen steps down and sits among the group.

"We'll talk strategy later. Tonight, I want to hear your stories." He sees his friends' postures shift. Shoulders straighten. Heads lift. "The mission Yahweh has given us is difficult, but we can rejoice in our sufferings, knowing that suffering produces endurance, and endurance produces character, and character produces hope. Not just hope for us, not just hope for

BethEl, but hope for the world. Don't forget what Uriel first told us when we arrived here at the camp. He said, 'You are the Light of the world.' Friends, the world is dark. We have seen that firsthand. It's darker than any of us could have imagined, but our Light shines brightest in the Darkness. Tonight, we will focus not on the Darkness but on the Light. I want us to share our stories of Light, even if it's just a glimmer."

A few smiles appear, ones Cohen hasn't seen in quite some time. He hears Adrielle shift behind him and gestures for her to come sit beside him. She doesn't move.

"I have a story." A timid voice speaks up. Cohen's eyes land on Kate. She's changed so much over the past several months—matured well beyond her eleven years. A weariness fills her face, an exhaustion that should never be seen on the face of a child, but in her eyes there is a spark, a tiny ember of light.

Everything within Cohen longs to fuel that waning flame, to fan it into an inferno. As Kate begins to tell her simple story, Cohen sees the transformation. The tiny ember sputters and sparks, grasping at hope like oxygen until the flame fills her eyes. Her face visibly lightens. A small smile tugs at her lips. She looks deep into the eyes of her team members as she shares her story.

Cohen witnesses the exact moment her Light jumps to another. That team member shares their story, and another fire is stoked. Their stories become gasoline, igniting and fueling the passion that had all but extinguished.

"Our time outside BethEl has been hard." Cohen turns as he hears Jesse's thick accent. "Much harder than I imagined. Like when I first met that man at the bar. You remember that story?" The team nods as Jesse continues. "His name is Nelson. He's a Unity scientist. Specializes in genetics and DNA mumbo jumbo. When I found that out, I had to ask God 'why?' Why would he put *me* with a guy like him? It makes no sense, but somehow, it's working. The way I explain the gospel is getting through to this guy. He asks lots of questions. Things I don't know. But he keeps coming back.

"Yesterday, I told Nelson about Jesus." Jesse's dark eyes meet Cohen's. "He's never even heard the name before." Emotion fills Jesse's voice. "He couldn't get enough of it. Kept saying, 'Jesus forgives *all* sins? Even mine?' Said he's done some bad things. Didn't say what. I didn't want to know. He's part of that orthodox sect." Disgust registers on Jesse's face then disappears. "But," he pauses to smile, "Nelson wants to meet again. Says he wants to know more about Jesus."

The spark catches; the fuse is lit; the dynamite explodes; and the fiery passion of the team returns. Laughter and celebration erupt all for the sake of one soul who heard the gospel. All for the sake of Jesus, a name long forgotten in this literally godforsaken world, a name that now resurfaces like a relic of ancient history—an unearthed fossil that could change everything these people know about their world.

"If a man who has a hundred sheep loses one," Cohen says, "doesn't he leave the ninety-nine in the open country and go after the lost sheep until he finds it? And when he finds it, he joyfully puts it on his shoulders and goes home. Then he calls his friends and neighbors together and says, 'Rejoice with me; I have found my lost sheep.'" The team smiles upon hearing the familiar parable. "I tell you that in the same way there will be more rejoicing in Heaven over one sinner who repents than over ninety-nine righteous persons who do not need to repent. Jesse's new friend, Nelson, may not have repented yet, but there is hope for his soul."

"And thanks to you"—one of the women on the team stands and looks to Cohen—"we have hope in our souls. Thank you, Cohen. We needed this."

The celebration continues late into the night. Like excited children on Christmas Eve, the Apostles are unable to sleep for the anticipation of what is to come. At some point, Adrielle slips away. Cohen doesn't see her leave but notices her absence at the meal.

The festivity wanes with the embers in the firepit. Adrielle isn't in her usual spot near Cohen. Instead he finds her outside the chapel, in the dirt, her back against a crumbling stone wall. She picks up a rock and tosses it. "If you're here to pull me out of my sour mood, I'm not interested. I prefer to wallow a bit."

Cohen sits beside her. "Fair enough, but you don't have to wallow alone." She shoots him a glare then fixes her eyes outward on the dark forest that surrounds them. Cohen follows her gaze. "It's amazing to think that this used to be a bustling town with the church at the hub. Now it's overgrown like some ancient civilization."

"Knowledge surpassed wisdom." Adrielle hurls another stone.

"What do you mean?" Cohen asks.

"Wisdom comes from God. It's pure, peace-loving, considerate, submissive, full of mercy and good fruit, impartial and sincere."

"James three seventeen."

She shakes her head. "I forget you have entire books of the Bible memorized."

Cohen shrugs.

"Anyway," she says. "Contrast wisdom with knowledge—specifically, the knowledge of good and evil. Knowledge gives the connotation of being something sought and obtained through the ways of the world. 'Knowledge is power,' the world says. Just look at how the world is structured now. The church is no longer the center of civilization; the education system is."

"I hadn't thought about it that way. That's really insightful."

"I have my moments." She picks at the sole of her boot.

"You had a moment tonight."

Adrielle winces. "Different kind of moment."

"Right. What was that about?"

She doesn't respond or meet his eyes. Cohen waits. With a sigh, she finally speaks. "Everyone loves you, Cohen. They always have, even despite your lack of Gifting." Her intended compliment stings. "You've never led a team before—didn't want to lead a team—but I have, and I wanted to lead. It's in my blood. Shepherding people is what I trained for in the Academy. It's what I do back home. But here, it's different. The team doesn't respect me the way they do you."

"They respect you."

"Okay, maybe they respect me, but they don't like me. No one likes me."

"I like you."

Adrielle turns to face him, eyes filled with sadness. "Not the way I want you to like me." She shifts the conversation. "I don't understand what I've done wrong. I'm a great leader in BethEl. That's what I'm told, at least." Her fingers begin to undo her braid. "But here, it's different." She runs her fingers through the wavy strands. "I wanted to prove myself to you, show you how competent I am. And if I'm being honest, I wanted to be better than you. For once, I wanted to be the best, the one everyone loves. I don't know—" She kicks at the ground. "That's all I've got."

Cohen considers his words carefully. "You're right. It is different here. Leading within the city of BethEl is completely different than leading out here. In BethEl, there is hope and light. Out here, hope and light don't exist. I'm no expert—"

"That's debatable."

He smiles. "But I have learned a few things while we've been out here. The power of a leader comes in their ability to spark hope and light. When the world feels darkest, people follow the one who carries the light. You have experience, strategy, tactics—all things that I don't have when it comes to leading. I need you, Adrielle. I can't do this on my own. We are better together."

"It doesn't feel like we're better together."

Cohen chuckles. "That's because you butt heads with me every chance you get!" He shoves her shoulder, and she punches his arm. "We have to be united. We can't work against each other. We need to come alongside each other." His eyes scan the side of her face. Her sharp features look even more striking in the hazy moonlight. "Look at me." She doesn't. "Seriously. Look at me." She turns to face Cohen. "I submit to your leadership." Surprise spreads across Adrielle's face. "Will you submit to mine?"

Her eyes search his. "Yes."

"Good." Cohen leans his head back against the wall to look up at the dim stars. He points. "Even they don't shine here." Adrielle turns her face upward. Silence lingers between them, broken only by the sounds of their team as they turn in for the night.

"You know"—Cohen finally interrupts the silence—"I do like you in the way you want." He keeps his eyes on the sky.

"But?"

"But it's complicated."

"Yeah."

"Yeah," he repeats. The sound of crickets fills the void. "I'm not sure what I'm supposed to do. You know, given the situation." Adrielle shifts beside him. He can feel her eyes on him. "What?" Cohen looks over at her.

"I know what you can do." Adrielle's eyes fall on his mouth. Before he can stop her, she closes the space between them and presses her lips to his. He wants to turn away, but his body betrays him. Adrielle pauses then pulls back, stands, and walks through the crumbling archway. She doesn't say a word. No goodnight. No explanation. She leaves nothing behind but the lingering taste of her lips.

CHAPTER 27

Music is the first thing to greet Cohen in the dream. The tune is familiar like a distant memory. Laughter erupts. Voices and scents reach him as he walks through the crowd of his BethEl family during a Shabbat celebration. Across the Common Gardens is Rachel, wearing the same white nightgown she wore when he found her. Cohen drifts through the crowd to get closer, but before he can reach her, someone comes to stand between them—Adrielle. Her face is a breath away from his. Cohen tries to push past her, but Adrielle remains steadfast. She runs her hands up his arms then interlocks her fingers behind his neck. "Dance with me," she whispers into his ear.

Adrielle takes the lead and pulls Cohen around the dance floor in a dizzying choreography. He searches the crowd for Rachel, but he's lost sight of her. Adrielle seems to notice he's distracted and redirects his gaze back to her. "Look at *me*," she whispers. Her dark eyes scan his face then land on his mouth. She traces a finger over his lips and leans in.

"Cohen?"

He pulls away from Adrielle. The crowd parts. Rachel stands in the center, hovering only a short distance away. As she says his name again, Cohen notices the blood that stains her body. Her short hair is matted, her beautiful face bruised. Adrielle clings to Cohen and tugs on his arm to pull him back into the dance. He pushes her away and runs to Rachel. "She needs me," he calls over his shoulder. Before he can reach Rachel, darkness creeps in to consume her like a thick smoke.

He stops before her. "Rachel?" She doesn't speak or move. A thin ribbon of blood streams from her nose then from her haunting blue eyes. It pours from her full lips. She reaches for him. He takes her hand. As soon as his fingers make contact with hers, Rachel vanishes.

***

Cohen sits up in his hammock. A thin sheen of sweat glistens on his forehead. He swings his legs over the side, pulls on his boots but doesn't lace them, then steps quietly through the camp. He passes Adrielle. Chestnut waves splay across her pillow and frame her peaceful face. He tiptoes past a few other slumbering teammates and wanders out through the arched opening.

Shards of stained glass crack beneath his boots as Cohen walks the perimeter of the old sanctuary. With the moon hidden by clouds, the darkness is thicker now, darker than he ever remembers. Whatever spark of light and hope he felt earlier that evening is now masked by the darkness that broods within him. The faces of the two women drift through his mind, but the haunting image of Rachel's blood-filled eyes lingers. Confused and overwhelmed, Cohen falls to his knees. As he did the night he found Rachel, he does the only thing he knows to do. He prays.

"Tonight was amazing, God. I saw your presence come and dwell among us as we shared stories. There was hope, but now . . ." his voice trails off. "I'm second-guessing everything," he whispers to the sky. "What am I getting myself into with Adrielle? How can I be an effective leader if I'm distracted? And this dream. Does it mean anything?" He sighs. "Maybe I'm just homesick." He digs his fingers into the ash and rubble.

"Then there's Rachel," he says. "I feel like I abandoned her. I'm her Finder, and I was supposed to be her Mentor." He pauses, remembering the look on her face the night he left. So lost, confused, but somehow still beautiful.

Since leaving BethEl, Cohen has caught himself thinking of Rachel on more than one occasion, wondering how she is doing, whether she made a full recovery, if her memories have returned, and if so, who was she before BethEl? Now Cohen wonders how long it feels like he has been gone to her. Will she still want him to be her Finder after being gone so long? Will the connection he felt with her still be there?

During his time in BethEl, Cohen has heard several stories about the Finder-Disciple connection. Still, he can't help but wonder if what he feels toward Rachel is different. He sighs, scoops up some of the dust, and lets it slip through his fingers.

"I don't know what I'm doing here, God. I'm stumbling my way through, making things up as I go along. Sure, the team likes me and follows me now, but what about when they need someone with a Gifting? I know that day will come. I'm not ready for this. I don't know how to be a leader. If this is a test for when I take over the Priesthood for Francis, then I'm failing. I'm failing you, and I'm failing these people."

"You're not a failure."

Cohen jumps to his feet and turns. A light-headed feeling consumes him. His heart beats too fast. "How?" he whispers. "How are you here?"

Rachel stands at a distance. Blood drips from the hem of her nightgown. She opens her mouth to speak, but before she can reply, Cohen bolts awake.

The hammock sways as he glances around the silent camp. It was all a dream. He rolls to his side and catches sight of something on his hands. Examining them in the moonlight, Cohen discovers a thin layer of dirt and ash clinging to his fingers.

CHAPTER 28

Images drift behind Rachel's closed eyes. Sand and steel. White walls and pale dunes. Oppressive heat and sterile smells. Light and dark.

Rachel peers up through the slats in the vented steel ceiling then rises from the floor. A crisp, white nightgown hangs loose around her flat stomach and bare knees. Steel walls box her in.

A metallic knock raps on the door, then it opens. A man in a white lab coat hovers in the doorway, beckoning her with his hand. "Time for your lessons," he says.

His fingers reach for hers. Rachel jerks away. "No touching." The man apologizes and leads her out the door and down the sterile corridor. After passing through several passcode-protected steel doors, they stop in front of an aged wooden one. The man in the white lab coat opens it and gestures for Rachel to enter. He doesn't follow her.

Rachel's bare feet pad against the cold stone floor. The entire tunnel is made of rock. Candles flicker against the dark walls and beckon her forward into the open space.

Statues of winged creatures line the circular cavern. A stone altar is erected in the middle, a young girl strapped to it. From where she stands, Rachel can see that the girl has soiled her nightgown in fear.

The smell of incense fills the room, signaling the beginning of her lesson. Rachel wants to vomit. A man's voice comes from behind her, but she cannot see him in the shadows.

"Go on," he urges Rachel. "Separate your mind as we've been practicing."

"I don't want to!" Rachel's voice echoes off the hollow cavern. "Don't make me do this again!"

A blow comes to the back of her head. Then another. Rachel spins with a kick. A fist hits her eye.

"No! I won't do it!"

Punch after punch. Blow after blow. Cloaked figures surround her and beat her until she snaps. Rachel's body is unleashed. She drops the cloaked figures one by one. Then her mind cracks. The last thing she sees is the fear in the young girl's eyes as she hovers over her. The last thing she hears is the voice of the man saying, "Do it."

The image of the dark stone cavern fades and is replaced with a dreamscape of blinding white sands. Heat envelopes her. Rachel's swollen, pregnant stomach presses against the nightgown as sand slips between her bare toes. A different man hovers nearby. Rachel recognizes him as the Guardian who tried to save her. A flaming sword flashes in his hand. His face and features are unclear.

Fear tries to keep Rachel from him. The sword sparks like a warning, yet she reaches toward him. Her fingers stretch for his.

Beneath her feet, the sand slips and pulls downward. The ground consumes Rachel. The desert is gone. Rachel is back inside the brightly lit hall. The man in the white lab coat opens the door to the metal cell and ushers Rachel in. The steel door closes with a hollow boom.

Moments later, the door opens again. A different voice calls her name. Familiar. Like the voice in the cavern. The man's head peeks in. "Good work today." He praises Rachel. "I have a present for you."

Rachel knows those eyes, knows that smile. Her mind reels to understand. The man in the gray suit reaches toward her. Rachel's fingers graze his as she accepts his gift—a striking red flower. That's when Rachel sees the blood under her fingernails. It pools around her cuticles like scarlet crescent moons. Like red paint. She finds the man's face again, but his appearance has morphed. Skin like onyx, eyes like death. The flower slips from her hand. Eyes drift down. Blood soaks the nightgown. This time, Rachel knows it is not her own.

***

Rachel bolts awake, heart pounding.

The darkness of the room reaches out and wraps its fingers around her. She draws the blanket tightly over her head and face. Breath heats the space in front of her. The rhythm of inhale and exhale is a comfort, but only for a moment.

The mattress shakes beneath Rachel as something launches itself from the floor and onto the bed. It scrambles toward her, rips the blankets from her body, and throws them onto the floor. Before Rachel can move or scream, it is on top of her, pinning her to her back. Her arms are by her head, held down at the wrists. The beast straddles her waist, hovering its face directly in front of hers; even still, Rachel can't see it through the thick black of night. Hot, sulfurous breath billows between them. Long, stringy hairs dangle from the creature's forearms and brush against Rachel. That's when she actually wakes from the dream.

Now released from two layers of dreams, Rachel realizes she is not in the parsonage guestroom as she thought. She's in the Sleep House with the other Dream Walkers. Her mind is alive. She's completely alert. But the monster is still there.

Rachel opens her mouth to scream, but her lips refuse to part, sealed by some unseen force. Her mind wills her tongue to move and form words, but it's made of lead. She cannot speak. Though she is awake, Rachel's body is paralyzed beneath the weight of a very real presence.

"Wake up!" her mind shouts to her body. "Wake up!"

The beast feels the internal struggle and senses the fight within her. It lunges at Rachel as a snarling bark erupts from the drool-covered fangs that she can now see. It chomps at the space between them, longing to devour her, but somehow unable to do more than threaten.

"Wake up! Wake up!" Rachel's mind screams so loud she is certain her teammates must be able to hear her, yet her lips never part. Her screams never escape her mind.

"Francis! Rabbi!" Her mind screams for those who are supposed to protect her while she sleeps. "Elias, help!" No one comes to her aid.

"Jesus!" The name slips out as a desperate plea.

The beast snarls and pulls back. She can feel the growl resonate in its gut before it spews from its mouth. "Jesus!" her mind pleads. The beast shrieks. Its talon-like fingers lock harder around Rachel's wrists. All its weight is held against her and presses her body into the tatami mat beneath her. "Jesus!" The beast screeches as it begins to vaporize. Rachel recognizes the power of the name. Her mind shouts it again. "Jesus!" Her tongue is loosed behind her still-sealed lips. The pressure on her wrists lessens. The beast's bark continues to thrash in her face, but its grip loosens. "Jesus!" The power is broken. Her lips part, and the name Jesus tumbles from Rachel's mouth. The beast vanishes.

Rachel's body is released from its prison of paralysis. She's on her back, hands near her head as if she were being held down.

Francis shuffles to her side. Her chest heaves. "Are you okay, my dear? You screamed. What happened?"

Tremors wrack Rachel's body as she tries to sit up. Her eyes scan the candlelit Sleep House. It's the middle of the night. Her teammates and Rabbi are spread throughout the room. None of them stir. "Oh, my dear," Francis mumbles. "I'm so sorry. It was my turn to intercede while Rabbi rests. I must have drifted off. Tell me, did you have a nightmare?"

Rachel's eyes dart through the open room as she searches for the beast's hiding place. Fear has never felt so raw. "No," Rachel whispers. She pushes the sweaty hair back from her face then extends her arms in front of her. The fingers of her left hand trace the bruises that have already begun to form on her right wrist. Francis examines the distinct finger marks then looks from her wrist to her face, eyes filled with questions. "It wasn't a nightmare," Rachel tells him. "It was real."

***

Neither of them able to sleep, Francis and Rachel sit quietly at a distance from the team so as not to disturb them. She sips a glass of water while Francis silently reads his Bible by the light of a candle. Rachel sets the glass aside and curls up on her mat near Francis's feet. He glances at her.

"Feeling any better?"

"No."

"Moments like these, you never forget. I had a similar experience once. I can still feel its presence on top of me when I think about it." He shakes his head.

"What was it?"

Francis hesitates. "Probably a Shedim. It must have slipped through because of the Breach." His tone suggests there is more he's not sharing. Rachel catches him glance in Rabbi's direction.

Rachel stares out into the room where her team sleeps, but her eyes only see the Darkness that attacked her moments before. "I Manifested that creature," she whispers.

Francis glances down at Rachel. "Preposterous. It was my fault, my dear. I dozed off when I was supposed to be interceding, and for that, I am terribly sorry. Do not even think such nonsense. You are not capable of creating such evil."

Rachel recalls the new images she saw in her dream, and she knows Francis is wrong. She shudders, rolls over to face him, and rubs her bruised wrist. "Can I ask you a question?"

"Anything, my dear."

"Why hasn't God healed you? Your arthritis—it seems painful for you."

His eyes look far away. "At times it is. More so now than it used to be."

"Haven't you gone to see the Healers?" Rachel asks.

Francis offers her a sad smile. "Yes, my dear. I have seen many Healers, but sometimes our healing doesn't come in this life."

"Why doesn't God want to heal you?" she asks.

"Oh, I believe he does."

Rachel waits for his explanation.

"Pain is not God's will, Rachel. Physical or otherwise. But there are forces at work in creation that oppose Yahweh, and there are consequences—often pain—as a result of their disobedience." Francis's face darkens.

"Free will?"

"Yes, my dear. Free will. Though God may be saying yes to our requests for healing, there are other forces who can come against it." He watches her. "Does that make sense?"

"I think so."

"Don't you worry, my dear. Someday, my pain will be no more." He smiles.

Rachel sighs and watches Francis as he goes back to reading.

"What is the meaning of the words?" she asks.

"What words?"

"The words you are reading." Rachel points at the Bible.

Francis tilts his head.

"They're the same words you said to me in the Chapel about my baby being the Lord's Anointed. Aren't they?"

The creases in Francis's forehead deepen. Then a soft smile forms. His knobby finger traces under the words as he reads in a whisper: "'And you, my child, will be called a Prophet of the Most High; for you will go on before the Lord to prepare the way for him, to give his people the knowledge of salvation through the forgiveness of their sins, because of the tender mercy of our God, by which the rising sun will come to us from Heaven to shine on those living in darkness and in the shadow of death, to guide our feet into the path of peace.'"

Rachel rubs her hand across the scar on her stomach. Francis doesn't notice.

"As you know from your studies, long ago, Yahweh promised his people a Savior, Jesus—the Messiah." Francis glances up from the ancient text. "He would be the one to redeem his people from their enslavement to the Darkness."

"The Nachash?"

"Yes, and all the evil powers who side with him. No one knew when the Messiah would come, but God's people were promised a forerunner, someone who would come before Jesus to herald his arrival."

"John the Baptist," Rachel recalls. "Cohen read me that story." The thought of Cohen brings a fresh wave of guilt as she thinks again of their last conversation.

Francis pauses at the mention of his absent Disciple. Rachel looks away. Even though she has Francis, Rabbi, and her teammates, Rachel can't help but think that if Cohen was still in BethEl, maybe the attack tonight wouldn't have happened. Maybe Rachel wouldn't even be caught up in this quest. Cohen would be her Mentor, not Francis, and she wouldn't have to face her nightmares or her past.

Francis interrupts her thoughts. "Yes, John the Baptist. He was Jesus's cousin, and a very strange fellow. He lived in the desert, dressed in camels' hair, and ate locusts." Francis chuckles when Rachel makes a face. "The problem with John was that many did not recognize him as the forerunner."

"Why?"

"Because he wasn't what people expected—an unfortunate theme among God's people. Many also didn't recognize Jesus, their Messiah, because he wasn't what they expected."

"What did they expect?"

"For the forerunner, they expected Elijah, a Prophet who lived long before Jesus did. He was a man sent by God to help turn the hearts of Yahweh's wayward followers back to him."

"Back to the face-to-face." Rachel's voice drops.

"Exactly." Francis observes her for a moment, but Rachel says nothing. "Of course, they didn't fully turn, or remain turned for that matter. There was only one way for Yahweh to redeem his people: the Messiah. So, Yahweh promised a Savior and one who would come before him." Francis flips back a few sections in his Bible. "Malachi, another Prophet, records Yahweh as saying, 'I will send my messenger, who will prepare the way before me.' Later, Malachi also said that the messenger and forerunner would be the Prophet Elijah. Even though Elijah had long been gone, many of God's people still expected the actual Elijah to return. Instead, what they were given was John, a man who came in the spirit of Elijah. A voice calling in the wilderness, as Isaiah the Prophet said, the one who would prepare the way for the Lord."

Francis leans toward her. "Now, here's where the story gets good. Yahweh sends the Messiah, Jesus, and he too was not what people expected. They wanted a militant leader to redeem them from their physical slavery and oppression to the Roman empire, not their spiritual slavery to the Darkness. Jesus came in peace.

He revealed Yahweh's true character of love. He was the Light of the world, shining in the midst of great Darkness, but very few understood who he really was."

Rachel remembers the sound of her own mind shouting his name only moments before she witnessed the presence of evil flee.

"Yahweh," Rachel whispers.

Crinkles form around Francis's eyes. "Precisely, my dear. Jesus was Yahweh, the Master of the Universe. He incarnated himself and became flesh and blood!" Francis's voice rises above a whisper. He quickly lowers it. "But do you know why he did it?"

The answer slips from Rachel's lips like an exhale. "So he could stand with us face-to-face."

Francis chuckles but his eyes pool with tears. He pats Rachel's hand. She allows his touch to linger a moment, surprised by the comfort it brings. "So much wisdom in such a small girl," he mumbles. She slowly draws her hand away and tucks it under the blanket. "You are precisely right, my dear. To once again physically be with us face-to-face.

"During his time on earth, many turned to Jesus and recognized him, not only as the Messiah, but also as Yahweh. They turned back to the face-to-face and became followers of the Way, which would later be called Christianity.

"Now, let's fast forward through Jesus's life, death, and resurrection. After being raised from the dead, Jesus ascended back into Heaven from where he came, but before he did, he made a promise to his people. He promised to return." Rachel watches the candlelight create strange shadows on her Mentor's face, but it is his words that grip her. "Tradition teaches that, once again, a forerunner will come, one to prepare the way for Jesus's return and herald his coming."

"The Lord's Anointed."

He nods. "Your child."

Rachel allows her gaze to drift outside the open Sleep House toward the garden. Francis returns to reading silently. The sound of crickets fills the room.

"How do you think it happened?"

Francis doesn't look up. "What's that?"

"Me. How do you think I became pregnant with such an important child?"

Francis clears his throat and closes his Bible. "I have wondered the same thing, my dear." He smooths his hand over the cover of the worn book. "Perhaps, in time, Yahweh will allow you to remember."

"That's what I'm afraid of." She whispers it so softly, Francis doesn't hear.

A heaviness settles over her body, and Rachel knows that sleep will come for her. She shifts on the mat.

"I'm right here, my dear. I promise not to doze again."

Rachel wants to tell Francis that it doesn't matter if he intercedes or not. The things that haunt her don't come from dreams. They come from her memory.

Instead she says, "Tell me about the Wedding Supper of the Lamb. You mentioned it once. When Rabbi was with us at the parsonage."

Excitement dances in Francis's eyes. He shifts closer. "I thought you would never ask. This is a perfect bedtime story." Rachel rolls onto her side. "While the Bible mentions the Wedding Supper of the Lamb, most think of it as an analogy for the way Yahweh wants to reunite himself with humanity. That is true, but there is more to it than that. The scriptures are deep." Francis pats his Bible. "Very deep. Tradition teaches that there is a surface meaning to any given story, and that there is also an allegorical or symbolic meaning. Then there is a deeper meaning that is only understood through study and inquiry, and finally, there is the deepest meaning—the secret spiritual meaning that only Yahweh knows and those to whom he gives the revelation."

Rachel's eyelids feel heavy. She pushes away the covers hoping the evening air will help her stay awake.

"Many have speculated and studied to understand the story of the Wedding Supper of the Lamb, but in BethEl, we have a legend." Rachel's blinks become slower. "From the time of the great flood of Noah's day, a legend has been passed down among a select group of people—the story of the Lost Ark. Not Noah's giant ark as many speculate, but a miniature ark, one fashioned after the blueprints of the original." Rachel's mind spins with questions, but she's far too tired to ask. "As the legend goes, during the many years it took Noah and his sons to construct the ark, Yahweh spoke to Noah. He told him stories." Francis holds up his Bible. "In this whole book, we only have five small chapters before we get to the story of Noah. There are a few things sprinkled throughout the rest of the text, but not much is known about the antediluvian world." Rachel peeks her eyes open and makes a face. "Just making sure you're still awake." Francis smiles.

"Antediluvian?" she mumbles.

"It means 'before the flood.'" Francis leans back in his chair. "The legend says that all of the untold stories from before the flood, ones we don't currently have a record of, were given to Noah verbally through Yahweh. Noah recorded them and placed them in the miniature replica of the ark he created to protect them from the waters during the flood."

"What happened to the stories?" Rachel yawns.

"No one knows. They were lost. Legend says Noah was the one who lost them, and after they vanished, he was never the same, prone to drunkenness and what have you." Rachel's eyes drift closed. Francis's voice becomes muffled. "But legend says the stories and the Lost Ark are still out there, and that contained within the collection is the story of the Wedding Supper of the Lamb." Francis pauses. Rachel's chest rises and falls.

"My dear?" No response. Francis smiles and pulls the blanket up to her chin. "But legend also says," he whispers, "that one day those stories will be found. At just the right time, before the return of our Messiah." He opens the Bible on his lap. "And these stories will play an integral role in the end times. They will help prepare the way for the Lord's coming." Francis glances down at the text then smiles. He takes out his pipe and lights it. "And these stories will be found by the Lord's Anointed, your child."

He takes a long draw from the pipe. "Good night, Rachel," he whispers. "Sweet dreams."

CHAPTER 29

"Eleven, twelve."

"Rachel, hi."

"Thirteen." Rachel grunts, finishes the push-up, then stands to mop the sweat from her brow with the front of her tunic. "Hey, Jubilee!" She pants while brushing the sand from her pants. She hates that even the Academy training-room floor is a reminder of her dreams.

"It's been awhile. How are you?" There's something different about Jubilee. Her voice is soft as she speaks, her complexion ashen. Even her usually wild hair is pulled back into a tame braid. Everything about her presence feels dim. She avoids direct eye contact with Rachel and folds her hands quietly in front of her.

"I'm well." Rachel catches her breath as she takes in Jubilee's appearance. "How are you?" It's been nearly a month since Rachel's last conversation with Jubilee. Over the past few weeks, Rachel's training schedule has eliminated time for socialization beyond her teammates. Rachel has barely seen Jubilee and only in passing at Shabbat. But the rigorous schedule has paid off. Rachel's skill level has advanced at an unprecedented speed. Even Francis, who has believed in her ability since the beginning, seems genuinely surprised by the swiftness at which she has advanced.

"I never see you at the house anymore." Jubilee's voice sounds like a whisper in the open expanse of the Academy's training room.

"Francis and Rabbi have me on a tight schedule," Rachel says. "Fitness first thing when I wake up, combat training with Elias on Monday and Wednesday mornings, technique and scripture with Micaiah on Tuesday and Thursday mornings, Friday mornings I'm with Rabbi, and every afternoon we practice Dream Walking drills."

"Sounds intense," Jubilee mumbles.

"It is. I rarely have downtime, and when I do, it doesn't last long. Like yesterday, I was sitting alone in the Sleep House, clearing my head. Then Rabbi walked in, dropped a book in my lap, and walked right back out." Rachel laughs. Jubilee doesn't. "Plus, we have to stay in the Sleep House at night," Rachel explains, "so Rabbi and Francis can intercede." She watches her friend's face. "It's a safety precaution."

Across the training room, Rivi drops down from a pull-up bar. She mops her face with a towel. "Hey," she calls to Rachel. "Quit jabbering and wrap it up. I'm finished already." She wipes the sweat off her long brown arms. "I'll see you back at the Sleep House."

"Be right there," Rachel calls after her. "I think she likes causing me pain," Rachel whispers to Jubilee.

Again, Jubilee doesn't even smile. Her eyes drift off to the far corner of the room.

"Hey," Rachel says. "I'm sorry I'm not around much anymore. Everything okay with you?"

Jubilee ignores the question. "You look good." She gestures to the definition that is beginning to form on

Rachel's arms. "I guess you have your strength back from before the accident." Jubilee's own body is thin, almost frail. She's a shadow of the vivacious young girl Rachel met when she first arrived in BethEl.

Reaching for her water, Rachel asks, "How's your training coming along? Graduation is not far off for you."

Jubilee offers a timid smile. "Hopefully I'll graduate by the end of this year."

"Hopefully?"

"Yeah, my progress has slowed a bit."

Rachel chugs her water and waits for Jubilee to explain. When she doesn't, Rachel asks, "Are you still training with Hayden? How's that going?"

A visible darkness comes over Jubilee. "Draining."

Sweat drips from Rachel's forehead to the floor. "How so?"

A distant look settles in Jubilee's eyes. "I don't know how to explain it. It's strange, but—"

"Jubilee, there you are." Hayden trots over, water and towel in hand. Rachel notes his surprise when he sees her. "Hi. You're Rachel, right?"

"Right. Nice to see you again."

"You should join us for a workout today," he says. Jubilee's eyes plead with Rachel to stay.

"Actually, I just finished. I need to get going." Water drips down Rachel's chin as she takes another swig from her bottle. She glances between Jubilee and Hayden. "Before I forget—Jubilee, have you heard from Cohen at all?"

Jubilee crawls onto the floor for push-ups. "No, I haven't."

"Who's Cohen?" Hayden thrusts his hands into his pockets.

"He's my Finder and—"

"Some guy," Jubilee says at the same time Rachel attempts to answer.

"Some guy?" Rachel begins to question Jubilee when Rivi reenters the training room from the other side of the Academy and gestures for Rachel to hurry. She holds up a finger to let Rivi know she will be there in a minute, but Rivi shakes her head and mouths the word *now*.

"I have to go." Regret fills Rachel's voice. "It was great to see you, Jubilee." Her gaze settles on her friend as her arms struggle to lift her weakened body from the ground. She takes another look at Hayden. Jubilee is right. There is something strange about him, but Rachel can't pinpoint it.

Without another word, Rachel walks across the room. Rivi is gone, already on her way to the Sleep House. Rachel casts a glance over her shoulder. Hunched on the floor is Jubilee's fatigued form while Hayden bobs up and down on the pull-up bar. He never once takes his eyes off Rachel.

***

The breezy Sleep House is a welcome relief after her workout. Rachel slips off her shoes and leaves them next to the row of others. As she straightens, two thick arms lock around her shoulders. Without thought, she deftly slips through and flips Elias onto his back.

He moans from his place on the floor. "Hey, that hurt."

"Well, that's what you get." Rachel wipes her hands on her pants. "You're only supposed to practice combat in dreams."

"I was testing you." Elias rubs his right shoulder.

"I think I passed."

The two of them walk to the center of the room to join the rest of the team.

"Quick reflexes. A great asset in combat," Micaiah says to Rachel while he gives Elias a once-over. "Don't worry, my friend." He slaps Elias on his bad shoulder. "There is always a day when the apprentice surpasses the teacher."

Elias winces. "Didn't take long."

"And she's right," Micaiah says as he settles onto his mat. "Combat is reserved for dreams—even training. You did deserve that."

Elias plops to his mat to sulk.

Rachel joins her friends on the tatami mats. She stretches out her worn body on the floor, as she has done countless times over the past few weeks. Rabbi already paces around the edge of the mats, not praying as usual, but wringing her hands.

Rachel props herself up on her elbows. "Where's Francis?"

Rabbi catches herself, releases her hands, and smooths them over her pressed uniform. "He should be here any moment. In fact" —she nods toward the far side of the Sleep House—"here he is now."

The distinct shuffle of sandals and swish of his robe fills the room. Francis enters, Bible in hand. He leaves his shoes with the others. The lines on his forehead seem deeper than usual, blue eyes dim, dark skin ashen. Bags tug at his eyes. Intercession has taken its toll on him, giving him no more than a couple hours of sleep at a time. His worn body comes to rest beside Rabbi, and for the first time, Rachel notices the dark circles that ring her eyes as well.

"It is time," Francis says. No greeting, no typical scripture reading or prayer, just a nod to Rabbi and an icy stare directed at the team.

Micaiah responds. "Time for what?"

"No more training. We must begin an active search for the child immediately."

Rachel sits up and crosses her legs beneath her.

"I heard from Yahweh last night," Francis says. "We cannot delay any longer."

Mouth dry, Rachel wipes her palms on the gray linen pants of her uniform. She clears her throat. "Is the baby in danger?"

Francis's face softens. "I'm afraid I don't have any details, my dear, but yes, the threat is imminent. We have no more time to waste with training. From now on, Rachel, you will always be the Dreamer. Everyone else, you will Walk in her dreams. Consider yourselves in full support mode." They nod their consent.

"My dear." Francis shuffles toward Rachel and struggles to his knees. Strong but wrinkled hands cup the sides of her face, dark against light, old against young. "You are ready."

Rachel hesitates then places her hand on top of his. "Are you sure? I don't feel ready."

A familiar chuckle escapes his lips. "None of us ever feel ready when Yahweh calls us, but, my dear, you have been chosen by Yahweh, brought to BethEl for such a time as this. Trust your training; trust your team; but more importantly, trust Yahweh. He will lead you. We *will* find your child."

Despite her fear and uncertainty about her past, Francis's words fill Rachel with confidence. "Okay," she whispers. For the first time, Rachel wishes she told Francis about the parts of her past she's been able to recall. Maybe he would have answers. Maybe he could put her mind at ease. She fights the memory of her blood-covered hands. Then again, maybe it's best he doesn't know.

Francis makes his way to the center of the mats. Each Dream Walker takes their position. Rabbi resumes her pace around the mats with hands splayed open in prayer.

"All right, my dear, picture the last place you remember seeing yourself pregnant with the child. Picture that location as vividly as you can. Make it real in your mind. Team, keep your focus on Rachel. This is not a drill."

Rachel lays her head back and slides her legs out against the mat. She focuses on clearing her mind. A soft chant fills her head with each inhale. *Jesus, Jesus, Jesus.* Perhaps the same power that saved her from the Shedim can protect her now.

A fragrant breeze drifts through the room. The powerful gust rushes through the garden and rattles the palm leaves on the edge of the open space. The wind rustles Rachel's hair. Goosebumps rise on her arms, but not from the breeze. The familiar sound of rushing water fills her ears. It's been weeks since Rachel's heard it. She lifts her head to see if her teammates hear it too. They lay motionless.

Something stirs inside Rachel. She doesn't know who she was before entering BethEl or how she became pregnant, but that doesn't matter now. Though her past seeks to haunt her, the anticipation of the truth propels her. Rachel reaches into her pocket and pulls out the red flower bloom, still vibrant and unwilted. A fire forms in her bones, a fierceness she can't hold in. Rachel clings to the blood-red bloom as if it is her only lifeline, her only way back from the nightmares she is sure to see.

Eyes slip closed as Francis recites a blessing in Hebrew. His voice takes on a methodical and hypnotic tone, then the counting begins. Breath slows. A thickness fills the room. Rachel feels the weight of sleep slip over her like a father covering a child with a blanket. Her instinct is to fight it, but that's not who she is anymore. Rachel is a Dream Walker.

Fear and uncertainty flee as a new strength fills her with each deep breath she takes. Fingers wrap tighter around the bloom so they won't slip open when sleep comes to carry her away. Eventually it does. Her body is still, her chest rising and falling rhythmically, fists clenched tight, while vibrant-red petals seep through her fingers.

CHAPTER 30

"Cohen, wake up!" Adrielle's face is directly in front of Cohen's when his eyes fly open. Her strong cheekbones are highlighted by the dim moonlight. Concern fills her deep-brown eyes. "You were having another nightmare." She whispers so she doesn't wake the rest of the group.

"I'm okay." He swings his legs over the side of the hammock and rubs his temples.

"Are you sure? This time, you were screaming in your sleep."

"Was I?" He tries to shake the images from his mind, but they are far too disturbing to forget.

"Want to talk about it? We can walk outside."

"Sure." He slips on his boots and follows Adrielle. Once outside the chapel, she reaches over and interlocks her fingers with his. They pace around the perimeter of their camp.

"I used to have nightmares all the time as a kid," Cohen says. "They eventually went away, but these past few months, I've had horrible dreams."

"Are your dreams always about the same thing?"

"Kind of, yeah. They're all different"—he hesitates—"but they all involve Rachel."

"Your Disciple back home?"

"Yeah."

"Why her?"

"I'm not sure."

"Tell me about them."

"They're pretty disturbing."

"Cohen, you can tell me. You might feel better if you tell someone about them."

He sighs. "Maybe you're right." He tries to shake the presence of evil that clings to him from the nightmare. "Well, like I said, all the dreams have been different, but they all involve Rachel, and each time, she's in danger."

"What kind of danger?"

"This time, I was with her in some sort of clinic. It was a bright-white room, and in the center, Rachel was lying on a gurney. I couldn't tell if she was asleep or unconscious. The strange part was—" Cohen stops and peers at Adrielle out of the corner of his eye—"Rachel was pregnant."

"Pregnant?"

"Yeah." Cohen sighs. "It was strange. There was a man in the room with her. He was dressed in all white and stood over Rachel, his hands on her temples. In fact, now that I think about it, he must have been some kind of spiritual being."

"What makes you think that?"

"Because light pulsed through his body, and when he touched Rachel's head, the light traveled through his arms and into Rachel. Her whole body glowed. The man closed his eyes and began to speak in a strange language. As he spoke, Rachel repeated every line even though she wasn't awake."

Adrielle shivers. "That's kind of creepy."

"Yeah. It gets worse. A terrifying creature entered the room. It slipped in through the walls and lunged itself at the man of light. As his body flew across the room, his eyes opened. He looked right at me and said, 'Find her.'

"Several more of these creatures slithered into the room. They jumped on the man and pinned down his arms and legs. Then a door opened on the far wall." Cohen shakes his head. "I'm not sure how to describe what entered. It wasn't fully human or fully animal. Its skin was covered in black scales that looked like metal plating, and it had yellow eyes. It touched Rachel's stomach, smiled, and then her body began to seize." Cohen releases a breath he didn't know he was holding. "That's when I woke up."

Adrielle stops and turns to face him. She takes both of his hands in hers. "What an awful dream, but you know"—she glances down at their joined hands—"it was just a dream. Cohen, you didn't abandon Rachel. Yahweh called you here. You can't beat yourself up for leaving her. You did what you were supposed to do, and you left her in good hands. You are here now. You need to stay focused on the present. Our mission is a stressful one. If I had to guess, I'd say it's the stress of being out here that causes your nightmares—that and an underlying feeling that you somehow abandoned Rachel. Which," she adds, "you did not."

"Maybe you're right."

"I know I am. This is where you're supposed to be." She smiles. "With me."

Cohen returns the smile, but on the inside he's still not certain.

"Now." She rubs her hands up his arms. "If you don't mind, I also had a dream I want to share with you. Actually, maybe I should show you instead of tell you."

Adrielle doesn't give Cohen time to respond before she plants her lips on his. He tries to pull away, but she locks her fingers around his neck.

Finally, Cohen stops fighting—stops fighting the kiss, the attraction, the emotions, his doubts, his calling. For once, he doesn't care, doesn't think.

Breathlessly, Adrielle pulls her lips away from his. "Good dream, huh?" She squeezes his hand. "Better get back before someone notices we're missing."

Cohen's senses come flooding back in the wake of her kiss. "You go," he whispers. "I'll be in shortly."

Now alone in the night air, Cohen crumples to the ground like a little boy. "I don't know what I'm doing, God," he says. "I'm so confused. If I'm on the right path, please show me." Cohen waits for a response, a whisper, a sign, a thundering voice, anything. But none comes.

He stands and turns to walk back into the camp. At the entrance, he pauses to utter one final prayer into the silence. It escapes from his lips like a dying breath. "Speak," he mumbles. "Please speak, Yahweh. Your servant is listening."

CHAPTER 31

A sickening smell pierces Rachel's nostrils. The assault on her senses draws her eyes open as she bolts upright. Burnt rice tries to smother her body. She jumps to her feet, ankle deep in the singed grains. Down the beach, people rake the rice out of the ocean and onto the shore. As her brain recognizes the change in location, Rachel peers down at her right hand and examines her ring. Yes, this is a dream, but her team isn't here. And in this dream, Rachel is not pregnant.

"Great," she says. "My first official mission and not only do I enter the wrong dream, I lose my team too."

The familiar chant of the rice rakers reaches her ears. It pulses through the air like a heartbeat. Despite the heat that radiates from the beach, cold chills shoot through Rachel's body as she listens to their haunting tune.

"Unclean, unclean. They have no part in the unseen. Separated from sea and love, they cannot enter the place above. Banished to burn, they shall not return. Unclean, unclean."

Rachel scans the shoreline as the chant begins again. Her team must be somewhere.

Though she has been in this dream before, Rachel can't help but notice a difference in the atmosphere. Somehow, the evil presence in this world has intensified. For the first time, Rachel regrets the training that has taught her to be Lucid and more present in her dreams. It makes the evil far too tangible. She remembers Francis's warning. "The Spiritual Realm is real, my dear. Your dreams are a gateway to enter that realm. Don't discredit what you see and experience as merely dreams. There is no such thing."

Rachel watches the workers more closely to see if her teammates landed among them. In practice, the four Dream Walkers always landed together in the same formation of their mats. The only time they didn't was the first time Rachel entered this dream. Once again, she is alone in this world.

As Rachel scans the crowd, she notices something strange about the people raking the rice—they aren't human. Their size is the first thing to give them away. At a distance, down the beach, it's difficult to gauge scale, but after watching them in the context of their surroundings, Rachel can better discern their size. They are tall—very tall—much larger than any human. Their naked bodies are lined with lean muscle. Only a black loin cloth covers them. It stands out against their pale, almost translucent skin. Hair is void from their heads and, as far as Rachel can tell, from their entire bodies. Like the two men in Rachel's desert dream, a soft metallic glow emanates from their forms. These are spiritual beings, that much is certain. What she doesn't know is which side they are on.

The strange upside-down beast still hangs from the wooden structure while it gorges itself on burnt rice. Rachel feels sick. She wipes away the sweat that beads on her forehead as her mind sorts through the dream's images. There are only so many places where three adult humans could hide.

There are far more places to hide an infant.

Rachel rubs her hand over her flat stomach, wondering if her baby or her friends are even in this dream.

"Hello, Rachel."

She jumps at the sound of the familiar voice. Rachel turns to find the man who tried to save her and her baby. His impressive form towers over her. Unlike the other spiritual beings on the beach, he is fully clothed in white. Blond hair curls around his face.

"It's you," Rachel whispers. "Who are you?"

"We will have time for introductions later. Right now, I must get you away from this place. You should not be here." The man reaches out his arm. "Quick, take my hand. We don't have much time."

Rachel hesitates and looks at his outstretched arm.

"Do you trust me?"

While every fiber of her being tells Rachel not to trust anyone from her dreams, she remembers Elias's words. Yahweh sent this man as her Guardian. He saved her once—or at least tried to save her.

She glances down the beach. The tall figures with the rakes have noticed her presence, and now they approach.

"We must go!" He urges her to decide. "Do you trust me?"

Without fully understanding why, Rachel's fingers reach for the man's hand. Her voice cracks. "I trust you."

"Good. It's time to go." As the Guardian's hand envelops hers, the beach and everything with it disappears. The landscape changes as they are transported to another realm. The new scenery comes into focus, and the man releases his grip from Rachel's hand.

Swirls of dust and sand settle around them. "Where are we?"

"Have a look."

Barren desert stretches as far as Rachel can see. She instantly recognizes this place as the desert from her dreams. It's exactly as she left it. She glances down at her body. Yes, *exactly* as she left it. In this dream, Rachel is pregnant. Her hands come to rest on either side of her stomach as it protrudes against the white nightgown.

"How is this possible? I'm pregnant now, but I wasn't just a second ago."

"In this land, the child is safe," he says.

"But it was in this land that my child was taken. You were there. You saw what happened."

"It's hard to explain."

Rachel's arms cross in front of her chest as she waits for a better explanation.

"That time was different," he clarifies. "You weren't fully in this land."

"I don't understand."

"When the child was taken, there was an intersection of worlds, which allowed the Darkness to steal the child."

"An intersection of worlds?" Rachel's mind sifts through the information. "The Breach," she whispers. The Guardian nods. She glances around the dreamscape. "Then what world is this?"

His eyes spark. "This, Rachel, is the Wilderness. Everyone comes to the Wilderness for a time. It is up to you how long you stay."

"Well, that's easy." Rachel sighs. "I don't want to stay here. Let's go. I need to find my team."

He chuckles. "It's not that simple, Rachel. No one chooses to enter the Wilderness, and while it is up to you as to how long you stay; you cannot just leave. People come to the Wilderness for two reasons—they have lost something or are waiting for something. For you, both are true."

"I know what I've lost—my baby. What am I waiting for?"

"That I cannot say."

"You're not a very helpful tour guide."

He smirks. "What is in your pocket, Rachel?"

"My pocket?"

"Yes, may I see it."

She hesitates then carefully removes the flower bloom.

Her Guardian smiles as he takes the flower from her hand. "You will find your answers, Rachel. Everything you seek, you will find." He runs his fingers over the petals. "Knock and the door will be opened unto you."

"You're starting to sound like Francis."

He chuckles. "I know Francis well. He is a good man."

Rachel peers up at him through squinted eyes. Sunlight bathes his already blinding presence. "Who are you?" she asks.

"You can call me Aleph."

"Are you an angel? I mean, a Malak?"

"Not exactly. Malakim are only one type of spiritual being—but I'm sure you already knew that from your training." A smile tugs at his lips.

"You know about my training?"

"I know many things, Rachel. I have been watching you for quite some time."

"So, you're a spiritual being?"

He nods.

"And you're here to help me?"

"I am here to guide you. My interference is limited. It is you who must choose to seek the truth."

Rachel folds her arms. "If you know the truth, why can't you just tell me?"

Aleph pauses and looks to the sky as if it might contain the answer. "I cannot tell you the truth because you already know it. The truth is in you, but you have forgotten it."

Rachel shakes her head. "Look, I'm really sick and tired of all the riddles. I'm just trying to find my baby and, now, my team. Can't someone just make sense for once?"

Aleph's face is unreadable. "I can only confirm or deny what you remember. To know the truth, you must choose to remember."

Rachel throws her hands into the air and starts to walk away.

"Where are you going?"

"Shouldn't you already know?" Rachel shouts over her shoulder. "I'm going to find my team." She doesn't look back. "And I don't need your help," she mutters under her breath.

"Guidance!" Aleph calls after her. "Not help. Guidance."

"Right," Rachel says. "Guidance. Well, I don't need that either."

***

Rachel trudges over dunes and through the thick sand. The Wilderness is eternal and infinite. Aleph was right. Rachel has no choice in how long she is here. In training, Rachel was taught that time ceases to exist in the Spiritual Realm. Now, she understands what that means. The sun doesn't move, and the stretch of sand has no end.

Fear returns as she thinks of the man in the gray suit. She has encountered him more than once while in this dream. She sees the curve of his hooked sword in her mind, feels the icy pain when the metal tore through her gut. Her shoulders shudder. She presses her hands against her stomach. The baby is still.

The faces of her teammates fill her mind. The fear becomes too raw as she imagines what may have happened to them. The terror becomes as real as the Shedim that pinned her. The heat, the sand, it all magnifies the horror of what she has seen over the past several weeks in her nightmares and memories.

She draws a deep breath. "Get a grip, Rachel." She can't allow the images in her mind to project into the dream, or worse, Manifest outside the dream.

She sucks in another deep breath, exhales, and utters, "Jesus." She chants the name as she walks, remembering the fire in Jubilee's eyes when she whispered the name like a prayer. "Jesus." The fear begins to dissipate. "Jesus." Confidence returns. "Jesus." Her feet are wet.

Rachel stops and looks down. She is standing in a stream. Her bare toes wiggle in the cool water. She wades farther in until the water encircles her ankles. "A stream in the desert," she whispers. The phrase runs through her mind. She's heard it before, in her training with Rabbi. "Forget the former things," she mumbles. She searches for the rest of the scripture in her memory. "Do not dwell on the past. I am doing a new thing." She repeats the phrase. "Do not dwell on the past. I am doing a new thing."

Rachel peers over her shoulder at the stretch of Wilderness behind her then back at the stream that unwinds before her. With the hem of her nightgown in hand, Rachel follows the current of the stream.

After what feels like hours of following the stream as it winds through the Wilderness, it eventually dead-ends into an ocean. Mist dances along the surface of the water. Archways rise and fall, holding up gazebos that float among the fog. Standing proudly against the backdrop of the sea is an ancient tower. It soars into the clouds.

"Rachel!" A voice draws her attention to the base of the building. Relief welcomes her as she sees Rivi sprint from the front entrance. Rachel runs to meet her. "We thought we lost you." Rivi wraps her arms around Rachel and holds on longer than necessary.

"I thought I lost *you*." Rachel says when Rivi finally releases her.

Tears fill Rivi's eyes as she places her hands on either side of Rachel's pregnant belly.

"Where is everyone else?"

Rivi meets Rachel's gaze. "They're already inside." There's something in her tone.

"What's wrong?"

"Nothing now." A rare smile parts Rivi's face. "Absolutely nothing." She leads Rachel toward the tower. "I'm sorry," she says. "I'm so sorry, Rachel. I had no idea."

"Sorry for what?"

"For everything. I didn't believe you."

As they near the entrance, the mist that envelops the lands parts to reveal other towers, domes, and structures that connect to the building. Intricate details are visible now. Ancient designs are inlaid with precious stones and tiles from foundation to cupola.

"What is this place? It looks like a palace."

"Don't you know? This is your dream."

"Yes, but I've never been in this part of the dream."

"Oh, Rachel." Rivi's words are filled with awe. "Just wait until you see."

As they enter the front tower, the grandness of the interior spills out like a giant gust of life. The ground floor opens all the way up through the center of the tower. Countless rooms flank the perimeter, each floor containing more and more rooms. None of them have doors.

"You found her!" Micaiah wraps his arms around Rachel. He pauses when her stomach presses against him. He backs away, but his hands linger on the sides of her belly. "I can't believe it," he whispers.

"Believe it." Elias walks up from behind them. "Good to see you, Dream Girl." The look of relief on his face gives way to something else as his gaze shifts to Rachel's pregnant belly. "What's this?" Elias gestures to the white nightgown.

Rachel's gaze drifts down the hall to where a man and a woman walk hand in hand. "I wear it in my dreams sometimes. I don't know why." Groups of people linger in the halls. They notice the presence of the Dream Walkers, but no one seems surprised or bothered by it. "What is this place?" Rachel asks.

From one of the other corridors, a large beast saunters toward them. Its massive girth fills the hallway. The marble floor trembles beneath its feet, and its snort echoes off the walls as it approaches. Thick hide wrinkles as its trunks-for-legs trudge along until it comes to stand before Rachel. As it nudges her hand with its horned face, she allows her fingers to trail over its scaly gray skin. The creature closes its eyes, blasts another snort from its nose, then it trudges away. Rachel follows it with her gaze. Other animals walk up and down the halls with the people. "That was a rhinoceros," she says, dumbfounded. "What is going on here?"

After a minute of no one responding, Rivi finally says, "We should show her around."

Micaiah leads them up a wide staircase. Each step is engraved with intricate designs on its face. The banisters on either side are carved with flowers, pomegranates, and vines. Two columns flank the top of the staircase. As they pass between them, Rachel notices the lotus flowers that decorate the capitals.

Micaiah leads her and the team around the perimeter of the tower where each room stands wide open. More people and animals walk through the halls. Joyful songs echo all around them.

"Take a look." Elias points to the nearest doorway.

Rachel walks from room to room and examines the elegance of each space. The living quarters are unique, as if each one is occupied by a different person.

"Does anything about this place feel familiar?" Rivi asks as they make their way around the tower and arrive back at the staircase where they began.

"Should it feel familiar?" Rachel glides her hand down the detailed banister. No one responds. There is something intriguing about this place but not familiar.

Their bare feet are silent against the cold, marble floor. Rachel gawks as they pass four small children who climb on the back of a lion. The giant cat bows and pounces like a dog, licking one of the little girls on the face. When it sees the four Dream Walkers approach, it freezes. Saffron-yellow eyes lock on Rachel and follow her as she passes. A door stands open at the end of the vaulted corridor. Micaiah keeps pace, unfazed by the beast.

"My Father's house has many rooms." Micaiah's bellowing voice bounces around them. "I am going there to prepare a place for you."

"I remember reading that passage of scripture with Rabbi. You think that has something to do with this place?"

"The wolf will live with the lamb, the leopard will lie down with the goat, the calf and the lion and the yearling together." Rivi quotes the verse from Isaiah. "And a little child will lead them." She turns to look over her shoulder and locks eyes with Rachel.

Giggles from the children ricochet through the hall. Rachel's hand presses against her stomach. The baby within her kicks.

No one says another word as they near the open door. Rachel slows her pace as she tries to process this land and what it has to do with her baby.

Micaiah, Elias, and Rivi disappear through the exit and into the daylight. Rachel shields her eyes as she steps through the carved doorway. It takes them a moment to adjust.

"Hello, Rachel." A man's voice welcomes her outside.

Holding open the door is a man Rachel is certain she has never seen before, yet something about him stirs memories within her. Dark, wavy hair and a thick beard frame his handsome face.

"I've been waiting for you. Would you like to come with me?"

Music and laughter from beyond the door draw Rachel's attention. A group of people dressed in white dance and sing. Her friends are among them. They too are now dressed in white and are oblivious to Rachel's absence or the presence of this man.

"They'll be okay," the man says. "They will be right here waiting for you when you return."

"Where are you taking me?"

"To show you something. Come." His beckon is familiar.

Rachel wavers. The man looks to be no older than Micaiah, yet his presence feels ancient. He extends his hand to her. "Come, Rachel."

She glances over at her friends then back at the man's hand. She hesitates then places her fingers in his.

He leads her down a cobblestone path that winds through the palace grounds and down toward the water's edge. From there, Rachel can see both the ancient archways that rise through the water and the growing group of people who celebrate under a vine-covered pergola near the shore. The music and laughter remind Rachel of her first Shabbat celebration with Cohen.

The crash of waves draws her gaze out to sea. In the nearest floating gazebo, two figures emerge: a man and a woman.

"Who are they?" Rachel asks. The two people now face one another, hands joined between them. The bearded man follows her gaze. An infectious smile spreads across his face before he turns back to her.

"Rachel." He reaches toward her. She takes a small step backward. His eyes reassure her as he places a tender hand over her unborn child. "In order to find the Lord's Anointed, you must remember."

"Remember? I can't. I was in an accident and—"

"You can, and you will." His smile widens. "You've met Aleph?"

"You know him?"

"Trust him, Rachel. He will lead you. I sent him to guide you."

"You sent him?

An eruption of laughter pulls Rachel's attention back to her friends and the celebration they've joined. The dancers clasp hands and form two concentric circles. The men form a ring on the outside, while the women circle up on the inside, facing the men as they dance in the opposite direction.

"Rachel?"

She can't take her eyes off the dancers. She has never seen such joy on her teammates' faces.

"Rachel?"

Her eyes finally lock with the man's. "What is this place?" she asks. "And who are you?"

Crinkles form in the corners of the man's bright eyes as his smile returns. He holds out a fist. Rachel notices something strange on his hand as his fingers uncurl to reveal what he holds—a ring.

"Take it," he says.

The music and dance fight for Rachel's attention, but she can't peel her eyes from the small piece of jewelry. Her fingers reach into his palm and wrap around the gold band. She brings it to her face to observe the patterns and swirls the metal creates.

"This is my ring," she whispers. She notes the bare index finger of her right hand. "How did you—" The centermost swirl of the ring morphs. It peels back like a blooming flower to reveal a bright sapphire gemstone in the center. The ocean-colored prisms and golden swirls entrance her. "This isn't right. This isn't my ring."

A shout of joy rises from the dancing crowd. Rachel jumps. The ring slips from her grasp and tumbles in slow motion. The sound of the ring hitting the cobblestone jolts her brain awake. The world around them trembles. Rachel looks to her friends one last time to see if they realize what is happening. As the ground quakes, the two circles of people each shift directions, their joy unbroken and undistracted. Rachel's eyes meet the man's as his face fades away. "Wait!" she calls to him. But he vanishes with the ocean and celebration. She drifts into darkness, the joy-filled singing the last thing to disappear as Rachel wakes from the dream.

CHAPTER 32

Francis approaches quietly, slips off his sandals, and struggles into a seated position beside Rachel. He dangles his bare feet into the water as she does. Rachel prays he will remain silent. Talking is the last thing she wants to do.

Her eyes trace the lines of the stone bridge that connects the main part of the Central Gardens to the island where the Sleep House and her team await her return. Even the bridge reminds Rachel of her failure. She notes its similarity to the ones in her dream.

"You left in a hurry," Francis finally says.

Heat floods Rachel's face. As soon as she woke, she ran out of the Sleep House without an explanation. She hoped no one would follow her.

"When can we go back in?"

"Tomorrow. You were in that dream for the better part of the day. For now, you and the team must try to get some actual rest."

"I'm ready now."

"It's not up for debate."

Rachel kicks her foot through the surface of the water. A few small fish scatter. "The team is mad at me."

"Mad, no. Disappointed, yes. They experienced a taste of Heaven. They wanted to stay longer, perhaps, maybe never return." Francis chuckles. "I know I wouldn't want to return from an experience like that. I'm quite envious."

"I lost focus. It was my fault. I fell out of the dream too soon."

"You still haven't told me what happened. All I know is what Micaiah shared."

"What did he tell you?"

"That you entered the new Heaven and experienced a glimpse of glory. Tell me, my dear, was your child there?"

She sighs and tosses a stone into the water. "Yes, I was pregnant. Again."

"That's a start. Any clues as to how we can locate the child?"

"I'm not sure."

"You are surer than you pretend to be," Francis says.

"A man was there. He told me that to find my baby, I must remember."

"Remember what?"

"I don't know." She huffs. "Just remember."

Stroking the stubble on his cheeks Francis asks, "This man who spoke to you, do you know who he was?"

"No."

"Hmm." Francis reaches into the folds of his robe and pulls out his pipe.

Rachel watches him from the corner of her eye. "Do you have any new information from the Clinic about me?"

Francis shakes his head. "We are still working on that."

"And the Breach?"

Francis's face darkens. "Still under investigation. And the mysterious thirteen new residents." His jaw tenses as he bites down on the tip of his pipe. "There are many puzzles we are trying to solve." His eyes are far away. "Any indication as to how you must remember?" Francis finally asks.

Rachel bites her lip. "There will be a guide. The guide will help me." The words come out cold and filled with regret. Maybe if Rachel would have listened to Aleph the first time, they would have found her baby by now. And if she would have told Francis about her memories—

"My dear." Francis removes the pipe from his teeth and turns to stare at Rachel. "I can't help but feel you are holding back from me." Rachel doesn't take her eyes off the bridge. "I've sensed you pulling away the past couple weeks."

"I'm just confused, okay." Her words come out harsher than she intends. "First, I'm thrust into BethEl, which would be difficult enough. But then I have no memories of my life before I got here. I try to adjust and fit in, but my Finder is taken away from me. Then I find out I have these weird powers called Giftings. I'm trying to learn how to use them and understand everything that's being thrown at me—" Desperation fills her voice. "And to top it all off, just as I start to build a new life here," she huffs, "I'm told the key to my future is in my past." She doesn't mention the part about being terrified of what she will find there.

A deep chuckle rumbles from her Mentor. "Ah, my dear, as the mother of the Lord's Anointed, you may be special, but you are not so unlike the rest of us. You make a classic mistake of believing you are separate from your past. Humans are not made to live in their pasts, but they are not detached from them either. Your DNA is encoded with the fingerprints of Yahweh. Your past is a road map to your future. Human identity comes from Yahweh, but somehow, you have left your identity buried in your past. That is why you feel so lost. You are not confused about your purpose. You know what that is. You were brought here to find your child. What you're confused about is who you are."

Rachel skips another stone across the pond. "So, what do I do now?"

"It seems to me that you have two missions: find your child and find yourself. I believe the two are intricately entwined. One will lead us to the other." Francis grunts as he comes to his feet. He shields his eyes and looks to the descending sun. "Tomorrow, we will send the team back in. You must meet with this guide. It's time, my dear—time for you to remember."

CHAPTER 33

Eyes trace the familiar wooden beams of the Sleep House ceiling as Rachel waits for the rest of the team to settle onto their mats. They enter the room silently. A mixture of longing and regret enters with them. A weight settles over the room. So much hinges on Rachel's ability to recall her past. She's the only one who can find the Lord's Anointed and the only one who stands in her way.

Francis and Rabbi enter next. The circles under their eyes have darkened. Francis's beard is scragglier than usual, and Rabbi's normally erect shoulders slump. Exhaustion lingers on the despondent faces of Rachel's team. Her head falls back on her mat. She has become a burden to the only people she cares about.

Rabbi speaks first. "Francis and I spent the evening praying."

"Did you take turns getting some sleep too?" Rivi asks.

Rabbi purses her lips. "No. Sleep is not important for us now. The four of you are the ones who need to sleep—well, dream."

Rachel hears Micaiah and Rivi mumble their concern for their leaders.

"As I said, we've been praying, specifically for Rachel's memory. It seems the answers we seek, and the child, will be found when Rachel can remember. We believe Yahweh plans to use the Spiritual Realm to access Rachel's memories. We need the three of you to assist in Intercession."

"Whoa, wait." Elias jumps up from his mat. "You want to send her in alone?"

"She will not be alone." Francis's voice sounds raspier than usual. "She will have five Intercessors."

Elias pushes back. "Yes, but technically, she will still be alone."

"It has already been decided." Rabbi's tone puts an end to the discussion. "The best way for all of us to assist Rachel in locating her memories is through prayer. We know circumstances are not ideal, but we also know that time is of the essence. The child is in danger—of that, we are certain. We must find it before it is too late. Only Rachel can remember. All we can do is pray."

Elias shakes his head then collapses back on his mat. His body is still as he surrenders to the will of his leaders.

"Francis, do you want to explain the process to them?"

He grunts his consent as he hobbles to the center of the mats and takes his seat. "While only Rachel will enter her dream, the three of you will each enter a dream of your own—a place where you have connected with Yahweh before." Elias catches Rachel's eye. "It is from this place in each of your dreams that you will pray in order to magnify your petitions. Rabbi and I will remain here to intercede as usual."

"Any more questions or objections?" Rabbi's voice is tired. No one responds. "Good. Shall we proceed?"

Francis locks eyes with Rachel. He doesn't even have to ask the question. He knows she doesn't feel ready. He was the one who told her she never would.

Rachel's future calls to her as much as her past. She knows she cannot escape either one. The collision of who she was and who she will be affects so much more than her own life. The ripple effects of this moment stretch not only into her own future but into the futures of the people she has come to love.

Rachel closes her eyes and nods her head, knowing that Francis sees the gesture. "We begin," his voice rumbles. He leans in and whispers only to her, "You will not be alone, my dear."

She doesn't reply, her breath now coming slow and steady and her mind relaxed and prepared to leave the Physical Realm. She reaches into her pocket for the comfort of the silky red bloom.

A sick feeling forms in the pit of her stomach. The flower is not there. She searches her other pocket. Nothing. Her heart rate rises as she checks her pockets once more.

Noticing her panic, Francis tries to calm her. "Relax, Rachel. Focus on my voice. We are with you in spirit."

Francis can assure Rachel that she is not alone, but inside she knows the truth. He has not seen the images that come to her when she is alone in sleep. He doesn't know the reality Rachel fears—that her past was not a good one, that her life before BethEl was utter darkness.

Rachel wants to call off the Walk, wants to tell Francis she can't go in, not without her flower. But she knows how stupid it will sound. The Lord's Anointed, her own child, waits for her. And though they don't know it, the entire city of BethEl waits for her. They wait in expectation for the Lord's Anointed because when the Anointed comes, so will the Messiah. So much hinges on this moment. Rachel will not fail them again, not because of a missing good luck totem.

"I can do this," she whispers.

To slow her racing mind, Rachel focuses on the sound of Francis's voice as he counts backward from one hundred. She inhales deeply, holds her breath, then lets it out as slow as possible. After three deep breaths, Rachel's body and mind have slowed. Francis's deep baritone reaches her ears and echoes in her mind as she enters Twilight. As she uncurls her clenched fingers, she relaxes the last part of her body and focuses on her Mentor's last few words. "Three, two, one."

***

Eyelids flutter against the piercing light then squint at the sun directly overhead. A comforting heat wraps its arms around Rachel as the ground beneath her shifts. She is back in the Wilderness.

Bare toes dig into the sand as Rachel pushes herself up from the ground and rubs her hands over her pregnant belly. The gold ring on the index finger of her right hand lets her know she has successfully reentered the dream. The baby inside her is still as a breeze sweeps across the dunes and ruffles the hem of the ever-present nightgown.

"Aleph!" Rachel spins in a circle searching for her Guardian and guide. The tower, the ocean, and Aleph are nowhere to be seen. The desert is as void as the first time she entered it, perhaps even more so. "Aleph!" she calls again.

The ground trembles beneath her. Rachel focuses her mind so she doesn't fall out of the dream, but the dune crumbles like a child's sandcastle on a beach. She falls to the ground and grasps at the sand that slips through her fingers. All around her, the ground swirls and pulls downward into a vortex funnel. Like sand in an hourglass, the Wilderness world flushes itself down some invisible drain and carries Rachel with it.

"Aleph!" she screams in panic, but the sound of her voice is muffled by the sand that fills her mouth. Rachel grasps in vain at the sides of the invisible funnel as it ushers her helpless body from one dreamscape into the next.

Before unconsciousness can swallow her completely, Rachel slips through the bottom and lands faceup on another patch of sand. The sky above her seals the hole from where she fell.

Motionless, she waits for her head to stop spinning. Eyes closed, her body pulses and trembles with her racing heart. She clutches her chest then places a hand on her belly. The baby still doesn't move.

When she finally opens her eyes, Aleph is standing over her.

"You scared me!" she shrieks. "Why did you do that?"

"You were looking for me. I was just helping." He smirks.

Rachel comes to her feet, hands on her hips. "That wasn't funny. And don't you mean guiding, not helping?" She brushes the sand off her nightgown. "Hey, wait." She points her finger in his face. "You have my flower! You never gave it back."

"What flower?"

"Big red one, about the size of my hand. The only flower I ever gave you. Any of this sound familiar?"

Aleph narrows his eyes. "Oh yes, that flower, of course." He hesitates. "I'm sorry, I don't have it with me."

Rachel huffs. "Some Guardian you are. Can't even keep track of a flower." She crosses her arms. "All right, let's not waste any more time. I know the key to finding my baby is in my memory." She draws a deep breath and blows it out. "I'm ready to remember."

Aleph blinks as he examines her. "You're ready to remember?" He rubs his chin. "Tell me, Rachel, are you also ready for the truth?" He pauses. "No matter how hard it may be to hear?"

Rachel's stomach twists. "No." She hesitates before saying more. "I'm not ready. But a very wise friend once told me that no one feels ready when Yahweh calls them." Aleph glances away as she speaks. "My friends need me to do this." She swallows. "I'm sorry. Will you still guide me?"

Aleph coughs, clears his throat, and turns back to look at her. He narrows his eyes.

"I want to know the truth," she pleads. "No, I need to know."

Aleph gives a slight nod, walks toward her, and slides his hand over her belly. Rachel stiffens. "You know that your child is in danger, yes?"

"That's why I came looking for you." She searches his face. "Is it too late?"

"Nearly."

Rachel wraps her arms around her belly. "What do I need to do? I'll do anything."

"There is a problem, a barrier we must eliminate. It's your friends."

"My friends?"

"Yes. Those who enter the Spiritual Realm with you, the ones who are praying for you."

"I don't understand. They're helping me."

Aleph shakes his head. "They impede your ability to locate the child. They don't understand your past like I do. They mean well and believe they do what is right, but this situation is unlike any they have encountered before.

"You are special, Rachel, and I think you know this deep down. Unlike those who have gone before you, you have the power and ability to interact with this realm without the aid of others. Your power is weighed down by the company you keep. If you want to find the child, you must come here alone."

"I am alone."

"No." He shakes his head. "There are Intercessors in this realm. They may not be here"—he points to the ground—"but they are with you. I can sense them."

"Then I will come back without them. Surely they will understand."

"They will not understand." His tone is emphatic. "You cannot tell them what you must do. They will continue to intercede from the Physical Realm. Their prayers hinder the whole mission!"

Rachel tilts her head. "That doesn't make any sense. How can their prayers have such a negative effect?"

"Because they pray for the wrong things."

"The wrong things?" She shakes her head. "Then tell me. What are the right things?"

Aleph smiles. "I will show you. Trust me, Rachel. Come to me. Come to me alone, and I will help you find the child."

"But—"

"I know what you are thinking," he says. "Why you? And how could you? After all, you're just you, nothing special. But see, that is where you are wrong. You, Rachel, are very special—chosen even, for a task that only you can achieve. Think about it: the strange circumstances under which you entered that bizarre town, your dreams . . . doesn't it make sense that someone so special would be chosen to be the bearer of someone special? It is you, Rachel. You are the only one who can find the child. I tell you the truth." His lips curl upward. "Unless you come alone, you endanger your friends and all of humanity."

Rachel shifts and glances around the Wilderness. "Okay," she finally whispers. "I'll do it. I'll come alone. I'll do anything to find my baby and protect my friends."

"Splendid."

"And bring my flower!" She points a finger in his face.

"Of course," Aleph grins.

"Okay, so how do I do it? How do I Dream Walk without them knowing?"

"Easy. You keep it a secret," he smirks. "You spend so much time at that little island, have you forgotten the house that belongs to you? Seems like a perfect place for some privacy. Come as soon as you can. I will be waiting for you." Aleph flashes a farewell smile. At the snap of his fingers, he expels Rachel from the Spiritual Realm.

***

A chuckle bubbles up and spews from Aleph's lips. He rubs his hands together. "Fool!" he bellows. "A deceiver in the desert—they fall for it every time." He laughs to himself. "Well, almost every time."

He turns to walk back through the desert sands. As he does, he sheds his light outward appearance like a skin. The white clothing and blond hair vaporize, revealing the onyx-colored scales and slithering form that hide underneath.

CHAPTER 34

A glass bottle shatters under Cohen's boot. He glances down to find a used hypodermic needle that was once inside the bottle. Now more careful as to where he steps, Cohen continues to pick his way through the dense forest that surrounds his team's base camp. He glances up at the limbs of a nearby tree then veers from the slightly worn trails his team members use. Whenever possible, they switch up their routines to avoid leaving a path to their camp. The litter of bottles and other paraphernalia suggests someone outside of their team has been too close to the chapel's ruins, but when? He can't tell how long the trash has been there.

Cohen shoves aside branches of saplings and thorny vines that swipe at his face. Up ahead, the brush thins. He treads as silently as possible, never certain that he or his team will be alone. Adrielle and the other Apostles shouldn't be back for a while. Cohen's final class at the university ended early today, and for whatever reason, he felt led into this uncharted area of the forest after he arrived back at the camp.

There are no longer any markings denoting the location of a trail, and the ground is oddly clear of litter. Thorns and thistles thin until they are all but gone. The usual dull green of the foliage gives way to a bright shade of chartreuse as Cohen ventures deeper into the woods.

His eyes shift to the ground to make sure he doesn't slip as he descends a mossy hillside. He continues forward then stops, foot midair. Carefully, Cohen places his boot down beside the item that caught his attention. A tiny white flower peers up at him from its mossy bed. Since he arrived at the camp, Cohen hasn't seen a single flower. Even the presence of this seemingly insignificant plant feels like a miracle, but there is something even more curious about it. Cohen has seen this type of flower before, and to his knowledge, they only grow in one very specific place—on the outskirts of BethEl where Francis found him. The same place where Cohen and his team exited the city so many months ago.

The flower is bent. Its petals lean as if to point Cohen in the right direction. As he follows, more flowers appear, sparse at first then thicker. He pursues their trail until he finds a patch of white at the base of the largest tree he has ever seen, towering up through the forest.

Cohen enters the space and stops. Unsure as to why, he removes his shoes, something he would never do in any other part of the forest. The moss is soft beneath his toes. The feel of it brings back memories from his childhood in BethEl as he sets aside the unworn boots.

As he enters the circular patch of flowers, something unusual catches his eye. Directly overhead, the air buzzes. He can see the atmosphere swirl and vibrate as he stands beneath the swarming cloud. The sky is teeming with gnats. Hundreds if not thousands of the tiny insects zip around the air in the most unusual of patterns. Cohen swats at the ones that drifts too close to his face.

"Don't!" a voice bellows from within the buzzing cloud. Cohen falls to his knees. "You stand on Holy Ground," the voice thunders again. Though it is not menacing, it still strikes terror in the core of Cohen's being. He presses his forehead to the blanket of moss and flowers as he waits to see if the voice will speak again.

Cohen's voice cracks as he asks, "Are you the Lord?"

"I Am who I Am," the voice says.

Cohen's breath catches in his throat as the presence of holiness and power washes over him. The air hums with life and warmth, infused with the scent of nectar and spice. The presence of Yahweh is palpable.

"Why?" Cohen whispers. "Why would you make yourself known to me?"

"Because I am pleased with you, Cohen."

"Pleased with me?"

"Yes, my son. I am pleased with you. You are a faithful servant, obedient and full of my presence." Cohen's head spins. He feels light-headed. "Yes, I am very pleased. You lead with love and come under others to lift them up, even when it costs you greatly. You represent me well."

The weight of Yahweh's presence crushes Cohen. At the same time, he never wants to leave it.

The voice bellows again. "You have led well on this mission."

"I have? I feel like we haven't accomplished anything," Cohen says. "We haven't made any progress since we left BethEl, and I don't know how we ever will."

The calm voice of Yahweh says, "Do not despise the day of small beginnings, my son. Consider the gnat. Such a small, insignificant creature, yet just one of these pestering insects can inflict great turmoil on a human when it flies into the eyes or mouth. A swarm such as these can drive a wild bull completely mad. One gnat is an irritant, but a thousand are unstoppable.

"So too you and your people shall be as a growing swarm of gnats. You may be small, but together, you are unstoppable, revolutionary, able to overthrow the strongest and most powerful of bulls."

"Like a mustard seed," Cohen whispers.

"Yes, my son, like a mustard seed. Though you may not see it, your team has already caused quite a stir. The bull is snorting and stomping. It fights back with all its might. That is why you must return."

"Return?"

"Yes, my son. It is time for you to return to BethEl. You are needed there."

"And leave the team? What about Adrielle?"

"Your team will be in good hands, and I will continue to guide Adrielle. But for you, it is time. You must return now. It is why I have led you here today."

"Right now? Shouldn't I at least go back and explain to Adrielle and the rest of the team?"

"No!" the voice commands. "Rachel is in danger."

Cohen's mind spins. "The dreams. You were warning me."

"Yes, and now you must go to her."

Panic grips Cohen's chest as his mind dredges up the horrifying images of Rachel from his nightmares. "How do I get back to her?"

"By my power. Rise to your feet."

Cohen hesitates then obeys.

"Run," the voice says. "As soon as you enter the city of BethEl, you must run! Run to Francis. There is not much time."

The thump of Cohen's heart thunders through his body. Fear for Rachel's safety overwhelms him. He should have known. Maybe then he could have returned sooner. But it's too late for that now. All he has is the present and the presence of the Lord. With a deep breath, he tries to settle his mind and body.

Above him, the swarm of gnats descends. The buzzing cloud opens to form a ring of the humming insects. They engulf Cohen and leave him with only the faint echo of the words of his Lord. "I will be with you."

A flash of light immerses Cohen then fades to reveal the familiar outskirts of his hometown. The gnats have vanished along with the dim world outside of BethEl. He breathes in the familiar and sweet air, preparing himself as the voice of Yahweh bellows around him, "RUN!"

CHAPTER 35

The residential area is empty when Rachel arrives. Guilt plagues her as she climbs the porch stairs to the tiny townhouse. Rachel didn't lie to Francis and Rabbi, but she wasn't exactly forthright. She can't tell them the truth; Aleph made that clear. But if a lie is what keeps her friends safe and helps Rachel find the child they have been waiting for, she can deal with the remorse. The front door clicks shut behind her.

"I do need space to process," Rachel mumbles as she drops her shoes by the front door. "I really do need time alone to understand these memories." She tries to convince herself of the story she told her friends as she makes her way down the hall to the bedroom. The vacancy of the house is oppressive.

With her palms pressed firmly against the casing of the doorway, Rachel stares at the bed in her room. She tries to process the emotions that swirl inside. Fear is absent, replaced by a sense of reckless courage that courses through her veins. "This is why I was brought here," she whispers to herself.

Rachel slips into the room, climbs onto the bed, and reaches for the drawer on the bedside table. Inside is the

Bible Cohen gave her. While Rachel has spent many hours over the past several weeks reading the scriptures, she hasn't seen this particular Bible since before she started training. She slides the aged book from the drawer and opens it onto her lap. The scent instantly overtakes her.

Rachel wishes she better understood the stories and the God contained within these pages. There is still so much she doesn't know, so much to learn. If only there had been more time. Perhaps then she would feel more prepared for what she is about to do, but there is no time for that now.

Rachel flips to the title page in search of the most powerful few sentences in the entire Bible. Not the words of some Prophet or Apostle or even God, but the words of a boy who believed in her.

Rachel, while you may not remember the truth of who you are, may you never forget God's goodness and love for you. Yahweh made you for a purpose. I can't wait for us to discover what that is. Reach out to him. Ask him for the answers. Seek him. Yahweh is eager to answer those who call on him. Cohen.

Rachel draws a deep breath, allowing the words to fuel her. She remembers the comfort Cohen brought her when she first arrived in BethEl. He became the only familiar face among strangers. Now, those strangers are her friends, her family. Rachel wishes Cohen was here now, wishes she could tell him she finally discovered the reason Yahweh brought her to BethEl. But most of all she wishes she could see his smile again. Her fingers trace the handwritten note. If only she could tell him how sorry she is for the things she said before he left.

Rachel closes the Bible and lies back on the bed. She must do this—for BethEl, for Cohen, Francis,

Rabbi, and the team. For her baby, and more importantly, for herself. Rachel must remember.

She laughs to herself. "I actually feel ready this time."

With the Bible clutched to her chest, Rachel begins the breathing pattern she has mastered over the past few weeks. She begins to count. "One hundred, ninety-nine, ninety-eight, ninety-seven."

At fifty-two, Rachel knows she is on the cusp of sleep. Slumber hastens to steal her away from this realm and usher her into the next. She skips the rest of the numbers and finishes the countdown in her mind. Five, four, three, two—

***

Rachel opens her eyes to the Wilderness scene. Sand swirls in the wind. As he promised, Aleph is waiting. He wears a strange smile.

"Oh, dear Rachel." He steps toward her and grabs her face with his hand. Squeezing her jaw and cheeks, Aleph forces her to look into his eyes. "Foolish girl." He tsks. Rachel's body is rigid, but the baby within her belly squirms. Fear seizes her.

"Aleph?"

"Silence!" He shoves her, and with little effort, Rachel's body careens through the air and lands in a heap of sand. His laugh sends an icy chill through Rachel's body. "I am not Aleph. I don't know where he is now, but I can assure you, I am not him."

Rachel watches as the façade unfolds. His appearance morphs into a human-like figure, tall and lean, body rippled with well-formed muscles. From head to toe he is covered in a metallic substance that looks like scales, black as onyx, but it is his face that strikes the most terror. Not because of his bald, elongated skull, or the two slits where a nose should be. It's not the menacing mouth that spreads from one cheek to the other without any lips to frame it. The horror comes from the yellow, reptilian eyes that blink back at her—the familiar eyes.

Rachel can feel the blood drain from her cheeks.

"Ah, it seems you are indeed getting your memories back." The creature crouches on the ground and leans his face toward Rachel's. "You remember me," he hisses, "don't you?"

Lips quiver. Eyes close as Rachel prays to unsee what she knows she can never unsee.

"Answer me!"

"Yes." The word tumbles from her mouth.

"Good." He stands. "Now as for that Aleph, you don't have to worry about him finding us. He doesn't make a habit of coming here."

"I—" she stammers. "I don't understand."

"My poor little sweet," the Watcher taunts her. "That little bump to the head really messed you up, didn't it?"

Rachel backs away. He stalks toward her.

"Let me ask you, Rachel—have you wondered why sometimes, when you enter the Spiritual Realm, it is a wonderful experience?" He mocks a pleasant voice. "And other times"—the evil growl returns—"your dreams are the makings of nightmares? Hmm? Do you wonder?" When she doesn't answer he continues. "It is because you, Rachel, are a very, very bad girl. You are evil to your core; that is your true identity. You have simply forgotten.

"But somehow, these miserably delightful people you met have managed to spark a hint of good in you.

That is why you can project on both the Light side and Dark side of the Spiritual Realm."

When the Watcher sees Rachel's confusion, he pauses. "You still don't understand?" He curses under his breath. "Let me put it into words you might comprehend. I know that stupid monk and teacher told you about the Breach. They aren't sure how it happened, but I know. It was you! You caused the Breach and endangered this entire town. Why? Because you are evil! How you managed to enter that town, I don't know; that is still unexplainable. But when you did, you ripped a gaping hole in the Veil that cloaked the city and made a way for one of my employees to enter. Because you humans are both physical and spiritual beings, the Breach is effective in both the Physical and Spiritual Realms. That is why when you dream, you keep falling through to different sides."

Rachel finally finds her voice. "But that's just the Spiritual Realm."

"Ah, yes. The puzzle is still too hard for you to solve. Perhaps you have met my dear friend Hayden?" The Watcher doesn't wait for her to answer. "When you escaped, I sent a team of my employees after you. Hayden was among them. Because you ruptured the Veil to that hidden town, somehow, he managed to enter it as well." He pauses and smiles. "Oh, I've been meaning to thank you." He leans toward her. "Turns out, Yahweh has been keeping many secrets from us. We didn't know about that hidden city, but now thanks to you, we do."

Rachel's stomach plummets. "And the others who came in with him?"

The Watcher shrugs. "A mystery even to me. They are not my employees. Perhaps they too stumbled in through the Breach. That, or Yahweh is up to no good."

His lip curls with disdain. “We lost contact with Hayden once he was inside the city,” he says. “No one knew where he was—even him. It took him several days of spying to begin to understand that strange place. Finally, he caught wind of a story—a girl who had been in a car accident. Now, that sounded familiar. Hayden peered into your window that night, suspecting it was you, but he couldn’t confirm until you literally bumped into him on the street. Around that same time, he discovered the other new arrivals. What good fortune! Then it was simply a matter of deception, a game my employees are all too familiar with.” The creature furrows it brow. “Of course, Hayden has struggled to complete his job of retrieving you since you have been quite occupied.” The creature steeples his fingers in front of his face. “Fortunately, I’ve been trying to connect with you too.”

“In my dreams,” Rachel whispers.

The Watcher nods. “Hide and seek—remember when we used to play that little astral projection game? You were always quite skilled at dream travel. Except this time, you didn’t know you were hiding, and when I found you, you didn’t remember me.” He shrugs. “It doesn’t matter now. Because while I have been entertaining you here, Hayden has broken into your home and is preparing to finish the job he started.”

Rachel stumbles to her feet. “No! You’re lying!”

The Watcher chuckles. “Not this time, Rachel. You opened the Breach, and now that we have you alone, we can carry you back through it.”

She presses a hand against her stomach. “And my baby?”

“The child belongs to us.”

“It was you! You were the one who—”

The Watcher pulls a sword from his side. The blade glimmers like black ice. "The one who gutted you?" His appearance morphs. Rachel's lips tremble. She steps backward. She knows those eyes. Knows that smile. The man's features are striking. Dark hair; cold, haunting eyes. Her heart stutters.

"Now you really remember me, don't you?" He reaches out to caress her cheek.

"Lord Alderman," she whispers.

"You must be careful, my sweet," he says, "for even Darkness can masquerade as Light." Lord Alderman pauses then sneers. "Just as you've done in deceiving those foolish Christians." He smiles. Rachel stiffens. "I'm proud of you. Now, it's time for you to come home where we can finish what you started."

Rachel backs away. "No." She shakes her head. "No! I didn't deceive them. You deceived me! I will not hurt them or betray them. They are my friends."

"But I am your family." He touches her cheek again.

She hesitates then backs away. "No!"

The man lunges for her. Rachel runs, but she doesn't make it far. Beneath her, the ground gives way to quicksand. Her ankles stick in the thick muck. She falls as the ground tugs at her.

Lord Alderman kneels in front of her, still in his human form, his face a breath away from hers. "It's too late, Rachel. I found you." He smiles. "And now, ready or not, here I come."

CHAPTER 36

Facedown on the bed, Rachel can barely hear her own muffled screams. Now awake, her fingers claw at the mattress as hands wrap around her ankles and pull her toward its bottom edge. With one swift motion, Rachel flips onto her back and swings her foot. Hayden moans as her heel connects with his temple.

She scrambles from the bed, dashes out of the room, and runs down the hallway of the townhouse. Hayden's feet pound behind her. Rachel's fingers wrap around the handle of the front door, but before she can swing it open, Hayden's hand slams it shut. She stumbles backward into the kitchen as he shoves her away from the door.

Evil flashes in Hayden's eyes as he saunters into the space between the kitchen and living room. He suddenly looks much older. In her mind, Rachel runs through her options. If she tries to run out the back entrance, Hayden will close the distance between them before her feet even leave the ground. She sees him eye the door.

"You shouldn't have left, Rachel." He steps toward her. "You had a good life. You know that anyone who tries to leave never escapes, and for those who do try"—Hayden chuckles—"it doesn't end well. Lucky for you, you've been missed. So, rather than end your miserable existence, I'm bringing you back." He smiles at his generous offer.

Rachel backs farther into the kitchen toward the island. Her back slams against the counter. Behind her, she hears the rattle of the knives in the knife block. Her mind races to form a plan.

"I don't understand." She lies to buy herself more time as she remembers her teammates' warning to never use violence in the Physical Realm. Her fingers glide against the counter.

"You know why I'm here, Rachel. I know he told you."

She stalls. "Who?"

"You know! Damn it, Rachel! Quit playing these games. You're coming with me."

Rachel's fingers wrap around the handle of the biggest knife. Hayden's eyes flick to her hand then widen. He lunges. So does Rachel. She grips the knife the same way Elias taught her to grip a sword. She swings at Hayden's bicep. Surprise flashes on his face as he grabs at the bloody wound.

Rachel dives in for a second attack, but Hayden blocks her. The force of his arm against hers causes the knife to fall and clatter against the kitchen floor.

Rachel ducks a punch then stands and swings her foot into his jaw. Hayden's eyes flare with anger. He lands a boot in her ribcage. She falls to her back but doesn't stay there. Adrenaline and fear mask the pain as her body moves with instinct. Rachel rolls across the floor, snatches the knife, and stands. She spins and extends her leg at the same time. Hayden doubles over as she lands a kick in his gut. He stumbles back against the island and chuckles. “You always were a good fighter, but you’re a little rusty.” He sneers at her.

Hayden launches himself from the island and barrels into Rachel. The full force of his body slams her back into the wall. She raises the knife, but he twists her wrist. Her grip falters. Hayden turns her body to face the wall and grabs a fistful of hair. Pulling her head back, he presses his body against hers.

“You thought you could escape.” His lips graze the side of her neck as he growls into her ear. “But we will always find you!” His free hand trails longingly up the side of her body before it whacks the back of her head and slams her face into the wall. She slides to the floor as Hayden releases her.

Rachel is stunned by the blow but not as unaware as she pretends to be. Hayden stands over her as she regains her wits. Before he can make another move, Rachel presses her hands into the floor and pushes her body upward, leg extended to drive into his groin. This time, Hayden gasps with pain and stumbles backward, still managing to block her path of escape.

Rachel doesn’t have time to think as her feet fly down the hall toward the bathroom. Fingers tremble as she locks the door behind her. The shower curtain still lays in a ball on the floor. Jumping into the bathtub, Rachel unlocks the latch on the window above the shower.

Hayden slams his shoulder into the door. “You cannot escape us!”

Rachel’s torso is only halfway through the window when Hayden crashes through the door. Hands wrap around her ankles. “Jubilee! Help!” She prays her friend is home. “Help!” Rachel screams for anyone to hear.

Hayden yanks Rachel back into the bathroom. Her sides scrape open as he pulls her back through the narrow window. "Even if she could hear you, she wouldn't come to your rescue. Didn't you notice the catatonic glaze in her eyes the last time you saw her? Jubilee's under my influence now." Hayden shoves Rachel down into the tub. Her head smacks the faucet on the way down. Straddling her, Hayden pins her hands under his legs. She squirms, but he's almost twice her weight. There's nothing in the tub she can use to gain leverage.

Hayden's laugh bellows as he turns on the faucet. His hand grips Rachel's face as he holds it under the water. Finding a cloth on the side of the tub, he forces it over her nose and mouth as the water continues to pummel her. Rachel can't breathe.

Muffled laughter is the only thing that reaches her through the thunder of water. Hayden's hungry hand runs up and down her body. "I see why the boss likes you." He chuckles. "It's a shame I can't keep you all to myself. I'd have my way with you, of course." His hand slides up her body once more before he wraps his fingers around her neck. "And then I'd kill you!"

Rachel sputters and struggles under the water. Consciousness begins to fade, but just as she is about to succumb to the blackness, Hayden turns off the water and frees her face from the washcloth. She wheezes and coughs as he drags her limp form from the tub. Rachel shrieks as his fingers grip her hair to pull her across the bathroom floor.

Pain shoots through her legs as she stomps her heel down on his toes. Knees buckle and give way beneath her.

Hayden erupts with laughter. "Steel-toed boots, love. Too bad you aren't wearing any." He crushes her bare toes beneath the weight of his. "Ah, see there. We can have some fun. I like it when you scream."

Rachel's eyes widen as he wraps his hand around her throat. His fingers constrict. "Look, Rachel, I know you want to stay and play, but I have work to do, so . . ." He releases his hand from her neck and slams her face into the sink basin.

The last thing Rachel hears is the sound of her skull cracking against the cold porcelain, followed by Hayden's sick laughter ringing in her ears.

CHAPTER 37

The front door to the parsonage bursts open. Francis jumps from his chair in the hearth room, startled from his nap. He hears panting in the front room.

"Francis!" a breathless voice calls. Recognizing it, Francis hobbles from his chair as Cohen stumbles into the room covered in sweat. His chest heaves as he doubles over and clutches his knees to catch his breath.

"My boy! What are you doing here?"

"Rachel." Cohen pants.

"Ah, she is in good hands. You'd be so proud of her—"

Cohen cuts him short. "Where—is—she?" He barely manages to get the words out.

"I'm not sure exactly. She went for a walk. Said she needed a break. She's a Dream Walker now, you know. I still don't understand, my boy. Why are you here?"

Cohen stumbles out of the room. Francis follows. "Yahweh told me," Cohen says. He doesn't look back as he bolts out the front door. "Rachel is in danger."

***

Cohen has never felt so fatigued. His lungs burn, his heart feels like it will explode, but he doesn't stop.

He's on their street now. Cohen passes his old home when he hears the scream. His body forces itself to the point of breaking. With each step he prays for Rachel's safety.

His feet pound up the front steps, his body screaming *Stop!* as he barrels through the front door. He freezes in the entryway. There in the hallway stands a boy that looks to be his age, but Cohen doesn't recognize him.

A look of surprise flashes across the boy's face as his eyes meet Cohen's. It's quickly replaced by a devious smirk. Cohen follows the boy's gaze as he looks down at Rachel's limp and bloody body cradled in his arms.

"Ah, ah, ah." He tsks as Cohen moves toward him. "She is ours now." The boy smiles at Cohen, turns, then walks through the wall.

CHAPTER 38

The sound of metal against metal rouses Rachel from unconsciousness. Her vision is blurred, but she manages to stumble to her feet. Balance returns to her throbbing body as she examines the tiny steel cube no more than two meters square. Other than a large vent in the ceiling, there are no openings. Dim light filters through the slits. Rachel looks to the gold ring on her finger. The taste of bile fills her mouth. The swirls and patterns are correct. This time, she is not dreaming.

Ignoring the pain, Rachel jumps and bangs her hands against the vent. It's locked in place.

The hollow rumble of Rachel's stomach tells her she's been here a while. As she pushes a matted clump of hair back from her face, her hand grazes the gash on her forehead. Memories of the attack materialize.

Rachel screams. "Hey! Is anybody out there? Help!" There is no response. "Hello? Someone! Help!" She shouts louder. "Is anyone there?"

Her heart races in her chest. Pulse thunders in her ears. The pressure in her head is unbearable. Her throat is raw.

Rachel crawls along the floor of the cell to search for any sign of another opening, but she is trapped in a steel coffin.

She jumps again and slams her open palms against the vent on the top of the cell. It doesn't budge. This time, as she jumps, she tries to gain leverage and reaches her fingers through the slits. Screaming, she drops to the floor as the edges of the metal slice through her fingers. Her clenched fists fill with blood.

"Help! Anyone, please!" Rachel pounds her bloodied fists against the wall then sits back and kicks the sides of her metal tomb. "HELP!" The only response is the faint metallic echo of her own attempts to be heard.

Fury rises within her but quickly turns to panic. Sobs wrack her body. Rachel wipes her nose on the bloodied sleeve of her gray tunic, then falls facedown on the cold floor, crying until she is light-headed. Eventually, she begins to hyperventilate. She rolls to her back and stares up at the vent on the ceiling, unable to control her rapid breath. Light begins to dim as a suffocating darkness closes in. Rachel tries to cling to the faint glimmer of light, but even that hope is soon consumed by the darkness as it draws her into its murky grave. For the first time in weeks, Rachel falls into a dreamless sleep.

CHAPTER 39

A booted foot prods Rachel's side and flips her onto her back. Eyes fly open to see a man in a black leather jacket. She scrambles to a corner of the steel cage. She didn't hear him enter. Looking to the ceiling of the cell, Rachel sees that the only entry is still sealed.

"Here," the man says as he sets a dirty plastic cup of water on the floor. A paper plate sits next to it, containing a very stale-looking piece of bread and a small mound of something unidentifiable. Rachel's stomach roars with hunger then lurches at the smell. She shrinks back into the corner like a cockroach.

"The boss sent me to ask you some questions. Also said to bring you some food. You know Lord Alderman doesn't like his girls too thin." Rachel can hear the smile in the man's voice. "Hey," he calls as if she were a dog. "I'm talking to you."

Rachel lifts her face from where she's buried it in her arms and shoots a hateful gaze through the bloody strands of hair that fall into her eyes.

"Man, Hayden sure did a number on you. Not sure the boss will want you back after he sees you. Personally, I think he should let Hayden keep you for himself. You know what they say: you break it, you bought it." He chuckles. "You'd like that, though, wouldn't you? Hayden says you like to play rough."

Rachel's body betrays her with a flinch.

"Yeah, I thought so. Well, let me say this. If you're not cooperative, I'll send Hayden in to do the questioning next time. Oh, I almost forgot." He pulls a clump of white fabric from his back pocket and tosses it to Rachel. "Boss wants you to put this on." As it falls to the ground, Rachel instantly recognizes the garment. A white nightgown, identical to the one Francis let her borrow, the same one she wears in her strange dreams. "I said put it on," the man repeats with more force. "What are you, dumb?"

Rachel's voice cracks. "Now?"

"Yes, now. I know you're Lord Alderman's favorite, but that doesn't mean you don't have to wear a uniform like the other girls." The man crosses his arms over his chest. A smile spreads across his face as he watches Rachel stumble to her feet. "That's a good girl."

Rachel waits for him to turn around, but he has no such intentions. She slips the gray tunic of her uniform over her head and winces as pain shoots through her arms and back. She can feel the man's eyes trail across her body as she struggles to remove her pants. Every movement sends fresh tears to her eyes. The man whistles as she bends over to pick up the nightgown. "If it weren't for all those nasty bruises, I'd be tempted to keep you for myself." He chuckles. "But seriously, you look awful." Rachel has never been so grateful to feel ugly.

Her arms struggle above her head with the nightgown. She can't see through the wad of fabric that bunches around her face. As she tries to find the hole for her head, calloused hands grope her hips and run up the sides of her torso. She shuffles backward and nearly falls. The man catches her and yanks the nightgown down into position. "Only helping," he says as he shoves her back into the corner. He laughs when he sees the look on her face. "The boss said to make you cooperate by any means necessary," he sneers. "Even touching. Now, let's start with an easy question. How did you escape?"

Rachel pulls the fabric down around her legs and tries to force some confidence into her voice. "I don't know what you're talking about." Instead, her words sound more strained than before. "Escape from what?" she tries again. Her voice is stronger this time, much stronger than she feels.

"So, you're going to be difficult, eh? Let me ask you again. How did you escape?" Rachel doesn't answer. "Damn it, stupid girl!" He lunges then collects himself. He sucks in a deep breath and smooths his hands over his well-pressed shirt. "Don't you know we can *end* you?" The words come through gritted teeth.

"I don't remember, okay! I lost my memory in the car accident."

"I don't believe you!" He spits out the words. "You're telling me you don't remember this?" He gestures to her holding cell. "The place where you spent the first sixteen years of your life?"

"No," she whispers. "You're lying." Her voice gets louder. "You're lying!"

Laughter echoes through the cell. "Lying is the boss's job, not mine. I'm honest to a fault, so let me help you with the truth if you can't remember.

"You're nothing but a worthless pawn in our game. Sure, the boss likes you, but that's only because, well, you know." Bile rises in Rachel's throat. "The truth is that you were born into this cell. I remember the day your mother squatted right there to bear you." He points to a place on the floor. "She was a bad woman. You didn't belong to us. You weren't one of ours. So the boss killed her as soon as you were born. We thought he should kill you too, but the boss didn't want to throw away such pretty genes—said he had a better idea. So we delayed our plan and waited until you were old enough.

"Time passed, and the boss learned of your *abilities*. It didn't take long for you to become his favorite. On your sixteenth birthday, we were ready to set things into motion, but that's when you escaped. Any of this ringing a bell?"

Rachel's body crumples. Her face lands between her knees as she tries not to be sick. Every word this man says has an echo of truth. Images from her nightmares emerge in her mind. Now, Rachel is able to sort the memories from the dreams.

"You are our slave, Rachel." He spits her name. "Still can't believe the boss let your mother name you. Now, tell me." He crouches in front of her trembling form. "Look at me!" He grabs a handful of matted hair and forces her face toward his. Her eyes squeeze shut, but she can still smell the liquor on his breath. "Look at me!" he screams. Rachel obeys. "Now, tell me. How did you escape?"

Her lips quiver. "I—I don't kn—" Before she can finish, he slams her head into the wall. Rachel's body slumps to the floor. The man's boot lands with a thump in her side. Without another word, he kicks over the cup of water. Rachel doesn't see or hear him leave, but she feels the icy water as it soaks into the dirty white nightgown.

CHAPTER 40

Cohen is on his hands and knees when Elias bursts through the front door. Chest heaving, he can hardly answer Elias's questions.

He shoves his way past where Cohen collapsed in the entryway. "What happened?" Elias repeats. "Dude." He nudges Cohen with his boot.

Cohen sits up, face ashen. "Rachel—"

"Yes, spit it out. Francis sent me immediately. The rest of the team is on the way. Tell me exactly what happened here."

Cohen shakes his head and clutches his chest as he tries to catch his breath. He stumbles to his feet, legs wobbling.

Rivi runs through the front door. Micaiah is right behind her. "Rabbi is on her way. What's going on here? Where's Rachel?"

"I don't know yet." Elias gestures to Cohen. "He's hyperventilating or something."

Cohen holds up a hand and clutches his knee with the other. He straightens after he settles his breath. "I ran. I was outside of BethEl. Yahweh told me she was in trouble, so I tried to get here as fast as I could. I was too late."

"Too late?" Micaiah says. "Too late for what?"

"To save her." Cohen nearly trips over the abandoned knife as he walks down the hall. Blood dots the carpet from the bathroom.

Elias follows close behind. He glances into the bathroom then punches a hole into the wall when he sees the sink basin covered with blood. Rivi grabs Elias by the shoulder and pulls him away from the bathroom. "Who did this?" Rage flashes across Elias's face.

"Hayden," a timid voice answers from the open doorway. Jubilee stands just outside the front door. Rabbi is next to her. "It had to be him."

"Blondish hair? About this tall?" Cohen holds out a hand to estimate Hayden's height.

Jubilee nods.

"Where did he take her?" The muscles in Elias's jaw tense.

Cohen walks over to the section of the hallway where Rachel and Hayden disappeared. His hand glides over the smooth wall where a few strange symbols are drawn in blood. Other than the markings, there is no evidence that anything supernatural took place. "Here," Cohen finally replies. "He took her through right here."

"Took her through?"

"She was unconscious. He held her in his arms then walked right through the wall. I saw it."

"The Breach." Rabbi straightens her shoulders and enters cautiously into the house. She examines the wall then turns to Micaiah. "You have to search for her. The three of you must go back in right away and search for her!"

"They won't find her." A worn and raspy voice fills the room.

"Francis." Cohen approaches his Mentor. "I tried to get here as fast as I could, but—"

"It would have been no use, my boy." Francis hobbles toward the hall. He chews the end of his pipe as he examines the bloody symbols on the wall. "Dark incantations," he mumbles. "I should have seen this sooner."

"Seen what?"

"The source of the Breach." Francis rubs his brow.

"Hayden?" Rivi asks.

"No." Francis sighs. "Hayden was not the source of the Breach. Rachel was."

CHAPTER 41

Pain sears across Rachel's face. She flinches backward as she wakes to someone dabbing antiseptic on her forehead. "There, there," a kind voice coos. "I've got you. My boys were a bit rough on you. You should have been more cooperative."

Rachel shuffles away from the strong smell of astringent. Her back presses against the wall. Legs draw to her chest. Lord Alderman comes to his feet. His gray shirt and pants nearly blend into the cold steel walls of her prison.

"It's good to have you back, Rachel. I hate when my property goes missing."

Fury rises within her. "I am no one's property!" Rachel stumbles to her feet.

"Ah." He smiles. "There it is. There's that fire I love! It's what makes you so powerful. Don't you see, Rachel? It's one of the reasons I chose you." He saunters closer. She tries to turn, but there's nowhere to go. He presses his body against hers. "Your fire and your pretty face. Yes, that is why I chose you." His fingers graze Rachel's cheek as he draws her face upward. "I like what you did with your hair, by the way. The color suits you." Lord Alderman's tender actions turn violent as he grabs Rachel's face and forces his mouth against hers.

Her jaw clenches. She spits into his face. Unfazed, Lord Alderman takes a step back, removes a handkerchief from his pocket, and wipes his cheek.

"Chose me for what?" Rachel asks through gritted teeth.

He ignores the question. "You loved me once, Rachel. In time, you will come to love me again. Didn't you notice the present I brought for you?" He bends down to pick up something from the floor. He straightens and extends the gift to her. In his hands, Lord Alderman holds a black vase. From the top, six iridescent-red flowers sprout, the only splash of color in the gray room.

Rachel furrows her brow. "Where did you get these?" As she touches the petals, memories unleash in her mind. She selects a flower from the vase. It's exactly like the one she Manifested and lost.

"Somewhere special." Lord Alderman's voice is soft but slicing. "They were always your favorite," he whispers almost tenderly. "Don't you remember?"

"I remember," Rachel whispers. She remembers everything. His praise and his gifts. His abuse and the horrible, violent things he made her do to earn his approval. The color of the flower against her palm reminds her of the blood he forced her to shed. She remembers the strange mix of fatherly care and violent commands. His sensual advances yet restraint as he promised to save her for a future time. The way he'd kill anyone who dared to touch her without his permission, yet his complete lack of regard when he'd slap her across the face. The way he used the word *Jesus* as a curse while beating her until she came to fear the name.

Rachel takes the vase of flowers from his hands. Lord Alderman reaches out to push the hair back from her face. When she meets his gaze, he smiles. “Good girl.”

Rachel hesitates then launches the vase. The scream that comes from her mouth is anything but human. The vase shatters. A flower slides down the wet steel wall. The tenderness in Lord Alderman’s eyes vanishes.

“Chose me for what?!” Rachel repeats the question.

Lord Alderman’s nostrils flare. The muscles in his jaw clench. He looks just as he did in her dream when he spilled open her pregnant stomach.

He composes himself, turns, and strides toward the far wall. He glances over his shoulder and eyes her head to toe, teeth gleaming in the dim light. “I thought you said you remembered.” Lord Alderman’s smile is the last thing Rachel sees before he disappears through the wall. “I chose you to carry my seed.”

CHAPTER 42

The nausea crashes in like a tidal wave. It barrels into Rachel's weakened body and knocks her to her knees. She dry heaves uncontrollably in the corner of the metal cell, but there's nothing in her stomach to bring up.

The memories come just as violently and assault her from every corner of her brain. Lord Alderman's words were the key that unlocked the final barred door of her mind. Hair falls in her face as she lurches forward. The smell of dried blood causes her to retch again. Rachel clutches her knees as the wicked images dance through her mind. There is no mercy from the memories. They hurl themselves one after another with no reprieve.

***

Sterile white walls surround Rachel. A welcome change from the metallic gray of her home. It's her sixteenth birthday.

Unfazed by her nakedness, she sits on the gurney, bare feet swinging as she waits for the doctor to return. Lord Alderman stands by possessively. Anxiousness marks his face.

Shoes click down the hallway. They stop outside the door before it opens. A bespectacled man enters, one hand thrust into the pocket of his white lab coat, the other waving a small digital tablet in front of him.

"I have good news for you, boss."

"You better."

The doctor takes a seat on a stool. "She's ready."

The corners of Lord Alderman's mouth twitch upward. "Wonderful news. Though I sense a 'but.'"

The doctor removes a stylus pen from behind his ear and swirls it across his fingers. "You're right," he says. "The 'but' has to do with her—shall we say—hardiness."

"Go on, Nelson. No need to speak in code."

"Very well." The doctor glances at Rachel without concern. "Conception should not be an issue. Our concern is the pregnancy and delivery."

"Isn't that always the concern? I thought we solved this issue."

"We have." He pauses before continuing. "To some extent."

Lord Alderman prompts him with his impatient eyes.

"As you know, we have made much progress in adjusting for size. Growth slows significantly after delivery, but the specimens are still born large."

"How large are we talking?"

The doctor glances at Rachel. "The smallest was seventeen pounds."

"See there, that should be fine," Lord Alderman says.

"Yes, but seventeen was a bit too small. It wasn't healthy. We terminated it shortly after delivery. On average, a healthy specimen is delivered at around twenty-one pounds."

"That seems reasonable."

The doctor sizes up Rachel with his eyes. "She is fully developed physically, but her hips seem too narrow. Perhaps you would like to choose a more"—he searches for the word—"robust host?"

Lord Alderman's glare lets the doctor know that he has proposed an outrageous idea. Nelson holds up his hands in defense. "Just be advised, we must get this right on the first try. If the specimen she delivers is not to your liking, you will have to find a different host. This one will not be viable after delivery."

"Understood." Lord Alderman tosses something into Rachel's lap. She stares at the white nightgown.

"Wonderful." Nelson stands. We can move forward with collecting samples from both of you today. My lab is prepared to create the embryo."

"That won't be necessary." Lord Alderman smiles at Rachel. "I have been waiting for this special day. I will take care of that part of the procedure myself."

***

Rachel stirs in her cell, trying to forget, but the memories still linger: sterile smells, bright-white lights, drug after intoxicating drug pumped through her veins. The tests, the whispers. Brutal staff and unsavory men. Their menacing smiles.

Then there were the lessons and the warped form of the gospel she was taught. The incantations, strange chants, and rituals. The beatings when she wouldn't cooperate. The blood that always stained her hands when she returned to her cell.

Rachel wasn't the only one. There were other girls, but they never understood her. Rachel was different, special. Given privileges that no one else was given.

Like access to a library with ancient books that reached from floor to ceiling. Lord Alderman didn't hide his favoritism. The other girls saw the flowers he gave her. They heard him call her "my sweet."

They just called her weird.

It didn't help that Rachel's powers were stronger than theirs—too strong. She didn't mean to do it. The blonde-haired girl made her mad. Rachel snapped. It was an accident.

Now Rachel sees herself at age nine cradling the beautiful face of a girl as blood soaks her golden hair. Rachel just wanted to be her friend. After that day, she wasn't allowed to play with the other girls anymore.

A haunting wail echoes through the metal chamber. "What have I done? What have I done!"

Laughter sifts down through the vents in the ceiling.

Rachel's torment seeps out as she moans through cracked lips. Nails claw the cold floor. Hands tear at the nightgown, longing to be rid of the filthy garment. She stands on shaking legs. Her feet stumble and head swims. Fists beat against the wall as her anger pours out in screams. Tears stain her cheeks and leave trails through the dried blood on her face. Her palms press against the metal. Fingers splay wide, her forehead resting between them. She can hardly hold up the weight of her own body. The strength she built the past several weeks diminishes with each passing day. Her forehead taps the wall as she rocks back and forth on her heels. Each time, it lands with a slightly louder thud. She beats her head into the metal.

"I'm sorry!" she wails. "I'm sorry!"

Her forehead splits. Fresh blood runs into her eyes.

"Please! Please, forgive me!" Her head hits the wall so hard, it knocks her off balance. She tumbles to the ground. Her bruised and swollen eyes close. Saliva clings to her cracked lips as she rolls to her back muttering the words, "Forgive me."

CHAPTER 43

Swirls of inky black dance in the basin of a motel bathroom sink as Rachel rinses the dye from her hair. She shuts off the water, reaches for the towel on the rack beside her, and squeezes water from the now jet-black tendrils. After raking her fingers through the wet, wavy strands, she swings them over her shoulder. Her hand grips the scissors. The reflection in the mirror stares back coldly. With a deep breath, Rachel makes the first cut. Over a foot's length of hair slips through her fingertips and curls like a snake in the sink basin. She continues to work her way around the back of her head, leaving little more than a chin-length bob.

After she finishes the cut, Rachel collects the strands and steps into the shower. Following instructions, she turns on the water and allows the hot stream to rinse the loose hairs from her shoulders. When she is sure she has rinsed well enough, Rachel drops small sections of her chopped-off hair into the tub. The black ribbons slither down the drain and out of sight. The water pools around her toes as the drain starts to back up.

“Give it a minute. It will go down,” a man’s voice calls from the other room.

Once every piece of hair is washed away, Rachel steps out of the tub and wraps herself in a starchy motel towel. She cracks the door just wide enough for the man to hear her.

"What am I supposed to wear?"

"I didn't have time to find something else." The familiar white nightgown slips through the crack in the door. "We're running out of time. Please hurry."

The smell of Rachel's past assaults her as she slips the garment over her head. For a moment, she felt clean. Now she is dirty once again. Goosebumps cover her skinny, bruised legs as she steps from the steamy bathroom into the cool motel bedroom.

The man waits for her, arms folded over his chest. A young man about her age stands beside him. Their whispers cease when she enters the room. Rachel recognizes both of them. She's only seen them a few times, exchanging glances as they passed in the hallway on the way to her lessons.

"You look good," the boy says. "Unrecognizable."

Rachel touches the damp ends of her freshly chopped hair. She can't remember the last time she had a haircut.

"Where are you taking me?" Her voice sounds raw.

"We are not taking you anywhere," the man says. "He is."

For the first time, Rachel notices the man by the far window. His back is to them, arms crossed over his chest as he stares out into the murky night. "I will take you someplace safe," he says as he turns. Even in the old florescent light, he is handsome. Defined cheekbones and a strong jaw frame his face. Blond hair curls around his ears.

"Why?" Rachel's voice cracks as she looks at the three men in the room. "Why rescue me?"

The man with the blond hair steps toward Rachel. Kindness floods his face. "Because, Rachel. You are worth it. Your life has a purpose, and it is not the purpose those evil men told you every day of your life. You were made for something more."

His words are foreign. The kindness in his eyes is unfamiliar. He smiles without a hint of evil or malice. "We must go. They will not waste time in searching for you."

The blond-haired man whispers something to the other two then leads Rachel to the door. She glances back at the two men who rescued her before she ducks into the hall. The door closes behind them, and Rachel stops. "Wait," she whispers.

The man stops and turns.

"Who are you?"

A dimple appears on his right cheek as he smiles. "You can call me Aleph."

CHAPTER 44

Silence fills the cell. No sound echoes from the steel box. A man unlocks and lifts the vented opening on the top of the cage then drops a small rope ladder to descend. He gags, still not used to the scent of human filth after all these years. "I don't know how you guys do it," he mutters while longing for the sterile scent of the lab. He pulls a cloth from the pocket of his white lab coat and covers his nose.

Nelson crouches beside the girl and begins to check her vitals. Fingers linger on her wrist as he searches for the faint pulse.

"Well?" A voice calls from above.

Nelson pulls the handkerchief just far enough away from his lips to be heard. "She's been here, what, ten days? Don't you guys feed her?"

"Won't eat."

"Water?"

"A little. Is she gonna make it? Boss wants to know. Said he'd like to still use her."

As Nelson examines Rachel's frail form, he feels a hint of remorse and a twinge of pity for the girl. It never bothered him before, but lately the conversations with his new friend at the bar have him questioning things he's never given a second thought. He pushes the hesitation from his mind and reminds himself that each girl's life equals a nice fat paycheck for him. Still, it doesn't motivate him the way it once did.

He reaches into his lab pocket, pulls out a syringe, then presses the needle deep into Rachel's veins. Nelson takes one last look at what used to be a pretty face then ascends the ladder.

"We can still use her, but her condition drastically reduces our chance of success. Best to keep her sedated. I need to get her to my lab."

CHAPTER 45

A warm desert breeze rustles Rachel's hair. She stirs. Thick arms hold her. She peers up into Aleph's face. Rachel's pregnant belly throws her off balance as she jumps from his lap. Her hands come to rest on the sides of her stomach. She falls to her knees and wails. "Oh, God! What have I done?"

Warm sand collects under her fingernails as she digs her hands into the ground. "Leave me, Aleph! Go away! I am evil!" Her screams disappear into the vast Wilderness. Not even a rock hears her cries to return them back as an echo. "Go!" her hoarse voice screeches. She throws a fistful of sand at him. "Get away from me!" She pelts him, but he doesn't move. Coming to her feet, Rachel stomps up to Aleph. Fists beat against his solid chest. "Go! Leave me!" She tries to shove his immoveable form. "Go away!" She crumples at his feet. Sand clings to her wet face. She cowers in his shadow, but he doesn't say a word.

Aleph crouches beside Rachel and picks her up from the desert floor. She claws at the sand, unwilling to be moved. Aleph wraps his arms so tight around her, she cannot fight. Tears come afresh as love penetrates her fortified walls. "I will not let you go," Aleph whispers into her wet hair. “Your story is not over. It is only the beginning.”

***

Long after her tears have dried, Rachel stirs in Aleph’s lap. She wipes the sand and salt from her cheeks and slides away from him. She grips the hem of the nightgown in her balled fists and clenches her teeth.

Aleph sits beside her. He watches but doesn’t speak.

“Now what?” Rachel’s voice is hoarse as she whispers.

“It’s time for you to make a choice.” Aleph’s legs stretch out in front of him as he speaks. He leans back on his hands.

Rachel’s gaze remains fixed on the stained garment she wears. “What kind of choice?”

“You decide what happens to the child. It can either be an instrument of Light or an instrument of Darkness. Your decision determines the outcome.”

“If I stop searching for my baby?”

“Darkness.”

“And if I find her?”

Aleph’s head tilts to the side. Quizzical eyes stare back at Rachel.

She looks down at her stomach and presses her hands on the unborn child. The baby squirms. “Her,” Rachel whispers. She looks up from her belly and into Aleph’s face. “It’s a girl. I remember.”

A hint of a smile pulls at Aleph’s lips. Rachel watches him then sighs. “Why are you still here, Aleph? Don’t you know what I’ve done?”

Aleph leans forward. “You once were a part of the Darkness, Rachel, but you chose the Light.” He pauses. “Will you choose it again?”

They sit in silence. The dreamscape of the Wilderness is more desolate than ever. Rachel's eyes scan the horizon. Sand and sky blur in a hazy line like water, like an ocean in the distance.

A thought occurs to Rachel. "A stream in the desert," she mumbles while rubbing her stomach. "She is a new thing." Rachel stands and faces Aleph. "I want to find my baby. I have to. It's why I was brought to BethEl." She reaches a hand down to Aleph. "Will you still guide me?"

With a grin, he takes her hand and stands. "Of course, but we must hurry. Come. It is almost time." Without waiting for Rachel, Aleph takes off toward the horizon. She struggles to keep up with his long strides.

"Time for what?" Rachel pants as she chases after him.

Without breaking stride, Aleph glances over his shoulder and says, "It's almost time for the baby to be born."

CHAPTER 46

Cohen stands in the center of Rachel's living room, arms folded across his chest as he watches Elias pace back and forth. "So why won't we be able to find her?" Elias stops just long enough to ask the question.

"Because she's been taken outside of BethEl." Rivi sighs as she pushes her thick bangs back from her face. "She's in the Physical Realm now."

"We search for things in the Physical Realm all the time," Elias says. "We can enter a dream to locate Rachel in the Physical Realm, just like we were trying to do with her baby."

Cohen's eyes widen.

"There is a problem with that." Francis takes a seat. "If what I suspect is true, then Rachel did not just cause the Breach. She *is* the Breach."

"I'm not following." Micaiah shoves his hands into his pockets.

Francis shoots a glance at Rabbi then continues before Cohen can interject. "It's hard to know for certain since nothing like this has ever happened here." He pauses. "But after hearing Rachel describe some of the things from her dreams . . ." Francis shakes his head. "It is clear to me that Light and Darkness wage war inside her, like a vortex or a black hole. You will not be able to find Rachel because it will be like searching for a void in a vacuum."

Defeat fills Elias's voice. "You're saying both she and her baby are gone?" Silence lingers in the wake of his words.

Finally, Cohen finds an opportunity to ask his burning question. "Her baby?"

Francis sighs. "My boy, you have missed so much while you were away."

"Is she really gone?"

Rabbi speaks up. "There is only one way we will be able to locate her."

Elias glances between her and Francis. "And that is?"

"She must choose the Darkness or the Light," Francis answers.

"She did choose the Light," Elias says.

"Yes, but it is one thing to choose good; it is another thing altogether to choose God." Francis pauses. "He has chosen her, just as he has with all of us. And just as each of us have done, Rachel must also choose him. If she chooses Yeshua, there is a chance we can find her."

"If she doesn't?" Elias's voice is flat.

"Then she is truly lost to us."

Rivi flops down on the couch. "But she is the mother of the Lord's Anointed. What about the baby?"

Cohen rubs his temples. "Wait. What?"

"It's true, my boy." It's the only explanation Francis offers. Instead of elaborating, he faces Rivi. "I believe Yahweh will still lead us to his Anointed. We have been promised that child for centuries. Unfortunately, we were never promised Rachel."

"But she's the one who is supposed to find the child!" Elias throws his hands into the air.

Cohen's mind swirls. "God moves in mysterious ways," he mumbles while he stares at a spot of Rachel's blood on the floor.

Elias glares. "Really? Fancy sound bites at a time like this?"

"I'm serious." Cohen looks up. "I think I have an idea."

Elias faces him. "Talk."

"If you guys can't locate her through dreams, maybe we can find her in the Physical Realm."

Elias narrows his gaze. "Do you know how big the Physical Realm is?"

"Yes, but—"

"Not to mention, we can't leave BethEl unless—"

"Unless you're chosen to leave." Cohen finishes Elias's sentence.

Francis arches an eyebrow as he lights his pipe. "Go on."

"I was chosen to leave BethEl, to enter into the Physical Realm. Maybe it wasn't a one-time deal. What if I can go back out?"

"Interesting." Francis rubs his stubbly chin.

"I think it's worth trying, don't you?" Everyone but Elias nods. "Yahweh didn't send me back to come this close and lose Rachel. I found her once. I will find her again."

A smile spreads across Francis's face. "My boy, it seems after all these years, your Giftings are beginning to make themselves known. You have heard the voice of your Father in Heaven. Not only that, you are obeying. True obedience is a gift very few possess." The team is silent. "Well?" Francis continues. "What are you waiting for? Godspeed, my boy. Godspeed!"

CHAPTER 47

Blinding light reflects off the golden domes of the palace as it pierces the sapphire sky. Rachel scans the familiar dreamscape. The entrance she and Aleph stand before is different than the one she entered with her team in a previous dream. From this side of the palace, Rachel can see the fullness of the estate as it stretches endlessly on the horizon.

Aleph gives Rachel a slight shove from behind. Her bare feet dig into the hot sand.

"Maybe this was a bad idea."

"Maybe. But it was your decision." The ocean crashes in the background.

"My decision, yes, but not my idea to come here."

"You did ask me to guide you."

"Right," she mumbles.

"Rachel, learn this lesson from the fig tree." Aleph steps beside her and points to a tree in the center of the nearest courtyard. It's covered with buds and young leaves. A few tiny flowers peek through the greenery. "As soon as its twigs get tender and its leaves come out, you know that summer is near."

"Riddles again?" As Rachel asks the question, her stomach cramps. She doubles over as pain sears across her back and abdomen.

Aleph takes her hand. "Rachel, it is time. Time for you to come face-to-face with your past, time for you to remember, and time for the baby to be born. Then you will find the child."

Aleph waits for Rachel to catch her breath then guides her up the cobblestone path and grand staircase. Two massive doors made of solid wood tower above them. Carved images of lotus blossoms and pomegranates bloom along the panels. Where handles should be, the wood is marked with the engraving of two handprints. They appear so tiny against the giant wooden plane. Rachel waits for Aleph to open the door, but instead, he nods to her.

"I don't know how—"

Aleph comes up behind her, guides his hands under her elbows, and lifts Rachel's arms to the height of the handprints. He slides his fingers around her wrists and presses her palms forward. Rachel's fingers nestle perfectly into the carvings. The wood wraps around her hands as if it was made for her, as if she herself, sometime long ago, had placed her hands in these very spots and branded them for eternity. The wood becomes warm underneath her fingers. Golden light seeps around the outlines of her palms. A hissing sound escapes from behind the doors as the oversized wooden panels swing inward.

Smoke tumbles out and wraps itself around Rachel's body. Like fingers, the thick haze latches on and draws her inside. Unable to keep her feet from moving forward, Rachel glances back at Aleph. He doesn't enter. Her eyes remain fixed on his face until the smoke devours him. Ahead, the billowing cloud parts and creates a tunnel.

A force pushes Rachel from behind, and the wooden doors swing shut. An echo bellows through the chamber as the entrance seals. The dark room fades to light as the smoke dissipates. The walls of the room and its ceiling can't be seen, each too far a distance away for Rachel's human eyes to measure. The smoke curls and unfurls in front of her like a beckoning hand. With hesitation, Rachel takes the first step. Her body trembles. A chill runs up her spine as her bare feet hit the cool glass floor.

"I can do this," Rachel whispers as she straightens her shoulders and lifts her head. "I'm ready." But even as she takes the first tentative step, Rachel knows she will never be ready for what awaits her in this chamber—the truth.

Rachel smooths her hands over her hair and glances down at the dirty nightgown. She is in the presence of greatness; she can sense it. Yet here she is in a filthy garment, covered with dirt and sand, stained with her blood, tarnished with the memories of the murderous acts she committed while wearing it. Her swollen stomach serves as a reminder of even worse things. The baby writhes within her.

Columns flank both sides of the aisle and stretch the full length of the corridor. Rachel counts the endless pillars as she passes them—anything to keep her mind off the uncontrollable tremble in her legs.

Now that the smoke has dissipated, light drifts down from above. The floor sparkles like a prism and casts rainbows of light over every surface of the grand hall. The colorful array reminds Rachel of a story Cohen read to her what feels like so long ago, the story of Noah and the great flood. To him, God had given a promise, a covenant of a new beginning. The sign of it was a rainbow.

Another contraction brings Rachel to her knees. Her palms press into the floor as she tries to breathe through the pain. From where she is crouched on the ground, Rachel can now see water trapped beneath the glass-like surface. Light emanates from the depths and reveals the silhouette of a strange, watery beast. It hums a mournful song.

The contraction passes, and Rachel continues down the corridor. The beast follows underneath her feet, its song louder as it ascends closer to the barrier between them. The music it sings echoes around the pillars and reverberates through the chamber. A high-pitched harmony accompanies the melody. A new song forms. The tune is familiar, though Rachel can't quite place it. She hums as words long to form on her tongue.

Beyond the next set of pillars, two cloaked figures emerge and come to rest on either side of the aisle. Rachel's pace slows. Terror forms in her gut as the unseen force of the room shoves her forward once again. Rachel stumbles in front of the giant, human-like beings. Now closer, she can see that what appeared to be cloaks at a distance are actually enormous wings.

With one set of wings, the creatures cover their faces. Another set covers their feet, and a final pair unfolds from their backs and fans the air like eagles preparing to take flight. Rachel's feet shift backward. The creatures' massive bodies fold to the ground, eyes and feet still covered, wings outstretched as if bowing. Rachel shuffles back farther. "No," she whispers.

"Yes," they reply in unison. They lift their voices high to be heard from their place upon the ground. "Holy, holy, holy," they sing, "is Yahweh, Lord God Almighty. Holy, holy, holy." Their words flow with the humming tune of the watery beast. Rachel still can't place the song, but the words fill her mouth.

"The whole earth is full of His glory." She joins the song. "Holy, holy, holy is Yahweh, Lord God Almighty. Who was and is and is to come." The chamber trembles at the sound of her voice. More winged beings appear from behind columns and come to bow along the edges of the aisle.

Rachel lowers herself to her knees to join them, but the nearest being catches her with one of his wings. "No, you mustn't." The creature raises its voice higher, and the others join with it. "Holy, holy, holy. The Bride of the Lamb has been made holy. Holy, holy, holy. Heaven and earth shall behold her glory."

The columns quake. Joyful laughter fills the chamber. Smoke forms at the front of the aisle. It bubbles up like a cloud during a summer storm. From it come flashes of lightning and peals of thunder. Rachel shields her eyes. Goosebumps cover her arms and legs. Hair stands on the back of her neck.

The billowing ball of smoke and storm drifts down the corridor. A familiar voice beckons from within. "Come."

Rachel's feet remain planted on the floor. It's the same voice that has called to her in her dreams, the voice like many voices, like the sound of rushing water. Now Rachel understands the meaning of the sound: he is calling to her. It's him. "Jesus." His name comes as an exhale from her lips.

The voice responds, "Come."

The corridor suddenly seems shorter. "Jesus," she whispers again. Her feet follow. Her pace quickens. She begins to run. With each pounding step Rachel passes more winged beings who bow on both sides of the glass aisle. They kneel between the columns and declare,

"Holy, holy, holy!" Rachel's entire being unites with the song. The beat of her heart, the pound of her feet, and the pull of her breath all sync to the rhythm. "Holy, holy, holy. Holy, holy, holy."

She can't stop the surge that courses through her. It draws her to the voice.

The corridor comes to a dramatic halt. The tower of smoke stands at the end, but Rachel's feet will not slow. She barrels into the pillar of cloud and falls headfirst into its storm, diving another layer deeper into the dream.

Inside the clouds, the haze disperses and reveals the now-familiar ocean scene. From where Rachel stands, feet planted firmly on the placid surface of the water, there is no land in sight. A pale, serene sky kisses the horizon; thin fog blankets the sea; and intricately-constructed bridges rise and fall through the surface. The exquisite masonry reminds Rachel of the bridge that leads from the Central Gardens to the Sleep House.

She drops to her knees on top of the water as a contraction rips through her body. The surface of the sea begins to give way. Her hands hold firm, but her legs sink. The sensation is familiar. Rachel is about to fall through to the other side of the Spiritual Realm, a darker side.

Her body convulses. Nausea tears through her as dark clouds form on the horizon.

Rachel tries to focus on her breath. She fixes her eyes on her gold ring as her hands begin to slip.

"This is a dream! This is a dream!" She fights to keep the truth fixed in her mind. If she can't hold to the fact that this is a dream, the experience will become her reality.

Another wave of agony washes over Rachel's body. Tightness grips her chest, but this pain is different from the contractions. Her breathing is labored. Sweat beads along her brow as Rachel gasps for air and clutches her chest. Her body is plunged into the sea. Her lungs take on water as her conscious mind loses its hold on what is true. Rachel thrashes for the surface, but flames burst in her chest and consume the last trace of her strength. As sudden as a light switch being flicked off, Rachel leaves the Spiritual Realm and reenters the darkness.

CHAPTER 48

"We're losing her! She's going into cardiac arrest!" The lab staff run around frantically. Their white coats billow behind them.

"Boss, please step out of the way!"

"If she dies, so do you!" Lord Alderman curses under his breath as he steps back into the corner of the lab.

"I need paddles over here!"

"Pulse is dropping!"

"Paddles!"

The whine of the charge fills the room followed by the thump of Rachel's limp body against the gurney.

"Again. Clear!"

Her arms and legs flop like limp noodles as the electricity courses through her body.

One of the machines screams as her heart flatlines. "Do it again!"

Her body convulses.

"Again!"

Her pulse returns.

"She's back." Nelson sighs. "Barely."

"Uh, Nelson." One of the lab staff waves him over. "You might want to see this."

"What's going on?" Lord Alderman pushes past Nelson so he can see the screen.

"This is her brain activity." The young scientist points at the monitor.

"I know what I'm looking at," Lord Alderman barks.

"Oh. So, you know what that means?"

Lord Alderman glares at the underling. "Unfortunately for you, yes, I do know what that means. Fools. You let her slip into a coma."

Terror flashes in the eyes of the lab worker. He takes a step backward.

Lord Alderman strokes his chin as he watches the screen. "Nelson?"

The head of the lab pushes around the other workers. "Yes, sir?"

"What does this do to our probability for success?"

"You mean, you want to move forward?"

"Yes. Do you have a problem with that?"

Nelson removes his glasses and rubs the lenses between the folds of his lab coat. "I suppose that takes us down to less than twenty-five percent."

"Less than twenty-five percent chance that the experiment will be a success?"

"No. Less than twenty-five percent chance that she will survive."

Lord Alderman hesitates. "So, we can still move forward with implantation?"

Nelson shifts from foot to foot. "Yes, but—"

"Then please continue." Lord Alderman takes a seat in the corner and folds his hands in his lap. "Nelson, don't look at me that way. Did you suddenly grow a conscience? You know what we do here. I care only about the child she will give me." He pauses. "Once I have what I want, she becomes disposable."

Nelson's hands tremble as he returns his glasses to his face. He's never cared about the girls before, never felt conflicted.

"Nelson?"

"Yes, sir?"

"Please continue the procedure."

He glances at Rachel's lifeless form. "Yes, sir."

CHAPTER 49

Rachel bursts through the surface of the sea. Her lungs vomit water. She gasps, filling her chest with air. The once serene ocean now chops and sways with the omen of a storm. A chill seizes Rachel's body as wind gusts through the land and salt water sprays her face.

A guttural scream escapes her lips as another contraction comes. The pain hinders her ability to tread water. The storm clouds in the distance darken. The baby comes faster now. Rachel tries to swim toward one of the bridges, but her body cramps.

"Jesus!" she screams, but her voice is swallowed by a growl of thunder. "Jesus!" She bellows his name into the wind. Lightning dances in the distance. Rachel tumbles through the water as the sea tosses her.

A violent wave heaves a wall of water in her direction. It crashes over her and pulls her body under. She kicks back to the top only to cough and gasp for life. "This is a dream." Rachel pants. She holds her right hand above the water and fixes her eyes on the golden ring. "I can control this—" She's knocked under by another wave.

"Jesus!" Her voice gurgles as her head breaks through the surface. "Jesus, please!"

Water shoots up Rachel's nose as her body is drawn under by another wave. The salt stings her nasal passages and burns into her forehead. The pain is familiar and conjures up new memories of her tormented past. Just as when she was a child, now, the name Jesus is not Rachel's salvation but a reminder of how evil she truly is. "Jesus will not save you," Lord Alderman used to tell her. "I am your only salvation. I am the only one who cares about you."

Rachel kicks to the surface and treads water. Tears mingle with the salt on her face. "I'm sorry!" She sobs. "Please, if you are there—" A scream comes through clenched teeth as her body cramps.

Water pummels Rachel from behind. Her body is pulled beneath the waves. Legs kick wildly. Arms grasp for the surface. Her muscles burn, and her strength diminishes as another contraction seizes her body. Rachel longs to succumb to the ocean and allow the waters to consume her. She sinks. Her conscious mind no longer cares what is a dream and what is reality; it only longs to die. But as she descends, her subconscious drifts to thoughts of Francis, her friends, and Cohen. If Rachel dies here, so does her child, the Lord's Anointed.

She swims for the surface. Finally, her head breaks through. Rachel sputters and gulps air. Above the water, the storm rages. The sky erupts with lightning and illuminates something in the distance. A tiny object approaches, floating on top of the waves. Another flash of lightning illuminates its blood-red hue as it spins and swirls. Rachel swims in its direction and thrusts her hand toward it. Her fingers wrap around the smooth petals as she grasps the flower.

Rachel presses the bloom to her lips, remembering what the flower meant to her before she came to BethEl, it's red hue the color of the blood she was forced to shed. But since the moment she Manifested the flower from her dream, it became a symbol of so much more—her purpose and now, perhaps, her child's redemption.

Rachel kicks harder and strains to lift herself as high as she can in the waves. "Aleph!" she shouts into the wind. "Aleph! Please, I need you! Aleph!" Her voice cracks. Lungs and throat burn from the salt water. "Aleph!" Her screams are drowned by another wave that drags her into the depths. Rachel's body tumbles. She cannot tell which way is up or down. Her arms flail, fingers tightening around the bloom.

Rachel's body is tossed by another wave, but this time she crashes into something. A hand wraps around her wrist and pulls her through the waves. Lightning illuminates Aleph's handsome face as he pulls her onto the surface of the water.

Doubled over, Rachel spews. Her body trembles. Her hands press into the surface of the water where she crouches. Like the glass floor in the palace chamber, the water surges beneath her, but Rachel remains firmly planted. She gazes up. Aleph's bare feet are standing on the water. She notices something strange. He extends a hand toward her. Rachel peers up at his open palm, hesitates, then takes it. She comes to her feet, standing on the water in front of him. Removing her hand from his, Rachel's traces Aleph's palm with her finger. "Sacrifice," she whispers.

"Sacrifice?" Aleph repeats the word.

Rachel meets his stare. "Sacrifice. It's what I must do for her to be saved." Rachel places a hand on her stomach. "It's what must be done for anyone to be saved." She pauses. "God is eager to answer those who call on him." She repeats the line from the note Cohen wrote in the Bible he gave to her. "And everyone who calls on the name of the Lord will be saved."

Aleph's dimple appears. "But you called on me?"

Rachel coughs and spits out water. "A friend once told me that the Lord has many names. He also said that, one day, I would learn those names."

Aleph's smile flashes like the lightning in the sky.

"You are Aleph," Rachel whispers. "The one who is before the beginning."

His eyes spark. "Before the beginning," he says, "I AM."

Again, Rachel touches the scar on his hand. "It was always you. You were my Guardian and my Guide. My Protector." She hesitates. "My Savior. You were with me the whole time. At times, I didn't recognize you, like when you gave me the ring with the sapphire, outside the palace. I saw the marks on your hand then, but I didn't understand."

Aleph nods. "At that point, I had chosen you, but you still had to choose me."

"I think I understand now." Aleph's eyes urge Rachel to continue. "Francis told me about this moment. If you are Yahweh, then you are Jesus. This is the moment of face-to-face. I have turned."

Aleph's dimple deepens. "That you have."

Rachel hesitates. "It's time, isn't it?"

"Yes, Rachel. The time has come."

"Time for my child to be born," she whispers. "If she is found here in the Spiritual Realm, it will lead me to her in the Physical Realm." Rachel takes a deep breath. "I am ready."

"Then you know what you must do?"

Rachel nods and holds out a trembling hand. "Sacrifice." Her lips quiver around the word. "Though she was a product of the Darkness, let her be innocent in your eyes. Let her be a child of the Light."

Aleph reaches to his side and unsheathes his flaming sword, the same weapon he used to defend Rachel and her child in a dream that feels as ancient as him.

A strange laugh catches in Rachel's throat. "The Sword of the Spirit. Elias would be proud." A wave of sadness washes over her as she thinks of him. She will miss him. She will miss all of them. "This is my purpose." Rachel tries to force courage into her voice. She touches her stomach. "But hers is still yet to be fulfilled." Rachel's hand trembles. Her eyes trail the hilt and blade of the sword. The engravings come to life as lightning flickers in the distance. Aleph steadies Rachel's hand with his.

With a deep breath, Rachel holds back a sob. The sword flashes with fire as she drags the blade across her stomach. Hot metal fills her gut. Blood and water pour from the opening.

A guttural scream erupts from her mouth as Rachel falls to the surface of the water, curling around the wound as she did once before in another dream. "I must die"—she gasps for air—"so that she may live." Aleph reaches down and scoops up the slippery child. Rachel's blood stains the hem of his white garment as he wipes the baby clean. Blood pools around Rachel in the water as her feet and legs sink beneath the surface.

Aleph rubs the baby girl's chest and blows into her nostrils. She wails.

Rachel laughs. Delirious with pain, her body sinks deeper into the waves. "She is the Lord's Anointed! A Prophet of the Most High." Rachel gulps air. "She will go on before the Lord to prepare the way for him . . ." Her voice trails off. "Forgive me, Aleph." She reaches for his hand. "Forgive me?" Tears stream down her cheeks.

"You are forgiven."

"I'm cold." With one hand, Rachel clings to Aleph; with the other, she clutches the flower. Violent-red water churns around her body and tugs at her dying form. Before her head slips beneath the waves, Rachel reaches up to place something in Aleph's hand. He uncurls his fingers. "Take my ring," she urges. "It's hers now."

Aleph places the gold ring over the child's finger and holds it in place. As it touches the baby's hand, the centermost swirl of the ring morphs and peels back to reveal an ocean-blue stone.

Aleph's peaceful eyes are the last thing Rachel sees as the watery grave seals around her. She clutches the flower bloom to her chest, remembering a Psalm Rabbi taught her as her body descends deeper into the sea. *Even if I make my bed in the depths, you are with me.*

The petals of the flower flutter in the current as Rachel sinks, its color reflected in the sea that consumes her.

CHAPTER 50

The sound of Rachel's flatlining pulse screams through the lab. Confusion etches the faces of the staff as they stare at her still form.

"Don't just stand there!" Lord Alderman says. "Do something!"

One of the technicians dashes over and begins to administer CPR. Another grabs the paddles. Nelson makes himself look busy in the opposite corner of the room.

"Nelson! Get over here!"

His hands fumble as he reaches for a syringe. "Just looking for this," he says from behind a surgical mask and makes his way over to Rachel. His eyes dart through the room to make sure no one can see what he is about to do. He pretends to puncture Rachel's skin with the epinephrine and spills the liquid onto the floor.

The paddles whir to life as another member of the lab staff tries to resuscitate Rachel's heart.

"Clear!"

Nelson takes a step back and watches the lifeless girl flop on the table.

"Clear!"

"She's not responding to the epinephrine!"

"Clear!"

Nelson hovers nearby and directs his staff. He catches his boss's gaze out of the corner of his eye.

"Call it," someone says.

The man with the paddles steps back and glances at his watch. "Time of death: 6:07 p.m."

"Son of a—" Lord Alderman turns and punches the wall behind him. His shoulders slump then straighten. His turn is slow. Face calm. Words composed. "How did this happen?"

"She was very frail, sir. Wouldn't eat for days. The preparatory drugs we administered sent her into cardiac arrest," one of the scientists says. "If it makes you feel any better, I don't think she would have made a good host. The specimen would have killed her in the first trimester. It's probably best we weren't able to go through with the pregnancy the first time before she escaped."

"Nelson." Lord Alderman's cold stare finds him from across the room. "What is your professional medical opinion?"

"I agree with my colleague." Nelson composes himself. "I did tell you from the beginning that she would make a poor host."

"You said we still had a twenty-five percent chance."

"Less than twenty-five," Nelson says. "And we didn't have a high success rate to begin with. In the coma, we could have still implanted the specimen, but to carry it full-term, well, it wasn't likely."

A flush of red spreads up the boss's neck. "Someone is responsible for this failure." He turns and stalks out of the lab. "I will find out who."

Nelson swallows the lump in his throat and touches the empty syringe in his pocket.

CHAPTER 51

A branch swipes at Cohen's face as he moves through the thick forest. Twigs snap beneath his boots. He can no longer tell if he is still in BethEl or if he has crossed over to the outside world. His only clue is the sky, and the tree cover above is too dense.

He still hears Elias's voice in his mind. He all but demanded to go with Cohen. Thankfully, Francis stepped in and handled the conversation. But right before Cohen left the parsonage, Elias pulled him aside and, with an intensity Cohen has never seen, he said, "Find her."

Now, Cohen tries to remember the direction Uriel led them when the Apostolic team first left BethEl. Before he left the parsonage, Cohen asked Francis how long it had been since he and the team left. His Mentor's eyes flashed with recognition as he asked the question.

"For me, it feels only a month," Francis had said. "But for you, it has probably felt much longer."

Nearly a year, Cohen wanted to tell him. Instead, he nodded to his Mentor and left. The only time frame that matters now is how long Rachel has been gone. To Cohen, it feels no more than a couple hours since he saw Hayden take her. But as Uriel once said, there is no direct correlation between time inside and time outside BethEl. At best, it's been a day for Rachel. At worst . . .

Cohen increases his pace and mumbles under his breath. "I need your help, Yahweh. I found her once before. Help me find her again."

His mind drifts to some of the things Francis said during their short reunion. Rachel is a Dream Walker now. Cohen can't help the twinge of jealousy he feels at learning his Disciple—along with everyone else in BethEl—discovered her Gifting before him. "This was a mistake," Cohen mutters. "I'll never find her." He pauses again, glances around the forest for a sign that he is headed in the right direction. When he finds none, he continues.

Cohen tries not to think about his discovery of Rachel having a child, let alone Francis's claim that the baby is the Lord's Anointed. From the time Cohen first entered BethEl, Francis instilled in Cohen the importance of this prophesied individual. At least once a year, Francis recounted the story of when the Lord told him he would one day see this promised child. Cohen never thought the arrival of the Lord's Anointed would hinge on any of his actions, but he can't think about the Anointed now; that's Francis's responsibility. The only person Cohen cares to find is Rachel. He prays she is still alive.

"I could really use some help here, God," he calls up to the sky. "A sign, a Malak . . ." He waits for a response. "Anything?"

Cohen doesn't see the fallen log before his face hits the ground. He groans as he pushes off the forest floor and reaches back to free his boot laces from where they snagged on the branch. Sitting up on his knees, he rubs his forehead then stoops to retie his laces. Something flashes in the leaves ahead of where he fell. Using his boot, Cohen kicks through the brush to expose an empty foil pill package. He straightens and glances around the forest. This isn't BethEl, and he's seen these empty wrappers before.

In the branches of a tree up ahead, Cohen finds what he has been looking for. No one would notice it except the ones who put it there. Two tree branches are snapped at odd angles to form a discreet cross symbol. A carved mark on one of the cross points denotes true north.

"Thank you," Cohen whispers. He turns and follows the compass, knowing he will see another a short distance up ahead. If he continues to follow the crosses, he should reach the camp and his Apostolic friends before nightfall.

To find Rachel, Cohen will need a team. Thankfully, Yahweh has already provided one.

CHAPTER 52

The cool touch of the glass floor brings Rachel's awareness back to her body. She sinks against the surface as her eyes slowly open. Smoke fills her vision. "I'm dead," she whispers while she stares into nothingness. The haze shifts and begins to part. Specks of light glimmer in the clouds as they dissipate.

The ornate details of the palace pillars come into view, stretching upward as far as she can see. The remainder of the smoke peels back, and for the first time, Rachel can glimpse what should be the upper limits of the palace temple; there is no ceiling. The columns stretch into eternity as if to hold up the vault of the sky. Rachel's heart flutters as her eyes glimpse the expanse. It is BethEl's sky, the same stars and planets, yet, somehow clearer and more brilliant than she has ever seen them before.

Rachel comes to her feet and takes in her surroundings. She stands in the palace, in the same spot where she first entered the cloud of smoke. Her hands graze her stomach. The baby is gone, as is the nightgown and bloody wound. A silky white garment now drapes Rachel's body. It hugs the curve of her hips and glides across the floor in a train behind her. In the glow of the light that now fills the temple, the starkness of it is almost blinding.

A chant begins to echo and bounces through the chamber. Rachel turns to see the source of the voices. One by one, the winged creatures step out from behind the columns. "Holy, holy, holy." They flank the aisle, lower to their knees, and prostrate themselves until their foreheads kiss the ground. "Holy, holy, holy." Rachel follows their lead and presses her body onto the glass floor. She unifies her voice with theirs. "Holy, holy, holy."

Another voice joins the song, this one louder, clearer, and more beautiful than the others. The voice approaches Rachel; she can hear the nearness of it. It pauses beside her, then a hand pulls Rachel to her feet. Her breath catches when she sees the voice's owner.

At the front of the temple, Rachel stands face-to-face with Aleph. A majestic throne glimmers behind him. Fabrics of gold, linen, and violet billow about him. A delicate gold crown with the appearance of twisted thorns graces his head.

"Holy, holy, holy," Aleph sings to Rachel. "I have made you holy."

Her legs wobble as she faces him. She follows Aleph's gaze as he glances around the expanse of the temple. "Is this Heaven?" Rachel asks.

"You might call it Heaven," Aleph says as his eyes continue to roam the chamber. "You are in the Throne Room, in the midst of my Divine Assembly." He gestures to the celestial beings. "A place not many enter—only those who are chosen for a special task."

"Chosen? My daughter is the one who is chosen." Rachel pauses. "Is she safe?"

Aleph chuckles. "You still don't understand?" Rachel shakes her head. "Rachel, *you* are the one who is chosen. *You* are the child, the Lord's Anointed."

Rachel is silent as she tries to piece his words together. "But I was pregnant . . . the experiment . . . I was a surrogate for—"

Aleph cuts her off. "The pregnancy never happened." He pauses to let the words sink in. "You escaped before it could."

"But my memories?"

"The mind is an interesting thing, Rachel, one of my greatest creations. During the accident, you lost your memory and, with it, your identity. You were always the Anointed; you just didn't know it. Your mother dedicated you to me right before you were born."

"My mother?"

"Yes, your mother, like you, was a prisoner of the Darkness. As a young woman, she was deceived, told that she was dedicating her life and body to a noble cause. Of course, that was a lie. Your mother was chosen by the Darkness as you were, but when she was found to be barren, they cast her aside. When she turned forty years of age and still had not produced a child, the Darkness planned to dispose of her. But before they could kill her, your mother escaped—for a time.

"During that time, your mother heard the truth of the gospel from someone you now know inside BethEl. The two of them fell in love, and by a miracle, your mother conceived. Rachel, you were never the one to bear the Lord's Anointed. Your mother was. From your mother's womb, I appointed you to be a Prophet—the one who will prepare the way for my return. And since that day, I have waited and hoped for this moment when you would choose to accept that calling in return."

Rachel's mind whirls as she tries to accept what Aleph is telling her. She lands on something that happened shortly after she was released from the Clinic. "Francis," Rachel whispers. She remembers the nightgown her Mentor let her borrow and the care with which he handled it. It was her mother's, a token of her previous life. "Is he—?

Aleph smiles and nods. "Yes, Rachel. Francis is your father."

Her hands cover her mouth.

"You have his blue eyes," Aleph says as he watches Rachel's response. "And your mother's fair skin. You are a perfect blend of the two. Looking at you, no one would ever guess you belong to either of them."

Rachel blinks back the tears that pool in her eyes.

"When Francis first met your mother, he didn't understand the danger that surrounded her. He sensed she had a dark past, but that didn't matter to him. He simply loved her as she was. When he finally learned of the evil that hunted her, he and your mother fled." Aleph shakes his head. "But your mother didn't make it. She was captured before either of them knew she was pregnant."

Overwhelmed, Rachel mumbles, "I had no idea."

"There is still much you do not yet know, Rachel."

"So Francis doesn't know that I'm his daughter?"

"No."

Rachel nods.

"Shortly after your mother's oppressors managed to recapture her, they learned of her pregnancy and assumed the child she carried was one of their own. They waited until you were born, but when they realized you were fully human"—he pauses—"they killed your mother.

"The Darkness tried to continue their work with you, but I do not forget my promises or the promises my people make to me. You belonged to me, Rachel, and so I sent help to rescue you."

Rachel remembers the men who helped her escape. "How did the car accident happen?"

"The man you know as Lord Alderman. He caused the accident. I had planned to take you somewhere safe, but when he showed up, I had to change my plans. I uttered a prayer and allowed you passage into the city of BethEl."

Rachel's voice is quiet. "Then I caused the Breach."

Aleph nods. "Though all the people in BethEl are unique, Rachel, they have one thing in common. They all were turned toward me before they entered. That's why they were brought to BethEl. Because I was reserving them for a time when they could help turn others toward me."

"Didn't you know there could be a Breach?" she asks. "Why would you allow me in if I hadn't yet turned?"

"Because I am God, Rachel. No matter what situation the Darkness throws at me, I can still manage to bring good from it. I did with your mother. And I did with you." Aleph smiles. "And I will continue to bring good from your life if you allow me."

Rachel offers a slight smile.

He continues. "After the accident, your mind pieced together what it could from what memories you had. Just as the baby was hidden inside you as you dreamed"—Aleph gestures to Rachel's belly—"so too the truth of your identity was hidden inside your mind." He taps his temple. "As the Healers told you early on, you were never pregnant. The child in your dreams was always a symbol of your identity and purpose."

"Why didn't you help me see that?"

"I did." Aleph smiles. "But you had to make a choice. I could not force you to choose. I am not a coercive God, Rachel. You should know that by now. You were chosen, but you also had to choose me. Thankfully, you did."

Out of habit, Rachel rubs a hand over her now flat belly. She takes in the image of the Throne Room and shakes her head. "You said, 'Not many enter here; only those who are chosen for a special task.'"

Aleph nods. "And those who choose to accept it."

Rachel hesitates. "What is the special task?"

Mystery kindles in Aleph's eyes. "I will show you."

At his words, the temple trembles. Smoke fills the chamber and disperses as quickly as it arrived. The scenery changes. Now outside the columns, Rachel can see the pure and endless sea. She searches the familiar surroundings and begins to recognize where she is. Together, they stand on one of the floating gazebos in the middle of the water. The peaceful ocean surrounds them; a graceful mist veils the land.

"Why do you keep bringing me here?"

Aleph doesn't respond but watches Rachel as she walks to the edge of the portico. Her fingers graze each column as she glides along the perimeter. Across the water, in another gazebo, two people emerge between the columns.

A man, dressed in white, walks to the center. His eyes are fixed ahead. The corners of his lips turn upward as a look of adoration creases his handsome face. Out of the shadows, the other figure steps toward him. A woman, beautiful beyond description, draped in a white dress. The fabric wraps around her hips and trails behind her across the floor.

"It's a wedding," Rachel whispers.

Aleph nods.

The groom steps forward and reaches for his bride's hands. He pulls her in close and cups her face. The woman leans her head back to gaze into the eyes of her betrothed. Rachel holds her breath.

"The endless ocean of this realm is a symbol of their boundless love," Aleph says. "This realm exists for them. They were made to love each other. It is the sole reason for their existence—to love and be loved." Aleph pauses and waits for Rachel to look at him. "I brought you here to witness this moment.

"I told you, Rachel. It is you. You are the Lord's Anointed, the one who will prepare the way for my return. The reason I have brought you here, and the reason I will continue to bring you here, is to bear witness. To witness the Aleph *and* the Tov."

"Aleph and Tov? Those are the first and last letters of the Hebrew alphabet."

"Precisely. The Aleph and the Tov, the Alpha and the Omega, the beginning and the end. The Aleph is the beginning. The Tov is the end, but not the end like you might imagine. It is a new beginning. The Tov is the covenant. It is the moment when I finally wed myself to the people who have betrothed themselves to me. You are witnessing a time that is yet to come. This is the Wedding Supper of the Lamb."

Before Aleph's words can fade, music erupts through the land. Rachel peers through the columns to find people, spiritual beings, and animals dancing and celebrating in the other gazebos. Everyone is dressed in white, their heads wreathed in flowers. Shimmering petals float in the sea around them, each one the color of crimson, just like Rachel's flower bloom.

"May I have this dance?" Aleph holds out a hand. Rachel doesn't hesitate as she places her hand on top of his scar.

Even though she doesn't know the dance, Rachel falls in step with Aleph as he leads her around the intimate dance floor. Joy fills the land, and Rachel finally understands why Micaiah, Rivi, and Elias never wanted to leave this realm.

Time disappears. It seems days must pass, or maybe weeks, but eventually, the music comes to a close. Laughter fades. The wedding party disappears, and all that is left is Aleph and Rachel.

"Is it over?" she asks.

"This isn't eternity yet, Rachel. This is a glimpse." Aleph's feet come to a stop as the final note of the song fades. "That's what witnesses do. They glimpse a moment in the story of the Kingdom of God, then they tell others about it."

"What do you mean?"

"I'm sending you back, Rachel." He pauses. "That is, if you choose to accept the calling." His eyes scan her face. "Because while the first part of witnessing is the glimpse, the second part is the telling."

Rachel glances out through the columns at the endless ocean then meets Aleph's gaze. The eternal sea is reflected in his eyes.

She offers a small nod.

Aleph smiles as he tilts Rachel's chin upward and speaks boldly over her. "You, my child, you are a Prophet of the Most High. You have glimpsed, and you will tell. You will be the one to go before me and prepare the way for my coming."

A wave of emotion washes over Rachel. "Are you leaving me?"

"I will never leave you. I am always with you, and I will lead you, just like this dance. Trust me. I know every step."

Rachel clings to his hand.

Aleph squeezes back. "I chose you, Rachel, and now, you have chosen me. This is why I brought you to BethEl. This is your purpose. Before I formed you in the womb I knew you, before you were born I set you apart; I appointed you as a Prophet to the nations. Today, you have accepted that calling.

"Therefore, you must go to everyone I send you and say whatever I command. Don't worry about what to say or how to say it, for it will not be you speaking, but me speaking through you." Aleph reaches out and touches a finger to Rachel's lips. "I have put my words in your mouth.

"You will not be alone, Rachel. I, the Lord, will be with you. I will never leave you or forsake you. You will also have the entire BethEl community on your side. And—" Aleph pauses—"I will send you a helper."

"A helper?" This time Rachel smiles. "Not a guide?"

"Yes." Aleph chuckles. "A helper."

"When?"

"When the time is right." He pats Rachel's hand.

"I still have so many questions."

"And they will be answered, but now, it is time for you to return."

Rachel bites her lip. "I know."

Aleph takes her right hand and lifts it for Rachel to see. He places the gold ring back on her finger. A sapphire gem glimmers in the center. Rachel's eyes get lost in the prisms of the stone.

"It's time to wake up, Rachel," Aleph whispers. "It's time to wake up."

Light flashes through the land, the brilliance slowly fades, and Aleph's face becomes a mist.

"Wait! What do I tell them?" Rachel calls into the encroaching void. "You said you would tell me what to say!"

Before Aleph's image completely vanishes, he says, "Tell them I am coming soon!"

CHAPTER 53

Inside the crematorium, Nelson administers CPR. He breathes into the mouth of the pale, lifeless girl and, after a glance over his shoulder, begins to pump his fist against her chest.

"C'mon, c'mon," he mumbles under his breath. "I'm sorry," he whispers to the body. "I thought letting you die was better than what they were about to do to you." Nelson pauses to push air into her lungs. "I know you are gone, but if there is any chance I can bring you back—" His voice cracks. "I can't do it anymore. I can't participate in this evil. If you only knew the things I've seen, the things I've done." A wail slips from Nelson's lips. "Forgive me—please forgive me." Tears fall onto the girl's filthy nightgown.

Nelson steps away from the body. His fingers tug at his hair while he mutters, "He said I could be forgiven. Jesse said I could be forgiven! Even for horrible things, even for this. Please," he sobs, "please, forgive me!"

Nelson removes his glasses and wipes his cheeks before returning them to his face. He continues to pump the girl's chest. "C'mon! Breathe!" His lips press against hers in one final attempt to restore what was stolen.

The girl gasps. Eyes shoot open. Lungs draw air. She coughs. Nelson jumps back from the gurney. Hands fly to his mouth. "My God," he mumbles.

The girl rolls to her side and winces as she tries to sit up.

"My God. My God."

Life fills her body. Color returns to her cheeks.

Nelson's body trembles as he stumbles toward the gurney and falls to his knees. "My God!" Unable to meet her gaze, he buries his face in his hands and begins to weep. His shoulders shake with each sob.

"Who?" The girl's raspy voice asks.

Nelson can't stop the tremors or the words that continue to bubble from his lips. "My God! My God!"

"Who?" she croaks again. "*Who* is your God?"

With a deep breath, Nelson does his best to collect himself. His hands drop from his face as he turns his eyes to the miracle girl. She peers down at him. With a voice that still quivers, he manages to say, "My god was once the lord of Darkness, but now"—tears stream from behind his glasses—"my God is Jesus."

Pink tinges the girl's previously ashen lips. She winces as she tries to smile. "Your sins are forgiven. Welcome to the Light."

CHAPTER 54

The metal floor sends a chill through Rachel's bare feet and into her wobbly legs. Strength returns with each step as Nelson leads her silently down a dark corridor. He turns and presses a finger to his lips. Underneath her feet, Rachel can feel the ventilation slits. Walking toe to heel, she tries to ignore the moans and wails that echo through the hall. Beneath the floor are countless girls and women, held in cages as Rachel once was. Nelson warned her before they left the crematorium, "There is only one way out, and you will not like it."

The corridor is long—too long—and every couple meters there is another vent. Rachel counts them, knowing that each one represents a life like hers. They are slaves, every one of them, and at one time, they were the closest thing Rachel had to friends. Now it doesn't matter that many of the girls didn't like Rachel. She doesn't think about the curses they hurled at her as she cradled the bloodied face of the golden-haired girl. Now all Rachel wants to do is wail with them, to tell them it will be okay—that in the end, something greater is coming.

Rachel falls behind, and Nelson grabs her arm to pull her forward. He points ahead where the corridor splits in two, leads her down the right side then a left turn and another left. Each tunnel seems longer than the previous one. Thankful that there is no way she will ever find her way back, Rachel silently prays that each girl would one day be so lucky.

The hall comes to an abrupt end. A menacing steel door stands before them. Nelson motions for Rachel to come close. "Hold your breath," he whispers. Before she can ask why, he punches a code on the door's keypad. Nelson pulls his shirt over his nose as air gushes out through the once-sealed chamber. Rachel immediately gags. Reaching over, Nelson pulls the collar of the nightgown up over her nose and motions for her to follow. The door echoes closed behind them, hissing as it reseals. In front of them, a catwalk stretches over a ten-meter drop. The smell of human feces and death rises from the pit.

"The dumping ground," Nelson whispers. His walk turns into a hurried stride. Rachel can understand why. The stench is unbearable.

The chamber is longer than it is tall, and they can't cross fast enough. Every few seconds, Nelson casts a glance over his shoulder. Finally, he grabs Rachel's hand and pulls her into a jog.

As they reach the end of the catwalk, Nelson sends Rachel down a small ladder ahead of him. He drops down beside her and whispers from behind his shirt collar, "Almost there."

He pushes her to the right and into a hall. At the end stands a door. Rachel can see the light that seeps through the cracks. The corridor is the only thing that stands between her and her freedom.

A sound bellows in the chamber behind them, followed by a hiss. Rachel recognizes the sound. Someone else has entered the chamber. Even in the dark room, Rachel can see the whites of Nelson's wide eyes behind his glasses. His hand locks around her forearm as he drags her to the door.

"This door opens at the back of the compound. We're in the middle of the woods. When I open this door, you run. Don't stop running, and don't look back. Get as far away as you can. Once they realize you're not dead, they will do everything they can to find you. Do you understand?"

"Yes, but what about you?"

"Don't worry about me." A somber smile forms on his lips. "Thanks to you and a special friend, I will be okay. I will see you again one day." Nelson's smile quickly fades. "I am so sorry, Rachel."

"I forgive you." She pauses then envelops him in an embrace. Nelson flinches, hesitates, then wraps his arms around her. "Thank you," she whispers.

"No, it is I who must thank you." He pushes her away. "There is no time left. You must go." Nelson punches in the code, thrusts open the door, and shoves Rachel out. With a final smile, he slams the door.

The sound of the lock as it clicks into place propels Rachel. Whether it's adrenaline or supernatural strength from Yahweh, she isn't sure. Her bare feet fly across the ground and carry her into the dense woods. Her energy has been depleted, but somehow new strength fills her legs. Her lungs burn, heart races—but she doesn't stop.

CHAPTER 55

Nightfall comes quicker than Cohen expected. He moves slower now, unable to see the ground clearly in the dim light of the worldly moon. The cross compasses in the trees have become less visible. He prays he is close to the camp.

Cohen stops when he hears footsteps approach in the distance. With his back against a tree, he waits. As the footsteps draw near, Cohen can tell it is the sound of a human. His eyes scan the area for somewhere to hide. If it's not someone from his team, he could jeopardize their mission and their safety. He shifts around to the other side of the tree, crouches, and silently asks Yahweh to hide him.

The sound changes its direction, and to his left, a teenage girl emerges from the thick brush, eyes on the ground, a backpack slung over her shoulders. Scrapes line her cheeks, and her clothes are torn. As she glances up, her eyes lock on Cohen. Fear registers on her face, then she runs.

Cohen stands, but the girl is already gone. He sighs as she disappears into the woods.

"Cohen?"

He freezes, then turns. Before he can say a word, Adrielle wraps her arms around Cohen's neck. Her lips brush against his ear. "I was so worried! Where have you been? Are you okay?" She pulls back to look at him.

Cohen glances in the direction the girl disappeared. "I'm fine. Yahweh sent me back to BethEl—"

"Why didn't you tell me?"

"I couldn't."

"Jesse said he had a dream you were safe, but"—Adrielle shakes her head. "Two weeks, Cohen. You've been missing for nearly two weeks. What was I supposed to think?"

Cohen winces. "Two weeks?"

"Yes." She waits for him to look at her. "What happened? Tell me everything."

"I will, but first we need to get back to camp. I need the whole team on the same page. Our work out here is not finished."

Adrielle interlaces her fingers with Cohen's. "This way."

Cohen notices some familiar landmarks as they near the camp. "What were you doing out here so late by yourself?" he asks.

Adrielle casts him a sideways glance. Her expression is unreadable.

When she doesn't give a response, he says, "I saw a girl. Was she with you?"

"I made a promise," Adrielle finally says. "I can't tell you anything about her. All you need to know is that Jesse isn't the only one who has planted a seed."

Cohen searches her face then smiles.

Ahead, the familiar dilapidated chapel emerges through the trees. "Thank Yahweh," Cohen sighs.

Adrielle pauses outside the building. She wraps her arms around Cohen's neck and presses her lips against his. He pulls away. "We can't waste time," he whispers. Adrielle doesn't say anything, but Cohen sees the hurt on her face. She follows him into the chapel where the team prepares for bed. They stop and stare when Cohen enters.

"Praise Yahweh!" one of the women cries.

Jesse approaches and wraps Cohen in a hug. "I knew you'd be back."

Adrielle crosses her arms. "You said you'd explain once we had everyone together."

"Right." Cohen peers out at the quizzical faces of his teammates. "I'm sorry I left without any warning. I promise, if there had been a way to tell you, I would have." Cohen catches Adrielle's eye. "Yahweh sent me back to BethEl. I had to leave immediately." The Apostles whisper among themselves.

"Why?" Jesse asks.

Cohen answers by saying, "It's been almost a year since we left BethEl. I know this mission has felt futile at times, but Yahweh sent us here for a reason. He had a purpose for each one of us when he chose us for this assignment, and we said yes to that." He pauses and makes eye contact with each Apostle. "My question for you tonight is, will you say yes again?"

CHAPTER 56

The sound of footsteps on the catwalk greet Nelson as he climbs the ladder. His eyes peer over the top to stare straight into a perfectly polished pair of shoes.

"Hello, Nelson."

Nelson steps up onto the catwalk, trying not to breathe in the stench.

"Please uncover your face in my presence," Lord Alderman says, seemingly unperturbed by the smell. Nelson removes his shirt collar from his nose. "Nelson, I'd love to ask you where you've been, but I'm not in the mood to listen to your lies.

"You've always been one of my most loyal subjects. So, imagine my surprise when I inspected the lab and found a small puddle of epinephrine on the floor where my dear Rachel breathed her last. You did not try to save her. You let her die!"

Years of concealed rage well up in Nelson—the disturbing and cruel acts he's seen, the blood that stains his own hands. "You're right," Nelson says. He reaches into his lab coat and grabs the empty syringe. He tosses it at Lord Alderman's feet. "I let her die!"

"You imbecile! I went to the crematorium; she wasn't there. What did you do with her body?" Lord Alderman's normally placid façade begins to seethe.

"I disobeyed your wishes." Nelson spits out the words. "I didn't give her an honorary burial as you requested. I tossed her body like the others." Nelson gestures to the festering pit beneath them.

Lord Alderman steps forward and wraps his fingers around Nelson's throat. The scientist's white smile beams against the purple that tinges his face. Nelson's voice comes out as a rasp as he tries to speak.

"What was that, fool? I couldn't quite hear you," Lord Alderman says. He loosens his grip to hear his colleague's dying words.

"I said"—Nelson wheezes, a smile still plastered on his face—"Jesus is Lord!"

Lord Alderman's face flinches. His fingers instantly lock around Nelson's throat in a strength that is anything but natural. A growl bellows from his gut. Breath like sulfur unfurls in Nelson's face as he watches his boss's human features vanish and morph. As Lord Alderman lifts Nelson's squirming body from the ground, his pale skin turns to scales as black as the dark room. Deep-brown hair disappears to reveal the bald, elongated skull. His nose flattens to the familiar serpent-like slits. Human eyes close and reopen to a burning yellow. He narrows his reptilian stare in the same way a snake does before striking its prey.

"Blasphemer! Do not mention that name in my presence!"

"Jesus—is—Lord," Nelson grunts. "And now—" he wheezes—"I am going to the one place you will never be able to go!"

The creature snarls. "You have made your bed, human. You have made your bed among the dead, and now you will lie in it!"

"Rot in Hell, Watcher!" Nelson's voice is cut short as his trachea is crushed. The beast hurls his body over the side of the catwalk. Collecting himself, the creature morphs back into his human form, wipes his hands on his pants, and casually walks back the way he came.

CHAPTER 57

Rachel's mind tells her she should be spent, but her legs somehow keep moving, pulling her deeper into the forest. There is no longer any daylight to guide her path. The presence of Yahweh leads her. The desire to return to BethEl propels her. She longs to see the faces of her friends—and Francis. She tries not to think about what she will say to him. Right now, she can only focus on how to survive.

As far as Rachel can tell, her pace hasn't slowed. Once, she thought she heard footsteps behind her, but she didn't dare look back. Not after Nelson's warning. She prays he is safe and wonders how long it will be before Lord Alderman realizes Rachel isn't dead.

The shadows of the landscape turn menacing as Rachel enters the deepest parts of the forest. With her gaze fixed on the ground, she leaps over fallen branches and stones. The nightgown catches on a patch of thorns and tears both the fabric and the skin on her thigh. She doesn't stop. Blood trickles down her calf. The bottoms of her feet are numb. She knows they too are tinged with the color of her blood.

A sharp pain radiates through Rachel's shin as she crashes into a fallen log. Her body careens through the air and tumbles down a hill before she lands flat on her back. The dull night sky of the outside world greets her. She is still a long way from BethEl.

The silence of the forest is broken by the crack of a twig. Rachel holds her breath. Feet shuffle somewhere nearby.

Her hands and knees scrape the ground as Rachel crawls to hide behind some brush. Stickers and thorns grab at her hair. A figure approaches. Rachel's eyes are barely able to make out the shape in the dim moonlight. She feels around on the ground for a stone, a stick, anything that she can use as a weapon while silently mumbling a prayer of protection Francis taught her. Fingers graze across the cool, solid surface of a rock about the size of her fist. She grips it, ready to fight if she is found. The footsteps stop directly in front of her hiding place.

Before she can think through her other options, Rachel bolts upright, stone in fist, ready to strike. Her arm reels back and swings forward. Fingers lock around her wrist and force her to drop the stone.

"Who are you?" a voice says.

The voice is familiar. "Cohen?"

"Rachel?" Before she can respond, Cohen pulls her into an embrace. His grip is so tight, it feels he might break her. The fatigue catches up with Rachel. She sinks into Cohen's arms.

He pulls back. "What happened? Where have you been? You're so thin. Are you hurt?"

Rachel shakes her head. The energy she felt moments before drains from her body. "We don't have time for questions. We must keep going. We have to get back to BethEl before they find us."

"Before who finds us? Hayden?"

A howl that is neither animal nor human echoes through the trees. "The Darkness." Rachel pants. "They know I'm here. They know I'm alive. We have to go!" She stumbles forward, forcing her legs to keep moving.

Cohen runs beside her then takes the lead. "This way. I have somewhere we can hide." Another howl rings through the night air, this time louder and closer. Cohen lengthens his stride, but Rachel can't keep his pace. The sound of hurried footsteps manifests behind them. This time Rachel knows it's not her imagination.

"I'm sorry," Rachel says. Cohen doesn't respond. He grabs her wrist and pulls her along. "This is all my fault." His grip is tighter; their legs move faster. She hears the sound of ragged breath behind them. Rachel's legs cramp. She stumbles, but Cohen's hands catch her as she falls. He immediately scoops Rachel into his arms and takes off in a sprint.

She hears his whispered prayers as her body bounces in his arms. "Yahweh, blind and confuse our enemies. Blind and confuse our enemies!"

The sound of footsteps fades behind them, but Cohen doesn't stop.

"How do you know where you're going?" Rachel asks. Cohen doesn't answer. His breath is ragged against her hair. His arms tighten around her frail and weary body.

"What is that?" Rachel sees a dark outline up ahead. Cohen's lungs heave. His sprint turns into a jog as they approach what Rachel can now tell is the remains of a brick-and-stone building. Cohen's pace slows again as he turns to face the direction they just came. Sweat beads his lip. They listen. Cohen lingers a moment then carries Rachel into the small clearing and through one of the building's crumbling archways.

Candlelight ahead warms Cohen's light skin and glows in his gray eyes. Even now—dirty, sweaty, exhausted—he is more handsome than Rachel remembers. She leans her head into his chest. She has never felt safer.

"How did you know about this place—" Rachel stops. Six people stand inside the entrance to the building. She flinches and grips Cohen, but the unfamiliar faces only show kindness and relief.

An older man with a thick accent approaches. "I can't believe you found her."

Cohen nods, still panting. "Please, all of you. Go get the others. Tell them we have her." The man nods and hurries out the way Rachel and Cohen entered. A striking girl with an angular face narrows her dark-brown eyes at Rachel as she exits behind the other man.

Cohen carries Rachel into the center of the building before he sets her down. He catches his breath as he walks over to a far corner and returns with medical supplies. "I think we're safe now," he says as he unrolls some gauze.

"Is this where you've been since you left BethEl? Is this your mission?" Rachel watches Cohen closely. "I can do that." She reaches for the gauze. "I mean—" she pauses when she sees his face. "You'll get my blood on you."

Cohen pauses. His eyes meet hers. "Why don't you just allow me to be your Finder?" There is no anger in his voice, no hurt or malice, but Rachel wonders if he remembers what she said the last time they saw each other. She certainly hasn't forgotten. He takes the gauze back from her. "Can I take care of you?"

Rachel presses her lips together. "Okay."

She watches him as he tends to her wounds. Cohen's voice is quiet, calm. "I saw Hayden take you."

His words are measured. "I don't think I will ever forget that. I thought I lost you."

There are so many things Rachel wants to say. To tell him everything that's happened since he left. To apologize for the way she hurt him. Instead, she places her hand on top of his. Cohen looks up into her face. "No, Cohen," she whispers. "You didn't lose me. Once again, you found me."

"Cohen." The girl with the angular face has returned. "We're all here now."

Cohen pulls his hand away from Rachel's. "Good." He finishes bandaging Rachel's leg, offers her a hand up, then walks toward the group of people Rachel now recognizes as BethEl's first Apostolic team.

"I'm Adrielle." The girl watches Rachel then extends her hand. Rachel looks at her a moment then accepts it. Adrielle's grip is firm. Rachel squeezes back. "Glad to see you're alive, Rachel." She releases her hand and turns to join Cohen and the rest of the Apostles. Rachel follows.

"I agree," Cohen says to the group as they approach.

"Agree with what?" Adrielle asks. She stands beside Cohen; her shoulder touches his.

"Jesse, tell Adrielle what you told us." Cohen nods to the older man Rachel first saw when they entered.

"I just have a feeling." Jesse taps his chest. "I think the Lord wants us to get out of here."

Adrielle folds her arms over her chest. "All due respect, but that's a terrible idea. Where would we go?"

"I think the Lord is ready to bring us back into BethEl. I can't explain it." He taps his chest again. "It's a feeling. Our work here is done."

"Our work here is *not* done." Adrielle exchanges a glance with Cohen. "What about Nelson?" she asks Jesse.

"Nelson?" Rachel pushes into the group.

Cohen explains. "A man Jesse developed a relationship with while we were here."

"There are other relationships that have formed too." Adrielle's eyes plead with Cohen.

He shakes his head. "I'm with Jesse on this one. I feel it in my bones. We need to get out of here."

Adrielle throws up her hands. "So, you're going to completely abandon all the work we've done here?"

"No." Cohen faces off with her. "All along we said that we are planting seeds. We planted them. It's Yahweh's job to make them grow."

"I can't believe this," Adrielle mumbles.

"Nelson was the name of the man who helped me escape." Everyone stops to stare at Rachel.

Jesse takes a step toward her. "What did he look like?"

"Dark hair, glasses, about Cohen's height. He's a scientist."

"Ay, Dios mío." Jesse's eyes widen. "He helped you escape? What does that mean? Escape from what? Did he say anything?"

Cohen places a hand on Jesse's shoulder. "Slow down."

Rachel scans the faces of the Apostles. "He did say something." She smiles. "He said Jesus is his God."

Jesse falls to his knees and begins to mumble in Spanish. He brings a crucifix necklace to his lips and kisses it. "I can die a happy man!" He takes Rachel's hand. "Thank you," he whispers.

Rachel sees the emotion in Cohen's eyes as he watches the exchange. Adrielle's face is unchanged.

“He’s the one for the ninety-nine,” Jesse says to Cohen as he stands.

Cohen hugs the man. “You’re exactly right, and now I feel even more confident that it’s time for us to go.”

“But what about the ninety-nine?” Adrielle protests.

“Adrielle, it’s decided. We’re leaving.” Cohen addresses the group. “Everyone, pack your belongings.”

“Leaving so soon?” A new voice echoes through the space. Rachel turns to see a man in a gray suit hovering in the opening. Moonlight filters through the holes in the roof and illuminates his cold but poised face as he steps into the crumbling chapel. “But I just got here.”

CHAPTER 58

Lord Alderman traipses across the soot-covered floor and brushes his hands on his pants. A look of disgust crosses his face as he glances around the dilapidated building. He scans the faces of the frozen Apostles.

Rachel's eyes lock on Cohen's. He steps toward Lord Alderman. "Can we help you?"

Lord Alderman's head snaps in Cohen's direction. "Are you in charge here?"

Cohen clears his throat, casts a quick glance at Adrielle, then says, "I am."

Lord Alderman's lips twitch into a smirk. "Good. I'll make this quick. You are harboring a dangerous fugitive. I've come to collect her." Cohen's gaze catches Rachel's. Lord Alderman doesn't miss it. "Ah, you already know—" he pauses and holds up a finger. "But wait." Lord Alderman assesses Cohen's expression. "You know her, but you don't *know her*."

"Who are you?" Cohen says.

Lord Alderman cocks his head. "Don't you recognize me?"

Adrielle whispers something into Cohen's ear. His eyes widen.

"Yes, it is me, *the* Lord Alderman, the most high power of the Unity. In the flesh," he adds. "So, now that we have that out of the way, who are you?" Lord Alderman takes another step toward Cohen, then circles him like prey. "There's something familiar about you, and I'll be frank: I don't like it." He shoots a glare at one of the other Apostles. "All of you. You reek of"—he snaps his finger to produce the word—"holiness." He sneers then runs his hands over the breast of his jacket. "You are from that hidden city," Lord Alderman says. "It all makes sense now. How long have you been here? How many of you are there?"

Cohen holds his head high. He doesn't even blink as Lord Alderman leers at him.

"Fine." Lord Alderman shrugs. "Don't answer my questions. There is an easy solution to this problem. I will kill all of you."

"No!" Adrielle steps forward.

Lord Alderman shifts his glare. "Ah, are you the voice of reason?"

"What do you want?" Adrielle looks fierce, but Rachel sees the slight tremor in her hands.

"You look like a smart girl. Why don't you take a guess?"

Adrielle glances at Rachel. "Will you kill her?"

"Adrielle, no!" Cohen tries to push her out of the way.

"Not now, boy. We're talking." Lord Alderman holds up a hand, and Cohen's body goes flying across the chapel.

A few of the Apostles scream. One rushes over to tend to Cohen.

Lord Alderman is unfazed. He looks Rachel up and down, hesitates, then says, "No." He faces Adrielle. "I will not kill her."

"Then will you let us go?"

A slow smile spreads across Lord Alderman's lips. Rachel recognizes the expression from when she was a little girl. She'd ask if she could play with the other girls after completing her lessons. *Of course*, Lord Alderman would say while wearing that same smile. He never did. Now, he leers at Adrielle. "Of course. Just give me the girl."

"He's lying!" Rachel says. "He will kill you! He'll kill everyone!"

Lord Alderman ignores Rachel. "Thirteen lives for the price of one," he says to Adrielle. "Now that's quite a deal.

Cohen stumbles back to the group. "Adrielle, listen to yourself. What are you doing?"

"Don't you get it, Cohen? She's not who you think she is! She's working with the Darkness. If we let her back in BethEl—"

"Listen—"

"No, Cohen. You listen. I will not allow you to jeopardize our entire team because she's blinded you to the truth." She points a finger at Rachel. "Now it's time to sacrifice the one for the ninety-nine."

"Adrielle—"

"Silence!" Lord Alderman's calm surface erupts.

Rachel feels a set of hands on her shoulders. She turns to see the man Cohen calls Jesse. He presses a finger to his lips and motions for Rachel to come with him into the shadows. Lord Alderman's attention is on Adrielle. "If you don't hand her over immediately," he says, "I will begin killing you one by one!" Lord Alderman jams a finger in Adrielle's face.

In the shadows, Jesse whispers to Rachel. "Yahweh has redeemed you from your evil past, just like

Nelson," he says. "Don't let anyone ever tell you otherwise."

"How do you—"

Jesse waves her words away. "You must go!" He ushers her to an opening on the back wall of the chapel. "Go, go!" He pushes her. "Run! May the Holy Spirit guide you!"

"Wait!" Rachel pleads with him. "Why are you doing this?"

Jesse's face is ashen. "Because I know what that man will do to you." He shakes his head. "Nelson told me everything." Jesse removes his necklace, kisses the crucifix, then places it over Rachel's head. "Go!"

Rachel turns to run out of the chapel. Once outside, she pauses to look back. "I can't leave them," she whispers. Before she can make a move, an invisible force grips her hair. Rachel screams as the pain sears across her scalp and rips down her neck. Her body is dragged back into the building, across a pile of rubble, and thrown at the feet of Lord Alderman. Jesse now lies beside Rachel gasping for air, an invisible vice around his throat. Rachel is pulled to her feet.

"Fool me once, Rachel, shame on you. Fool me twice, shame on me. Fool me a third time, and you'll wish you were never born." He slaps her across the face. "I taught you better than this."

Behind Lord Alderman, Rachel can see Cohen's wide eyes. He tries to get to Jesse.

"Nobody move!" Lord Alderman demands.

Behind him, Cohen silently snatches up a wooden board and rushes at Lord Alderman. An unseen force knocks the plank out of his hands. "I warned you!" Lord Alderman bellows as he raises his hand. Without touching him, Lord Alderman draws Jesse's body to his feet by his neck. His face is purple, eyes wide. Lord

Alderman looks at Rachel. "Remember your friend, Nelson, back at the compound?"

Rachel's lips tremble.

"Unfortunately, you didn't get to watch him die, so this time, you must witness the consequences of your actions." He turns back to Jesse.

Tears fill Rachel's eyes. "No!"

"Goodbye!" Lord Alderman sings.

Jesse's body is hurled across the room and collides with a nearly intact statue of an angelic soldier holding a drawn sword. The finely carved blade impales his chest. Jesse gasps as blood trickles from his mouth.

"Oh, dear," Lord Alderman feigns surprise. "Must be a fallen angel."

Rachel falls to her knees. Her eyes well as a sob catches in her throat. A firm hand comes under her arm and drags her to her feet.

Lord Alderman's cool eyes narrow. "Are you done playing now, Rache—what is this?" He grasps the cross around her neck. Rachel takes the opportunity to spit in his face. Immediately, Lord Alderman's handsome façade is replaced by the horrifying image of his true identity. Around them, the Apostles scream and wail, but Rachel can see nothing except the face of evil and the dying form of Jesse behind him. Her eyes fall on the blood-covered sword that juts from his chest. "I asked you a question," the Watcher hisses.

"I don't have to answer. I no longer belong to you." Rachel draws out the words, not taking her eyes off the sword. "Or the dominion of Darkness."

"No."

"I belong to the Kingdom of Light."

"No!" the Watcher barks in her face. He grabs her by the chin and forces her to meet his gaze. "What are you staring at?"

Everything comes together in Rachel's mind. *The sword.* Francis said it is the Word of God. And the Word of God is Jesus. "In the Physical Realm," Francis told her, "the Word dwells unseen within us, slipping out when we open our mouths and speak in accordance with Yahweh's will."

The Watcher shakes her. "I demand you answer me!"

Rachel remembers the mysterious look in Francis's cool blue eyes as he said, "But when we enter the Spiritual Realm through our dreams, we are able to wield the Word as the sword and weapon it truly is in defeating the Darkness."

Rachel calmly meets the yellow stare of the monster. "I told you. I don't answer to you anymore. I answer to Jesus."

The Watcher's head snaps back on his shoulders. He growls something incoherent. His reaction reminds Rachel of the Shedim that attacked her.

"Jesus," Rachel repeats louder. He yanks his hand back from her face as if her skin were made of fire. "Jesus!"

He shrieks.

Cohen and a few of his teammates join Rachel in the chant. The Watcher quivers with anger. The other Apostles join in. The name Jesus echoes like a song through the decaying chapel. Once again, the house of God is alive with the name.

"This is not over!" The beast bellows. "I will destroy you!" His fangs lash at her.

Rachel doesn't move. The chant continues in the background. "I am no longer under your dominion," she says. "You are under mine. According to the power and authority given to me, Jesus rebukes you, Watcher! Go back to Hell where you belong!"

Evil screeches pour from the monster's mouth as his body vaporizes into the night.

Rachel collapses to her knees. The chant fades. No one speaks.

Her body trembles uncontrollably. Rachel sees Cohen rush to Jesse's side. The youngest Apostle begins to cry as a woman wraps her arms around her. Others run to help Cohen while several fall to their knees in praise. Adrielle stands at a distance staring at Rachel, but she doesn't say a word. Rachel buries her face in her hands, collects herself, then makes her way over to Jesse.

Gurgling sounds come from his mouth as blood continues to spill from his body.

"His lung is punctured," Cohen says. His voice is void of emotion. "We can't move him. The sword is the only thing keeping him alive. For now." He doesn't look at Rachel.

Jesse slowly lifts a hand and motions Cohen closer to him. The other Apostles place tender kisses on the man's forehead then slip away silently. Cohen takes Jesse's hand and kneels beside him. Rachel shifts a little closer.

Jesse's voice rasps. "Do not weep for me." Cohen chokes back a sob. "What did I say?" Jesse's full lips pull into a smile. Cohen coughs out a laugh. "This is not your fault." His eyes stare at Cohen then drift to Rachel. He raises his eyebrows as if to make sure she knows he speaks to both of them. Then his gaze falls on Cohen. "I am proud to call you my amigo, but I am more proud to call you my leader."

Jesse coughs uncontrollably. Blood spatters Cohen's shirt. His eyes drift upward. "Ay, Dios mío," he whispers. "I see him. I see him." Jesse's eyes fall on Cohen one more time then widen. A full smile forms on his lips. "I see him." His final breath bubbles from his mouth. His head slumps. Body surrenders.

Cohen stares at the man for a long moment then gently closes his eyes.

CHAPTER 59

Adrielle whispers to Cohen as he and Rachel approach. "What in BethEl was that thing?"

"It wasn't from BethEl," Rachel mumbles.

"Of course it wasn't." She narrows her eyes at Rachel.

"We need to get out of here."

"No. You have some explaining to do." Adrielle glances over at Jesse's body then blinks several times. When she turns back to Rachel her eyes glisten.

"We don't have time. The Watcher is not dead. Or alone," Rachel adds. "There will be others. We have to get out of here."

"We can't leave him." Adrielle motions to Jesse's body.

Cohen shakes his head. "Adrielle, Rachel is right. We need to go."

"But Jesse—"

"He's not in there anymore. You know that."

Adrielle looks away.

"He would have wanted it this way." Cohen glances around the chapel ruins. "He is in the house of the Lord. Both his body and his spirit. Adrielle, if you want to honor the man, then we need to follow through on what he felt Yahweh was saying. Yahweh is ready to bring us back into BethEl. It's time to go."

Adrielle sighs, walks away, and begins rounding up the group. The Apostles are so shaken, it only takes a few minutes for them to pack and be ready to leave.

Rachel pulls Cohen aside. "Hey, I have a weird idea, but I think it might be a way for us to get back to BethEl." She can tell from Cohen's face that he isn't sure how to respond or even interact with her. She sees the weight of his grief, and despite Jesse's dying words, she knows that, like her, Cohen feels responsible for Jesse's death.

"Rachel, that's great, but you know people don't enter BethEl by their own choice. Yahweh—"

"Yahweh chooses those who enter," Rachel finishes for him.

He searches her face. Nearby, a strange howl rings out.

One of the men shouts, "Are we all ready? We need to go!"

Another howl echoes against the chapel's falling walls. A shiver runs through Rachel's body.

"It sounds like it's right outside," one of the women whispers.

Cackles and howls surround the building. Cohen looks to Rachel. "You said you had an idea?"

"Okay everyone, circle around!" Rachel shouts to the team. The sounds of the forces of Darkness fill the night and threaten to drown out her voice. "Hold hands, everyone!"

Adrielle pushes past a few people and takes Cohen's right hand. He reaches over and grabs Rachel's with his left.

"What are we doing?" someone shouts. "We're sitting ducks! We need to get out of here!"

A man begins chanting the name Jesus under his breath.

"Listen to Rachel!" Cohen says. He looks to her. "Whenever you're ready would be great."

"Everyone! Close your eyes." The team follows Rachel's command. "Try to mimic my breathing." She exaggerates the inhale and exhale of her breath. "Focus on BethEl." She hesitates. "Picture it as clearly as you can in your mind." She forces confidence into her voice. Under her breath, Rachel whispers, "Please, Jesus, let this work."

One by one, each Apostle falls to their knees, light-headed from the breathing pattern. Rachel kneels beside Cohen and fixes her eyes on her ring. The sapphire stone, now Manifested permanently in the gold filigree, reminds her of the endless sea; the swirls of metal remind her of the dance; and as she thinks of all the dreams she's had while wearing the ring, Rachel is reminded that she is chosen.

"Rachel?" There is hesitancy in Cohen's voice.

"Focus!" she says. Under her breath, she whispers, "I choose you too, Yahweh. I choose this calling."

The presence of the Darkness encroaches on all sides. The scent of sulfur and death fills the air. Evil laughter bounces off the stone and brick, but the image of BethEl is locked in Rachel's mind. She prays the others have a picture as clear as hers. "Please, Jesus, let this work," she says. Rachel counts down in her head.

Five. Four.

"Rachel?"

Three.

"Rachel?"

Two.

"Rachel!"

"One!" She shouts the word into the night.

A flash of light surrounds and engulfs the entire Apostolic team. The ground trembles. Spindly fingers reach for them on all sides but are quickly swallowed by the blinding light. Cohen's hand tightens around Rachel's. The powers of Darkness screech as the brilliance overtakes them. Their shrieks fade as the light subsides.

***

The blustery gale dwindles to a soft breeze, and the song of birds greets Rachel and the team as they huddle on the ground. Rachel opens her eyes and rises to her feet. The forest is consumed by the daylight that drifts in through the tops of the trees. The scent of flowers floods the air.

"We did it," Rachel murmurs as she peers up at the familiar BethEl sky. Daylight shines on the perimeter, while in the center, the vastness of the cosmos unfolds with visible planets and galaxies. It's somehow even more awe-inspiring than the first time she saw it.

Cohen stands beside her. "No, you did it, but how?" Wonder fills his voice. He shakes his head as he looks at her. "Yahweh has to choose."

"He did." Rachel smiles. "He chose me. And I chose him."

Cohen scans the group. He takes note of each Apostle's presence before he turns back to Rachel. "What do you mean?"

Rachel glances around the forest of the outskirts of BethEl and draws a deep breath of the sweet air. She meets Cohen's gaze and says, "Yahweh chose me. Cohen, I am the Lord's Anointed."

CHAPTER 60

Magic unfolds in the BethEl Common Gardens. Flowers erupt with a chorus of blooms, their heavy scent mingling with the aroma of the feast. Lyrical voices drift through the evening air while the jangle of tambourines keeps the beat. Amidst the beautiful chaos, Rachel retreats to a quiet space in a corner of the garden to watch the Shabbat celebration from a distance.

Hugs are shared with abandon as Cohen and the other Apostles make their first public appearance since their return. A pang of jealousy hits Rachel as she watches Jubilee jump into Cohen's arms. Now released from the dark shadow of Hayden's presence, her spark has returned. Her emerald eyes flash all the way from across the lawn as she wraps her arms around Cohen's neck. Rachel looks away as Jubilee plants a kiss on his cheek.

"I don't think it is a coincidence that your return should coincide with the evening of Shabbat," Francis's familiar baritone greets her. Rachel pats the ground beside her and offers a hand to help him sit down. He stretches his knobby legs in front of him and leans back on his hands for support. "I am getting too old for this, my dear." He chuckles.

Francis takes her hand in his and waits for Rachel to look at him. "I think, somehow, I must have always known it was you." He kisses her knuckles. Rachel glances away. "My spirit knew"—he touches his chest—"but my mind is still a silly old man, slow to the ways of Yahweh. Ah, there's that smile. You have been somber since your return." Francis waits for her response. Rachel doesn't offer one. Though he knows her identity as the Lord's Anointed, Rachel still hasn't found the words to tell Francis that she is his daughter, a fact she still struggles to believe despite Aleph's insistence that it is true.

"I know it is much to take in," he says. "It will be much more once we make the announcement to BethEl. The demands on you will be great. Much is expected of the Lord's Anointed, and much is predicted."

Francis's words remind Rachel of a story she had since forgotten. "The Lost Ark?" she asks.

"Ah, you remember." He sounds surprised. "I thought you were asleep that night. Thought I was talking to myself, but what's new?" He chuckles as he removes his pipe from the folds of his robe. "When you're my age, talking to yourself is common practice." Francis's tone grows serious. "But you are right, my dear. It is predicted that the Lost Ark and, more importantly, the stories within it will be found by the Lord's Anointed. Your arrival is a catalyst." He points over to a small group of people. Rachel recognizes four of them from the mysterious group that arrived after her. "Like them." Francis chuckles and shakes his head. "Rabbi and I were so confused and concerned about their arrival. And rightfully so, it turns out, since there was a deceiver among them. But even after Hayden was gone and you had returned, there was fear in my gut. But Yahweh set me straight."

"How so?" Rachel asks.

"He reminded me that his ways are not my ways. God does things differently. We should not always expect him to do things the same way as us or even in the same way he has done them before." Francis smiles. "I suspect there will be more unusual things to come. But we need not concern ourselves with that tonight." He pats her hand.

They sit quietly side by side until Rachel breaks the silence. "I assume Cohen talked to you?"

"About forfeiting his role completely as your Finder and Mentor? Yes. He and I both agree that it will be best for you to continue under my training." Francis watches her. "Cohen is not abandoning you, my dear. He would never do that. He is doing what is best for you."

Rachel watches as Jubilee grabs Cohen by the hand and pulls him into the crowd to join the others in a boisterous dance. Adrielle hovers nearby, eyebrows furrowed, fidgeting with the end of her braid while she watches Cohen and Jubilee. Layers of red and orange skirts sway about Jubilee's ankles, mimicking her hair as it tosses about her head. Francis follows Rachel's gaze. "She loves him, you know."

Rachel's voice is flat. "And he loves her."

Francis nods. "Dearly. It's precious to me. You don't see that kind of love outside BethEl—the innocent love of a brother and sister."

"Brother and sister?" Rachel turns to look at Francis. He fights back a smile.

"Why, yes. Didn't you know? Sweet Jubilee is only a couple years younger than Cohen. She arrived in BethEl after him, took to him immediately, and started calling him her big brother. Cohen, of course, adored her. He took his role as big brother seriously. They've been the best of friends ever since." There's a spark in Francis's eyes. "Ah, silly me. I thought you knew." His smile is no longer contained.

"In addition to mentoring you, I will continue my training with Cohen," Francis says. "Since my bones are old and weary, I will likely combine your training. I hope that is all right. You don't mind working with Cohen, do you?" Francis nudges her arm.

Heat floods Rachel's cheeks as she swats at Francis and tries not to smile.

"All jokes aside, my dear, these next several months of training will not be easy. Cohen is strong in ways that I am not. You will be wise to learn from him." Francis falls silent and allows the music to fill the space between them. The scent of cherry tobacco fills the air.

When he doesn't say anything else, Rachel rises to join the party. Francis catches her hand and signals her to help him to his feet. She stumbles under his weight as he leans on her for support. "Your strength will return," he says, gesturing to her frail form. "You have eaten, yes?" Rachel nods. "Good. Eat again." He points to the food. Elias waves from a nearby table when he sees Rachel look his way. She waves back and tries to pull her hand away from Francis, but he doesn't let go. "Enjoy these moments, Rachel." His face fills with sadness. "Enjoy these sweet times. They will be few."

"What do you mean?"

"We are coming into a time"—Francis coughs to clear his throat—"the end of the last days. And mark my words, Rachel, there will be terrible times in the last days. There will be great distress, unequaled from the beginning of the world until now, for as it was in the days of Noah, so it will be at the coming of the Son of

Man. The outside world is much darker than you realize. Soon you will see.

"You remember the dry bones from your vision when you first arrived?"

"How could I forget."

Francis nods. "The bones are the remnant, the Church, both Jews and Gentiles. They say, 'Our bones are dried up and our hope is gone; we are cut off.' That is why you must prophesy to them and say, 'This is what the Sovereign Lord says: My people, I am going to open your graves and bring you up from them; I will bring you back to the land of promise. Then you will know that I am the Lord. I will put my Spirit in you and you will live, and I will settle you in the land of promise.'

"The dry bones have waited long enough, Rachel. They have been dead and dry for far too long. But the Lord will pour water on the thirsty land, and streams on the dry ground. He will pour out his Spirit on his offspring, and blessings on his descendants. He will breathe new life into his people and restore them."

Rachel's mind drifts to her dreams. "Like a stream in the desert," she murmurs. "God is doing a new thing."

Francis beams. Tears well in his eyes. "Indeed, he is, my dear. Indeed, he is." He pats her hand. "The time is now, Rachel. The Lord is saying, 'Come!' Let the one who is thirsty come; and let the one who wishes take the free gift of the water of life. Blessed are those who wash their robes, that they may have the right to the Tree of Life and may go through the gates into the city!'" Francis's voice is filled with enchantment.

"My dear, I know you have seen him. I know you have stood face-to-face with him. Don't ever forget that. Don't ever leave the space of face-to-face, so that when he appears you may be confident and unashamed before him at his coming."

Francis's eyes search hers. "I'm confusing you."

"It's okay." Rachel chuckles. "It's a lot to process."

"Yes," Francis says. "My dear, I know you do not fully recognize your mission now, but you will. You have ears to hear and eyes to see. I promise, when the time comes, you will also be given a mind to understand."

He pauses then asks, "In your training with Rabbi, did you ever learn the story of Zechariah?"

"John the Baptist's father?"

He shakes his head. "A different Zechariah, a Prophet. There is a small book about him near the end of the Old Testament." Francis continues. "In one of Zechariah's visions, a Malak woke him from his sleep and asked him, 'What do you see?'

"Zechariah said, 'I see a solid gold lampstand with a bowl at the top and seven lamps on it, with seven channels to the lamps. Also there are two olive trees by it, one on the right of the bowl and the other on its left.'

When Zechariah asked for an explanation of the vision, the Malak told him that the two olive trees symbolize the two who stand by the Lord of the whole earth, the two Anointed Ones.'" Francis pauses to watch Rachel's reaction.

"Two? Two Anointed Ones?"

"Yes, my dear. It seems so. Remember when I told you that Elijah would come before the Messiah to herald his way?"

"Yes, but you said it was the spirit of Elijah who came in the form of Jesus's cousin, John the Baptist."

"Correct, and I also told you that tradition suggests another will come in the spirit of Elijah as John did, and this time, before the return of Yeshua. We have searched and waited for that person—the Lord's Anointed—you.

"But we've become so entangled in that mission it seems we failed to see what is right beneath our noses. Yahweh reminded me of this in a dream last night. I simply saw a vision of a lampstand and two olive trees, as Zechariah saw, and I heard these words, 'There will be another.'"

"Another like me?"

"Yes, my dear. You are only half of what we have been searching for." Francis watches Rachel's expression. She blinks but doesn't speak. Francis continues. "Zechariah's vision is mentioned another time in the Bible, in the New Testament."

"By Jesus?"

"No." He pauses. "It is not spoken of again until the end. In the book of Revelation. Rachel, you are one of the two Witnesses."

"Two Witnesses," she repeats under her breath. "Aleph said he would send me a helper."

Francis waits for her to continue. When she doesn't, he urges, "Go on."

"There is so much to tell you, Francis." Rachel sighs. "I did see him. I saw Yahweh. I stood with him face-to-face, and he spoke to me. He said the reason he brought me to him was to bear witness. To witness the Aleph and the Tov."

"The beginning and the end," Francis says.

"Yes. Francis—" she hesitates. "I saw the Wedding Supper of the Lamb."

A tear rolls down Francis's wrinkled face and follows a crease until it lands in his beard. "You saw it?" Awe fills his voice.

"I did." A smile uncurls on her face. "It is beyond words."

"You must try to use your words, my dear. You must! I have waited for this moment my whole life. I have been waiting for *you* my whole life." Rachel bites her lip. "You are the Lord's Anointed, the one who will use your words to declare what wonders you have seen!"

Rachel takes one of Francis's calloused hands in hers and traces the lines of his palm. Each crease tells a story, each line a marker of a journey traveled, all connected and held together by Yahweh. Now, each thread of his past converges in this moment. She looks up at him. Aleph is right. She has his eyes.

Though he never knew her, this man devoted his whole life to Rachel. Everything he did was for her and for his God. She wonders if, somehow, his spirit also realizes that in another life, he would have been more than just a Mentor, that maybe, he still can be. She wants to tell him, but not tonight. There will be plenty of time for that.

Rachel looks up into Francis's face. "You're right. I have to speak. I must use my words. That's what Witnesses do," she says, recalling Aleph's words. "They glimpse a moment in the story of the Kingdom of God. Then they tell others about it. The first part of witnessing is the glimpse. The second part is the telling."

Francis's blue eyes flash wildly against his ebony skin. The colors of the fading daylight reflect like fire against his dark pupils. He squeezes Rachel's hand. "Then tell you must! Come with me." He holds her hand as he shuffles toward the crowd. "I can think of no better moment than this to make the announcement to BethEl. You must tell us your story."

Francis leads Rachel to the center of the celebration. He motions for Cohen to join them and help gather the attention of the crowd. Rachel shifts from one foot to the other as she stands beside Francis.

Music fades, and everyone takes a seat at the long oak tables in the Common Gardens behind their homes. Cohen whispers something to Adrielle then comes to stand on the other side of his Mentor. He places a hand on Francis's shoulder then beams proudly over at Rachel. At one of the nearest tables, Micaiah, Rivi, and Elias sit together. All three offer an encouraging smile, even Rivi. Elias winks.

Francis squeezes Rachel's hand then clears his throat. "People of BethEl, as you know, our city life, as of late, has not been normal."

Chuckles drift through the crowd. "Have we ever been normal?" someone shouts. Laughter erupts.

"Good point." Francis laughs. "But ever since this young lady crashed into our lives, even our normal has been disrupted." Francis glances at Rachel. "Many of you know Rachel. We have come to love her as one of our own. I know many of you beseeched the Lord in prayer when you heard of her abduction. Today, we celebrate the return not only of the Apostolic Assembly of BethEl but also the return of Rachel." Applause fills the air. Francis holds up a hand to silence the people. "But it's not even just her return that we celebrate." The residents of BethEl look to one another. Confusion etches their kind faces. "And with that"—Francis nods to Rachel—"I give you the floor, my dear."

A tremble works its way through Rachel's legs and up her spine. Francis gives her a little shove. Everyone stares and waits for her to speak. She clears her throat and whispers a silent prayer. Words come out with a power that surprises her.

"I would like to tell you what happened while I was gone." Rachel swallows. "I wasn't just taken from

BethEl; I was taken away in the Spirit." Murmurs fill the courtyard. "I saw him. I saw the Great and Mighty I AM. With my own eyes, I saw him in the flesh, and he spoke to me."

She pauses, glancing first at Francis and then at Cohen. Their warm smiles and kind eyes fill her with strength. Rachel finally knows what is true: she is the Lord's Anointed, chosen for such a time as this.

Rachel focuses on the captive audience, the people who have become her family and, soon, will be comrades in the mission that is to come. They cling to her every word and wait to hear what she has glimpsed. With the strength of the Spirit and the Prophets who have gone before her, Rachel's lips part. Breath fills her lungs as she releases the words that burn inside her.

"Face-to-face, I stood with the Lord," Rachel proclaims. "And here is what he said to me. 'Behold, I am coming soon!'"

EPILOGUE

Francis sits in the hearth room of the parsonage, his pipe clenched between his teeth. The usual comfort of the cherry scent and slow rhythm of his rocking chair do nothing to aid his troubled mind now. Even the scent of the cold hickory ash in the empty fireplace doesn't bring him solace as it usually does. A Bible lies open on his lap. His tired eyes scan the scriptures, but his mind cannot focus on the words. A gentle knock on the front door diverts his attention. The door opens without him calling to the guest to invite them in.

Rabbi enters through the front hall and into the hearth room.

"Junia. Hello." Francis closes the Bible. "Please have a seat." He gestures to the empty chair across from him.

"Where are Rachel and Cohen?" Rabbi asks.

"Out. He is helping her with her lessons today."

"Are you sure it's a good idea to have them both live here with you?" she asks as she crosses her long, slender legs and leans back into the chair.

"I enjoy having them around. They help keep me in order." Francis waves his pipe through the air. "Plus, Cohen is a good cook."

Rabbi's full lips turn upward into a smile but only for a moment. "And Rachel's training?"

"It's only been a week since she's been back." Francis pauses. His brow furrows. He hopes Rabbi doesn't read him as she always does. "But she is doing well. Having them both here makes training simpler on my weary bones."

Rabbi's eyes narrow. "How is your pain?"

"Manageable."

"You're lying."

"Junia—"

"Ever since Rachel returned, you've seemed, I don't know, weighed down." Rabbi folds her hands in her lap and begins a steady rock. Her smooth mocha skin looks even darker in the dimly lit hearth room.

Francis stares into the empty fireplace. "I miss Abigail. That is all."

Rabbi's face softens. "Rachel has stirred up memories?"

"Yes," Francis whispers. "She hasn't told me much, but I worry. If there was enough Darkness attached to her past to cause another Breach—"

"Francis," Rabbi cuts him off, "Rachel is not like Abby. Rachel has turned. The Darkness has no claim over her. She is a child of the Light."

"I know." Francis blinks back tears. "But she is still a child, nonetheless."

"She is the Lord's Anointed."

Francis nods.

"This will not be like the last time," Rabbi says.

Francis nods again but doesn't speak. He runs his fingers over of the hem of the white nightgown he has tucked underneath his Bible. "I worry their pasts are somehow connected." Francis's mind drifts back to the shared vision he and Rachel had when he first met her in the Chapel. In the vision, Rachel wore a white nightgown. He didn't notice it then, but over the last week, the images of the vision came back to him. This time he couldn't escape the familiarity of the white nightgown.

"Francis?"

"Yes, Junia."

"You know why I am here."

Francis pulls his gaze away from the fireplace to meet Rabbi's. He doesn't respond

"Francis, we have to tell them. They deserve to know."

"It's too soon. Rachel has only just returned."

"Francis."

"Junia, please—"

"We have to tell the other Elders."

Francis stops and presses his lips together. "She's so young. So new to her faith—"

"Francis, you may be a man of God, but you are not Yahweh. You do not get to make these decisions."

Francis's gaze falls to the floor. "I'm just concerned she's not ready."

"No." Rabbi shakes her head. "That's not what this is about. No one is ever ready for Yahweh's call on their life. You know this as well as I do. There's something else going on here." She points a long finger at him. "What is it?"

Francis clears his throat and shakes his head. "Nothing, Junia. Nothing. It's just me being a silly old man concerned for a girl I have grown to care for."

Rabbi tilts her head. "We all care for Rachel. But the others need to know. We have been waiting for this moment, Francis. All twelve cities of BethEl have now been established. The Lord's Anointed has been found. Francis—" Rabbi's voice chokes. "He told her he is coming soon! This is it! We are coming into the last days, and finally, the people of BethEl Twelve and the other elven cities will manifest their purpose!"

Her emotion stirs him. "I know." He sighs.

"It's time. You must tell them that we've found her."

Francis nods. "I will. I will leave tomorrow for BethEl One and call together an Elder meeting. You will stay here?"

"Of course."

"And what will you tell everyone of my absence?"

A smile tugs at Rabbi's lips. "What we always tell them. That you are taking a Sabbatical."

Francis sighs. "I am becoming weary of all this sneaking around."

Rabbi leans forward in her chair. "Soon we will be able to tell them the whole truth. It's all in Yahweh's timing."

Francis shakes his head. "I can only imagine how it will hit them when they learn that we are not the only ones."

"Don't worry about that now," Rabbi says. "You just focus on what you need to do tomorrow."

"Right," Francis whispers. "Thank you, Junia."

"We're in this together."

"I know. And for that I am grateful."

Rabbi stands to leave. "Any idea how long you will be gone this time?"

Francis leans back in his rocker and takes a long draw from his pipe. Smoke lingers around him as he lets it uncurl from his lips. "Yahweh only knows, Junia. Yahweh only knows."

Look For

Witness

Bethel Book Two

Coming 2019

Sign up at hrhutzel.com for updates on *Witness* and the entire Anointed series.

Building a relationship with my readers is one of the best parts of being a writer. I occasionally send newsletters with updates about new releases, special offers, and other news about the books I'm writing.

And if you sign up for my mailing list, I'll send you a free digital copy of *The Story of Life*, my bestselling, debut novel.

You can sign up to get updates and your copy of *The Story of Life* here: bit.ly/thestoryoflife

Enjoy This Book?

You can make a big difference!

I am so grateful for my committed and loyal readers! Your reviews are one of the best thank-yous I can receive.

Reviews are the most powerful tool I have as an author when it comes to bringing my books to the attention of other readers.

If you enjoyed this book, I would be very grateful if you could spend just five minutes leaving a review (it can be as short as you like) on the book's Amazon page. You can jump right to the page at this link: bit.ly/reviewanointed

ACKNOWLEDGEMENTS

Writing *Anointed* was unlike any other writing experience I've ever had.

My first book was written in a Holy Spirit-inspired frenzy, similar to the emotional bliss that accompanies a brand-new romantic relationship. That book was born of my spirit.

My second book was written out of the struggle and pain of discovering what it truly means to be an author; what it is to pursue a God-given dream; and what it's like to surrender myself to a power that is greater and higher. That book was born of my humanity.

But like the gospel of our Savior who is both human and divine, *Anointed* was born of both my flesh and spirit—a story inspired by the *Ruach ha-Kodesh* (the Holy Spirit of God), entrusted to a mere human, formed and shaped through her experiences, wisdom, trials, and errors. It's the kind of partnership God desires to have with all of us, if only we allow him.

Yeshua is the foundation, and we are called to build upon *him.* 1 Corinthians 13:10 tells us to be *skilled* builders and to consider carefully how we build upon that foundation. I've learned the hard way that the key to being a skilled builder is to never build alone. That is why, upon the foundation of Christ, I organized a series of pillars who not only help uphold the vision for this book but also extend it beyond the places I can reach. This book is not the result of one human's efforts, but of a body of people who emanate light, love, purpose, and faith. They are my team, and without them, this book would not exist.

Thank you first to my husband, David, who continues to be the central pillar of what I am building. You are the one who holds *me* up. Without you, I would surely fall.

To my family and friends, thank you for your unwavering love and support.

Thank you to my team of contributors. To my editor, Karli Jackson, you have brought so much to this story, and it is truly a better tale because of you. I am honored to partner with you in crafting these stories. To Nat Akin, you are a master of detail; thank you for putting the final polish on this manuscript. To Greg Boyd, my theological consultant (aka, the Official Heresy-Sniffer-Outer), thank you for bringing your knowledge and expertise to the table and helping to ensure that the true gospel of God's love is what shines through in this book.

To my Board of Protectors, Christine, Stacey, David, RaeLynn, Jack, Tatiana, and Terri, you are some of the most important people on my team. Thank you for covering me with your prayers.

A huge thank-you to my Financial Pillars who helped make the publication of this book possible: Tatiana Anthony, Renee Berkemeier, Stacey Berkemeier, Dan Bisig, Patty Bracken, Megan Carlton, Ronda Crosby, Jerry DeAngelis, RaeLynn DeAngelis, Lyn Gentry, Shirley Kaiser, Christine Luken, Angela Nienaber, Miriam Pacheco, Paula Reitsma, and Pat Spanagel.

And finally, to the One who continues to unveil himself to me. You are infinite. How could I possibly think I could capture every facet of your essence in a book? I guess I will just have to keep writing. And with your blessing, I will. May the beautiful, divine dance that is spirit and flesh be evident not only in this book, but in every breath and heartbeat of my life.

About the Author

H.R. Hutzel (Heather Rae) never aspired to be a writer or dreamed of writing a book. But that all changed when she prayed a very dangerous prayer—she told God she would do *anything*. Now, not only is she a bestselling author, she is a speaker who helps readers and audiences experience the biblical story in surprising, inspiring, and challenging ways.

Heather lives in Cincinnati with her husband and their beloved golden retrievers, Westen and Finnley. When she's not writing, you'll find her digging in the garden or hanging out in the hammock with a good book.

To inquire about booking H.R. Hutzel for a speaking engagement or to find out more about her and her books, please reach out at hrhutzel.com.

Made in the USA
Lexington, KY
24 April 2019